Cold Flood

Cold Flood

R. J. Corgan

2017

Cover art and maps by Justus Lyons

First Printing: 2017

Seventh Edition

ISBN: 978-1-387-29536-4

https://RJcorganbooks.com/

For Kate, Matt, and Scott

Icelandic Pronunciation

á - the "ou" in "house"

ð - the "th" in "father"

í - the "i" in "Maria"

j - the "y" in "yes"

ó - the "o" in "sole"

ö - the "u" in "urgent"

ú - the "zoo"

æ - the "aye"

See Appendix for definitions of Icelandic and geologic terms.

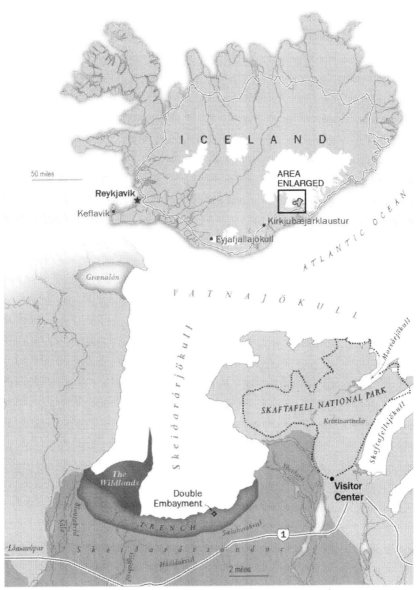

Skeiðarárjökull, Skaftafell National Park

Prologue

Pénzesgyőr, Hungary

ANDREA SPRINTED through the forest, her feet blindly finding purchase on the soft earth. Branches slashed her cheeks and snagged her hair. Glancing back, she saw flashlight beams pierce the mist between the tree trunks, their white blades searching for her. She scanned the landscape ahead, desperate for any sign that she was on the right path.

Nothing.

She ducked behind the shelter of a fallen tree, pausing to rest.

Things were not going to plan.

She fought to control her breathing, reducing her heaving pants into hushed, measured gasps. Closing her eyes, she felt the damp kiss of the tree's bark, cold and alien against her neck. Her pale hands were covered in grime, her manicured fingernails crusted with mud. Her long black hair had been tied up in a knot, but spilled out as she fled, and was constantly falling across her eyes. She wore only a rain jacket, a t-shirt, sneakers, and skinny jeans. No phone, no gun.

Breathe, she thought. *Just breathe*. Opening her eyes, a gossamer thread glinted in the faint morning light, drifting down from the shadowy canopy above. A silkworm dangled from the delicate strand, parasailing through the forest with ease, oblivious to the drama unfolding around it. She focused on the tiny creature as it floated off into the mist.

If only it were that easy, she thought.

Huddled deeper into the husk of the tree, she listened as the voices in the woods called to each other, sometimes distant, sometimes seeming to be right beside her. She willed herself to remember the way back to her vehicle. Instead, her mind was trying to comprehend how it could all have gone wrong so quickly.

The call had come in just after midnight. Still blinking sleep from her eyes, she had thrown on whatever clothes were at hand, jumped in her car, and entered the coordinates into her GPS. Heading out of Munich at full speed, she had been thankful for the lack of traffic in the dead of night. She would swear she hadn't been followed. Yet, despite reaching the target without incident, she was ambushed as she made her way back through the forest. Either her pursuers had tracked her phone, or they had known where she was going all along.

Had she been in her own territory, she would have had a chance. She could have made a feint to throw them off, doubled back to her car, and then fled to a safe house. Here, though, this deep in a strange woodland on the outskirts of a tiny town two hours southwest of Budapest, she didn't know the terrain. She had no allies, no safe haven, no plan, and no weapons. She possessed nothing except the panic belonging to a creature of prey, frantic to keep ahead of the pack.

She waited. One minute. Three. Ten. The gaps between shouts became longer, the voices farther apart. Or so it seemed. A trick?

Have to risk it.

She peered over the edge of the trunk. She saw nothing but the sun cresting the treetops, bleeding through the boughs like a broken yolk.

Go!

Sprinting, she threaded a path through the tree trunks. She headed west where her vehicle was parked a kilometer distant. Or so she hoped.

She heard a cry of alarm, followed by an exultant shout.

They had spotted her.

A shot rang out, its deafening echoes reverberating through the trees.

Her heart pounding, she dug deep, tapping into her last reserves of energy. As she ran, she gave silent thanks to those who had planted this forest. Unlike the wild woodlands of her youth, this one had been planted with evenly spaced trunks and minimal undergrowth. The layout allowed her to quickly zigzag between the trees, putting their sturdy girth between her and gunfire.

Nearing the brink of exhaustion, she heard shouts growing closer. A crackle of thunder rolled through the trees: the sound of her pursuers smashing through the undergrowth. They were closing in. She staggered up a steep rise and almost cried out in relief as she recognized a distinctive outcrop of slate, its surface dripping a scraggly beard of dark green moss.

So close. Her car was parked just at the end of the valley. She slid down the embankment, rolling like a child into a pile of leaves, her head giddy with relief. Stumbling into a final run, she headed toward the lights of her car.

Lights?

She hadn't left-

A mixture of shame and terror tightened her chest. They had followed her. Not just through the forest. They had followed her car. Of course, they would know where she had parked.

Stupid! I'm so stupid!

Another shot rang out. Still stumbling, she veered off to the right, her feet skidding in the leaves as she picked up speed. She ran in a blind panic, not caring where.

Out of options. Out of time.

She headed east toward the rising sun, fighting to keep her pace steady, to push through the pain that burned her thighs, to see through her tears that blurred her vision.

The sound of rushing water reached her ears. She sprinted toward it, hoping to put it between herself and her pursuers.

She exploded out of the trees to find herself on the edge of an embankment. Below, ribbons of steam rose from the turbulent surface of a roaring river. The gray light of dawn made it difficult to ascertain the channel's murky depths. The cliff itself was less than ten meters high, but the river below was at least fifty meters across. She paused, trying to gather the nerve to leap into the water's unknown, and potentially lethal, embrace.

Her foot suddenly flew into the air unbidden, slamming her backward onto the rocky ground. The impact knocked out the last of her breath. She stared up at the sky blinking stupidly, her exhausted brain finally processing the sound of the gunshot. The pain in her foot roiled across her body, its white fire lighting up her nervous system in stages, before finally forcing a cry from her gasping throat.

Frantically, she crawled to the cliff's edge and reached into her pocket to fling her prize into the river in a final act of desperation. Her hand came up empty save for the lining of her jacket. She groaned. She must have dropped it in the forest. It could be anywhere. Rolling onto her back, she found that she was laughing hysterically at the ridiculousness of it all, of the stupidity of her situation.

Andrea didn't recognize any of the goons who stepped into the clearing. In her head, she had envisioned being chased by professionals clad in black camouflage, bristling with military gear. Instead, she faced five men of varying heights wearing an array of jeans, hoodies, and t-shirts, dressed as if they were going grocery shopping. Average, everyday, blue-collar workers. Except for the handguns, of course.

"Hi boys," she managed between ragged coughs. "He couldn't even be bothered to show, huh?" She had arranged a handover in three days' time in Marienplatz, Munich's central square. A public place where she would have had backup, body armor, a handgun, and a get-away car. Her buyer had obviously decided he couldn't wait and sent his men to take it from her at the source. For free. "What's the matter with you guys? Doesn't anyone believe in supply chain economics anymore? Un-American, that's what this is."

The men frowned, not comprehending. She searched her memory for any Hungarian phrases, but the only ones she could remember were swear words. Naturally.

"I hate to ruin your day, but I don't have it." She sat up slowly, holding up her sweaty palms, empty except for the grime of the forest floor still plastered to her skin. "Honestly, I have no idea where it is."

One of the men, his face half-hidden beneath the hood of his jacket, stepped closer. "The problem with young people today," he began, his German colored with the hint of an accent she was unable to identify, "is that you are all about the energy, the ambition, but you want nothing to do with patience."

Andrea lowered her hands to the ground for support, pulling her injured leg close. The man's tone was conversational, but his gun never wavered.

"I don't have it," she repeated, wishing her voice would stop quavering. Very slowly, she began using her arms to pull herself backward, scooting closer to the edge.

"This is new to you, yes?" If the man noticed her progress, he gave no sign. "But this is a very old game, one we have played for generations..."

"I told you before," Andrea said, her voice a whisper now, "I don't have it."

An electric disco beat tinkled in the air, dancing in the space between them.

"I believe you." The man pulled out his ringing phone and held it up. "Hush now, daddy's talking."

His accent had slipped, but she still couldn't place it.

He turned away to answer the phone, speaking into the receiver in low, murmurous tones. He held the gun loosely in his hand, tapping the nuzzle against his leg impatiently.

Andrea eyed the river below, her adrenaline and terror masking the pain in her foot. She suspected that she was slipping into shock. She wasn't sure it mattered anymore.

Maybe they'd just walk away, she thought giddily. *Maybe they'll forget about me and start searching through the forest. Maybe...*

The man tucked the phone into his pocket and nodded to the others. They raised their weapons and advanced as one.

Christ.

Andrea lunged for the river. As she crested the cliff's edge, she felt two abrupt punches slam into her shoulder. The impact of the bullets only succeeded in pushing her over the edge faster. She screamed with newfound pain as she fell, trying to twist, to straighten her dive, but instead, she slapped belly-first into the river.

The shock caused her to gulp in lungs full of frigid water. Her knees bounced and cracked against the river's cobbled bottom.

Too shallow! Too shallow!

She tried to move her arms, tried to swim, but found that her muscles refused to respond. As the roar of the rapids filled her ears, her body shook with irregular tremors. Although her eyes remained open, darkness swallowed her vision and the cold hand of death stilled her heart.

***

The hooded man peered over the cliff and saw the broken body of the woman drifting in the water below. He shook his head in disgust. "Amateurs."

Waving the others back the way they had come, he placed a call with one hand, while searching in his pocket for a cigarette with the other. He waited patiently as the Internet call dove in and out of the series of routers and blind IPs. He used the time to light up.

"We're gonna need a cleanup crew," he said in German. "No, no sign. We can look, but in this forest, you'd have a better chance of finding a virgin in Vegas."

The response came as a series of deafening shouts. The man held the phone away from his ear and shouted back. "What about the other one? You want us to retrieve that one too?"

Another shout.

Then nothing.

He put the phone back in his pocket. The others had paused, staring at him from the darkness between the trees. He shrugged, then in Hungarian said to the men, "Sounds like he wants try a different approach."

He took a long last drag from his cigarette and looked around the forest. The tree trunks were frosted with early morning sunlight and in the undergrowth, fairytale mushrooms peaked out their heads, crowned with dew. It could take weeks to search properly. Months, if ever. He peered down into the river. The young woman's body, twisted and broken, had lodged between a knuckle of boulders in the river. "Getting that body out will be a nightmare." He sighed, blowing out a cloud of smoke. "Such a waste."

Chapter 1

Day One

AS KEA Wright watched, the stream swept off the edge of the flat mountaintop and slipped effortlessly up into the sky, as if trying to touch the belly of their plane. Here at the edge of Iceland's southern coast, the harsh ocean winds were strong enough to blow waterfalls vertically into the air. Gravity itself seemed to behave differently in this little island country, one of Iceland's many unexpected wonders that kept her coming back year after year.

The plane banked north, turning away from the Atlantic Ocean, and headed toward the Vatnajökull icecap. Gigantic mushroom-shaped mountains lurched up into the sky, standing proudly atop a vista of still pools and rushing streams. While the Ice Age sheets had since faded into the mists of time, they left behind their legacy in the form of these flat-topped mountains and sheer cliffs. As the lava extruded into the glaciers, these table-top mountains, or *tuyas*, had grown one layer at a time, melting their way up through the ice, and now stood as lonely sentinels of a distant past.

She caught a ghostly glimpse of her reflection in the window: freckled nose, tired green eyes, and a fringe of ginger plastered to a greasy brow. It had been a rush job trying to get a flight above the field site before the volunteers arrived. She had barely enough time to tuck her hair into a ponytail and baseball cap; she hadn't stepped foot in a shower for three days. If they could wrap up this flight and finish prepping the camp before noon, she might have time to brush her teeth.

A sudden jolt sent her forehead against the window. Too late, she threw her hands out to brace herself but only succeeded in dropping her camera. It bounced off her lap and clattered onto the floor.

"Sorry about that!" A cheery voice boomed into her headset as the plane completed a tight turn, skimming toward the glacier's eastern edge.

No, you're not, Kea thought. She forced herself to take several deep calming breaths, partly to regain her temper, but mostly to try to keep down her breakfast. Last night's farewell for the previous batch of volunteers had involved a feast of smoked salmon and numerous shots of the potato mash Icelandic vodka, locally known as the 'Black

Death,' that dealt a brutal kick. She had vague memories of participating in a drinking game with Isadora, one of the locals, who ran the park's visitor center. Isadora had won, as always, while Kea had found herself among the ranks of the other wounded warriors who spent most of the morning stumbling around like zombies after a ride on a tilt-a-whirl. This little flight had been Marcus' idea. No doubt he was directing the pilot to take the most turbulent route.

She reached under the seat for her camera, her fingertips only just brushing its casing as she fought against the confines of her safety belt. She took another deep breath and unbuckled the clasp, wedging her other arm against the seat lest the plane perform any more suicidal acrobatics. She managed to retrieve the camera in time to see a blanket of ice fill her window.

Vatnajökull.

Europe's largest ice cap, Vatnajökull, rested on a nest of slumbering volcanoes. A plume of steam emerged from a series of curved crevasses signaling the country's most famous crater: Grímsvötn. The constant volcanic heat melted the overlying ice, filling the caldera with water, and causing ice above to collapse. The resulting circular depression always reminded Kea of a ruined soufflé. The tremendous volume of meltwater generated during eruptions was enough to float the ice dams that impounded Lake Grímsvötn, allowing the water to rush out during a sudden flood, a *jökulhlaup*. The force of the floodwaters was strong enough to rip apart the glaciers, sending house-sized chunks tumbling out across the plains.

Steadying herself against the window, she took as many photographs as she dared as they flew around the depression in the ice. The volcano had been dormant since 2011 and, while it appeared to be puffing away like a chain-smoker, there didn't appear to be any elevated activity compared with what they had seen most of the summer. She thought back to the photographs of past eruptions that captured the billowing ash clouds, riotous with lightning that stretched twenty-kilometers high. Looking at the tremulous gray wisps that drifted above Grímsvötn now, she sighed.

Maybe next year we'll get lucky.

Gulping down another upwelling of bile as the plane turned back towards the ocean, she forced herself to look over the stubble of Marcus' crewcut and out through the cockpit. The pilot, a scraggly little man whose name she still hadn't learned to pronounce after all these years, was saying something to Marcus that she couldn't hear. Their microphones were off, she realized, her conspiracy theory gaining ground.

Marcus, though stocky, was a well-marbled mixture of muscle and fat. Former military, he had fallen victim of one too many nights of beer and pizza at the university with the undergraduates, regaling them with tales of battle in the Middle East. Late to the academic world, and surrounded by those more qualified than him, he fiercely attacked anything that stood in his way. Whatever he lacked in years of research, he made up for it with fieldwork, reveling in it as if he was a general leading a battalion.

At least, Kea thought, *that's probably how Marcus sees himself.*

She bet that he had retired as a junior lieutenant, graduating late from the University of California Burlingame, where they both now worked in San Diego. Today, however, sitting in the cockpit, he was in his element. He had even dug out an old leather bomber jacket for the trip.

He'd also be more tolerable, Kea reflected, *if his attitude toward women wasn't firmly fixed in 1954.*

Ahead she could see the sprawling mass of ice known as Skeiðarárjökull stretching out before them. Skeiðarárjökull was comprised of three glaciers that flowed together on the slopes before spilling out onto the plain below and merging to form a glacier front that extended more than twenty-three kilometers across the valley. Racing toward it at this low altitude, she could only see a small portion of the glacier's mass. Filthy with dirt and ash, the low front of the ice slumbered on the edge of her view as they sped across the outwash plain Skeiðarársandur.

"How close can you get?" Kea pointed to where the Skeiðará Rivers emerged from the glacier's eastern edge, the slender streams twisting like gnarled roots as their braids crisscrossed their way out onto the plain.

"As close as you like," the pilot replied. "There aren't any winds now, so no problem."

"Couple of east-west passes along the front, please." She gestured to where the blackened ice along the margin appeared irregular, pitted from the extensive melting of the underlying ice. Only a couple of years ago, they had been able to lead research teams out onto the glacier on foot this far east, but the rapid retreat of the glacier in recent years had thinned the ice, resulting in treacherous pools and dips that might drop them into the freezing waters with little warning.

"It doesn't look great," Marcus commented airily.

"No, it doesn't," Kea agreed mournfully. The eastern region of the glacier contained meltwater streams that flowed under sub-zero temperatures due to the intense pressure of the overlying ice. It was a key portion of her research – or had been until recently. No field team meant no data. No data meant no publication, which no doubt delighted Marcus. His field area, however, was untouched by the melt. She just wished he didn't sound so smug about it. "Fly as low as you can, please."

"Sure thing." The pilot made a wide sweeping turn, approaching the edge of the ice at a low elevation.

With the glacier margin alongside the plane, Kea could take detailed photographs of the region through her window. The outwash plain still abutted the ice in one location, making passage a possibility, but this late in August, the many pools and shifting ice blocks meant they couldn't risk taking a team out there. Besides, if their research on the glacier's internal response to the recent rapid retreat was correct, this location might be one of the main outlets during the next big flood.

"It's no good," Kea concurred. "We probably won't be able to cross with a team here again 'til winter."

"Shame," agreed Marcus, barely able to contain his glee.

"I don't know what you're so happy about," she snapped. "This means we'll have to keep using the rafts by the Double Embayment," she said gloomily, referring to the main outlet of the most recent large-scale flooding event back in 1996. Because it was located near the center of the glacier margin, getting onto the ice from there involved crossing a lake. In addition to the delay caused by rowing out to the ice, just getting to the rafts involved a long drive and a four-kilometer hike with all their equipment, a journey that took longer every year as the margin steadily retreated.

"Good workout for the shoulders," Marcus mimed rowing with his arms. "Besides, safety first."

Never mind the fact that it's closer to your field site, Kea thought spitefully. She still had a project or two she could conduct in that region, but her focus was on groundwater, which meant she could spend most of her time on the outwash plain, on reassuringly solid ground.

The plane shuddered again as the pilot forced it into another sharp turn.

Cretin.

Kea wiped her hair out of her eyes with the back of her hand. Beads of sweat made her brow cool and clammy as she felt another wave of nausea churn her stomach. Although it was too dangerous to step foot on the ice in the section of the glacier below her, capturing the evolution of the drainage patterns as the glacier retreated might help her produce another paper.

She forced herself to take as many photographs as she could of the adjoining outwash plain. It wasn't much, but at least it was something. She felt the contents of her stomach heave again. "This should be the last run I'll need," she managed to gurgle.

"Yes, yes," Marcus nodded enthusiastically. "I'll just need a few more passes over the Double Embayment."

Kea placed her feet carefully on the floor and rested the crown of her head against the seat in front of her, praying quietly to the treacherous god Bacchus to just make it through this.

***

Twenty minutes later, Kea staggered out of the plane and offered up her breakfast to the gravel runway. Between retches, she saw the two men watching from the cockpit. She could swear she saw Marcus slip the pilot some cash. Since they had prepaid for the flight with the Geology Department's credit card, the two men must have made some kind of bet. She made a vow to do something about it, once she stopped spewing fluid out of her nostrils.

The landing strip was located only a couple of miles from the park but between the variable weather and their restricted funding, they had only managed two flights this field season.

The jeep ride back to Skaftafell National Park was made in silence. Kea spent most of it blowing her nose clean of debris with a wad of tissues she'd found in the glove compartment.

As they pulled out of the airport and onto the main road, Marcus pointed excitedly. "There they are, right on time!"

Kea squinted. Heading toward them along the highway was a battered green jeep, trundling along with a wobbly trailer packed with gear. It was one of theirs, returning with supplies from Reykjavik.

Looming behind the vehicle towered the sheer cliffs of Lómagnúpur, marking the western extent of the field area. Standing more than three thousand feet in height, the basalt massif stood as tall and ominous as a castle built by giants, sheltering the glacier within. It made the jeep look like a cheap child's toy, about to be squashed underfoot.

Marcus gave a merry little toot of his horn in greeting. Tony and Julie, their two graduate students, gave a mock salute before speeding on ahead towards the park.

"It's a bit sad," Marcus commented. "Last supply run of the season. Probably our last flight too."

"Ten more days and home," Kea said, the acrid burn of bile still lingering in her mouth.

Just don't say anything. Let it go, she thought. *He's just pissed Dr. Carlyle left you in charge and not him. Just get through the next ten days.* "I can hardly wait."

"Thank goodness this new team showed up," Marcus observed. "Otherwise, we'd be shutting down early. Eco-Observers seems to be struggling more each year to deliver volunteers."

Kea nodded. Eco-Observers, or EO for short, was a non-profit organization that provided university research teams with eco-tourists from all over the world to help with data collection – if the tourists were willing to pay a sizeable sum. While EO provided volunteers of all ages, sometimes private companies often sent full teams, partially for team building, but mostly for the tax break.

Numbers had been down again this year, however, and they nearly shut down operations last week as they didn't have any volunteers to fill the final ten-day sprint. Then last month, unexpectedly, Eco-Observers headquarters notified them that not one, but two companies would be sending volunteers to help the scientists collect data at the last minute. Great news for the data collection effort, but it meant two more weeks with Marcus.

"Janie and I are headed to Mexico for three weeks after this," Marcus continued. "What are you and Jason planning to do once you get back?"

Kea felt as if she had just been punched in her chest. Unable to respond, she stared out at the expanse of Skeiðarársandur that stretched out to the sea, its flat, endless surface fading into the horizon. She lost herself in its vastness, unable to discern where the shimmering water met the bright blue sky, desperately trying not to dwell on her recent wreck of a relationship.

Just don't say anything.

"Sorry," Marcus realized he'd gone too far. He sputtered for a bit, his fingers twitching on the steering wheel as they tried to find another topic to occupy them. "I forgot about..."

"You're pissed off that he left me in charge, aren't you?" Kea turned to address him directly. *Better out than in. Unlike my breakfast.*

Marcus blew out a long breath, his hands visibly tightening on the steering wheel. "I'm sure he knows what he's doing. Besides, it's only for two weeks."

Gee thanks. Kea turned back to watch the landscape scoot past the window. "I didn't ask for it, if that's what you're wondering." *I asked him not to,* she didn't add. She knew her strengths lay in geology, not entertaining tourists.

"Yes, well, I'm sure it will be fine." Marcus' vice-like grip on the steering wheel remained unchanged. "Besides," he pointed at the trailer in front of them, "I'm very excited that the new equipment is finally here..."

"What new equipment?" Kea turned from the sea to examine her companion.

"The... the new gear our friends bought us," Marcus stammered, obviously realizing he'd said too much. "You know, the gear your friend requested..."

Kea frowned. The gear in question was supposed to be arriving along with the tourists in a bus that hadn't come yet, which Marcus must know.

Upon learning that EO had hooked in the two new companies, Kea had offered to handle the coordination with one company, T3, while Marcus agreed to liaise with the other, Corvis Engineering. Lately, she was starting to wonder exactly what Marcus had been up to, as Corvis kept sending him new mobile phones and some other devices that he refused to show her. For now, she kept her thoughts to herself and focused on the jeep in front of them, curious as to what the trailer might contain.

Marcus changed conversational tracks as they pulled into the park road, blathering on about how much grading he still had to do for the online course he was teaching over the summer. Kea tuned out, randomly nodding encouragingly, as she stared out the window. The sky above was filled with the hulking body of Oræfajökull, the massive snowcapped volcano that watched over the park like a benevolent god.

They followed the quiet road toward the base of the mountain until it opened into a vast parking lot teeming with buses and sport utility vehicles. Driving past the park's tiny, white-walled visitor center, they trundled onto the dirt road through the campsites before easing to a stop beside the main research tent, a battered, green and black affair some twenty meters long.

Once Marcus had parked, Kea helped Julie and Tony unload the paper towels, canned goods, and other sundries from the rear of the jeep, stacking them on the grass. Tony, who had not partaken in the festivities last night, appeared annoyingly refreshed, his sharp chin peppered with a carefully groomed five o'clock shadow. Slender and lanky, his clothes were rumpled in such a way to appear fashionable yet outdoorsy. He effortlessly lifted the heavy crates of milk and orange juice out of the vehicle.

Julie, on the other hand, appeared to still be hungover. The collar of her rain jacket was askew, exposing the nape of her neck; her pale complexion was stuttered with anime tattoos, the shapes of the odd little creatures marked by slashes of yellow, ocher, and violet. Her slender frame and raven black hair made Kea feel ancient, even though they were separated only by a decade. This morning, at least, they had a hangover in common, and both moved at the same sluggish pace.

Kea helped her hoist bags of groceries out of the jeep while Marcus and Tony unloaded some sci-fi looking silver crate about a meter square and hastily headed off in the direction of Marcus' tent. They couldn't have looked guiltier if they were attempting to smuggle a body in a bulging rolled-up carpet. She was dying to know what was inside. "Good trip?"

"Meh," Julie shrugged. "Dropped off the professor at the airport okay. Shopping was a bit of a beast though. The height of the tourist season is the worst time to try to buy all this food." She grabbed another bag of bread that threatened to tumble out of the jeep. "April would have been much easier. Plus, that probe took up too much friggin' space in the trailer."

"About that," Kea said, trying to sound casual. "What is this probe of which you speak?"

"The laser probe Corvis had waiting for us at the airport."

"Laser probe, huh?" Kea attempted a bored tone, her mind whirling. "Fascinating."

It took Julie a moment, but then her eyes grew wide as she realized that Kea was still none the wiser. "He didn't tell you, did he?"

"Not exactly, no." Kea hoped she didn't sound as annoyed as she felt. It would be unprofessional. "So, are you going to tell me what it is, or am I going to have to pull out the thumbscrews?"

Julie stuffed the last loaf into a large bag and started waddling toward the main tent with her bundle, the food seeming about to topple at any moment. "I didn't get to see the thing, but apparently it measures water isotopes and methane concentration in real-time as you drill down into the ice. Provides information about atmospheric conditions when the ice was formed. Basically, you can zap and get instant paleoclimatology as you go down."

"Sounds very swank." Kea made a mental note to do some research once she got back to the visitor center. She moved ahead of Julie and helped her through the flap into the main tent. "And very pricey. Where'd he get it?"

"On loan from the French," Julie dumped the food onto the table then headed back to the jeep with Kea trailing in her wake. "He thinks he'll get loads of publications out of it."

Kea let out a slow sigh, like a kettle about to boil, and counted to ten. When she opened her eyes, she spotted the tour bus in the distance, driving along the wide arc across the outwash plain. "It looks like they're just about to turn off the main highway." She checked her watch. "That should buy us another ten minutes or so before we have to put on the meet and greet."

Julie groaned. "I don't think I'm up for being either meet-y or greet-y right now."

"How about I'll handle the welcoming committee with Marcus," Kea offered. "While you and Tony get a head start on unloading anything that needs to go in the coolers?"

"You sure?" Julie asked. "You're wearing your '*I wanna thump something*' face. The one you wear when undergraduates ask to reschedule exams."

Kea shook her head. "Marcus and I will be fine."

"If you say so." Julie opened the rear of the jeep and started to stack boxes of cucumbers and tomatoes onto the grass. "All I know is that the temperature always seems to drop a couple of degrees when you two are together."

Kea grunted.

"On the ride out this morning, Carlyle mentioned that he put you in charge. I can't imagine that's going over well…" Julie trailed off, obviously hoping Kea would provide more information.

It certainly hadn't gone well. Kea wasn't quite sure what her mentor had been thinking, particularly given her rocky history with Marcus. The man practically lived in the classroom, ignoring the publishing that was so crucial to a university career. When her tenure came through last year, any conversation with him became strained. Now they were both Assistant Professors, competing for a single promotion slot to Professor.

When Kea didn't rise to her bait, Julie pressed, "He has been doing these fieldwork teams for more than a decade. You've only been doing them for what, a few years?"

Kea nodded. Indeed, she had raised this point with Carlyle this very morning. Looking back, he seemed to find the whole affair entertaining.

"His expertise lies in teaching," Carlyle had commented. "While yours is research as well as teaching. If he wants to get promoted, he knows he needs to step up. In the meantime, you're the most qualified ranking personnel to lead this team in my absence."

"I just wish you hadn't, that's all." Kea had folded her arms across her chest. "It's like poking a bear. An angry, armed, NRA dues-paying bear."

"It's just two weeks," Carlyle had reminded her.

"Exactly," Kea had snapped. "Why do it? It will just serve to irritate him further."

"It'll be good practice." Carlyle's blue eyes widened slightly before adding, "for next year."

Kea had considered that for a long moment. "Are you saying that I'll be a team lead next year as well?"

"Not just one team, the project lead," Carlyle had announced with pride. "I'm retiring from fieldwork."

It had taken Kea a moment to digest that.

"I'll still be teaching, of course," Carlyle continued, "but no more disappearing for three months at a time in the summer, I'm afraid. My wife finally put her foot down."

"That's the entire field season," Kea gaped. "You want me to run all the teams?"

"You'll be fantastic," Carlyle had reassured her, as he put on his pack. "You're always fantastic."

"Of course, I'm fantastic," Kea had replied automatically. "It's because I spend my entire time here doing research."

Carlyle had narrowed his eyes. "Are you implying that I don't?"

"I'm pointing out that you spend a great deal of time on these trips researching whiskey." Kea corrected. "The rest of your time is spent taking care of the volunteers. Which is not why I'm here. I didn't spend the last twelve years in school to be a babysitter."

"You'll be fantastic," Carlyle repeated blithely.

"I wish you'd stop saying that." Kea had sighed, contemplating the prospect of being the permanent project lead. "Honestly, I don't know how you manage all of these trips. The money, the logistics..."

"Remember," Carlyle had waved her objections aside, "these volunteers have traveled from across the world to help, to see the landscape, and to learn. When things get tough, just take a deep breath."

"That's it?" Her nostrils had flared in frustration. "That's your advice? Breathe?"

"Breathe." Carlyle had contemplated his walking stick for a moment, a ridiculous collapsible thing with a brass puffin fitted onto the handle. He had placed it carefully down on the table before heading out to the jeep. He had paused before adding, "Well, that and try to bring them back alive."

Back in the present, Kea shook away that ominous memory, and firmly repeated to Julie, "Marcus and I will be fine. Now, what was the name of the other company that sent volunteers?" she asked, trying to navigate the conversation to safer ground. "T3? What does it stand for again, TeleTech or something?"

"It's your friend's company," Julie admonished, referring to Bruce, Kea's old classmate, who was a team lead on T3's software development team. She paused and dug into the pocket of her grimy jeans, pulling out a crumpled copy of the itinerary. "If you can't remember, why should I?"

Kea grimaced. She had last seen Bruce in high school, only coordinating the logistics for this trip via email. She couldn't remember the name of his wife, let alone his company. It had been a godsend funding-wise, although she had been surprised that he had reached out to her so unexpectedly.

Julie scanned the page. "Looks like your friend's company is called Thaumaturgical Telecommunication Technologies."

"That's a mouthful." Kea attempted to repeat the name but failed. "What does it mean?"

Julie shook her head. "Doesn't say. Only their slogan: '*We make miracles happen.*'"

"Well," Kea muttered, "a few of miracles would make a nice change of pace... Right, if you grab Tony and finish unloading the trailer, I'll head over and play hostess. And Julie..."

"Don't worry," Julie tapped a jar of chocolate hazelnut spread. "I'll stash your precious cargo in the toolbox. Your addiction is safe with me." She winked before heading back to the storage area.

Kea stopped by her own tent long enough to drop off her wallet and camera. She pulled on her dark green long-sleeve t-shirt with '*Eco-Observers*' emblazoned across the front in friendly white letters. Trotting behind the main tent, she grabbed her clipboard and a battered cardboard '*Welcome Team!*' sign, and then walked across the grassy campground filled with sealed tents and empty lawn chairs. Most of the campers were out hiking for the day, although a few odd stragglers hauled laundry bags back and forth to the main building.

As she weaved through the tents, she saw the tour bus arrive at the visitor center, along with some cars pulling in behind it. She was close enough to see the first passengers step off the bus. A large man with black framed glasses and a head as bald as a turnip spotted her and started waving.

Bruce.

She was struck by how old he looked before it occurred to her that he might be thinking exactly the same thing about her. High school seemed so far away. Although she could tell from his frame and body language that it was Bruce, his loss of hair and substantial weight gain made him seem like a cheap stunt double. Hopefully, despite her similar mileage, she didn't appear as worn.

Then again, Kea reflected, *time has been no good friend of mine.* She gave Bruce a hearty wave and picked up her pace. Just then, a woman's scream redirected her attention to the rear of the bus.

Cursing under her breath, she changed direction to intercept the yelling. She waded into the crowd of volunteers clustered around the luggage compartment at the rear of the bus and forced a smile.

Chapter 2

"CAREFUL! THAT'S a six-hundred-dollar espresso machine!" The indignant voice belonged to a woman with a tremendous explosion of quivering black curls. Wearing a pristine yellow jacket, she clutched desperately at a massive orange suitcase that lay half-open on the sidewalk. Marcus held the other handle, watching helplessly as its contents tumbled around in the breeze. The woman lunged into the pile of clothes and junk food and emerged triumphantly hugging the expensive coffee maker.

"Hello," Kea ventured as Marcus fumbled with the cookies and bags of potato chips that tumbled out of the suitcase. She knelt carefully so as not to crush any of the cupcakes and helped stuff everything back into the suitcase. "I'm Dr. Kea Wright."

"Bonnie." Bangles clattered on the woman's wrist as she shook Kea's hand. "Don't worry, I've nearly got it sorted out."

Kea noticed that Bonnie's lips were perfectly glossed and her hazel eyes were nestled inside deft strokes of cerulean eyeliner. Kea remembered wearing make-up herself once when she was a teenager. Before geology entered her life. Now she wore dust, dirt, and sunburn as a badge of honor.

Marcus frowned at the motley array of gadgets and foodstuffs as Bonnie packed them back into the case. "You did read the welcome guide, didn't you?" he asked, referring to the materials that were shipped to all volunteers. The documents stipulated the appropriate gear and provisions for fieldwork in a sub-Arctic environment. "You are aware that this is a *camping* expedition?"

"Of course," Bonnie replied as if addressing a toddler. "I just like to be comfortable. Plus..." She shoved a DVD player into a cushion of rumpled silk lingerie. "I have three seasons of zombies to catch up on."

Kea eyed Bonnie's haul. In Iceland, where a large bag of chips could cost up to twelve dollars, this woman would be very popular. Add the DVD player to the equation and Bonnie would be a superstar if they got rained in for days at a time. She just hoped that somewhere in all that mess the woman had packed some actual field gear.

Kea pulled the roster out of the volunteer folder and scanned for the woman's name. "Bonnie... Bonnie Clark?"

"The one and only," Bonnie answered cheerfully.

Kea ticked the box next to her name, hoping that Bonnie hadn't heard Marcus mutter, *'We can only hope,'* under his breath.

Ignoring him, Kea examined the rest of the arrivals. While some were still watching Bonnie re-pack, others gaped in wonder at the world around them. They all wore the standard green Eco-Observers T-shirt, but that was where any similarity ended. Composed of men and women of many races, the group was clothed in a hodgepodge of jeans and cargo shorts, fanny packs, sun hats, and jackets. Most had already abandoned their gear on the sidewalk, a growing heap of sleeping bags, tents, and rucksacks, in order to take photographs of the scenery.

"Can everyone please check in with me?" Kea raised her clipboard in the air to get their attention. The next few minutes were a blur as she put a checkmark next to fifteen names. It happened so quickly, she had barely registered their faces.

Bruce patiently waited his turn in line, before enfolding her in a huge hug. She let out an *'oomph'* as he forced the air out of her lungs. Patting him gently on the back, she pried herself free.

"Long time." Bruce stood back and considered her, a gentle smile on his face.

She grinned back. He looked exhausted. His complexion was pallid, and deep circles wallowed beneath his eyes. Dusty silver scruff peppered his chin in odd patches as if he had tried to shave while drunk. His belt was on its last notch as it half-heartedly struggled to contain his paunch. His appearance was in stark contrast to his pictures on social media pages she'd seen, although in her experience, those were notoriously misleading anyway. She forced her smile a bit wider and said, "You look great!"

"And you're still too kind by half," Bruce laughed. "You look amazing. How long have you been out here?"

"Three months or so." She rubbed her neck, trying to remember the last time she had slept in a real bed. "We spent most of June in our tents though - it rained for six weeks solid."

"I hope we have better luck than that," Bruce said. "Sounds miserable."

Kea shrugged. "On the plus side, this far north of the equator, we get about twenty-two hours of daylight. When we get a good weather day, we can cram in twice the work. Anyway, let me get everyone settled then we can catch up over a drink later."

"Best news I've heard in weeks," Bruce smiled. "It's a date."

Kea joined Marcus in front of the group. "Welcome to Skaftafell! I'm Dr. Kea Wright and this is Dr. Marcus Posner."

A gust of wind fluttered the brim of Marcus' absurd fishing hat, its long flat tail making it appear as if he was sporting a green mullet. While he insisted that the hat kept the rain off his face and the sun off his neck, the wide brim made his gnomish body appear even shorter. It didn't help that he had a habit of wearing green waterproof trousers. The ensemble made him look like a leprechaun.

Kea wondered, as she had so many times, whether he intentionally appeared ridiculous to catch people off-guard.

"If you'll follow us, we'll take you to your new home for the next ten days." Marcus led the team through the visitor parking lot and out onto the main campground.

Kea brought up the rear, making sure no one was left behind, although she lost sight of Bruce in the process.

"Excuse me!" called a breathless voice.

Kea turned to see a middle-aged woman jogging around the bus. She had a world-weary, been-there-done-that air of confidence about her. Judging by the look of her new boots and outer gear, she wasn't strapped for cash either.

"Dr. Wright?" The woman extended a hand. "Lexie. Lexie Girard."

"Great to finally meet you. We've never had a reporter on our trips before." Kea had exchanged a flurry of emails with Lexie over the last few weeks. "We're very happy that you could join us."

"Not all, I'm thrilled to be here," Lexie gushed.

"If you need anything, just let us know. We practically live in that thing," Kea nodded to the main tent. She noticed the large camera bag under the reporter's arm. "We've also got a generator in a spare trailer by the jeeps."

"Thanks! That'll help." Lexie hefted the straps on her shoulders. "I'll be shooting and recording as much as I can for the piece. Let me know if I'm ever in the way or if there's anything that's a must-see."

"Sounds fantastic." Kea was genuinely grateful. The advertising could mean they wouldn't be so desperate for volunteers next year. "When will the article get published?"

"EO usually updates its website every couple of weeks," Lexie explained, "but this piece will probably be in the annual mailer in the fall. With any luck, expect to see a spike in volunteers signing up for next year after it goes out. Um…" She looked over Kea's shoulder. "I think you're being hailed."

Kea turned to see Julie waving to her from the entrance of the main tent. Kea said a quick goodbye to Lexie and jogged ahead to join the graduate students handing out laminated maps to the volunteers.

Tony had changed into a loose linen shirt and baggy cargo pants as if he was ready to head out to the clubs. He'd obviously spent time primping for the arrival of the new volunteers and seemed to be scanning the new female volunteers with a player's eyes.

The new arrivals were disheveled, their hair tossed and askew, their clothes crumpled, eyes still heavy with sleep. She felt a rush of sympathy for them. Most had arrived on the early morning flight into the airport located at the westernmost end of the island. After picking up their luggage and stumbling into a bus, they were whisked across the black alien wasteland of steaming volcanic plains before arriving in the capital, Reykjavík. It would have then taken them another six hours by bus to reach Skaftafell. Since some volunteers had traveled from as far away as New Zealand, they may have spent anywhere from twelve to thirty-six hours just to get there, not to mention the jet lag.

Watching them shift and mutter, Kea was finally able to place what was bothering her. Normally, volunteers wound up chatting and mixing with the others during the long drive and numerous stops, from the city. Looking at this group, however, she noticed that they were split into two distinct factions. It wasn't too surprising, considering they were from two different companies, she thought, but the glares the teams exchanged set off her Spidey senses.

"Okay, everyone!" Marcus released a trio of enthusiastic claps to get their attention. "At UC San Diego Burlingame, we've been working with Eco-Observers to run this research expedition for several years now. Indeed, some of us have been coming to Iceland for more than a decade, others a fair bit less." He let his gaze linger on Kea.

Kea had never seen him so happy, so confident. He was positively beaming. Given the demotion Carlyle had handed out this morning, this wasn't the reaction she'd expected. Either Marcus was putting on a brave face, or he was up to something. Or both. She matched his hyper-focused gaze, but the anger she saw smoldering in his eyes made her realize that she was sailing into uncharted waters.

Here be dragons.

"Now," Marcus turned his attention back to the volunteers, "we're going to do quick introductions, then we'll help you set up your tents."

This was the part that always went too fast for Kea, although she did her best to keep up. At the university, on the first day of classes, she normally had digital photographs to help her put faces to names of the new students. In the field, all they had was a list of names. She had studied the medical forms last night, but nothing really stood out, although she was constantly amazed at how many people were allergic to dairy. The most dangerous condition listed for this season was one woman who had asthma. She made a mental note to look up who that was later.

The volunteers went around one by one and gave their first name and town or country of origin. Kea caught a few names that rang a bell. Gary. Derek. Fernando. Bonnie, of course. A giant bear of a man named Max. The two men who had carried Bonnie's bags, Jon and Erik. A Russian father-daughter team, Andrei and Nadia. Tiko and Amirah. Bruce, of course. A striking woman named Zoë and her teenage son. She missed a handful of other names.

As the group dispersed, Kea assisted as best she could by untangling poles and rain flies as they set up tents. Most of her time was spent reassuring them that they wouldn't be washed away by a flood or buried by a volcanic eruption. She noticed that the group seemed to be placing their tents up in two separate camps, or at least as far apart as they could in the space provided. She made a mental note to ask Bruce if he had any idea what all the tribalism was about.

Kea paused at the sound of hushed grumblings. A peculiar man with wiry gray hair was muttering to himself as he knotted a cluster of guide ropes to a peg. She considered going to his aid, but he seemed to be in the middle of a full-on discussion with his tent. His beak-like nose was perched atop a scraggly beard and the collar of his flannel shirt curled up on each side as if the shirt wanted to take flight. Although she couldn't hear much of what he was saying, he seemed to be threatening the knots with a fiery death if they didn't immediately unravel.

"First sign of madness?" whispered Julie by her side. "Or wizard?"

"I have to admit," Kea said as she ushered her graduate student away from the man, "the longer I've been out here, the more I catch me talking to myself. You'll understand..."

"... When I'm older?" Julie teased.

"When you start teaching undergraduates," Kea replied archly.

"Check out the bros." Julie pointed to the two men in their late twenties, or early thirties, who looked almost identical. They had taken off their shirts to indulge in the bright sun. Their skin was dark, riddled with spiraling tattoos that skittered up torsos before wrapping around their bulging necks and vanishing beneath quaffs of perfectly spiked hair.

Kea felt for a moment as if she had walked onto a photo shoot for a pin-up calendar. As she checked her clipboard for names, she tried to recall the last time she had stepped foot in a gym.

"Jon and Erik," she remembered at last. "They're with T3. I think I heard Max say they're cousins."

"Who's the cougar?" Julie asked.

Kea looked up. Bonnie had joined the two men and was handing them two large plastic margarita cups filled with some beverage.

What else had that woman packed in her suitcase?

Jon, the taller of the two men, caught Kea staring at him. She looked away quickly, feeling her cheeks flush.

Here for the science, she reminded herself, *I'm here for the science.*

"Interesting," Julie observed. Bonnie was giggling and laughing at the young man, the woman's eyelashes fluttering like the wings of a butterfly on crack. "I've never seen one hunting in the wild before."

"That's enough." Kea grabbed Julie's shoulders and turned her around. "Stop gawking and get back to work."

As Julie stalked off a huff, Kea lingered long enough to see her force her way into the conversation with Erik, much to Bonnie's evident dismay.

Just ten days, Kea mentally reprimanded Julie. *Just wait ten days. Then, when this expedition is over, you can flirt with whoever you want.*

25

Shaking her head, Kea continued her rounds assisting volunteers. Nearing the edge of the group, she locked eyes with a slender woman with long dark hair.

Zoë Forbes.

During the round of introductions, Kea had made a point of identifying her. Even at this distance, she noted Zoë's slim, athletic figure. Her dark braids swept down her back to fall across her trim waist, while her lithe legs stabbed down into hiking boots that seemed ridiculously large for her frame.

Walking over, Kea smiled awkwardly, realizing that her cheeks were flushed for the second time that day. "It's nice to finally meet you!"

"Same," Zoë shook her hand.

Kea, spellbound by the woman's copper complexion, her dark, languid eyes, and the warm touch of her skin, discovered that she was holding her breath. She forced herself to exhale, slowly.

Zoë pulled the teenage boy over. "This is my son, Cole."

Cole had his mother's raven hair and narrow face, his eyes two dark specks framed by soft, delicate lashes. His clothes were rumpled, a mixture of flannel and an ill-fitting long sleeve t-shirt that drooped across his thin, angular frame. Teenage angst hung about him like a dreary cloud, tugging his shoulders down and making his every move appear reluctant, burdensome. Despite this affliction, Kea had the impression that he would someday grow into a very large man indeed.

"Have a good trip?" Kea asked, shaking Cole's hand.

Cole's hazel eyes scrutinized Kea for a moment before dismissing her outright. "Was long." He turned back to his tent. "Mom, the knots are still all tangled."

Zoë winced, but Kea waved it aside. "It's okay, I just wanted to say thank you again for stepping in at the last minute."

"Not a problem, Bruce said you needed help, and I'm glad we came." Zoë stared at the glaciers above them. "It's amazing here."

"Did you have any trouble at customs?" Kea asked.

"Nope, the permits you arranged were perfect." Zoë waved at the boxes by her feet. "Should be ready to go whenever you need them."

"Thank you again," Kea smiled. "I can't tell you how much this means..."

"Mom!" Cole pleaded.

Despite Cole's size, the whine in his voice caused Kea to dial down her estimate of his maturity. Not for the first time, Kea wondered if she'd ever have children of her own, or if she'd wind up drowning them at the first sign of a tantrum.

"Sorry." Zoë moved to help her son. "See you in a bit!"

Walking away, Kea couldn't help looking back at Zoë and found herself thinking, *Just ten days... ten long days indeed.*

While the volunteers continued to set up their tents, Kea took a moment to return to her tent to change into a pair of sneakers. As she was lacing up, her phone gave a quiet *ding*. It was a notification of an email from a colleague at one of the New York State universities with the subject heading: *'Thought you might want to see this.'* The attachment contained a submission to a popular scientific journal. Opening it, the sight of the article's title and the main author made her blood boil.

"That bastard," she breathed.

Kea scrolled through the document, gulping it down in flashes of black and white as it flickered across the screen: Marcus had submitted an article for publication on the effects of terrain on glacial flooding, using data they collected together during the previous field season. She flipped through to the analysis and references. Not only had he not included her as a co-author, but she also wasn't listed in the acknowledgment section, nor in the references.

Calm, Kea reminded herself, *remain calm. Marcus hasn't written a paper in decades, it's probably rubbish.*

It had better be rubbish.

She connected her phone to her laptop, transferred the file, and began to read the paper on the larger screen, as the noises from the camp settled into a background hum. It only took ten minutes to come to the throat-clenching conclusion that while the document wasn't groundbreaking, it also wasn't a complete insult to the scientific community.

It might actually get published, she realized with growing horror. She started digging through her hard drive, trying to find her original data files. *Was he working with her processed data or did he use the raw data?*

"What the hell do you want?" A voice whispered hoarsely just outside her tent.

Startled, Kea nearly tossed her laptop into the air.

"Why did we have to come here?" The voice was less than a foot away. It was male, foreign, and angry.

"Keep your voice down." A large silhouette settled across the rear of her tent. Given its size, it could only belong to the bear of a man, Max.

Kea found that she was holding her breath. She was suddenly hyper-aware of how stifling the humid air inside her tent was, how even the faint daylight had managed to boil her laundry, creating a funky, ripe stench.

I should make a noise, she thought responsibly. *Rattle around a bit to let them know that I'm here, that they should move on.*

"A team building exercise? Now?" The accent clicked. New Zealand. There was only one in their party. Derek. "After what happened to Andrea?"

Very slowly, Kea closed her laptop to hide the glow of the screen. She sat up straight and listened intently.

"Can you think of a better time?" Max's deep voice rumbled like the sound of boulders rubbing together in a river.

"Any time other than now." Derek gesticulated wildly, the shadows of his arms dancing across Kea's tent. "We were already six months behind on production."

"A couple of setbacks-" Max protested.

"Setbacks? Seriously?" Derek's voice went up a notch.

Due to the distortions of the shadows on the fabric of the tent, Kea couldn't tell if Derek was pulling his hair out or just tugging violently on his knit cap.

"A couple of setbacks," Max repeated, his tone hardening. "It just means we need to be more focused as a team and learn how to work together."

"My team," Derek said slowly, "knows what we're doing, we're not the ones-"

Ding. Her phone's email notification chimed merrily.

Kea froze, her eyes frantically searching the profiles that rested against the tent wall for signs that they had noticed. The shadows lingered for a moment, then slipped away, the conversation aborted.

Kea let out a long sigh as she considered.

Drama to the left, drama to the right.

She glanced at her phone. The email was a reminder about open enrollment for health benefits.

Damn.

At least they didn't know it was her inside the tent. Although, she supposed, they'd work it out at some point, unless she spent the rest of the trip inside her tent. She closed her eyes and took another breath.

Tempting, but dear god it stinks in here.

She opened her laptop and stared at the paper again. She'd have to talk to Marcus. She sent off a note of thanks to her colleague and examined the data files again in case there was some data that he missed.

After running several searches, she found nothing on their shared drives. Anything she really wanted to get her hands on was undoubtedly on Marcus' laptop.

Shrugging off the dread at having to confront Marcus, she found herself more concerned with the variables she wasn't familiar with: the volunteers themselves. She pulled up the roster. Max and Derek belonged to T3. She peeled off a sticky note and made a list of the team members and their respective companies, T3 or Corvis, for future reference.

It was another five minutes before she realized she was late for the team huddle. Swearing, she crammed her laptop into her pile of laundry and bolted for the main tent.

***

After giving the group an overview of the camp, the leads let the volunteers loose on the visitor center café for an early afternoon dinner. The remainder of the evening was left open for the volunteers to take a flight over the glacier, or in most cases, simply turn in early.

Kea would gladly have hit the sack as well, but she had a mountain of receipts to document, papers to grade, and field equipment to check. However, she made a point of visiting Bruce after dinner. She found two empty folding chairs waiting for her outside his tent and his legs and rump sticking out of the tent flap. She coughed politely to announce her presence.

"Oh, ah, sorry," Bruce called from inside the tent. She spied him hurriedly tucking something small and blue into the space under his sleeping bag before crawling back out.

"I brought you some hot cocoa." Kea brandished a thermos and a couple of plastic mugs. Pouring the drinks, she noticed that Bruce had changed into sweats and an Icelandic sweater, gift-shop fresh. It had been so long since she had seen him, and he appeared so changed, that she found that she didn't quite know what to say.

"You okay?" Bruce spoke first, eyeing her warily as he accepted a mug. "You look like someone threw a wet cat at you."

Kea shook her head. "Just a bit irritated with a colleague right now. He's normally just annoying, but he's upped it to a new level this week. Plus, it turns out he made a special arrangement with Corvis to get some new gear out here."

He looked puzzled. "How is that any different from me getting Zoë and her toys out here for you?"

Kea narrowed her eyes. She was in no mood for people who used facts against her in arguments. "It's very different," she replied, wounded. "Epically different. I *told* everyone what I was doing. I didn't go sneaking around with crates acting like they contained the Ark of the Covenant."

Bruce just chuckled quietly. "You're welcome."

"What? Oh, yeah, thanks again for arranging that," Kea replied sheepishly. "What's her story anyway?"

"Zoë? We use her sometimes for some testing and evaluation. She's independent so we can contract her out for short gigs. Lost her for a while, guess she and her wife had a messy divorce last year, but she's been helping out quite a bit lately."

"Really? How interesting," Kea replied. *Wife? Divorced?* She filed that fact away in a drawer labeled: '*Yay!*'

"And you?" Bruce prompted. "How has life treated you since high school?"

"Well, I spent nearly all of that time doing indentured servitude, or as they call it in academia, a Ph.D. Then, I spent last spring dealing with a messy breakup myself," she admitted. "But now I'm drowning in work and busy doing the whole avoidance thing with this expedition, which is just lovely and distracting. Essentially, that's fifteen years of me in a nutshell." She took another sip of her drink and found herself wishing for marshmallows, wondering why it was so easy to sum up her life so quickly. "Your turn."

"Pretty much the same," Bruce considered. "College, followed by office work, then start-up company. Still married, although marriage can be just as messy sometimes..."

Kea got the impression the conversation was heading somewhere unpleasant if she pulled on that thread, so she fell silent again. She examined the lines that crinkled his temples and the loose chins that jiggled when he shifted in his chair. His hair, once light brown, was riddled with silver and gray strands. Mostly bald, the crown of his head was studded with groves of freckles that shone under a slick of grease. His voice was the same as she remembered, yet tinged with a harsh rasp that made him sound wiser, aged.

She wondered if time really did imbue knowledge, or if he, like her, still felt as if she were still the same person she was at sixteen, forever a stranger in a body that seemed to creak and groan in protest more each year. She gave a little shudder and gripped her mug tighter, enjoying the warmth that seeped into her skin.

"We're very happy that you guys could fit us in at such short notice," Bruce said, seeming to want to move the conversation to safer ground.

"No problem," Kea said. "We were short on volunteers, and you guys fell into our lap. Great timing."

Bruce laughed. "Tax write-off for us, plus team building. Two birds..."

Silence sat awkwardly between them.

"Are you going on the flight over the glacier tonight?" she asked, wincing as she remembered her own recent excursion.

"Yeah, I'm part of the second group." Bruce checked his watch. "Headed out in about a half-hour."

A dozen blond little heads bobbed and weaved in the grass field before them, the children squealing with delight as they chased after a soccer ball. Farther away, a horde of teenagers played their own game while the parents cheered every goal. The sound of the supportive families felt so different from their own new batch of volunteers. Kea found herself anxious to fill the silence between herself and Bruce.

Once more Bruce beat her to it. "This break up..."

"I'd rather not talk about it," Kea said with a sigh, then contradicted herself. "I'm not sure if the problem was him or me."

"Him?" Bruce's eyebrows wiggled in surprise. "That's a change."

Kea narrowed her eyes. "It's about the *person*," she reminded him, "not about what's between their legs."

"If you say so," Bruce stared into his mug. "If I recall, you dumped me for that dreadful girl, Tina, wasn't it?"

She laughed. "It was the fifth grade for god's sake. It's not like you and I ever really dated." She chuckled longer than she should have, vividly remembering breaking up with him all those years ago. Although they remained friends, they had drifted apart during high school and had only stayed in touch since then through the odd social media post.

Kea studied him again out of the corner of her eye. Aside from a less than healthy diet, Bruce seemed to carry a weight heavier than his years about him, that caused his head to droop and his back to bow. She was afraid to ask, worried it would require far more than hot chocolate and she wasn't feeling up to playing therapist tonight. Instead, she resorted to empty platitudes. "It really is great to see you, honestly. It's just today… I've been put in charge. It's making my stress levels skyrocket."

Bruce nodded. "I don't know how you do it. I can't imagine taking care of complete strangers who swap out every couple of weeks."

"It can be... exhausting," Kea agreed, taking another sip. "I haven't even filed the accounts yet for the last expedition. Nor applied for a grant for the spring."

"You take on too much, like always." Bruce sounded worn and tired as he spoke, as if knowing she would disregard his advice as soon as he said it. "You can't be responsible for everyone. You'll burn yourself out. Or drive people away."

"You sound a lot like Jason." Kea stared into her drink, tracing the chaotic circles of chocolate residue that lined the inside of her mug. "Apparently, I spent too much time working, and not enough time scrumping."

"Is Jason the ex you aren't talking about?" Bruce asked with a grin.

"Exactly," Kea said firmly. "Talking about it no more will I. The day has been long enough."

"What about that one?" Bruce indicated the edge of the field with his chin. "He looks like trouble."

"Who?" Kea followed his gaze to see Tony walking along the line of tents, his hands jammed into the pockets of his windbreaker. "Oh, him. That's Marcus' graduate student."

"He seemed very friendly with the girl at the visitor center," Bruce observed with amusement.

"Yes," Kea agreed carefully. "He's quite a fan of Ísadóra." She hoped Tony knew what he was doing. The young Icelandic woman's father ran a supply store in Reykjavík. In addition to owning the company they were renting the jeep from, Ísadóra's father was a tremendous tank of a man.

"Is he a good guy?" Bruce pressed.

"Tony?" Kea considered. As far as she knew, Tony was engaged to Jennifer, a biology graduate student back at the university. Over the last two months with no Jennifer around, Ísadóra appeared to have fit the bill. "He's... very good at his job." She took another long sip, letting the drink warm her throat. Exhaustion numbed her mind, lowering her defenses. "I have to say..." she gave her friend a long, honest look. "You look like something Death threw up."

Bruce roared. "Now that's the Kea I remember. And thanks."

"Anytime." She laughed along with him, but followed up with, "So, what's up?"

"Long days." He rubbed the bridge of his nose and gave a little snort. "And longer nights. We lost a key person recently, Andrea, who was just fantastic. Not that start-ups aren't tough enough."

"I got that impression." Kea remembered Max and Derek mentioning Andrea. "Tempers do seem to be running high."

"Yeah well, we've all had a rough couple of months. We're hoping this," Bruce gestured at the kids, the mountain, the sky, "gets everyone to chill out a bit."

"This ain't Turks and Caicos," she pointed out. "I can't promise to chill them out, but I can guarantee eight days of hard labor."

"Like I said," Bruce smiled grimly, "team building."

To Kea, team building exercises implied resolving pre-existing conflicts, airing embarrassing personnel issues, and sometimes resulted in discrimination lawsuits. In short, drama.

"While it is great to see you," she said carefully, "I do feel the need to remind you that our team is here to do science." She recalled how the group had shifted their tents into two separate encampments. Even at dinner in the visitor center, the split between the teams had been even more marked, with the Corvis group taking their food back to the main tent. "Not to mend emotional divides. Otherwise, we'd charge a lot more.

"We're not direct competitors," Bruce explained. "Corvis does engineering, and we're just software development. We have teamed up on a couple of projects, but lately, things have been a bit strained, financially."

She waited, but this time Bruce seemed content to let the conversation stall. For the sake of her own team, she pressed one last question. "Is there anyone I should watch out for?"

He seemed hesitant to reply. "In what way?"

She considered how to phrase the question without being offensive. "Well, you know, aggressive, reckless troublemakers. That sort of thing."

"Kea, we're two startup companies made up of engineers and developers desperate to make a fortune," Bruce answered quietly. "We're all aggressive, reckless troublemakers."

Kea stared sadly at the gooey remains of the hot chocolate powder that hugged the bottom of her mug. "Oh goody."

Chapter 3

Day Two

KEA STARED at her reflection in the jeep's mud-spattered side mirror. A tired face smeared with streaks of white sunblock blinked back from behind the scratched frames of her old glasses. While she could get away with wearing her contacts around the shelter of the grassy campsite, the high winds and loose grit on Skeiðarársandur made them impractical. The unfamiliar weight of the frames on her nose made her feel insecure and awkward, as if she were back in grade school.

She gripped the armrest fiercely as Julie turned off the highway and juddered onto the dirt track that led toward the glacier Skeiðarárjökull. Glancing at the volunteers crammed in the back of the jeep, she saw them chatting and laughing, oblivious to the shaking and skidding of the tires. The instant coffee had done little to reinvigorate her spirits, and as she watched the landscape bounce past her window, she willed her brain to wake up.

The track traversed an old floodplain, an irregular expanse of sand that stretched out for kilometers on either side, covered with patches of moss and fine grass. The land was pockmarked by huge circular depressions that grew progressively wider as they drove closer to the glacier. It looked like someone had carpet-bombed the entire plain. These gaping cavities, called kettle holes, were formed by gigantic ice blocks that had been ripped out of the glacier margin, stranded and buried by the floods.

Julie took another turn too quickly, and Kea's stomach lurched as they sped up the dirt ramp to the Háöldukvísl dam before screeching to a halt. With a sigh of relief, Kea stepped out to supervise the unloading of the volunteers. She used the opportunity to survey the dam. Plowed into place from sand and gravel by the Icelandic Roads Authority, the dam was erected due to concerns that flood waters would wipe out the highway bridges, as they had in 1996.

No danger of that now, Kea thought, looking across the vast trench that lay between the dam and the snout of the glacier. To the east lay Öræfajökull, its crisp white peaks basking in the bright morning sun.

To the west rose the dark wall of Lómagnúpur, its upper reaches swathed in mist. To the north, between the dam and the glacier margin lay a series of broad lakes and innumerable swarms of braided streams and channels that crisscrossed the depression. In the 1940's, the ice would have nestled right up to the jeep, but today the glacier was a dark form that slumbered up the valley, four kilometers distant.

She often thought of the glacier like a giant thumb pressing down on a hose. The bigger the thumb and the harder it pressed, the more river channels were squeezed out onto the sandur. Now that the thumb was retreating up the mountain - more like an index finger now - it left the remaining river, the Gígjukvísl, draining the middle of the enormous valley. While still an imposing channel in its own right, the Gígjukvísl was nothing compared to the five channels that had dominated this plain for a century. The retreat of the drainage basin into the depression left the Háöldukvísl drainage channel, and the dam, high and dry.

Kea shielded her eyes from the sun and considered the rapid retreat of the glacier over the last decade. It seemed as if it was crawling shamefully back into the embrace of its mother, Vatnajökull. I've given up for now, the glacier seemed to be saying. But I'll be back, just you wait. Someday.

I hope so, she thought mournfully.

Marcus called for everyone's attention. He had propped up a large, laminated map on the back of the jeep and started scribbling on it with a dry erase marker.

"The first word we'd like you to learn," Marcus began, not waiting for Kea to join him, "and my personal favorite, is *jökulhlaup*. This is the Icelandic term for large floods that emerge from a glacier. *Jökull* means glacier, while *hlaup* means running. These large-scale outburst floods may be caused by the release of water trapped within the glacier due to melt, severe rainfall, or even volcanic activity. Here we have not just volcanic activity as a source, but additionally, Lake Grænalón," he pointed on the map to a spot in the mountains where a large lake lay alongside the glacier, "which can also drain if the water can generate enough pressure to lift the ice dam."

Marcus seemed so energized, so eager to please the crowd, that Kea couldn't help but wonder why the thought of destroying his career delighted her so much. If only he would just stay out of her way and let her get on with her work.

Or, she reflected, *am I just still holding a grudge against Carlyle for engineering this whole scenario?*

Both, she decided. Definitely both.

As Marcus reeled off figures of the last great flood in 1996, Kea noticed that most of the team appeared to be paying attention, or at least taking photographs of the landscape and nodding occasionally. Bonnie was smiling politely, but Kea could tell that her mind was somewhere else. One girl in a tank-top, Nadia, was playing a game on her phone, furiously jabbing away with her thumbs. She appeared unimpressed when Marcus revealed that the flood's discharge had rivaled that of the Amazon River. Several of the other volunteers were blinking slowly, trying to keep awake.

Kea walked to the front of the crowd and caught Marcus' eyes. She gently rubbed her throat, hoping he'd take the hint. Oblivious, he looked past her and continued discussing the implications of glacial overburden pressure on sub-glacial drainage regimes.

"We want you to understand why we're here," Kea chimed in when Marcus paused to draw breath. "The big 'what is this all about,' if you will."

Marcus finally took her cue. "Indeed. These floods and the surges, the rapid advances, are all mechanisms that we think would be similar to those at work within continental ice sheets that were active during the ice ages. The retreat of the glaciers here, and the resulting exposed landforms, provide us with an opportunity to understand the processes that may have formed the similar landscapes under the ice sheets during the last ice age…"

Kea drifted back to check on her equipment in the trailer while Julie and Tony took up the narrative, thanking the volunteers for their time. Without their assistance, they pointed out, they would never be able to collect all the data they needed for their graduate work, given that the glacier itself was over twenty kilometers across.

Once they had finished wrapping up the safety briefing, Marcus herded the team across the dirt parking lot, Dr. Carlyle's walking stick held high, Kea noted. She had spent ten minutes this morning searching through the crates looking for the wretched thing.

I should have guessed he'd steal it.

"We're going to head down into the proglacial depression," Marcus said, waving to the bottom of the steep slope, some thirty meters below. "From here, it's a forty-minute walk to the glacier margin, but it's fairly level. Just take it slow and steady. Remember, we're not splitting up into teams until after we cross the lake and get on the ice. All right then, let's head out!"

Kea, still fumbling in the back of the jeep's trailer, shook her head in irritation. Once again, Marcus hadn't waited for her but had taken the lead, leaving her to follow up from behind. She unlocked the secure box in the trailer where they kept the valuables and, with more force than necessary, shoved aside the satellite phones, emergency cash, and spare batteries in order to pull out the air compressor. She tucked it into her pack, locked the box and then, making sure no one was looking, hid the keys in the wheel well. They had learned from past experiences that it was better to keep the keys with the vehicles. It was difficult to evacuate someone for a medical emergency if the person with the keys to the vehicle was several kilometers away on a glacier.

She stood back up and nearly yelped in alarm: Tony's head peered over the edge of the trailer, a delighted grin on his face. His sudden appearance was surprising enough, as he normally went out of his way to avoid her. His joyous expression also meant that he had something he wanted to share, and that was never a good thing.

"Did you hear what went down last night?" Tony came around the side of the trailer, pure delight etched into his face.

No 'hello' or 'good morning? Kea sighed and placed a hand against the trailer to steady herself. "No… what happened?"

"Sometime last night, someone dropped anchor right in front of Max's tent." Tony grinned. "He stepped in it this morning."

"I'm sorry," Kea said as calmly as she could, "I have no idea what you're talking about-"

Tony giggled. "Someone left a huge, steaming pile of-"

"Enough!" Kea cut him off once the realization hit her. "You're kidding me, right? Please tell me this is a joke."

Tony shook his head, still smirking.

"Why didn't someone say something?" Kea rubbed the bridge of her nose with her fingers, mentally trying to will the problem away. "You sure it wasn't a dog or something?"

"No dogs around. I overheard Erik and Jon talking about it on the ride out." Tony helped Kea lift her bag out of the trailer. "Max was livid, apparently."

"I can imagine." The thought of a man as large and as powerful as Max angry and soiled, did little to calm Kea's nerves. "What happened?"

Tony shrugged. "I guess they buried it."

"That's not-" Kea held up a hand to stop him from providing further details. "I meant, who did it?"

He pulled a face. "Didn't say. They were muttering about team Corvis, of course. My money is on old Gary."

Kea groaned. "I'm so not equipped to deal with this."

"True," Tony said thoughtfully, "I suppose if we could get our hands on a genetic test, we could find the owner-"

"Stop," Kea snapped. "Just stop." She paused, watching as the team marched away across the cobbled plain, stretching out like a line of ants as they receded into the distance. "If no one's bothered to complain, then I guess we do nothing."

"Seriously?" Tony seemed outraged that she wasn't going to escalate the matter further.

"We tell Marcus and Julie," Kea said calmly. "And when we regroup at the lake, we'll deliver a lecture on safety and remind them to leave the shenanigans for another time. Besides," she added reasonably. "It could have been anyone. There are hundreds of campers at the site and many of them spend every night drinking." She pulled on her pack. "No need to create a crisis if there isn't one," she added as they began the slow descent down the slope to the plain below. "And try to stop enjoying this so much."

***

As they hiked toward the ice, the group descended a giant staircase composed of dry river bottoms and lake beds. Sands and rocks of different textures formed the base of each terrace, showcasing flow conditions that had been dominant during various phases of past floods. They continued down into the widest, and lowest level, where vast plains of gravel were deposited during the most recent flooding event in 1996. The uneven terrain made for an arduous hike, particularly for those hauling the heavier gear. The long hike was unavoidable, since the shorter route along the eastern portion of the glacier was unstable, adding another two hours there and back every day. They spoke sparingly, intent on the view and carefully watching their step as they trudged across the plain.

Eric and Jon had been drafted as the main workhorses. Between them, they carried the thirty-pound bundle that held Kea's love child, a new 'miniaturized' piece of gear she had convinced her old university to loan her, after much begging. Even in its miniature form, the device was still about the size of a large ice chest. She and Bonnie each had batteries stuffed in their packs to power it, no small weight either. Andrei, Marcus, and Derek took turns marching with Marcus' thermal drill strapped to their back, the laser probe case carried between them.

The Ground Penetrating Radar kit was scattered between Julie and her team, while Fernando and Cole assisted Zoë with her gear, two large lightweight boxes that sporadic gusts of wind threatened to knock out of their grasp.

As Kea marched, the glacier margin and lakes in the distance bobbing up and down every step, never seemed to get closer. The plain was several kilometers wide, filled with nothing but sand, cobbles, and yawning kettle holes. Some rocks on the sandur were the size of her fist while others exceeded two meters in diameter.

Iceland had delivered another rare, gorgeous day, lit with bright sunshine and startlingly clear blue skies. The air in front of them shimmered as the sun warmed the sandur. White, football-sized rocks stood out against the dark sands, their forms crumbling into brittle sheaves like potato chips. Though broken, they still retained their overall shape, each slice separated by millimeters.

Freeze-thaw action, Kea judged, studying the decayed rocks. While not as dramatic as a flood, the alternating process of freezing and thawing that occurred in this region could destroy even the most durable of materials. She couldn't help but stare at the fragmented rocks as she marched onward. No longer whole, but still retaining the overall shape of the form it once had. She felt an aching sympathy for the rocky corpses.

Oh dear, Kea thought, *I'm sympathizing with stones, that's a new low. I may have even hit rock-bottom.*

Wincing at her own pun, she saw that most of the others were now far ahead. Shrugging, she forced her feet back into their plodding rhythm as she pressed on across the valley. She was so deep in her own thoughts that she didn't notice that Nadia had slowed down to keep pace with her until she asked a question.

"Everyone's talking about the glaciers retreating," Nadia commented. "But the map in the visitor center showed them much further up the valley when the land was first settled. Like this was all grass and forest and stuff."

Kea noticed that the young woman had yet to break a sweat despite her pack. Her slender legs were hidden in her snow pants, and the arms of her jacket were tied around her waist. She wore a bright pink tank top that Kea wouldn't have had the nerve to wear in a hundred years.

"This area used to be very different a thousand years ago. Much more populated," Kea agreed. She nodded to her graduate student who was a few paces ahead of them. "Although Julie's the historical expert..."

Julie shot Kea a *'gee thanks'* expression. "The Little Ice Age lasted approximately from 1500 to 1900 AD," she spouted. "When the glaciers extended much further south of where they are today. Before that, however, the climate was thought to be much warmer. From the location of abandoned farms and churches, we can infer the positions of many glaciers that terminated far up the valley. Buried birch logs have been found at the foot of Skaftafellsjökull, suggesting that they'd been transported out from beneath the ice by floodwaters..."

"I use an electromagnet," a gruff voice boomed beside them, its southern drawl thick and syrupy. "Doesn't leave a trace."

Kea turned toward Gary, wondering who the comment had been directed at. Gary stared back.

Not me, she realized. *He's not looking at me.*

Instead, his gaze was focused somewhere about two feet above their heads. After a moment, he turned back to stare at his feet, and he carried on hiking as if he had never said anything at all.

Kea exchanged a puzzled look with Nadia, as if to ask, *Am I supposed to ignore him?*

Nadia just rolled her eyes. Under her breath, she added, "He does that on conference calls all the time." She continued walking.

Kea quickened her pace to keep up with Nadia and away from Gary. She slowed once again when she had caught up with another gaggle of volunteers.

"This is taking forever," Cole complained.

"We can't camp any closer than Skaftafell, I'm afraid," Kea explained. "And as for the walk, try to think of it as a way to clear the brain before the real work begins."

"Are all the glaciers here retreating so quickly?" Reynard, the young German with wild curly blond hair, had joined their group. A couple of other volunteers were also slowing down to listen.

"Worse," Kea answered, happy to return to the safety of lecture-mode, although she kept track of Gary out of the corner of her eye. "Many are practically galloping away. When the ice is retreating upslope, like it is here, it appears to move even faster. As a glacier retreats out of a valley, it can even get beheaded."

"Beheaded?" Lexie asked, recorder in hand.

"When a glacier stagnates, it can melt unevenly. As it retreats, either due to topography or because it's buried by debris, it may leave the front of the glacier behind." She pointed to where the lakes lapped against the white and black crust of the ice margin. "That's where you'd think the glacier begins, but we're probably standing on ice right now." She waved her hand at the barren sandy plain that extended around them for kilometers. "The ice may extend nearly two kilometers south of here. We get glimpses when the rivers down cut, eroding away the overlying sediment, and expose the buried ice. Using radio waves, scientists have found buried ice hundreds of years old up to fifty meters beneath our feet."

"It's sad to see them wasting away so fast," commented Amirah, a middle-aged woman with long black hair. Tucked within her jacket, her tiny chin was ensconced by a silver and gold scarf that set off her dark complexion.

Kea nodded sympathetically. "On the plus side, the retreat exposes features below, within, and above the ice for us to study. By examining these, we can better understand the internal mechanics of the glaciers, which in turn gives us insight into how landscapes were created during the last ice age."

Before they're all gone.

Catching up with the rest of the volunteers, they paused for a break. She used the opportunity to pull Marcus aside.

"Everything all right?" Marcus pulled out his water flask as they walked.

Aside from you going behind my back and publishing without me?

42

She kept walking until she was satisfied that they were out of ear-shot of the others. "Have you had any interaction with Gary yet?"

"He's a little quirky, but he seems okay," Marcus replied with a shrug. "He talks to himself a lot, but that's nothing unusual for a volunteer."

"True," she admitted.

Marcus took a long drink, gulping down the water. "Remember that goth guy from last year? Dressed all in black, said he was a vampire or some nonsense."

"Trevor?" She remembered the pale, twenty-something young man from Boston. Harmless, but odd. Definitely odd. "I quite liked him."

"Takes all sorts," Marcus nodded. "But we'll take all the help we can get."

"To be fair," she reflected, "for a vampire, he was very good with the survey gear."

"Of course, I forgot, you like everyone. Well, there's hope for old Gary then." Marcus smiled ingratiatingly. "Just add him to the Watch List," he added referring to their mental register of people to keep an eye on in the field.

"Marcus," Kea shifted on her feet, her boot rocking a large cobble back and forth. He seemed to be up for conversation, but she was unsure where to begin. She didn't want to reveal her source, so she chose her words carefully. "I was thinking of submitting an article on some of the terrain work we did last season." She watched him as he paused before taking another drink. "I was going to ask..." She thought she saw his back stiffen, and she felt her courage flee her. She was just too exhausted to confront his treachery directly. Instead, she pivoted. "Would you be interested in collaborating on it?"

There we go, she thought. *Easy out. Just add me to the article. No harm no foul.*

"Yes, well..." Marcus turned toward her, his face contorting into a puzzled frown. "That's something to think about."

Yes, Kea thought. *Yes, it is. Come on, Marcus, let's adult together.*

"To be honest," Marcus's lips smeared into a greasy smile, "I've always been concerned that the error on your survey points was too far out of range to be useful. But yes, I'll have another look. It would certainly be good to get back in the publishing business again. It's so hard to keep up with you these days."

Kea found her lips plastered into a pained smile. At that moment, she suddenly understood why it was ill-advised to smile at dogs. Canines bared their teeth before ripping out the throat of their prey. She felt like tearing that insipid grin off his face. A slew of choice swears danced on her tongue, but she was acutely aware of the volunteers wandering nearby. "Do let me know if you change your mind," she managed to say at last.

Still gagging on her anger, Kea returned to the group and cast her eyes up to the sky, pleading for the heavens to give her patience.

When they arrived at the edge of the lake, she joined the graduate students and helped them retrieve the rafts and oars they'd hidden behind a boulder after their previous crossings. She attached the air pump and flicked the switch, watching with satisfaction as the rafts began to inflate.

Kea moved to a group of volunteers who were peering into the depths of the lake. The surface was steeped a dark brown, its waters thick with sediment. Massive slabs of ice broke the surface every hundred meters or so. Like giant slumbering turtles, they occasionally turned as the melting sun overbalanced their mass.

"Is there really no other way across?" Lexie asked, skipping a rock on the surface of the lake. Her pebble hopped over the water three times before thwacking into a floating chunk of ice.

Kea shook her head. "Not really. The rivers and lakes block most of the glacier now. There is one section farther east of here where you might just make it across, but we'd never risk the equipment or all of you."

"What's so dangerous about it?" asked a man with perfectly trimmed dark hair and a playful smile.

Fernando, she reminded herself. *Puerto Rican, in his mid-thirties, polite and judging by his bare ring-finger, single. Fernando, Fernando, fit Fernando.* She hoped the mnemonic would work. A recovering introvert, her role as team lead demanded that she be gregarious and engaging. It was exhausting, but necessary.

"There are a lot of upwellings at the edge of the eastern margin," she pointed to the mossy green cliffs. "The water there is forced up the

44

slope of the depression. You can even see small fountains spouting up through the ice in some locations. But the ice is thin and very treacherous. Here, the rafts might take longer, but they're much safer."

Observing the two distinct groups milling around the lakeshore, she grew more concerned about the team dynamics. Last night, she and the other leads had discussed the ramifications of going up on the ice with divided – and hostile – teams. They had decided on mixing them up in smaller groups in the hopes of building camaraderie. Looking at them now, she was questioning the wisdom of their decision.

She surveyed the volunteers again, mentally ticking off names. The group closest to her was team Corvis which included the father-daughter Russian combo, Andrei and Nadia. Andrei, a tall oak of a man with wide shoulders, kept a watchful gaze over his daughter through his wire-rimmed spectacles. Although only eighteen, Nadia was the same height as her father, but with a slender frame, one that Kea had already caught Cole ogling more than once.

This entire field team seems to be drowning in hormones, Kea reflected. Shaking her head, she toyed with the idea of adding saltpeter to the next shopping run.

Also on team Corvis was Amirah, who seemed to have more silk scarfs than Kea had underwear and Gary, a data scientist from Alabama. He stood quietly, apart from the group, content to observe. At least he'd stopped muttering.

A good twenty meters away, standing by the rafts were Jon and Erik, the muscular cousins, who were part of T3. Max, in contrast to the two sports models beside him, was a large man, his girth swathed in folds of fat and carried by a sturdy frame. He waved his hands expressively as he talked, with an air of authority that Marcus could only dream of. While Kea hadn't had a chance to speak to him yet, she had dug up his form and was unsurprised to see the words *'VP'* and *'CEO'*, in the *Occupation* box. Derek and Fernando, also T3, stood at the fringes, keeping their distance from both each other and the rest of the group.

Zoë waved a bottle of sunblock at Cole, who was patently ignoring her. Zoë was with T3, but as a freelance contractor. Kea wasn't sure where that placed her, however Cole wasn't part of either group. For that matter, neither was Lexie. For a reporter, she was far less inquisitive than Kea expected, often remaining silent for long periods, content to take photographs, more interested in landscape shots than people.

At least, Kea thought, *she wasn't filming everything I say. Yet.*

Bruce sat on a boulder between the two groups, basking in the sun and lustily devouring a muffin. In stark contrast to yesterday, he seemed to be the only one truly enjoying himself.

Good for you, Kea thought with a smile.

Once the rafts were fully inflated, and life jackets were handed out, Marcus and Andrei helmed the oars of one boat, while Tony and Fernando manned the other, volunteers sandwiched in between. Kea waited until everyone was across before taking the last raft, now manned by Jon and Erik. The two men seemed to revel in the exercise. Sitting behind Bonnie, Kea couldn't help but marvel at the outlines of their muscles, visible even through the bunched fabric of their jackets.

Despite the warmth of the day, wisps of mists scudded across the surface of the water, slipping between the boats and the shifting masses of ice. Erik pointed at the cliffs that soared up to the east a few hundred meters distant. "What is that thing?"

"Double Embayment." Kea considered the hundreds of meters of sand and gravel that towered above them. "The main outlet of the 1996 jökulhlaup deposited all of that sediment as the flood tore out the ice and inundated the plain. After the glacial margin retreated, it left behind huge chunks of buried ice, insulated from the melt by the flood deposits. While the rest of the clean ice has melted away and the glacier retreated, anything that was covered by the flood remains elevated, like those cliffs. It's called inverted topography."

"Mountains become valleys, valleys become mountains?" Jon asked.

"Something like that," Kea nodded. "The floodwaters poured out of the glacier margin there. It ripped out a canyon of ice hundreds of feet high. When the ice melted away, it left this area where the lake had been, high and dry. There's still ice buried in those cliffs though, insulated deep under the sediment. Could last for decades or even hundreds of years, depending on how much the climate warms up or if the ice advances back into this region."

An echo reminiscent of thunder rumbled down from the mountaintops. The sky above them was clear and blue, not a cloud in sight. Several of the volunteers cringed, no doubt fearing an eruption.

"What was that?" Bonnie's eyes darted from peak to peak in fear as the echoes faded away.

"Icefall." Kea pointed to the east where the beast of Oræfajökull dwelt among the mountain peaks. Between two peaks, the white frosting of a glacier filled a u-shaped valley, but it stopped abruptly atop a sheer cliff. "That's the glacier Morsárjökull. See how the middle doesn't quite reach the valley floor? It has retreated to the point where it can no longer connect downslope to the base of the cliff, but it's still advancing, as the ice accumulating behind it keeps pushing. As a result, what's left drops off the edge of the cliff in chunks. What you heard is the sound of the ice blocks falling."

Another rumble echoed from Morsárjökull. While they were too far away to see any icefall, the sound of the impact filled the valley. In the ensuing silence, they continued to drift between the icebergs in the lake, awed by the world around them.

"Well," Erik said slowly. "It's not dull."

Kea realized that she had been so consumed with inflating the rafts and answering the questions that she'd forgotten to lecture them again on safety and to set aside their rivalry. On the beach opposite, she spied Max watching them, a smug grin on his face. She began to worry that her reluctance to address the excrement incident might escalate into something else.

"Look out!" Bonnie cried in terror.

Beside their raft, an iceberg ten meters high lurched sideways. Like a whale emerging from the deep, the berg's underbelly rose out of the lake, frothy water cascading down its sides. Kea watched helplessly as the nose of the raft lifted out of the water.

Jon shoved at the rising wall with his oar, while Erik frantically paddled away. Coming to her senses, Kea added her paddle to the fight. With a tremendous yell, Jon shoved once more, launching them away from the rising ice. Paddling furiously, as the glacier shifted once more, they were able to ride the wave out of danger.

They watched, captivated, as the iceberg completed its rotation, exposing a fresh jagged surface to the sun's warm light.

Kea watched the ripples spread out across the lake. "Dull is never a problem here."

Chapter 4

ERIK STEADIED the raft as Kea splashed to the shore. Jon tied a rope to a boulder to serve as an anchor as the other volunteers hopped across the many shallow streams weaving in and out beneath the glacier's lip. A small group of stragglers took pictures, standing on an unusually flat patch of gravel. She caught sight of a tell-tale jiggle of the sand under their feet.

"Careful," Kea cautioned.

"Gloop ahoy!" Julie cried as she stomped on the gravel and watched the surface quiver like a pudding skin.

"Gloop?" Nadia gently eased her own foot onto the gravel as if stepping on a landmine.

Julie pressed the toe of her boot into the ground near Nadia's foot. Water seeped out of the sand, pooling around the base of her boot.

"The sediments here are saturated with water," Julie explained. "So, watch where you step, or you may find yourself getting-"

Nadia squealed as the sopping sands engulfed her foot, sinking up to her knee. In a panic, the girl flailed her arms to steady herself.

"—glooped," Julie finished.

Andrei moved to his daughter's side and helped extract her foot from the quicksand. As Nadia pulled her leg out, dollops of sludge and water slid off her boots onto the cobbles.

"It's too shallow here to be dangerous," Julie assured her. She jumped into the gloop and her own feet sank about fifteen centimeters. She pulled out a foot, causing a loud slurping sound, and they all watched as sludge rushed back in to fill the gaping hole.

"I think that's enough fooling around," Marcus frowned. "Once we all reach the next marker, we'll stop for a quick snack." He rapped the strange tank strapped to his back with his knuckles and waved everyone on their way. "Let's go!"

Kea watched the group drop out of sight as they crossed the convoluted terrain. Andrei lingered on the periphery, watching as his daughter interacted with the others. He looked, Kea realized, like every other helicopter parent she'd seen on a student's first day on campus.

"How's it going?" Kea grabbed her water bottle and took a long sip.

"It is amazing," Andrei waved at the features around him. "The complexity is... refreshing."

Kea wiped her chin with the back of her hand. "It's a challenge certainly, but with geology, there's always a logical answer." *Unlike so many other things in life*, she thought as she watched Zoë lecturing Cole. The teenager was pouting about something, once again seeming to completely ignore his mother.

"To make sense of all this, I think you are all detectives, of a kind." Andrei's thin lips pulled back into a smile.

"There are so many processes at work it can be tricky to sort out." Kea conceded. "To make things even more complicated, this glacier also surges, which can create landforms similar to floods. Plus, of course, the glacier can come back through again and override all the features completely."

Andrei raised an eyebrow. The Russian was no longer watching his daughter, which was a good sign. Kea pressed on, happy to help him focus his attention on something else. Nadia, for her part, seemed oblivious to her father's scrutiny and appeared to be flirting with Fernando.

"A surge," Kea explained, "starts with a rapid increase in velocity of the ice in the upper part of the glacier's accumulation area, but it may take several months before the wave reaches the front of the glacier."

Lexie appeared beside them, taking photographs as Kea demonstrated the contortions of the glacier mechanics by waving her hands and scooting her feet.

"When a glacier surges," Kea continued, hoping she didn't look too ridiculous, "the excess ice and changes within the internal structure alters the drainage network beneath the glacier. It switches from the conduit system to a distributed one. This happens when the ice moves faster over an irregular ground surface. Small cavities between the ice and the ground develop narrow links between them, perpendicular to ice flow."

Kea pressed her palms together, applying pressure. "The resulting increase in water pressure, combined with the reduced friction caused by the presence of the basal cavity system, may actually increase the sliding of the glacier over the bed. Since it's moving faster, this sliding maintains the pressure that permits the linked cavity network that preserves the increased water pressure. This loop is preserved until the wave hits the front of the glacier, then it collapses."

"In my job," Andrei began after a moment's thought, "new technologies are taking the same approach to big data. Rather than try to process millions of records all at the same time on one machine, the data is divided up into tiny chunks and processed across several boxes. Distributed. Very efficient and very powerful."

"Nature usually has the solution if you're willing to look for it. She's had a few billion years head start." Despite herself, Kea found herself studying Marcus in the distance. "It's interesting to see the results after enough pressure is applied. You never know what might happen..." She turned back to Andrei. "Is that what you do at Corvis? Big data?"

Andrei gave a noncommittal shrug. "This and that. I'm an engineer, but we all dabble. You mentioned that at the end of a surge, another flooding event occurs?"

Kea nodded, amazed at his lack of subtlety at dodging the question. "When the surge reaches the front of the glacier, large volumes of water may be released in a jökulhlaup. That flood may also excavate ice canyons and transport large ice blocks. As a result, it isn't just volcanically generated events that can cause jökulhlaups."

Andrei appeared to consider the implications. "With all these things going on all the time, all creating similar features, how do you know if you've had a surge or a volcanic flood?"

"You just have to take the time to piece the puzzles together," Kea responded.

"Yes." Andrei nodded again. "Like I said, you are detectives, all of you."

"Not really," Kea sighed. "More like historians, of the rock kind."

It was well past noon before they made their way through the interlacing networks of streams and eventually found an area where they could climb up onto the main body of the glacier. Even up close, the ice was freckled with black specks of ash and dirt. Cobbles, embedded in the ice, were dropping into the dirt, melted out by the warmth of the morning sun.

They came to a rise where Jon stopped and placed a tentative hand on a large black pile of mud and ice about a meter high. He looked askance at Kea.

"Dirt cone," Kea nodded at the irregular muddy mass of ice that squatted before them. It resembled a termite mound about to tumble on its side. "As the dirt melts out of the ice, it can collect and actually serve to insulate the ice. Melt occurs at different rates depending on the amount of debris, causing the irregular shapes." She reached out and wiped the brown, slimy film of grit with the tip of her glove, exposing the ice beneath. "Even a thin layer of dirt or ash can serve to insulate the ice, slowing the melting process."

"It certainly makes it much more difficult to see where you're going," Jon commented. "It's more like the surface of an alien planet than the snowfield I'd imagined."

"This next bit is a little tricky." Kea pointed to a massive ridge of gravel that rose out of the ground before them. Over ten meters in height and hundreds long, the ridge snaked away from the lake, burrowing into the lip of the glacier like a worm into an apple. "The melting has been more rapid than we expected in this area. Stick to the path as best you can."

The ridge was an esker, a landform composed of sand and gravel deposited within or beneath the ice by meltwater channels. Laid down at the height of the 1996 flood, the ice had retreated around it, leaving only the sediment, now hundreds of meters thick, standing above the landscape. Atop the esker's head lay the main checkpoint and the site of most of their scientific studies.

As they approached, she saw that Marcus' group had already reached the esker's summit. She heard his voice drifting down as he droned on about his favorite topic. "Unlike a river, eskers are made of sediment deposited under the ice, but above ground. Now that the ice is gone, you can just drive a backhoe up and dig away, no need to mine anything. There's been a lot of interest recently in the thousands of eskers in Canada, because they may contain large quantities of gold..."

Shaking her head, Kea followed the others as they threaded their way through the maze of smaller ridges that crisscrossed the area, making a beeline as best they could for the esker. Fractures filled with sediment during the flood created a honeycomb of intersecting angles they had to navigate. She held back from lecturing the others, aware that they needed to concentrate on their footing as, on either side of the ridge, the shallows were filled with deposits of sand, icy water, or large pools of goop. She paused to watch Marcus and the others wind their way across the terrain.

"Now that's a murder," Derek said as he joined her at the edge of the ridge.

"Sorry?" Kea asked in alarm, shifting so that she was further away from the edge of the ridge.

"Them lot," Derek nodded back at Gary, Andrei, and Amirah who were coming up from behind, picking their way carefully across the fracture-fills. "Flock of crows. You know, a murder."

"Corvis…" She frowned for a moment before realization dawned. "That's the constellation of the Crow, right?"

"Bunch of munters," Derek observed.

Kea wasn't aware of that particular New Zealand slang word but got the impression that it wasn't complimentary. Now that he was so close to her, she was struck by the shaggy brown hair atop his head and the spikes of red scruff that sprouted from his chin. Tall and improbably thin, he appeared composed and confident, a stark contrast to the fidgety shadow that she had observed ranting at Max yesterday.

He'd be quite handsome, Kea thought, *if I hadn't seen him go Tonya Harding on Max.*

Derek leaned in closer over her shoulder, as if to get a better look at the glacier. She pulled back reflexively, but still caught a whiff of his cologne, thick and musky. She stepped aside and cleared her throat, making a show of cleaning her glasses. As attractive as he was, there was something about him that set her on edge. Perhaps it was his display from earlier that seemed so at odds to the aspect he presented now. Or perhaps she had glimpsed something in his eyes, a hunger that she found unsettling.

She wanted to move further away from him but needed to find out more of what was at the heart of the rivalry that might pose a threat to the safety of her expedition. "You're one of the T3 crew then?"

"Just the last year or so." Derek pulled out his sunglasses and popped them on, their silvery surface hiding his dangerous brown eyes.

She averted her gaze and instead kept a careful eye on the other volunteers as they made their way toward them. Bruce seemed to be enjoying himself, his arms splayed out like wings as he moved across the tops of the thin ridges. Erik and Jon were moving more sedately, with the 'crows' trailing behind. For once, she regretted taking the lead as she saw Julie and Cole struggling with their gear at the end of the line.

"Only a year?" Kea knew technology jobs were plagued by high turnover, but it made his loyalty, or anger at least, hard to grasp. "Forgive me for saying so, why all the hate towards the… crows?"

Derek turned his head sharply to consider her. While his eyes were still hidden, Kea wondered if he worked out that she eavesdropped on his conversation with Max yesterday. Hastily she added, "I can't help but notice your teams go out of their way to avoid each other at every opportunity. With all the stares and glares, I feel like I'm chaperoning a junior high dance, with boys on one side of the gym and girls on the other."

Derek shrugged, shifting his gaze back toward the ice. "We had a contract thing fall apart recently. Plus, they didn't tell us they were coming on this trip as well."

"So, you've all worked together in the past?" Kea noticed that Bruce nearly took a swan dive off one of the ridges but was relieved to see that he was just fooling around. While some of the pools were only a few feet deep, the dark water in others held hidden depths, as well as other dangers. Not to mention frigid temperatures.

"In a way, yeah, but we all tend to work remotely." From his voice, Kea couldn't tell if the situation depressed him or was a tremendous relief. "This was the first time I've met some of them."

Kea couldn't help it. Her mouth dropped open in astonishment. "You've never met them before?"

Derek shrugged. "Video chat mostly. We're developers, coders. Not much with the chinwag. Very introverted. I mean, a couple of us have met, and we've all met Max…" he trailed off and seemed reluctant to expound further on the topic, his eyes fixed on the volunteers who had almost reached them. "To be fair, it's a bit tricky to hang out at the water cooler from six thousand miles away."

"Not much different from the online courses I teach," Kea conceded. "But then again, they never have to make a trip to get here. How are you handling the jet lag?"

"Nothing I can't handle. I'm sure," he added with a cheeky grin, "I'll be up all night."

Kea gave him a withering look. As a result, she completely missed what happened next. A yelp of alarm caused her to turn and catch a glimpse of Erik losing his footing. He launched out his arms to try to steady himself, nearly knocking Gary straight in the chest. The older man either ducked out of the way in time or caught part of the blow and stumbled to his knee. Erik's arm continued its path as he fell, knocking out Andrei's leg from underneath him.

Kea could only watch helplessly as Andrei tumbled head-first in slow motion off the narrow ridge and vanished out of sight. Erik and Gary managed to remain atop the ridge, albeit on their hands and knees, scrambling to find purchase.

Her heart racing, she leaped from ridge to ridge back along the way she had come. She came as close as she dared and helped Erik stand upright. Below, Andrei stood waist-deep in a pool of gloop. He must have fallen face-first as he was entirely covered in the muck. Seeing Kea's concerned expression, Andrei gave a thumbs-up to indicate he was okay.

Hearing peals of laughter, Kea turned to see Nadia cackling at her father's predicament, snapping pictures with her phone. Surprisingly, Cole was already helping Andrei out of the pool, and Julie was pulling out her waterproof emergency bag with spare clothes that all the leads carried.

Kea made herself take a series of long, calming breaths, doing her best to stop from ranting like a lunatic. She had only lost her temper on an expedition once before when a handful of students had ignored her warnings and wandered out onto an area of thin ice and nearly got themselves killed. When she bellowed at them, rather than be terrified, they regarded her quizzically, as if she were a mewling kitten caught in the rain. It was only after that she realized her words had come out in the wrong order and were mixed with flecks of spit.

Calm, she reminded herself. *Keep calm. Accidental, surely?*

She studied Erik's face, but found she couldn't read his expression. Max, however, who was watching from a vantage point a few ridges over, was radiating joy. Revenge, it had seemed, had been delivered.

On Andrei? Or was it meant for Gary?

Andrei would be cold and wet, but otherwise unharmed, she reasoned. Where he had fallen, the gloop was shallow and not exposed to the frigid waters of the lake.

Not that anyone would have known that, she thought.

Certain that Andrei would be okay, Kea retreated to the safety of a wider ridge that merged with the back of the esker. She remained there and counted off volunteers as they passed, shooing Derek along, lest he try to hit on her again.

Following the last of the volunteers up the slope, she was relieved to see that the team had safely reached the summit of the esker. They were already on their second snack break as Tony and Marcus started setting up the research gear. She took out her own lunch and munched, mentally gauging her inner demons.

Food first, establish calm, then reprimand.

On her right, Tiko chomped noisily on an apple. She had spread out her jacket so she could recline on the ice and soak up the sun. Reynard had done the same, using his cap to cover his brow. Beyond him, Lexie took a deep breath from her asthma inhaler then lit up a cigarette.

Shaking her head in amazement, Kea finished her sandwich and rummaged around in her lunch bag for a candy bar. She noticed that Jon had sat down beside her and was systematically consuming two sandwiches at once, stacked upon each other like a layer cake. Crumbs and bits of cucumber filled the air, winding up more on his face than in his mouth. Somehow his slovenly behavior did nothing to detract from his handsomeness. He was simply too ridiculously hot to be real.

She tried to focus on her own food and not openly ogle him.

"That poor bastard." Derek was watching the sky, the snack bar in his hand forgotten.

Kea followed his gaze and saw a gull wheeling in an arc across the blue sky. A larger, darker bird shot toward it and slammed into the gull, sending feathers scattering. The gull cried out, its wing damaged. It flew on, but the beat of its wings was irregular, twitching. It appeared to be rapidly dropping in elevation, plummeting towards the earth.

"Skua," Marcus said, barely glancing up from unpacking his box of equipment.

"There's another one," Jon pointed as the gull was again attacked, this time from a second large brown bird.

"It's mate," Kea explained. "They hunt in pairs."

"They're huge." Lexie deftly lit another cigarette, her attention riveted on the scene above.

"The Great Skua," Marcus nodded referring to the large brown birds with the white streaks across their plumage. "They can have a wingspan nearly four feet across. They'll wear the gull out with their attacks and drive it further from the coast. Eventually, it will tire, and then they'll have their lunch."

"Brutal." Erik was lying on his back, his jacket spread out on the ice beneath him. His eyes were hidden by shades, his expression unreadable.

"Do skua ever attack people?" Bonnie asked Kea.

"You should be fine as long as you don't get too close to their nests," Kea added, remembering some of her own encounters on the sandur. "If that happens, they tend to dive at your head, often from behind."

Bonnie frowned at the sky, not reassured. "What do you do then?"

Kea shrugged. "Duck."

"It's... fantastic. Simply fantastic," a voice wheezed above Kea's head.

She craned her neck and saw Bruce standing beside her, sweat pouring off his forehead. She had been keeping a watchful eye on him throughout most of the hike, concerned that he would overexert himself. Now, however, she saw an expression of awe stenciled across his face.

Kea envied that. She always had - and always would - love working out here, but she missed that moment when Iceland first took her breath away. Turning back to the others, she could see variations on all their faces, although Jon and Erik were doing their best to be nonchalant about it, casually taking pictures with their phones. Bonnie, it seemed, was doing her best to chat up Erik, while Julie stood by, a disapproving scowl stenciled on her face.

Kea offered Bruce a pouch of granola. "Feeling better?"

"Sleep does wonders." Bruce smiled back but waved away the food. "I'll be very sore tomorrow, but it'll be worth it."

Kea looked across the ice to Max and Derek. Their heads were bent in conversation and they seemed to be ignoring the vista around them. "Everything okay in T3 land?"

Bruce followed her gaze and just snorted. "As good as it gets." He turned back to look out to the sandur, as if to block his coworkers from his vision. "We just need a few days off. Just a few."

"Amen to that." Kea felt like she could use a good three months off after this trip.

"You up for more hot cocoa tonight?" Bruce asked hopefully.

"Work permitting," Kea nodded. "I just have to have a throw down with a colleague."

"Naughty." Bruce edged closer, taking off his baseball cap to whisper in her ear. "Who's the lucky one?"

"That's not what I meant you moron." Kea shook her head when she realized he was kidding. "Shut up," she laughed. She felt normal again, in control, ready. She packed up her trash and other belongings and stood in front of the group.

"Okay guys," Kea rallied her best angry teacher voice. "Last night, we gave you a safety brief for the camp, and this morning, we gave you a brief before we left about how to be safe during fieldwork."

For all the good it did.

"Now I heard rumors of an incident last night," she paused for effect, scanning the ranks. Expressions of confusion and curiosity stared back. She wondered, not for the first time, if the incident had occurred at all. She pressed on. "Just now there was a minor accident," she nodded to Andrei who now wore an oversized tie-dye t-shirt, "but one that could have been much worse."

The team looked bewildered. It was as if she'd announced a pop quiz to a freshmen lecture hall.

Either they were excellent actors, she thought, *or they really have no idea what I'm talking about.*

"Whatever is going on, I don't care," she continued, her confidence slipping. "It stops now. We are in a hostile environment up here and will be for the next week. If this continues, any of it, if we suspect anything is going on between your two groups, then we're off the ice and done for the season. We work together or not at all. Am I understood?" She heard her own voice waver and crack as certainty deserted her. The group looked around as if she were, quite possibly, losing her mind.

There was an awkward moment of silence. Even Marcus looked at her oddly. He stepped up beside her. "Yes, thanks for that... Okay everyone, gather round. I want to show you the new bit of kit from France that the folks of Corvis have provided for us."

Feeling slightly embarrassed, Kea stepped back and hovered at the edge of the group. She felt, rather than saw, Julie beside her.

"How'd I do?" Kea asked quietly.

Julie shrugged. "You know when you were a kid in the backseat, and your mom would get fed up and say that if you didn't stop whatever, she'd turn the car around? Except, you knew she'd never follow through? A bit like that."

"That bad?" Kea kept her eyes fixed on the volunteers as they listened to Marcus expound on his latest toy.

"The content was good, the delivery, not so much," Julie tried, and failed to sound supportive. "What was that all about anyway?"

Kea related the story that Tony had told her of someone laying a stretch of pipe outside Max's tent. Julie rolled her eyes and groaned. "Probably a drunk camper... I hope."

Kea's eyes flickered back around the group and caught Max staring at her, a playful smile pulling at his lips. "I'm not sure of anything anymore." She noticed some volunteers huddling around Zoë as she opened her equipment cases.

"What are those?" Derek's hands twitched as if he were a child eager to play with a new toy.

"They're prototypes my company was working on for a while before we started to..." Zoë paused, "pursue other avenues. Never flown above a glacier before, though. I'm a bit worried about the air up there," she waved up to the mountains. "I've been warned it might get quite choppy."

"Zoë's going to help us map the area," Kea added. "Both with imagery and lidar."

"Lidar?" Derek poked at one of the little propellers before Zoë swatted him away.

"Light Detection and Ranging," Zoë explained. "The drone fires pulses of laser light at the ground, calculating the distance between the earth and the drone. The laser is fired in rapid succession, building a three-dimensional point cloud of elevation data. We can drape the imagery we shoot over the resulting surface and create a detailed model of the terrain."

"It looks... pricey," Derek said, although beside him Max snickered in derision.

"Some more than others," Zoë agreed. "The degree of accuracy depends on how well the drone can track its position with GPS and how well the sensors are kept stable during the flight. Kea's given me the flight plans for the different sites, so these guys will be piloting themselves. Or at least that's the plan."

"That's Romulus," Cole pointed to the larger of the two drones sitting on the gravel. Romulus appeared to be little more than an assemblage of cameras with an odd box strapped underneath. The cross-shaped frame was made of blood-red plastic with four propellers mounted at each end. "And that's Remus." The second drone was jet black, about the size and shape of a basketball with a square assemblage resting on top, its six propellers flush within the frame.

"Resolution?" Max asked, a curious expression on his face.

"Depending on how low, and how safely, I can fly them in these conditions," Zoë emphasized, "probably about four centimeters."

Beside Zoë, Julie began to unpack her own gear. She carefully unfurled a length of wires onto the ice, then connected them to a large padded box strapped to her chest. In a matter of minutes, she had also assembled two large plastic rectangular frames made of white PVC pipes. She handed one to Cole, who acquiesced to the sudden recruitment with a strange grunting noise. She motioned for him to stand facing her so that they stood a meter apart. A loose wire connected the two lengths of tubing, which connected the box on Julie's chest to the frames she and Cole held.

"Marcus has asked me to give you all a brief on my dissertation project, so here it is." Julie tapped the device on her chest. "Ground-penetrating radar, or GPR, uses radio pulses to create a picture of the ice's internal structure. Basically, it allows us to see through the ice and map any features inside it." Julie nodded at the frames she and Cole were holding. "These antennae send high-frequency radio waves down into the ice, which bounce back up to the surface where we collect them. When the waves encounter an object or layers of sediment, it changes or scatters the waves that we can detect when they return."

Reynard stepped closer to inspect the device. "What's the range of the signal?"

Julie fiddled with the chest unit. "It depends on the material and the amount of water. In this area, we're probably looking to get reflections up to thirty meters deep in the ice." The unit emitted a loud beep, and she nodded to Cole. "Okay, now we move together. You take one step back, I take one step forward."

Cole looked behind him and gingerly took a step back as Julie moved toward him. Kea watched with the others as Julie indicated for Cole to step again.

"Each transect is gridded out ahead of time," Marcus picked up the narrative so that Julie and Cole could keep moving in tandem. He pointed to the rope laid out on the ice in a simple grid pattern. "The grids provide two-dimensional slices of the underlying surface," he continued as Julie and Cole performed their slow dance.

"When we get back tonight," Julie continued, "I can reconstruct the two-dimensional slices into a full three-dimensional model if anyone wants to see what's beneath our feet."

"Right!" Marcus rubbed his hands together as if washing them clean of Julie's project. "We'll break out into teams and rendezvous back here later." He looked at his watch and glanced at the sky. "It's just about noon, and since the sun doesn't set till about ten o'clock tonight, we've got plenty of time. Let's meet up back here around, say five?"

"Team GPR, with me," Julie waved over Amirah, Bonnie, and Erik.

"Thermal drill team?" Marcus asked the group. Tony, Bruce, Derek, Jon, and Reynard raised their hands. "You're with me."

"Everyone on Team Kea," Kea raised her arm, "follow me."

"Anyone on the drone team," Tony called out, "remain here with Zoë."

Kea was surprised to see how annoyed Cole looked as he skulked over to join his mother. In contrast, Nadia, Lexie, and Tiko hovered by the drones, watching Zoë as she prepped the control unit.

Marcus led the remaining teams upslope. Kea followed up the rear in case anyone needed assistance. Some of the younger members of the team didn't have much difficulty, despite never having walked on a glacier before. Others moved more cautiously, their limbs sticking out like scarecrows as they tried to find their glacier legs. She matched strides with Bruce, grateful for his slow and measured pace. The walk back to the jeep would be strenuous, and she was happy to save her energy and her calves.

In front of her, Jon and Erik whispered conspiratorially as they fell into step behind Max, shooting glances over their shoulder back at her.

No, she realized with a chill, *not at me. At Bruce.*

Bruce seemed oblivious to their attention. Instead, he kept pausing to take pictures, even stopping to pop interesting rocks into his satchel. Kea felt as if she were escorting him on a seaside jaunt and couldn't help but smile at his antics. She caught Derek staring at her again, and she met his gaze with a look that she hoped would melt steel. He looked away, guiltily.

At least he's not hitting on me anymore.

As if hearing her thoughts, Derek looked back at her and blew her a kiss.

Kea groaned.

***

"It looks so... organic," Erik dumped his pack next to Kea's equipment.

After another hour of hiking, they set up at a location near the glacier's western edge. Here, the ice was covered with tephra, as if blackened with soot. The undulations of the glacier surface and a dense forest of dirt cones that surrounded them obscured their view of the other teams.

"Eh?" Kea looked up from her mini-computer. Erik stood atop a hillock of ice and stared down into the proglacial depression that stretched between the glacier margin and the abandoned elevated outwash plain.

Erik was decidedly anti-fabric, Kea noticed. The man wore only a black tank top, his biceps flexing with every gesture. His well-defined lats gave his torso a perfect V-shape that she'd only seen on *Baywatch*.

While the sunlight was bright and warm, she was content inside her jacket. She plopped down on the ice, crossed her legs, and plugged a storage drive into a port on the side of the crate.

"The esker," Erik waved at the landforms below them. "The way the flood deposits spew out from the esker's mouth, all the kettle holes. It looks like an open wound."

"The event was certainly violent," she agreed, keeping her eyes on her work. "But that wound is a pattern we hope to find repeated throughout the historical record so we can identify other periods when jökulhlaups occurred."

She heard the artificial click of his phone as Erik took pictures of the landscape. As the shutter sounds moved closer, she noticed he was taking photographs of her. She posed with a grin, squinting in the bright sunlight.

"Your job is pretty awesome." He snapped a few more pictures of the glacier. "Who wouldn't want to come to work every day?"

"I'm not complaining," she shrugged. "Well, not much. At least not in the last hour. How about you? What does T3 actually do?"

"We used to do a lot of software development for telecommunications companies." Erik fished around in his pack and withdrew a candy bar. "We got new partners recently and now we do a bit more in the realm of deep learning and artificial intelligence."

Glancing up from her equipment, Kea noticed Nadia strolling in their direction. She saw no sign of the others, but she wasn't too bothered. Since calibrating her equipment could take time, she gave them permission to wander around while she finished setting up, reminding them to remain within shouting distance.

"You guys build artificial intelligence devices?" Kea turned back to Erik.

"Not exactly. We partner with larger companies as needed. You know how it is." He seemed reluctant to provide any more details and wandered further away, taking more pictures as he went.

"He's a good guy, really, just shy," said a gruff voice behind her. "Not as bad as Jon, though."

Kea swiveled on her rear to see Max standing behind her, eating a sandwich. She nodded absently and turned back to peer intently at her screen. The sunlight was so bright that it was difficult to tell if the computer was even switched on. "Bruce mentioned that your team… has a wide range of personalities."

Max grunted. "We're an unusual bunch, I admit, but start-ups always attract the odd ones. It takes a certain kind of person to throw off the safety nets and start your own company."

"I suppose," Kea said. She used her lunch bag to shield the screen and was relieved to see that the computer was already halfway through its booting sequence. "It does sound exciting though. I take it the idea is to get bought out at a certain point?"

"Depends on who you ask," Max commented. "I kinda like not working for a big company. Of course, if the buy-out's big enough, who am I to say no to retiring early in the Caribbean?"

"Is that likely?" Kea asked. "Not being nosy, just wondering if I should start my own someday."

Max laughed loudly at that. She wondered if she should feel offended.

"We'll see. We've got some products in the pipeline that we're excited about." He sounded thoughtful, not as brash as Kea had come to expect. "Had a couple rocky starts, but we think we've got some great ideas that are ahead of the curve. The trick is to find a niche before anyone else does."

"You're preaching to the choir," Kea replied. "Academia's no different. You have to find a research project, collect the data, and publish before anyone else just to survive."

"Competitive," Max agreed. "But for less profit, I imagine."

"It depends on the field," Kea admitted. "But when it comes to glaciers, most aren't in it to earn the big bucks."

Max snorted. "Is anyone else out here on the ice doing similar work?"

"Not that I know of," Kea said. "Although we're only here for a short time, so you never know. This site does get teams from all over the world."

"Aren't you worried about other scientists stealing your research?" He sounded almost excited at the prospect.

If you only knew, Kea didn't say. "It's possible, but the community's fairly small. Once you get a reputation for doing that, you'll have a hard time finding other people willing to work with you." She tried to focus on the instrument in front of her, rather than let herself get aggravated by dwelling on Marcus again.

"Must be nice to have that kind of transparency." Max packed away the remains of his lunch. "Industrial espionage costs us a small fortune."

"That's not to say it doesn't happen," Kea said. "I know some academics will do nearly anything for tenure."

One might be on this glacier right now, she thought as she watched Max wander away.

"What does this do, exactly?" Nadia, bored with sightseeing, squatted beside the ice chest, frowning at the knobs and readouts.

"It's a magnetic resonance sounding device," Kea proudly tapped the casing. "We lay out those wires and use them to measure the electrical field. The MRS sends an electric pulse through the wire hoops, applying an electrical field into the subsurface. Then we switch off the field and measure the magnetic resonance, that is the time it takes for the water molecules to return to their original magnetic state."

"Okay," Nadia said. She waited for a beat. "Why?"

"It's a fairly common technique used to measure the level of groundwater in aquifers," Kea explained. "It's usually done on a ground surface, but for now..."

"For now?" Nadia asked.

Kea shifted uncomfortably on the ice. "I saw a talk where someone did this on the ice sheets in Greenland last fall, and I've been dying to give it a go ever since. Of course, the talk was about an aquifer near the surface of the ice, describing water flowing through compacted snow. We've got a completely different situation here, so I have no idea what I'm going to find, if anything."

"Kind of sounds like you're making this up as you go along," Nadia teased.

"Does it? How fascinating." Kea kept working, intent on her task. "Hand me that bit of wire, will you?"

Nadia was silent for a full thirty seconds. "Why do you think it won't work?"

"I didn't say it wouldn't work, I just don't know what I might find..." Kea began, uncertain about how much detail to go into. "Most of the water in Alpine glaciers flows through crevasses, conduits, and moulins but not through an aquifer."

"What's a moulin?"

"Hmm..." Kea grumbled as she attempted to thread the wire back into the adapter. Not for the first time she regretted not having flashcards so she could just hand definitions out when asked. "As the ice melts on the surface, some of it burrows a path straight down, like a well or a giant plug hole. Some may grow over a hundred feet wide and several times that deep. And you know what they say, once you go down a moulin ..." She let her words trail off.

"Yes?" Nadia prompted.

"You never come back out," Kea finished with relish.

Nadia frowned as if sensing that Kea was messing with her. "Is that true?"

"Well, bits of you might," Kea admitted. "This close to the margin, some do flow out the front of the glacier straight into the lake. Most, however, flow down to the ice-rock interface. If you did eventually come out the front of the glacier, it'd be a bit of a case of the Humpty-dumpty's."

"That's horrible," Nadia said in disgust.

"That's science." Kea tucked her pencil in her mouth.

There was another pause, a minute this time, until Nadia finally asked, "Wait, are you saying you really *don't* know what you're doing?"

Kea smiled wryly. "I have planned out, to the letter, nearly every day of this twelve-week expedition." She sat on her heels, reflecting on how long, and yet how quickly, the last four months had passed. "Sometimes," she continued, "you have to try something different, test something strange, just to see. I spend most of the year cooped up in my office reading about experiments other researchers are trying all over the world, and it gets my creative juices flowing. Now, this may not tell me anything at all, but if it does, you'll be in the acknowledgment section."

***

Four MRS surveys and an hour later, the batteries clocked out. Kea mentally kicked herself for not remembering to pack a spare, although she wasn't sure it would have made a difference. Compared to the readings she had taken on dry land, the data she collected here was puzzling, to say the least. The Greenland work had been done on compacted snow, not glacial ice, which might explain why her data was off. *Although there had been that one paper on Svalbard*, she remembered. She considered sending the authors of that paper an email later to check the settings they'd used on that glacier because, quite frankly, a lot of her readings were complete nonsense.

It was only going on three o'clock, and the sun was still high in the Arctic sky so, with the help of the volunteers, Kea packed up her gear and relocated the team to a site at a lower elevation near the western edge of the glacier. Here, the massive cliffs of Lómagnúpur trapped the moist winds and causing frequent rainfall. That, combined with the vast amounts of tephra on the surface of the glacier, resulted in thousands of streams and rivulets that incised into the ice. The intricate drainage network had carved out a badlands of irregular hills, tiny narrow valleys, and chasms. Speckled with dark tephra, the skin of the glacier was irregular here, scalloped into sharp ridges that towered above the streams. She had nicknamed the area the wildlands.

After depositing their gear in a pile, she pulled out the one bit of equipment that was not battery operated. Indeed, it was reliable, durable, and downright juicy.

"All right team, this morning we asked everyone to grab two apples." Kea held up one in her hand. "Does everyone have some left?"

The team waved their apples in the air, apart from Fernando who admitted to eating his. Kea gave him a spare she had in her pack. "You now hold in your hands the forefront of fluvial mensuration technology. So, whatever you do, don't eat it."

She broke the group into three teams and held up a handful of little red flags. "I'm going to place these markers up and downstream. Please don't go beyond them as the terrain gets too dangerous. One person will release the apple while the other will time its path downstream to each marker I've paced out."

Kea handed stopwatches to Gary and Nadia. "The apples will likely get stuck in the smaller channels. If it's safe, rescue the apple and start from a clear point. We're interested in sampling the stream's velocities, so we just need distances and times."

She held up two metal sticks with small-finned torpedoes on one end. "I have two flow meters. I'll be using one to take readings in the larger channels. I'll leave the other with you, just please take turns. It's very simple, just lower the fins into the water and record the readings shown here." She tapped the readout at the other end of the stick.

After setting up the flags and making sure the teams could take their own measurements, she worked her way up one of the larger channels, slipping and sliding as she went. She climbed out of a small valley and stabbed the last flag into the ice to demarcate the northern boundary of the safe zone. She surveyed the team working in the canyons below her. She could only see two team members in the twisting valleys - Gary on a rise taking notes and Nadia chasing after an apple, cursing fluently in Russian whenever it got away from her.

Kea dropped down the channel and tucked her pack onto the safety of a ledge. The water was a meter deep here, but the ice walls were narrow enough that she could comfortably straddle it with her crampons nestled into either side. She lowered the flow meter into the icy stream to take a few test readings.

She reached for her notebook but realized it was still in her pack. Reprimanding herself for not snagging someone to assist her, she tucked the device under her arm and, after a couple of fumbled attempts, managed to pull out her notebook and jot down the measurements.

By the time she took a few more readings, she found her rhythm for juggling the device and her notebook. She took a dozen more before leaning against a channel wall to rest. She checked her watch: nearly four. Time to get back to the rest of the group and head down off the glacier.

She inhaled the cool air, relishing the rushing sounds of the streams and the solitude of her surroundings. With the utmost reluctance, she pushed herself away from the wall and reached up to the ledge to retrieve her pack. Its base slipped on the ice and slid into her arms faster than she expected. As she fumbled with the pack, the flow meter slipped out of her hand and tumbled into the channel below. The device clattered as it knocked against the ice and bobbed downstream, seeming to wave farewell as it floated away.

With forced calm, she made her way out of the channel and moved to a rise to look for the flow meter. Thankfully, the device wasn't going anywhere. It had wedged itself within a constriction in the channel about twenty meters downstream. The slope was gentle, but the meter was well beyond the safety marker.

Rather than risk going after it, she sat back and pulled out a cucumber and butter sandwich. The break was partially to give herself a moment to calm down, but also an excuse to spend a few more minutes to enjoy the landscape before she rejoined the volunteers.

Looking up into the blue sky, she knew that this stunning weather wouldn't last long. The katabatic winds would soon be blowing cold air down from the ice cap now that it was late afternoon. She hoped to have the team off the ice soon. Rubbing out a cramp in her leg, she heard voices from below her.

It was then that she heard something else, this time from the east. It sounded like the peal of a gull, but louder.

Skua kill?

Curious, she moved further along the rise, leaving her pack at the channel's edge.

Drawn by the sound of rushing water, she followed the sound upward and found where another channel plummeted down into the center of the glacier through a moulin, one of several scattered across the area. The slopes around the maw of the pit glistened from the spray of the waterfall. The clear blue of the glacier's heart gleamed tauntingly from within its darkened depths. The spray from the water pouring into the hole generated a mist, obscuring the dark shadows within. She edged closer and felt the cool tickle of moisture on her cheeks. It was difficult to discern against the taint of black tephra along the rim, but there looked to be a dark splash of dark red on the grimy ice in the shadows.

Sign of a skua kill? There were no feathers in evidence. She looked up into the sky, scanning for the birds, but saw none.

She sighed. It didn't sound like any gull she'd ever heard. Better safe than sorry. Carefully extracted the little radio she kept in the water-resistant jacket pocket, she called for Marcus. Only static answered.

Must be out of range, Kea thought.

That wasn't too unusual, as the radios only functioned well via line of sight. Despite adding new radios to last year's budget, the university never came through with the funding. Also per usual. She pushed the *talk* button again. "Julie, do you copy? Over."

Once more, the radio remained silent.

She tried again. "Julie, Kea here. Do you copy, over?"

Suddenly, the radio crackled to life. "Oh, hey."

"Zoë?" Kea asked in alarm. "Where's Julie? Over."

"She's still GPR-ing," Zoe replied. "She gave me the radio because she's got her hands full. What's up?"

Relieved, Kea remembered why she was calling. "Everyone okay down there, over?"

"Yup," Zoë replied brightly. "Why?"

I'm just being paranoid, Kea thought. *Marcus and Tony are well east of here, and my team is below me.* However, the cry echoed again in her memory, and it set the hair on the back of her neck on edge.

Still, talking to Zoë gave her an idea. She had planned on using the MRS all day, but now that was a bust. Even mapping the drainage channels had only become an activity in a pinch when the MRS died. A detailed survey of the features, however, would be perfect. Plus, if there was anything unusual going on out here, the cameras would see it. "Where are the drones now? Over."

"I lost Romulus... had some issues. But Remus is nearly finished with the last grid you asked for. Um... over?" Zoë finished uncertainly.

"Can you fly it over to me?" Kea asked. "I might have a new area to map. Let me get you the coordinates. Over."

Kea pulled out her GPS. The digits on the readout refused to settle.

"Damn," she whispered. She pushed the button on the radio again. "We're roughly a klick west from the glacier margin and about three klicks over from the western cliff. You should be able to see me from up there. Can you map the area for me? Over."

Silence.

Kea sighed. "Please? Over."

Zoë's laughter intertwined with the static. "Of course, sorry. The winds are kicking up. I'm just trying to re-direct Remus to you, but I'm going to have to swap out his batteries first. It may take a bit."

Kea signed off and struggled to put the radio back into her pocket, her cold fingers clumsily pulling the zipper beneath the Velcro flap. She stopped in mid-motion, her attention caught by the sight of a tiny object wedged in the mouth of the moulin, about a meter down. It was an oblong, segmented object about ten centimeters long. It looked like some kind of stick insect.

"Hello there," she said quietly, reaching out for it. "Who are you?"

Its surface was oily, causing the sunlight to scatter in an iridescent shimmer, like the wing of a dragonfly. Moving closer, however, she couldn't discern any wings emerging from its length, nor any legs for that matter. To get any nearer to the object required her to lean too far into the pit, and its slope was dangerously slick from the rising mists. Craning her neck, she considered it for another moment, deciding it was probably just a bit of volcanic rock.

"I wonder," she said, carrying on her conversation with the rock, "if I go senile, will I even notice?"

A terrified scream tore through the air, causing her to freeze.

That was no bird.

It had come from her apple team below. She turned and dashed away from the moulin, pausing only to grab her pack, and cast a look of regret at the abandoned flow meter before heading downstream as quickly as she dared. The wildlands were not meant to be navigated at speed. Her boots slithered across the streams and cobbles, and she chafed the palms of her hands steadying herself against the channel walls. As she pulled herself through the channels, nightmare scenarios of what might have happened flashed through her mind, each one worse than the one before.

The only thing they had to do was stay between the markers, Kea reminded herself. She had done this same exercise with many teams before. *Not a problem, it's never been a problem, it's fine,* she told herself over and over, trying to turn hope into reality.

Using the screams as a guide, she emerged breathless at the edge of an ice canyon. Before her, Gary was on the ground, convulsing. Max squatted by his side as he tried to steady the man's head. They were all precariously close to where the glacier ice sloped away into a crevasse that led straight down into one of the lakes.

What the hell was Gary doing so far outside the safety markers?

"What's going on?" Kea knelt by Gary's head, the sharp crystals of the ice gouging into her knees. "What happened?"

"He just keeled over," Nadia said in a hoarse voice, terrified.

Gary seized again. His face was pale, his forehead freckled with beads of sweat, breath wheezing out of him in gasps.

"Gary, can you hear me?" Kea pulled off his gloves. No medic alert bracelet. She felt for his pulse. His heart was racing. "Can you tell us what's happening?"

He did not, or could not, reply.

Kea continued searching for clues, her eyes never leaving Gary's body.

"Anything else?" she asked the others. "Did anyone notice anything else?" She knew that she was shouting, aware that her hands were shaking with adrenaline. She fought to control herself, aware her rising panic could become infectious.

Calm down, you're scaring the others, she reasoned. *Keep calm. Heart attack?*

She tried to remember if there was anything on his medical form about a heart condition, but even in her panicked state, she knew none of the volunteers had listed anything like that. She would have flagged it.

Stroke?

"Gary, can you hear me?" she asked, hearing the tremor in her own voice.

Still no response.

Kea reviewed his symptoms: sweaty, shaking, fainting. She felt his brow, but his temperature felt fine. He wasn't cold, not clammy, not burning up.

Not hypothermia, then. What was it?

Fernando jogged toward them, groping around inside his pack. He knelt on the ice beside Gary and pulled out a juice box. "Gary, can you hear me? Can you drink this?" He slipped the end of a straw between Gary's lips. "It's going to be okay."

Kea sat back on her heels. For one terrifying moment, Gary didn't respond. Another moment or two went by, and his lips pursed the straw. Relief flooded through Kea as Gary began sipping some of the juice.

"Hypoglycemia?" she asked, cursing herself for not recognizing the signs.

Fernando nodded. "My little sister's diabetic. Give him a few minutes." He turned to the group. "Anyone have an apple left?"

***

With every stomp of her boots, Kea tried to quell the rage that boiled inside her. By not monitoring his condition, Gary had put lives at risk, his as well as those of the other volunteers.

She understood it was tricky to manage diabetes. That she could forgive. The pure rage that burned inside her stemmed from knowing that he had forged his medical form. That she had been lied to.

How had he done that?

She made a mental note to dig up the form.

After Gary finished the juice and a candy bar, they found themselves with nothing to do but wait. Adrenaline still sloshed around in Kea's system, although it had begun to ebb as Gary began drinking the juice. The realization that he would be okay, that they wouldn't need an air rescue, was a blessed relief.

When Gary began speaking again, however, and he sheepishly admitted that he'd lied on his medical forms, Kea's adrenaline came back full force. This time fueled by anger. She found his lie difficult to digest. It made her want to grab him and scream.

On the return trip across the ice, she kept her eyes trained on Gary the entire time. Anxiety had joined the adrenaline and anger. She knew he was better, that nothing would happen to him, that he was safe, but she was still shaken to her core.

As soon as they reached an unobstructed view of the depression, she managed to get hold of Julie and Marcus on the radio to share what had happened. They agreed to head back to the jeeps as soon as possible. The rest of the hike off the glacier passed in a chaotic blur.

When her team reached the lake, Kea made sure she was in Gary's raft, her eyes boring into his back. It was only once they had crossed to the other side and Marcus offered to take over, that she started to calm down. Now she trailed behind the other volunteers on the hike across the depression, falling back to her standard rearguard position, waiting for her mind to reboot.

Gary would be grounded for the remainder of the week. His only option was to sit back at camp or remain with a team that worked a site near the jeeps. Julie had mentioned wanting to take some measurements of the kettle holes. That was safe. Or he could help sort out the gear at camp.

The air around Kea grew hazy and red. Pre-occupied, she had veered too far east and walked straight into the middle of a dry lakebed. The winds blowing off the glacier combined with the warm, dry weather to lift the fine clay into a miniature dust storm. The dust cloud blew around her, a fine mist that reduced visibility to less than a few meters.

Kea tucked away her glasses and fumbled in her pack for her goggles. She zipped up the collar of her jacket to encompass her nose and mouth. With her hat, her goggles, jacket, snow pants, boots, and gloves sealed, she was completely enclosed, like an astronaut walking on the surface of another world. It helped her detach from her anger and focus on making it through the dust cloud.

Perspective, Kea reminded herself. *Perspective and scale. They were going to be okay. Everyone was okay.*

She crested the rise at the edge of the dry lake basin. The cloud of sediment fell away around her feet as her boots touched the gravel and cobbles once more. Leaving the tranquility of the red mist made her sad, but she found that her steps were now confident, more purposeful.

Ahead, the jeeps parked atop the wall of the depression were visible and the last of the volunteers were already climbing up the slope. By the time she arrived at the parking area, the teams had loaded their bags into the trailers. Skimming the crowd, she spotted Gary's gray head in the back of one of the jeeps.

Almost home.

Marcus addressed the group as he stowed his gear. "Everyone's fine, just a bit of a slip." Over the radios, the leads had agreed to downplay the event for Gary's sake. "Please make sure you've stowed all your gear in the trailers, including the high visibility jackets and helmets."

After the volunteers dispersed to the jeeps, Kea walked over to Marcus.

"Well, you know how my day went," she said. "How was yours?"

Marcus smiled. "It really could have been much worse. This sort of stuff keeps us on our toes."

"You okay?" Julie stepped closer, watching as the volunteers filed into the back of the vehicles. She smiled sympathetically at Kea.

"I'm better now," Kea said. "But I did have a lot of time to think on the way back." She held out an empty palm. "Keys?"

Julie pouted but handed over the keys to the jeep. "Did I do something wrong?"

"I've just had enough excitement for one day," Kea climbed into the driver's seat. She pulled out her phone from the glove compartment, booted it up, and tucked it into her jacket pocket before starting the engine. Heat flooded the cabin as the vents gusted out their dusty breath. "Ready for a headcount?"

The volunteers nodded and Julie began counting. When she finished, she paused, then counted again.

The hair on the back of Kea's neck started to stand up. "Is everything okay?"

"Um... I don't know," Julie said softly. "I think we're one short."

Kea turned around and counted for herself. The rear of the jeep was lined with double benches that had been knee-to-knee full on the way out. Now there was a gap. She turned back around to face the steering wheel. Fighting down a rising panic, she reached for the jeep's CB radio. "Marcus, do you copy? Over."

There was a delay, then she heard Marcus say, "Roger. Over."

Kea checked her rear-view mirror again. "Doing a head count. How many do you have? Over."

Another pause before Marcus's voice crackled over the static again. "Nine here. Over."

"Are you sure?" Kea fought to keep her voice steady. "We only have eight. Over."

"Nine. Over," Marcus confirmed.

"We're one short. Count again. Over." She turned off the ignition, jumped out of the vehicle and threw open the back doors.

Julie got out and ran to join her. "How can we be short?"

Kea started calling names even though she could see everyone crammed onto the benches.

Julie counted off before arriving at the same conclusion, her chorus of profanities following Kea as she jogged down the hill to the other jeep. Marcus was already at the back door calling the names on his list. Still one short. Nausea clawed up the back of Kea's throat as she realized who was missing.

"Who is it? Who did we miss?" Tony asked.

Kea let out a long breath.

"Bruce," she said dully. "Bruce is still out there."

Forgotten in her pocket, her phone finished its boot cycle and started to chime repeatedly with a flood of text messages and voicemail notifications.

Chapter 5

"EVERYONE BACK in the jeep, now!" Kea pounded on the rear of the vehicle. "Tony, shuttle them back in this one, get them out of the other one and leave it here. Julie, wait here until Tony comes back for the others."

She ran to the other jeep and started pulling the dazed volunteers out of it telling them to *'Go! Go! Go!'* She tore off a corner of the trailer's tarp and dug for her pack. Marcus was at her side, phone crammed between his chin and shoulder as he related the situation to the authorities, all the while helping her dump the scientific gear out of the packs to lighten the load. Julie handed them the extra food and clothes they kept stashed under the seats, plus spare radio batteries, water bottles, and emergency blankets.

How is this happening?

She scanned the outwash plain but saw nothing but endless gravel and dark gray sand. Skeiðarárjökull lurked in the background, but its black-encrusted ice gave up no secrets, no sign of a high visibility vest, no sign of a jacket.

Bruce, where the hell are you?

The question screamed in her head, over and over again, making it hard to concentrate. Her hands refuse to obey her commands, her trembling fingers slipping and fumbling with the claps as she tried to strap on her pack. Too panicked, too cold, too weak.

God dammit.

She turned back to the jeeps and saw Corvis volunteers clustered around one of the trailers, whispering to each other. The T3 team was still in the second jeep, their pale faces peering out of the windows. They all looked confused, frightened.

"When was the last time anyone saw Bruce?" she asked repeatedly, moving from one group to another. They all shook their heads. No one had seen him since they had been on the ice.

Swearing, Kea pointed to Jon and Erik. "We're going to need your help. Julie, help them get packs sorted." She moved back to the cliff edge and stared out across the plain, hoping to make Bruce appear by sheer force of will.

Nothing.

Marcus joined her, putting away his phone. "They're sending out a search team, but it may take some time for them to get here."

"We have to go back," Kea said, her throat dry. "He could have fallen in a kettle hole, slipped off a ridge... he could be anywhere."

He was on your team! she wanted to scream at Marcus. *How could you let this happen?*

Not now, she reminded herself and forced three long deep breaths to steady her temper.

Why Bruce? Why not someone else?

Stop. Shut it away, shut the ugly thoughts away. Bruce first, recriminations later.

Footsteps crunched on gravel behind her. Jon and Erik. "Right guys, we're going to head back the way we came, back to the lake, but spread out. Brisk pace, but be careful."

"Cole, give me a hand." Zoë's voice carried across the parking area. Kea turned to see her unstrapping the tarp of the jeep. The jeep Kea had tried to order Tony to drive away. The jeep with the drone equipment in the trailer.

Stupid, I'm so stupid.

Kea jogged over to the trailer and helped Zoë pull off the tarp. Together they lifted the crate out onto the gravel and popped open the lids. She caught Zoë's eye.

"The batteries have some juice in them, but I can't make any promises at how far they'll go," Zoë said in response to Kea's unspoken question. "We're probably out of range of the ice margin here, but I'll get as close as I can." She laid out Remus and began to prep the blade assembly.

"Right." Kea nodded to Julie. "Radio us if you see anything. We gotta go."

Kea jogged back over to the cliff edge and saw that Marcus and the other two men had already started downslope to the outwash plain, their dark forms obscured by trailing clouds of dust. She went over the edge, half-leaping, half-falling down the soft sands of the slope.

Just hold on, Bruce, we're coming, just hold on.

***

Marcus kept ahead of them, his strides urgent while Kea stumbled across the uneven terrain. Much younger and fitter, Erik and Jon kept a measured pace, either wisely conserving their energy, or because they knew that their efforts might be in vain.

As fast as they were moving, Kea judged that it would still take forty minutes to reach the raft, at which point the search and rescue teams should have their helicopters out, or at least Zoë's drone would be airborne.

Unless Bruce had fallen into a kettle hole...

She forced herself to walk faster. If he was spotted, she wanted to be there on hand to help. She couldn't just wait at the parking area and do nothing but wonder what happened to him.

The marching helped her re-focus. This wasn't the first emergency they'd faced. In the past, they had dealt with broken legs, rolled ankles, and sprained shoulders. All avoidable, all people just being careless. They had never lost anyone, not with the buddy system they used. Well, only once, but that had been a couple who had thought it was romantic to squirrel themselves away in a kettle hole for an hour of fun. Then, as now, panic helped no one, yet a nervous fear twisted her stomach into knots, causing bile to scald the back of her throat.

She scanned the skies. Nothing. Still nothing. "Moron."

"Sorry?" Jon asked.

Kea shook her head, realizing she had verbalized her thoughts. She had been so focused on looking ahead, she hadn't noticed that she had edged closer to Jon who had overheard her cursing. "I called him a moron. Bruce, I mean. The last time I saw him…"

"I'm sure he's fine." Jon placed a hand on her shoulder. "We'll find him."

Part of her wanted to smack away his hand, while another part of it wanted to hold it tight. She settled for walking faster, letting his grip fall away as she moved ahead.

"You were with Bruce up on the ice, right?" Kea struggled to re-member the teams. Bruce had been on Marcus and Tony. "With Reynard and Derek? Did you see anything, notice anything?"

"Yeah." Jon increased his pace to match hers. "I mean, no, didn't see anything. Nothing really happened. He drilled a few holes," he waved at Marcus's form in the distance, "'til his equipment broke. We mostly just waited around a lot."

Kea mentally cursed Marcus and his precious new gear. He hadn't mentioned anything about a malfunction. Not that they had any time to talk since Gary's episode. "Waiting around?" she fished, knowing from experience that volunteers rarely waited patiently anywhere for long, not in a playground as fantastical as this.

Jon shrugged. "We had to wait a long time, more than once. I'm not sure he really knows how to use that gear of his."

What a surprise.

"Anyone go wandering off?" Kea pressed.

"Yeah, a little," Jon considered. "We messed around taking some photos and stuff, plus bathroom breaks. We kept together though." He sounded defensive, and she thought she heard a *that-wasn't-my-job* tone in his voice. "Until we heard about you and Gary."

"The lake," she pressed. "Did you see him cross in the raft? Who was the last one over?"

"Not sure, honestly." Jon sounded annoyed.

Kea wanted to scream, to swear, to hit something, but in truth, her own memories were far from certain. She hadn't wanted to bring Jon and Erik along on this search, but she was worried that if they found Bruce, he might not be in any condition to walk. There was no way she and Marcus could carry him out if he were injured. She mentally flinched at the thought.

They hurried on as fast as they could, spreading out in an arrow formation. Marcus pressed on ahead, while Kea, Erik, and Jon fanned out in his wake. When she was certain that the cousins couldn't hear, Kea listened to the messages saved on her phone again, the receiver pressed tight against her ear. Joanna, their main liaison with Eco Observers, sounded faint and breathless. Kea could barely hear Joanna over the wind of the outwash plain. "I've been getting calls from the wife of Mr. Bruce Thompson. His wife is very concerned that he could be-"

Kea tripped, the toe of her boot catching the tip of a large rock. She caught herself with the palm of her hand as she hit the ground, her skin stinging from the gravel. Shaken, she squatted on her heels and took a moment to survey the land ahead. They were within the lower drainage basin now, walking across the last wide floodplain that abutted the lake. Remarkably, they had made excellent time. However, there was still no sign of the rescue teams behind or above.

She pressed rewind and tried to catch Joanna's words. "But his ex-wife is very concerned that he may be about to do himself some harm."

Ex-wife??

Kea shook her head. One crisis at a time.

"I'm still not clear on the exact details, but his ex-wife apparently came home unexpectedly and found a rather troubling letter addressed to her."

Kea imagined Joanna looking side-to-side to see if anyone was within earshot. "I don't think she was supposed to be there. I bet she broke in, but anyway, she thinks he may be... *suicidal.*" Joanna made the term sound like a particularly exotic disease and, while concerned, she could hear the excitement in Joanna's voice.

Suicidal.

That was all she needed on this trip. She forced herself to stand up and continue walking, edging around a twenty-meter-deep kettle hole and searching the wide basin for any sign of her missing friend. Nothing.

He had seemed troubled, it was true. Kea remembered the brief time they had spent together last night. His eyes had been haggard, lined with deep circles, and he seemed worn, beaten. Angry, even. Yet today he had seemed energized, excited to be on the glacier and to see part of her world. The two Bruce's seemed at odds with each other.

What do I know? she considered. *I can barely keep track of what's going on in my own head.*

Marcus had reached the lake's edge, and she saw see him starting to inflate the rafts. Kea scanned the empty skies above.

Where was the drone? Where was the rescue team?

Frustrated, Kea looked back to the jeeps. They had descended so far into the basin that they were out of sight of the parking area. Waving Erik and Jon on, she hiked up to a small rise overlooking the lake's edge and raised the radio above her head, hoping for reception. After a moment of clumsy semaphore motions, the radio gave a burst of static and then relayed the clipped syllables of Cole's voice.

"There you are," she heard Cole reply as she managed to secure the signal. "Wondered why you weren't responding."

"Any luck with the drone?" She turned to look out across the lake, searching desperately between the floating blocks of ice for any sign of Bruce.

"Yeah, mom's driving," Cole said excitedly. "She said she had to use the inverter to give it a little charge from the jeep first. Doesn't think it'll last long though. Heading toward you now, but she says it hasn't seen anything yet."

"Roger," Kea said, relieved. "We're going to wait here by the lake." She headed back down the hill where the men were gathered around the raft. "Stop that, stop that, stop that, *stopthatstopthat*!" She called, her words running together as she skidded to a stop in the sand. "We're not going across."

Marcus didn't respond. Instead, he shoved the raft into the water. Jon and Erik stood by awkwardly, looking between the two leads.

"Marcus, we need to wait for the rescue team," she implored. "We'll just be making things worse if we're all scattered across the ice."

Marcus glared at her, his eyes dripping with pure hate. Or so Kea thought at first, so used to his venom. Instead, she saw an expression she had never seen on Marcus' face before: guilt.

She felt it too.

"Okay. We go, but we stay together." She nodded to the two other men, and they clambered into the raft. They pushed off the shore, and with all four manning the oars, they slid quickly into the middle of the lake.

The mists that had clung to the dark waters in the morning had fled with the heat of the day. Instead, a cool wind stroked the surface of the lake into low ripples that rocked against the prow of the boat. The ice blocks that had appeared almost mystical in the morning fog were now ominous and threatening. They loomed over the little craft as the boat threaded between them.

Glancing south again, Kea caught a glimpse of the drone flitting back and forth across the sky. She put down her oar and pulled out the walkie-talkie again. When she judged that she'd have enough time between bergs, she tried Cole. "What's up, any sign on the plain? Can you check out the ice? Over."

There was a long pause before Cole finally answered. "Nothing yet. Mom's worried about going out on the ice, that's out of range. She's going higher up to see if she can see anything on the glacier. So far nothing, over."

"Kea." Jon put a hand on her arm. This time she didn't pull away. "Over there." He pointed across the lake, to a space between two of the bergs. She felt her heart clench in dismay. There, she saw a flash of bright red bobbing in the water: Bruce's hat.

"Marcus!" She nearly swatted him with the oar. He and Erik had already changed course to intercept. "Cole!" She barked into the radio. "The lake, can she get coverage of the lake? Over."

Another agonizingly long pause before Cole responded. "She's going to try, no promises. Over."

"We think we see... something of his," she finished cautiously, unwilling to say anything more, terrified to draw any further conclusions. "We think we see something that may belong to Bruce," she repeated. "It's in the center of the lake, just east of the Double Embayment. Over."

As they drew closer, she couldn't see any other sign of her friend in the water, causing her to feel simultaneously relieved and disappointed. She watched in horrified fascination as Erik fished the hat out of the water with his oar. She plucked it off and carefully examined it for any sign of damage or injury but found nothing. With a peculiar scientific detachment, she used her phone to mark their discovery's GPS on the map.

"Now what?" Erik asked.

"We keep going, all the way to the landing site." It was the first thing Marcus had said during the entire boat ride. His voice was so low and hoarse that she almost didn't recognize it.

"Guys," Cole's voice crackled in the air between them. "Good news, bad news."

Kea thumbed the radio. "We copy. Go ahead. Over."

"Well, good news, bad news, worse news," his voice trembled, exacerbated by the static.

"Cole," Kea snapped, "out with it. Over."

"Hey, Kea," Zoë's voice emerged from the receiver, calmer but layered with sadness. "Look, we've spotted the relief team, looks like choppers on its way, they should be there in five. I lost the Remus though, batteries gave out. Think it landed in a lake, but before it went down, I think I found him. Julie gave me your number. If you have any signal there, I'm sending a screen grab to your phone now. It's not good, I'm afraid. Kea, I'm sorry. He's in the water."

Kea yanked her phone out of her pocket. One bar of signal registered. She held it up to the sky, willing, and dreading, the text message to come through. It took only a moment before the friendly *'ding'* chimed to tell her it had been received, but it seemed to take forever for her phone to display the image. It took her even longer to process what it held. Although taken at an oblique angle and slightly pixelated, it was enough for her to discern the form of her friend floating in the icy waters of the lake. Face down.

Bruce.

Chapter 6

Day Three

A DELICATE sail of ice drifted across the lagoon, its serrated ridges glistening in the sunlight, its angular reflection mirrored in the still waters. Inside the crystalline skin lay bubbles of air trapped from centuries ago, or even longer. A frozen breath, trapped in time.

Behind it, thousands more icebergs drifted lazily across the lagoon. In the distance, the low front of the glacier Breiðamerkurjökull lurked on the horizon, its low front shedding gigantic blocks of blue and white into a lagoon that was now twenty square kilometers across, the deepest lake in Iceland.

"Vodka?" Julie slapped a plastic cup into Kea's hand.

Kea peered at the clear, warm liquid within. "Wherever are we going to find any ice?"

Julie snorted, then stalked down to the water's edge. She broke off a large chunk of translucent ice and huffed and puffed her way back. She snapped off a couple of smaller chunks and plopped them into Kea's cup.

"Thanks." Kea stared blankly into her drink.

"No problem." Julie waved out to the lagoon. "Next round is on you."

"Thank you for bringing me here." Kea nodded at the majestic landscape.

The lagoon, Jökulsárlón, was *'just around the corner'* from Skaftafell. It was only a half-hour drive, but it seemed like another planet. Unlike Skeiðarárjökull, with its massive outwash plain, Breiðamerkurjökull abutted the ocean before retreating upslope, and the deep basin filled with water, forming the vast lagoon that stretched before them.

They had parked the jeep by the road and wandered away from the rest of the tourists until they found a spot where they could pretend that they were alone to escape the claustrophobia of the tents and the questioning stares of the volunteers.

Cause I have no idea what to say to them, Kea thought.

"What on earth are you holding?" Julie asked.

Kea looked down at the small plush toy clenched in one hand. It was brown and furry with bright blue hands, nose, and tail.

"It's a platypus," she said sadly. "I found it in Bruce's tent after the police went through his stuff. I had a toy like this one when I was younger. I loved them so much, it earned me my nickname."

"Platy?" Julie ventured cautiously.

"I wish." Kea shook her head. "Try the other end. It was a cute name when I was six, but not so nice in high school. Bruce must have brought it for me." She stared at the glossy, black button eyes of the creature. It was adorable.

Speaking of toys... she thought. "Remind me to apologize to Zoë," Kea said, referring to Remus, the drone that didn't make it back from the search. "We'll have to find some grant money somewhere to cover the cost of her drones." The batteries had given out, Zoë said, or else the winds had been too strong. Another body on the sandur.

The body.

Kea couldn't believe that she was using that term to describe a volunteer. To describe her friend. Bruce.

Everything since they'd found him floating in the water had seemed so surreal. Help had arrived in the form of Slysavarnarfélagið Lindsborg, which was quite a mouthful, even for Kea. ICE-SAR, or Icelandic Association for Search and Rescue, was much easier to get her tongue around. Kea and her team were still in their raft when the ICE-SAR chopper roared overhead. The sandur was a busy place the rest of the evening as the rescue teams flitted across the sands with their little all-terrain vehicles.

All that fuss, she thought, *far, far too late.*

Kea heard an alarming splash in the lagoon. She watched as an iceberg the size of a house overturned, exposing a belly of clear blue ice to the sun. The ripples spread outward, each ring slowly kissing the shore at her feet. The berg displayed a new face, a new personality exposed to the cruelty of the sun.

Another victim.

ICE-SAR retrieved the body from the water and, after she and Marcus identified Bruce, his body was whisked back to Reykjavík. Rosmannsson, the chief inspector, spent several hours interviewing all of them. As she re-played the messages on her phone to him, she saw the sadness in the inspector's eyes, and her own shame reflected in them.

I didn't know, Kea kept repeating, both out loud and in her head. *I didn't know. I was on the last raft. I should have radioed for a head count, but I was so focused on Gary.*

Technically, part of her rationalized, Bruce was on Marcus and Tony's team. Marcus held the responsibility for his team members, but at the end of the day, she was the team lead. She knew in her heart that she had failed Bruce.

"Do you know," Kea began slowly, "that this isn't the first time?"

"How do you mean?" Julie perched her elbows on her knees.

"I don't think it's common," Kea said, "but I got the impression when I called EO HQ that it has happened at least a couple of times. Different projects. Different parts of the world. Every once in a while, people use these trips to... die."

"Hold that thought." Julie stood up, walked over to the jeep, and opened the back door. She fumbled for something under the rear seat, before returning with a pack of cigarettes. She lit it up and took a deep breath before letting out a long, billowing stream of smoke through her nostrils. "That's disgusting."

"Yes," Kea agreed softly. She pictured Bruce sitting at her tent having hot cocoa and trying to match it with the person described in Joanna's voicemail. To the figure floating in the water. "Yes, it is."

"What did the messages say? I mean," Julie corrected herself, "what did his wife say?"

Kea forgot that Julie had not been present during the interactions with the police. She lifted her cup and stared at the ice chip that floated on the surface, fascinated by the tiny flecks of sand that peppered its frozen translucent heart.

Alcohol seemed suddenly so mundane, so every day, so useless.

Kea put the cup back down on the ground. "Usual suicide note stuff. You're better off without me..." She found couldn't finish, the effort of having to form words was too exhausting. Besides, the note had been read to her via Joanna. The police, after listening to the messages, thanked Kea politely, then reached out directly to Joanna and Bruce's ex-wife themselves.

"If you could choose where you were going to die," Julie said eventually, "where would it be?"

Anger stirred within Kea once more. She found her voice rising, her emotions causing her syllables to tremble like ice in a glass. "He put the team at risk, he-"

"I know, I know." Julie raised a hand to placate her. "I just mean, I kinda get it. Unhappy job, unhappy life. Where was he living again? New Jersey? Just wanting to end it all somewhere, beautiful, somewhere amazing."

"That's no excuse," Kea insisted.

"I get it, I do." Julie raised her hands in surrender. "I'm not making excuses for him, I'm just trying to, you know, put myself in his place, trying to think about what was going on... inside." She tapped the side of her head.

Kea placed her palms against her cheeks and sighed. She'd spent the last fourteen hours trying to figure out what had been troubling her friend. As well as attempting to salvage her now-ruined career. Bruce had died on her watch, the team was a bust, as was her leadership.

"I'm such an ass," Kea announced.

"Probably," Julie agreed. Then asked, "In what way, specifically?"

"Never mind. What are the other volunteers saying? Do they want to stay or go?"

"They're fine, I think," Julie said. "Marcus spent the last hour trying to get a feel for their mood. At least, they appear to be fine. It sounds like Bruce didn't earn himself any friends in his job…"

Kea frowned. She had spent most of the evening placing calls to EO and the university. She hadn't spent much time with the volunteers, but they had seemed shocked, somber. No one, she reflected, had cried or anything. It didn't surprise her that the Corvis team didn't seem rattled as they had only met him yesterday, but she assumed his own team members would be a little more disturbed.

Flashes of the rest of the night popped into her head. She had met with Julie, Marcus, and Tony in the main tent following the questioning by the police. It was the first time they had all been together since they had shouted at each other at the jeeps. The '*How could you*'s?' and '*Who was responsible?*' had been hurled back and forth ad nauseam. In the scramble following Gary's incident, the hike off the ice had passed in a panicked haze for everyone, something no one wanted to admit. It was Julie who pointed out that if Bruce had planned this all along there was nothing that any of them could have done.

During the shouting, Kea had found herself staring at a map of the expedition taped to a whiteboard. The locations of the ablation stakes that Marcus' team had installed were marked out in little red dots. The final site was more than a kilometer away from her team and at least twice that from any other team.

Bruce had been alone out there, she thought grimly. *With no one to talk him out of it, no one to save him.*

"A few of the T3 team members said they didn't really know Bruce outside of some monthly video teleconference calls," Julie continued. "The folks from Corvis never even met him 'til yesterday, let alone knew that he was planning to commit..." She didn't seem to want to say the word suicide.

Julie took another drag. "They came here to work on the ice, and they want to keep doing it. So far everyone has said they wanted to stay." She tapped some ash onto the beach. "I think they feel bad but they just got here and want to stay for the rest of the expedition."

"That's it?" Kea was astounded.

"To be honest, the only one asking any questions was Lexie," Julie frowned in distaste. "But I imagine she's only after a story. I think a few of them worked directly with Bruce, but to be honest... they just want to keep busy."

"I thought they'd be at least a little wigged out." Kea shook her head, part of her mind working out future logistics. They had learned that, if the investigation wrapped up quickly, there wouldn't be a funeral for at least a week. She was frantically thinking of how they could get all their equipment shipped back to the university early without getting charged a fortune.

Not to mention the fact that a news crew could descend on the camp shortly. Eco Observers HQ had given her the standard *'Nothing to say at this time, please contact this number for an official response regarding the incident'* to parrot to the media, but she tried not to think about it. The last thing she wanted was more people tramping around the campground.

"Did he seem depressed to you?" Julie asked.

Kea paused. "He certainly seemed off the night before, although yesterday morning... he seemed to be a bundle of energy." She watched the icebergs drift past, wishing that she could just sail away on one of them.

"To be honest," Kea said after a moment, "I guess I don't really know him. I mean, it's been a couple of decades, but it still feels... I'm still..."

"Furious?" Julie offered.

"That as well..." Kea trailed off, not certain she wanted to put her emotions into words.

"But?" Julie stubbed out her cigarette and tidily tucked the bud into the pack's wrapper.

"As horrible as this sounds," Kea found that she hated herself all the more because it was true, "I can feel my career slipping through my grasp."

Silence.

"I don't seriously think anyone will blame you. But yes," Julie added, "that is pretty awful."

"Yes," Kea agreed, repulsed by her own priorities. "Either way, research is done for the season. Not to mention the bloody MRS is still up there."

"Weren't you listening to anything I've been saying?" Julie waved her hands in frustration, splashing vodka out of her cup. "The volunteers want to stay. Hell, they're chomping at the bit to get back on the glacier. Tony and I are taking a team up to Skaftafellsjökull in the morning, just to get them out of their own heads, if you want to come. There's not much trouble they can get into up there."

Kea closed her eyes and mulled the idea over. Skaftafellsjökull was a tiny glacier in comparison to Skeiðarárjökull and only a ten-minute walk from the visitor center. The path to the glacier was paved, and even once on the glacier itself, it was so small it would be easy to keep track of everyone. There were no hazardous areas, no large crevasses, no moulins. In short, there was no reason not to go.

If she were honest with herself, she just wanted to stay here alone and watch the world drift past.

Forever.

"We're just going up a few hundred meters," Julie continued. "Should keep them out of trouble. No crevasses, no moulins, no drama. More of a stroll. I need to test out my equipment anyway. I broke one of the sensors yesterday."

"I just..." Words continued to evade Kea's tongue. "It doesn't feel right."

Julie stood up and offered out a hand. "It might do you a lot of good."

Kea stared out across the water, feeling just as lost as the blocks of ice that slid across the lagoon and out to sea.

Leave me alone. Let me have my space, let me have my time.

All the things she wanted to say. To scream. To shout.

Mr. Platypus stared up at her from her hand.

As a lead, she didn't have a choice.

Patting Mr. Platypus on the head, she tucked it into her jacket pocket and sighed. "Okay," she said, pouring the vodka onto the beach. "But can I have some coffee first?"

***

Returning to the campsite, they found the volunteers were already milling around the trailers, anxious to gear up and go out onto Skafta-fellsjökull. Or at least to get out of their tents and away from camp.

Tony was handing out bright orange reflective vests, and Marcus was busy inspecting the volunteer's packs, cramming in batteries and other equipment where he found space and anyone willing to share it.

Marcus looked haggard and pale, his hair in complete disarray. He hadn't slept either.

He still had Dr. Carlyle's puffin staff though, Kea observed, tucked tightly into the crook of his arm. She had to restrain herself from yanking it away and beating his head in with it.

"Here," Julie's voice distracted Kea from a pleasingly violent train of thought. She handed Kea a vest, radio, and clipboard.

"Thanks," Kea started checking off names as she saw team members. Most of them gave her nothing more than a cursory glance before going back to their selfies or group photos with the bright peaks of Öræfajökull as a backdrop.

In some ways, it was as if nothing had ever happened.

Kea wasn't sure how she felt about that.

"Crap," Julie groped around the bottom of the trailer. Max and Bonnie stood waiting patiently while she fished for safety vests. "We're short."

Of course, we're short, Kea nearly snapped. *It's probably lying at the bottom of the lake or washed out to sea.* Instead, she said, "There are spares in the back, I'll grab them." She made her way around the main tent to the supply area and picked up a box that held extra vests,

90

stopping along the way for a quick couple of finger dips from the hazelnut jar. Feeling slightly more together, or at least well-sugared, she handed the box to Julie to distribute.

When she was certain everyone was present and accounted, Kea called them to gather round. For once Marcus hung back, letting her talk. "We're going to head out to the visitor center, then follow the trail round to Skaftafellsjökull. Once we get on the ice, we're going to stick together. No one is to let anyone out of their sight. It's a quick hike, and we'll only be a couple of hours. Right, let's go." She motioned for Marcus to take the lead. He held his walking stick aloft in one hand, using the other to keep a tight hold of his hat that was in danger of being yanked off his head by a morning breeze. The volunteers streamed behind him as they wove their way through the tents. Cole appeared to be chatting up Nadia right in front of her father. Zoë followed a short distance behind, watching her son anxiously.

Despite the circumstances, Kea found herself smirking. Watching the juvenile boy flirt with the elegant, if pouty, Russian teen was like watching a penguin try to fly.

Are we really doing this? Kea asked herself. The normalcy of it all struck her as absurd. The calmness, the eagerness of the other volunteers to step out onto another glacier, it was just… she sighed.

Focus on the now. Focus on the work, Julie had said. The funeral will happen soon enough. There will be time to grieve later.

Kea shook her head and followed the others.

As they marched, she watched as Marcus fielded questions from Lexie, Derek, and Bonnie, who clustered around him. Fernando and Amirah followed behind. Jon and Erik were attempting to entertain Lexie, fighting for her attention like pups eager for a bone. Behind them marched Reynard and Tiko, the odd ones out. Gary, grounded, had been tasked with washing the jeeps.

Even before the incident, Kea felt like an outsider on every team. Being a lead scientist meant she was treated as an entertainer, a guide, or even a surrogate parent. Over the years, she had only caught glimpses of what really went on between the volunteers: the friendships, the drama, the love stories. As the days passed, she knew, conversations would drop to whispers when she approached. On the last night when liquor was deployed, defenses would be lowered, and she would gain some insight into what was going on, but rarely before.

Today she felt more alone than ever.

She turned her attention back to the landscape. The trail that led from the visitor center was paved and flat, snaking through the short grass and scrub that stretched out in all directions. To their left, green slopes rose steeply to the mountain cliffs. Even the dark gray cliffs were shot through with a vibrant green, as lichen and other small plants clung to the vertical surfaces.

Kea caught up with the volunteers as the path curved around the base of the mountain to reveal the snout of Skaftafellsjökull. The little glacier lay at the end of a wide, rocky plain filled with numerous small streams and stagnant pools. The front of the glacier itself was blackened and sooty, its low tongue gradually rising northward up to the ice cap. Looking at the sagging muddy front of the glacier, she couldn't help but feel as if it looked like an old man contemplating his glory days.

Bonnie came to stand next to her. "It's... not quite what I was expecting. I mean, it's so... dirty. Even more so than the other one."

"Not enough blue?" Kea asked.

"Too much... yuck." Bonnie caught herself and added, "I mean wow... and yuck. Yuck-wow."

"It does get cleaner as you go up the glacier," Kea assured her. "And a lot whiter."

"Is that all dirt?" Lexie asked, snapping away with her camera.

"Glaciers are known as dirt moving machines." Kea found comfort in the familiar words of past lectures. "Do you see those bands there?" She pointed to the black-striped whorls and loops that shot across the glacier surface. "Those are made of ash, tephra. The tephra falls onto the ice during volcanic eruptions and is transported down the glacier over the years toward the snout. The ice itself moves at different rates, which is why those bands curve and twist like that. You'll see it as we get closer." She rattled off some science-speak, barely registering what she was saying. The coffee had given her the energy for the hike, but her brain was still numb, switched off.

Kea noticed Tiko lagging behind the group, her breath shallow, her face pale.

Just out of shape? Or in shock?

Fernando appeared to notice too, hovering on the periphery. He exchanged a concerned glance with Kea but seemed reluctant to engage.

Kea matched Tiko's pace and forced her best impression of a smile. "How's it going?"

Tiko nodded but didn't reply. Her eyes were swollen, her cheeks flushed red. Perhaps she had been crying, although for all Kea knew it could simply be from lack of sleep. Or anger.

"If you're not feeling up for it," Kea said kindly, "I can head back with you."

Tiko shook her head in irritation and stalked up the path, leaving Fernando and Kea to follow at a distance. Kea winced. "I never know what to say sometimes. Or, always."

"It's not you," Fernando said quietly.

"Were she and Bruce close?" Kea judged the gap between Bruce and the young Georgian to be at least twenty years and almost two hundred pounds.

Stranger things, she thought.

"Yes and no." Fernando plunged his hands into his jacket pockets as a fresh gust of air berated them. "He was our manager if that's what you mean. They've already had a rough year, and now this happens."

"Bruce mentioned something about losing someone else on his team, but not that they, you know, died or anything."

"What?" Fernando looked confused. "Oh, Andrea? She didn't- she just didn't show up one day. I think she moved to one of our competitors. Always happens. She keeps posting about how awesome her new job is on social media. Shame though. Andrea was one of the best." He seemed to look through Kea, his eyes narrowing. "No, that's not what she's upset about."

"Then..." Kea prompted, feeling like she had lost a thread.

"She saw him kill himself, apparently. She told the police this morning." Fernando looked at her strangely. "Sorry, I thought you knew."

***

Kea and Fernando caught up with the rest of the volunteers just as Marcus launched into a new lecture.

"A glacier has two zones," Marcus began. "The region where ice is being added by snowfall is called the accumulation zone. The ablation zone, on the other hand, is the area further down the glacier where melting is taking place. The line where these two zones meet is called the zone of equilibrium. In the case of a retreating glacier like this one, the equilibrium line is moving further and further upslope. As the line moves up the glacier, more and more of the snout wastes away."

Kea picked her way through the group as they gathered around Marcus in a loose semi-circle. She noticed that Reynard and Derek had separated from the pack, their heads close together, deep in conversation. Spying Julie at the far side of the group, Kea made her way across to her.

"We're currently standing in the ablation zone," Marcus continued, holding up a metal rod. "Our goal is to measure the rate at which the melting is occurring. One way to do that is to drill into the ice and insert ablation stakes and measure how much ice has melted from year to year. The trick is getting the sticks deep enough into the ice..." He put down the rod and crouched next to a cylindrical metal tank.

It occurred to Kea that since Bruce was drilling up on the ice with Marcus yesterday, he may have heard this same lecture. This could have been the last thing he heard before he died.

Poor bastard.

"This is a thermal ice drill and uses butane, just like regular camping stoves." Marcus tapped the tank. "As it boils water, the steam allows us to drill through the ice with this." He held up the metal wand. "You could always use a hand borer instead, which is basically like a giant corkscrew, but you can only get down a few meters with one of those. With this baby, we can go down nearly eight meters." He patted the gray metal casing affectionately. "We have placed several more of these across the glacier, but we're installing this one today to replace one we lost. Or at least I hope we can. Had a bit of trouble with it yesterday, but I think I've got the seal fixed."

Kea noticed Reynard turning abruptly away from Derek, his hands visibly quaking in anger. Derek caught her looking at him and glared defiantly back before turning to watch Marcus' demonstration with feigned interest.

Shrugging, Kea finally reached Julie and nudged her away from the rest of the group. "Why didn't you tell me Tiko saw Bruce fall?"

Julie seemed puzzled by the attack. "I thought the inspector told you."

"Why the hell didn't she say something before?" Kea fought to keep her voice a low, raging whisper.

"Like before we left him there? Like when we asked everyone? Like any sane person would do?" Julie sounded just as angry as Kea felt. "I have no idea."

Kea bent her head closer. "What happened, exactly?"

"I wasn't there," Julie said. "But Amirah told me that when the inspector asked Tiko why she didn't say anything, she just said she saw Bruce running and jumping, but she didn't see the actual fall because of the angle. Too far away. She just thought he landed on another level. She said she didn't realize what she had seen until after they found his body. She had no idea he was trying to off himself. Who would?"

Unfortunately, at that moment Marcus paused in his lecture, permitting the word 'body' to float through the ranks of the team. Shamed into silence, Kea and Julie stepped apart as Marcus finished connecting the hoses to the butane tank.

After much fussing, and a good deal of swearing, Marcus sat back on his heels and gave a grunt of success. The volunteers waited for something flashy, but after several minutes of the device doing nothing more than emitting a low rumble, their excitement waned. The device had to achieve the correct temperature and pressure to operate the drill, Kea knew that they were waiting around for water to boil.

Looking for a distraction, she took out her GPS handheld device to mark the location of the drill site. The digital readout flickered, alternating constantly. She gave it a hearty slap.

"Everything okay?" asked Bonnie.

"GPS can be tricky up here," Kea frowned at the sky. "We don't get a lot of coverage this far north, so there are periods when the satellites dip below the horizon. It requires patience, but you can usually get enough signal during the day, although you may have to wait twenty minutes."

Bonnie held up her cell phone. "I've got plenty of signal."

Kea pointed toward the road. "On this glacier, we're close enough to the highway to get a decent cell signal. Sometimes we get Wi-Fi coverage from the Face-Googles," she waved up at the invisible high-altitude balloons and other toys the big companies had recently released around the globe. "We're not really in their loop, so it can be hit or miss. Ah, there we go," she corrected herself, seeing the display flicker into life, "seems to be fine here."

She looked downslope to the base of the glacier. Apart from a couple of areas where the ice bowed and humped, they had visibility straight down the gentle path to where they had walked onto the ice. Nowhere for anyone to get lost, nowhere for anyone to hide, no place for anyone to jump. Now that she had a moment to think about it, she tried to picture what Tiko could really have seen from her position all the way over at the Double Embayment…

A hissing startled her as the drill finally spat to life. Marcus moved it into position above the ice and began slowly lowering the wand down into the surface of the glacier. The rod disappeared into the ice a few centimeters at a time. Before long, the wand had vanished from sight, leaving only the black tubing to mark its descent.

The volunteers pulled some snacks out of their bags and squatted on the ice, waiting for something interesting to happen. Normally, they'd be in for a long wait, but not today. Even Kea was surprised when an angry snarling sound began emitting from the borehole.

Marcus swore under his breath and started tinkering with the tank. After a few minutes, he powered everything down and withdrew the hose and drill from the ice, checking along its length for damage.

"Anything I can do to help?" Kea asked.

"No," Marcus snapped. "Just an issue with a valve seal," he said in a calmer tone. "I thought we'd fixed that." He turned back toward the volunteers and flashed them a reassuring smile. "I'll take another stab at fixing the old girl tonight."

Kea tilted her head. It was still only just after noon, but she didn't have any other activity to keep the volunteers entertained. "Back to camp?"

Marcus nodded and began packing up his gear.

"All right, everyone," Kea called. "Have a look around to make sure that you've got all your stuff and we'll head back down. Slowly," she added for emphasis.

The team was far more energetic on the hike back down the glacier. Despite her words of caution, she watched the younger members race each other downslope. As she followed at a more sedate pace, she made a mental note to dig out the moleskin from the medical kit to treat the inevitable blisters that would appear later.

Bright flashes of neon purple caught her eye as Reynard sped into view, his trouser legs rolled up, exposing brightly colored socks and porcelain white calves. He wore only a T-shirt, exposing freckles that shot up his bare arms like a rash. There was a similar explosion of melanin peppering his neck and cheeks. She deliberately increased her descent to keep pace with him.

Reynard noticed her gaze. "I didn't expect to get a tan. Not in Iceland anyway."

Kea cracked a smile. She desperately wanted to know what he and Derek had been arguing about. *Act normal*, she told herself, *engage, relate*. It was the exact opposite of what she wanted to do, which was to let everyone walk off the glacier so she could remain up here, all alone.

Tell a story, said a quiet voice inside her head. It was the same voice that quelled her panic whenever she had to present in front of packed lecture halls. *Escape into a story*.

"I had a colleague once, back when I worked in Hawaii, who wore shorts one day when we were walking on the lava flows." *Not the brightest person in the world*, Kea remembered, *and one who wouldn't stop trying to get into my pants.* "The lava field was covered with pahoehoe, so it was basically a plain of twisted ropes of black volcanic glass." Telling the story became easier as she remembered standing under the burning sun in Hawaii. She had been surrounded by endless black fields of glass that stretched out around her like a vast pool of tar, tens of miles wide. "He wore plenty of sunblock, but it wasn't until he got back later that night that he hadn't considered the sunlight being reflected up his shorts. Which would have been fine, if he'd been wearing underwear. Poor guy roasted all his goodies."

Reynard made a sound like a goat being kicked. Even though she knew it must be laughter, the noise still startled her.

He smiled, his blue eyes and perfect teeth beaming in the sunlight. His crooked nose and sharp chin made for a peculiar profile, but one, she noticed for the first time, that was oddly handsome.

"You may need that soon." Kea nodded at the jacket wrapped around his waist. "It can get chilly pretty fast. The cold air from the ice sheets up here is much denser than the warmer air by the coast. It causes katabatic winds, as the air rushes down into the valleys below."

Reynard grinned, his expression suggesting he already knew this. He paused at an area where the ice leveled off into a gentle plateau. "Are you going up to Svartifoss tonight?" he asked, referring to the waterfall nestled in the mountain high above the campground. "Julie said she would take us."

"I've already been up a few times this season." Tourist sites were the farthest thing from her mind right now. "You should go up though, it's quite a sight."

"I may." Reynard's eyes flickered from her to the view and back again. "I am sorry. I heard he was a friend of yours."

Kea felt as if she'd stumbled. It was like he knew why she was talking to him.

Am I that obvious?

"Yeah, well, I'm sorry too." Kea found herself wondering again what she really knew about Bruce, and, for that matter, what kind of friends had they really been? *But if the game was already up...* "I have to ask, what happened up there?"

Reynard fixed his gaze on the ocean which simmered just below the horizon. "The drill, it was taking forever, kept breaking. We all got bored. We had lunch. Then coffee." He squatted down and started picking cobbles out of the melting glacial crust. "Then more coffee. Marcus was very angry, shouting."

Reynard flicked rocks down the glacier as they walked, one by one. Normally, Kea would have stopped him on principle, but since there was no one downrange of his projectiles, she said nothing, hoping he'd keep talking.

"He shouted at Tony, then they were both arguing." Reynard spoke in a lower voice now, the cold breath of the glacier threatening to steal his words. "Drill still wasn't working. Rest of us, we started wandering around, to kill time, let them cool down."

Kea closed her eyes and lowered her head. She could picture it all too clearly. On the ice, it would be easy enough to lose track of someone, particularly in an area full of dirt cones and active drainage channels. She pictured the map of the area in her head again. "But Bruce must have been gone for ages. How could you not see him? What on earth were you and Derek doing?"

Reynard glanced sharply at her, fixing her with a hard stare for what seemed like a full minute. Abruptly, he tossed the last rock down a narrow crevasse. "Photographs," he said, patting his bag. "I want to capture this." He pulled out his digital camera. "All of this beauty. Not... not men squabbling. I've seen enough of that for a lifetime."

Kea watched as he walked down the slope. She couldn't help but feel that she'd hit a nerve somehow, but she couldn't put her finger on what. Everyone insisted that they felt fine, but there was an air of electricity she felt whenever she spoke to anyone. She was afraid of getting too close and get zapped.

All I want, Kea thought as she looked out to the sea, *is a long, warm bath, with a bottle of wine. While I'm dreaming, I'd also kill for a full body massage, a pizza, and a-*

Movement on the terrain below caught her attention. Atop a series of slight rises in front of the margin, Tony held a survey-grade GPS staff aloft, looking for all the world like Gandalf. Shielding her eyes, she squinted at the little figures of a few volunteers who followed him.

"What's he up to down there anyway?" she muttered to herself.

"Mapping the moraines," Max's sonorous voice caused her to flinch.

She jerked around to see the large man standing behind her. She hadn't heard him approach, which she found unsettling. The rising winds must have covered the sound of his boots on the ice.

"Is that what he said?" Kea shifted, keeping Max in her peripheral vision and watched as Tony walked along a narrow ridge that ran parallel to the front of the glacier margin. There was nothing remarkable about the recessional moraines that he was surveying. The thin ridges were left behind following the retreat of the glacier margin, like ripple marks on a beach. Tony hadn't mentioned needing to map them.

Still, she considered, *perhaps he was just filling time while they waited for everyone to come down. Just trying to keep busy.* It was what she was doing up here too.

As she watched the others file off the ice and onto the plain, she noticed Derek and Reynard together once more. Reynard's hands were gesturing wildly, up the glacier.

At me, Kea realized.

Derek caught Reynard's arm, appearing to calm him down. She watched as they re-joined the rest of the group, but caught Derek giving her a quick, not so casual, sidelong look before stepping onto the sandur.

Kea found herself reluctant to follow. Up here on the ice, it felt as if she was part of another world. One without people, without drama.

She squatted down on her knees and made as if to tie her shoe, in case the others wondered what she was up to.

What am I up to?

"Great question," she breathed to the glacier.

Humpty Dumpty sat on a wall... The grotesque nursery rhyme played in her head as she stood and walked.

Who had been up on that wall?

Bruce had been with Tony and Marcus and...

Who else?

She ticked off names on her fingers: Reynard, Derek, and Jon.

Who else was on the ice?

Her apple team of course, but they had spent most of the afternoon in the wildlands.

Who did that leave? The GPR team?

She'd have to double check, but she thought it had consisted of Nadia, Tiko, and Lexie, along with Zoë and Cole on the drone team by the esker. She tried to picture the locations of the teams on the ice, the distances between them, and Bruce somewhere out on the ice, falling to his death into a crevasse or pit. She envisioned his body being dragged by the harsh waters through the chaotic innards of the glacier before finally emerging, battered and broken, into a proglacial lake.

Kea pulled out the little plush toy. "Bruce, what on earth were you all doing up there?" The platypus refused to answer.

And why didn't you give me this?

The night they had spoken, the conversation had turned quickly to ex's and breakups, so perhaps it wasn't the best time to give gifts, she admitted, but if he was really going to end it all, why bring the toy all the way to Iceland then not give it to her? Did he know she'd find it afterward, or did he just intend to give it to her later?

She cast her eyes up to the sky, searching the heavens above.

Bruce, what the hell were you thinking?

Chapter 7

LATER THAT afternoon, Kea was hacking out lumps of dried clay from her boots with a sliver of rock when the chief inspector called. She listened politely, thanked him, and hung up, all the while staring at the clumps of sand and grit still embedded in her sole as the reality of Bruce's death hit home once more.

She forced herself to finish cleaning her boots before she rounded up the team leads behind the jeeps to give them the news. Unable to meet their eyes, she kept her gaze trained on the volunteers that were sitting out on the grass in front of the main tent, enjoying the blue sky and sunlight. Safe.

"They completed the autopsy," Kea announced, fixated on a pair of furry boots Bonnie was wearing. They seemed oddly out of place, Kea thought, although absurdly comfortable. "As the medics noted yesterday, he took quite a beating when the waters carried him through the glacier and out into the lake."

An image of Bruce's body, broken and battered, leaped back into her mind. When asked to identify him, she and Marcus had been faced with a nightmare. The head had been smashed to a pulp, his limbs fractured, the bones bent in horrific unnatural directions, the pale flesh swollen and torn.

That's science indeed.

Boots, she reminded herself, focusing again on Bonnie's footwear: booties with dangling laces that had furry little balls on the end, like little bunny tails.

"They said his lungs were full of water, indicating that he was breathing when he drowned." She paused, blinking stupidly at the boots. The others said nothing. Something niggled at the back of her mind, something that didn't add up.

Eventually, she found that she could speak again, but her voice sounded chalky and foreign to her own ears. "They checked with the local authorities back in the states, and the note checks out. It's his signature. They've ruled it a suicide. The body's being shipped back tomorrow. We're to collect his tent and things and mail them to his family. We're all free to go."

Marcus puffed up his cheeks and blew out the air like a sagging balloon. "Right then, that's that. We still have six field days left. I'll ask the others if they'd like to stay and help."

"That's that?" Tony barked. "That's all you have to say? He's dead for Chrissake-"

"We had nothing to do with any of this," Marcus held up his hands. "It's just a very unfortunate-"

"Will the both of you stop!" Julie slammed her fist against the hood of the jeep.

Kea flinched. The volunteers across the field were all staring at them.

All this mess could have been avoided if I had stepped up, if I had just insisted that the others report head counts.

She caught Max looking at her. He was too far away for her to know for certain, but it seemed like he was smiling. Mocking.

If. If. If. If I had done a million other things differently.

"ENOUGH!" Kea bellowed, surprised at her own outburst. The anger welling up inside her pushed aside her doubts, her insecurities, her grief. She lowered her voice, fighting for control. "Enough. We're not doing all that again. Marcus is right, getting home sooner won't help Bruce. For all we know, this is the last season we may have funding, given the way budgets are going. The equipment is here, and so are we. Let's finish the work, then pack out as planned. If anyone would like to go to Bruce's funeral, there'll still be time after we get back."

In truth, Kea knew she would be the only one of their group attending, but she wanted to extend the offer. Worse, a part of her had no desire to go at all. She had no idea how she could even begin to explain to his family what had happened on her watch, but she knew she had little choice.

"Now," she continued, riding the wave of confidence that her rage provided. "Julie, please inform the others. If they'd like to stay and assist, they're more than welcome, but no one, and let me make this absolutely clear, no one other than the four of us are going out on the ice again. If the volunteers want to stay, they can help with the ground surveys, but other than that, no one leaves our site. Tony, I'd like a word alone, please."

Marcus, to her surprise, nodded and exited without a word, Julie in tow. Tony hovered by the rear of the jeep. Shifting his weight from foot to foot, she was reminded of an errant child called to the principal's office. She folded her arms across her chest and considered him. "Two questions."

Tony stopped fidgeting and leaned against the jeep, crossing his arms defensively.

"What were you doing out on the moraines today?" she asked in her most matronly tone.

That seemed to throw him for a moment, which was what she wanted.

"Marcus asked me to update the margin position." He seemed annoyed. "To track the recession."

"Oh." Marcus had been so obsessed with the new equipment, she hadn't heard him talk about anything else.

"What happened up there with Bruce?" she pressed. "Did you see anything?"

"What? No." Tony's demeanor changed from defensive to pleading. "We were just fixing the stupid drill. We weren't paying attention to anything much else."

As he sputtered and whined, Kea could tell he was telling the truth.

"I should have done a head count," he lamented. "But I was too focused on loading the rest of the volunteers into the rafts. I'm... I'm sorry."

"It's okay." Kea waved for him to stop. "I was just hoping that, oh, I don't know. Never mind. Look, why don't you break out some of the beers for dinner." She waved to one of the boxes next to the supply trailer. "It might be good for folks to let off some steam."

Leaving Tony to unpack the booze, Kea felt the urge for another chocolate fix. She knelt by one of the plastic tubs that held the toolkits and pulled out the jar of hazelnut spread. Sucking a dollop off the top of her finger, something clicked in her head. She popped open the lid of the tub that contained their records and started digging.

Thanks to their non-existent filing system, it took ten minutes to find their original equipment manifest. List in hand, she returned to the trailers and started counting. As Julie had noted this morning, they were short on the high visibility vests. Not just one, however, but two.

More than just Bruce's was missing.

Kea counted them once more to be sure, and again came up two short. She sat at the base of the trailer wheel, her mind churning. It was odd, but not unusual. Volunteers treated the flimsy vests pretty badly. It wasn't as if they hadn't gone missing on past trips.

Am I looking for evidence? Of what? That something worse happened to him?

It was not, it had to be said, the most damning of evidence. In fact, the absence of the vests was the opposite of having evidence.

She sighed. Short of searching everyone's tents, and searching all the glacier and sandur, she'd be hard-pressed to find the missing vest, but for the first time since losing Bruce, she felt as if she might have put her finger on something that could help her figure out what had happened to Bruce out on the ice.

***

"So, there I was on the glacier, holding one of Julie's GPR antennas." Bonnie addressed the team as they finished their dinner. "But I can't see where I'm stepping. I realize I'm about to fall into a crevasse behind me when Julie reaches out with both hands. I'm so relieved because I think she's going to save me at the last second. Instead, she just says, 'Sorry Bonnie,' grabs the GPR out of my hands and down I go butt-first into the crevasse!"

"To be fair," Marcus grinned, "it is expensive equipment."

"So is my ass!" Bonnie protested.

The tent filled with laughter. The mood of the team had lightened, if only for a moment. She took her plate back to the washtub and slipped it into the tepid water to soak. During supper, she had done little more than push food around her plate. She hovered by the tub, listening to the conversation at the main table.

"Didn't sleep at all last night," Erik said. "Not only doesn't the sun set here, but those sounds the birds were making were crazy."

That would be the Icelandic snipe, Kea thought. She considered pointing it out, but people tended to not believe her when she tried to tell them snipe were real birds. Too many people, it seemed, had fallen for a snipe hunt prank in their childhoods.

"What's that?" Cole pointed to a circular emblem on the inside of Max's left bicep.

"Every time we start a new project, I get a new tattoo," Max flexed his muscle. "When we complete the project, I get it filled in."

The tattoo appeared to be an outline of an ant standing atop a blade of grass, although from where Kea was standing, she couldn't quite make out all the details. The blade had been colored green, but the rest remained a stark outline of black ink against Max's leathery skin.

"How many tattoos do you have?" Cole leaned in closer for a better look.

"Eight so far, but you're not allowed to see all of them, kiddo," Max said with a chuckle.

"Eight?" Bonnie asked. "I only counted five last night!"

Oh dear. Kea shifted down the length of the bench a safe distance, where Julie was showing Jon and Reynard the data she had collected.

"Here's the unprocessed data." Julie pointed to a mess of squiggles on her display. "I'm going to run some basic tools to take out a lot of the noise in the data that we don't want to see."

"De-wow?" Reynard pointed to a tool button on the screen. "What is 'de-wow'?"

Julie smiled. "Wow is just a name for removing the errors caused by two antennas being positioned too close together. It's one of the processing steps involved in cleaning up the data."

Jon pointed at another icon on the screen. "And TWTT?"

"Two-Way Travel Time. It's the time that it takes for the signal to go down into the ice, then come back up and be collected by the receiver," Julie explained. "Measuring the length of time for the signal to return, and in what pattern, allows us to discern the structure of the ice. Okay, here we go, processing has finished." The screen flickered, revealing a more coherent image of flecks and lines, although to the untrained eye it still appeared to be nothing more than a grainy mess of streaks.

"What are those?" Jon waved at some streaks that the processing algorithm appeared to have made thicker, more defined.

"Layers within the ice." Julie followed the path of several of the lines across the screen with the cursor of her mouse. "You can trace the continuous layers. Sometimes its layers of debris, other times its differences in the thickness of the ice itself. Since we mapped out a grid pattern, we can reconstruct the surface in three-dimensions and really understand the structure."

"And that?" Jon pointed at a large distortion in the data.

"Erratic." Julie traced its outline. "A boulder in the ice."

"A meteorite?" Reynard's voice rose in excitement.

"That's an option," Julie admitted. "But more likely it's just a rock carried by the glacier. Don't get me wrong, a glacier can carry and move objects like meteorites, but there'd be more disturbance in the surrounding layers. Although, that's not really my specialty. It's far more likely this is just a boulder, scraped off from a cliff... I'll probably run the rest tomorrow morning. I just wanted to check to make sure the data recorded-"

"But with this," Reynard pressed, "you could find a meteorite?"

Julie shook her head. "It wouldn't really be a good tool for that. I mean, yes, this could find an object lodged in ice, but you'd rather use, and I'm just guessing, but a magnetometer? Metal detector? I dunno really."

Despite Julie's omnipresent smile, Kea detected an edge in her voice as she tried to hide her impatience. She couldn't blame her. She remembered being a graduate student all too well. How the work stretched into endless years of data processing and sourcing citations. Given how much work Julie had in front of her, Kea considered, chatty volunteers weren't going to be much help.

Since Reynard seemed eager to ask more follow-up questions, Kea motioned for them to move away from Julie so she could finish her work. "Anyone for a cup of cocoa?" she asked sweetly, feeling like a stewardess.

"Yes," Reynard said. Jon nodded his affirmation. Julie flashed her a grateful smile as she turned back to her screen.

For the second time that day, Kea found herself waiting for water to boil. As she spooned out the cocoa mix and poured the water, she noticed Zoë hovering around her son. Cole was playing a round of poker with Bonnie, Max, and Erik. After serving the others and pouring one for herself, Kea used the opportunity to hand Zoë a cup of cocoa. "How's Cole holding up?"

Zoë pulled an odd face and paused for a beat before responding. "I honestly don't know." She studied Cole as set down two face cards and laughed triumphantly. "The joy of having a teenager is that they barely speak to you, and when they do, it's not generally pleasant." She took a tentative sip of her drink. "You have to learn how to read them in other ways."

"You sound like a narrator from the nature channel," Kea re-marked.

"It's a bit like studying animal behavior... and just as smelly." Zoë turned back, and Kea found herself staring into Zoë's dark, soulful eyes. "If you're asking about how he's handling the incident, he seems fine."

"And his father?" Kea ventured, realizing that she wasn't sure if he was in the picture or not.

"He sees him sometimes. More often now." Zoë said in between sips. "He's still an asshole though, but he tries to help. A little. He taught Cole to play poker." She waved over to Bonnie's gang. "That's something I've only just discovered."

"Well," Kea said kindly, "I suppose you can't help what his father may let him get up to."

"No, that's not what I meant," Zoë said. "Cole's spent the last couple of years putting up so many walls, that I'm not sure I'll ever see all of him."

Zoë's face carried the exhaustion of motherhood, her forehead and mouth creased with dark shadows. Despite the weariness of her expression, it only made her appear more beautiful.

"Sometimes," Zoë continued, a faraway look in her eyes, "I'm not sure I want to."

***

Refreshed from a long shower, Kea headed back toward the main tent, where the sounds of laughter and conversation drifted across the grass. As she made her way through the field, she passed Zoë's tent, where she could hear her scolding Cole. While she couldn't make out the words, the tone suggested that the rest of his trip was going to be unpleasant. Kea reached the entrance of the main tent, only to nearly collide with a hastily exiting figure.

"Sorry," mumbled Tiko, her face flushed. She held open the flap and stumbled over her words as she brushed past Kea.

"Not even slightly odd," Kea muttered. Inside, she found only a handful of volunteers. Nadia played solitaire while Gary sat at the end of the table reading one of the scientific journals that the team had left out. Derek sat across from Amirah who was doing some knitting. Of what had troubled Tiko, Kea could see no sign, but seeing the hungry look that Derek was giving Kea, she could hazard a guess.

Amirah, dressed in a sweatshirt and practical pants, welcomed Kea and poured her a cup of cocoa. Amirah sported gold bracelets, earrings, and a lovely silk scarf that blazed with the hues of a Pacific sunset. A soft jingling noise followed her as she busied her hands with her own mug.

"Love the scarf. Fabulous," Kea commented, eyeing the cocoa cautiously. It was still only nine o'clock. If she wasn't careful, she was going to be up all night. "Where did you get it?"

"Oman," Amirah said proudly. "My home."

"Corvis certainly is a global company," Kea commented. "It's really amazing to see such a mix of people."

"When I started the company, I wanted to ensure that it contained a diverse workforce," Amirah said. "It is very important to me."

Kea could have kicked herself. This whole time she had assumed that Andrei was, if not the owner, then at least the lead presence for Corvis. *And I get upset when people think Marcus is my boss*, she thought wryly. "Did you make the decision to bring the Corvis team to Iceland?"

Amirah nodded. "I am not the biggest fan of camping." She made a distasteful little flicking gesture as if warding off a fly. "However, these glaciers are a sight that I have always wanted to see."

Amirah didn't say 'before they're gone,' but over the last several years Kea had heard similar sentiments from volunteers. The glaciers were retreating right before their eyes. Volunteers often came to see the ice in all its glory, or to see what there was left of it.

"How about you?" Amirah asked. "Where are you from?"

"A small town in Vermont, but I've always felt at home here in Iceland," Kea admitted. "It's warmer here than where I grew up, but in many ways, the climate is very similar."

"Minus the glaciers," Amirah pointed out.

"Well, yes," Kea laughed. "Although ten thousand years ago, there was an ice sheet more than two miles thick sitting on top of my little town, which is hard to imagine. We still get aftershocks from the isostatic rebound as the land is still responding to the removal of the weight of all that ice. Did you know the Great Lakes are spilling southward? They're pouring down into the United States, like a bucket being gently tipped over." Seeing the deer in headlights expression on Amirah's face, she paused. "Sorry, I switched into lecture mode again there."

"Not at all," Amirah replied with a smile. "I came here to learn."

"Well, we appreciate you all helping," Kea said.

"Hard work is the best way to see the world." Amirah replied. "Not that spending a week by a pool is torture, mind. But by working somewhere, you really get to know a place, the bad and the good. And the people..."

Kea noticed Amirah looking at the group of card players.

"Is Tiko okay?" Kea asked. "She seemed a bit off when I passed her just now. I mean, I know yesterday..."

Amirah nodded. "Awful. I hope she will be fine. She was playing cards with the rest of them, but most everyone went to the cave."

Kea wasn't certain, but she thought Amirah's gaze lingered on Derek as she commented.

Poor Tiko.

Kea would have to have a word with Derek if he kept hitting on everyone in sight.

Alarmed, Kea grabbed Amirah's arm. "I'm sorry, what did you just say just now?"

"Bonnie and a few of the others." Amirah, taken off guard by the physical contact, regarded Kea with wide eyes. "They said they were going to check out some ice cave they found on the internet..."

Kea released Amirah from her grip, worried she would frighten her. More calmly, she asked, "Do you remember where?"

"S... something." Amirah attempted to mutter half-heard Icelandic syllables. "I think."

"That's terribly helpful," Kea replied frostily. "Was it Skeiða-rárjökull perhaps? Skaftafellsjökull? Svínafellsjökull?"

"That's it," Nadia called from across the table. "The Svína one."

"Oh, that's all right then." Kea felt the knot in her stomach relax a bit. Svínafellsjökull was a good two or three miles away. "It's not like they have a car or anything. What were they going to do, walk there?"

"They were," Nadia confirmed, "but then Bonnie met a guy in the parking lot who offered to give them a lift. They left about an hour ago."

"They *hitchhiked?!*" Kea lunged for her jacket, patting them quickly to find the keys to the jeep, all the while spewing choice expletives.

"I don't know why you look so worried," Nadia commented. "Bonnie said she decided not to bring the snow tubes."

***

The jeep bucked violently as Kea turned off the highway and onto the service road leading toward Svínafellsjökull. "What the hell were they thinking?"

"They probably just wanted to get out of camp for a bit," Julie guessed as she looked out of the passenger window. "You gotta admit, the ice caves are pretty cool."

"Yes, in January, they're amazing," Kea enthused. "Fantastic ceilings of blue ice, dreamlike vistas." She wrenched sharply on the wheel to avoid a large pothole. "In August, at the height of summer, it's a goddamn death trap."

"Calm down." Julie sounded thoroughly bored, although Kea noted she was holding onto the door handle with a tight grip, her knuckles pinched white. "They probably can't even get across the way the water is right now. Besides they're adults. I doubt they'll go walking into the middle of a river."

"Really? We're really having this conversation?" Kea downshifted violently, grinding the gears as they lurched up a muddy embankment. "Where have you been the last couple of days? You've obviously not been working here!"

"Sorry." Julie breathed out a long sigh, obviously fighting to remain calm. She let go of the handle. "Who are we chasing down anyway? I've got a lot of work I could be doing right now rather than playing adventures in babysitting."

"From what I can gather, it's Lexie, Derek, Jon, Bonnie," Kea paused deliberately for emphasis, "and Erik."

Julie frowned at the news. "Can't you get this thing to move any faster?"

***

The month of January, despite the bitter cold and seemingly endless dark, was the perfect time to explore Iceland's glaciers, for the scientists at least. Kea had only visited twice during the winter, but when the rivers and lakes were frozen solid, they were able to reach areas that were off limits during the warmer seasons. Although the sediments and all their secrets remained trapped beneath the frigid grip of the winter snows, to Kea the ability to effortlessly stride across the expanse of lakes and winding rivers, to stroke the snout of the glacier was like approaching a slumbering dragon and tramping around its treasure trove without any fear.

The long nights also held their own wonders. Aurorae flickered and danced across the velvet black skies. It was no surprise that the Norse folk were so deeply tied to their mythology. Above them, the gods fought and warred at what seemed an arm's length away, their battles flaring up so bright as to light up the darkest of nights.

During her most recent winter visit, Kea had explored one of the largest ice caves in Iceland, formed where an englacial lake had drained away and left a vast chasm. Fractures and fissures bled cracks of light that reflected across scalloped walls and ceilings carved out of the clearest turquoise. Around her, the ice breathed with life, groaning with thunder as the glacier shifted in its sleep. To Kea, it was as if she was walking through the heart of a living, breathing blue diamond.

Tonight, even at this late hour, the sun still shone brightly, revealing a morass of shifting silts and stagnant mud that pooled in front of the glacier Svínafellsjökull. The jagged, narrow margin seethed drainage channels, interlacing streams that could burn with their icy touch. The snout was comparatively small, only a kilometer across, its margin less than a kilometer from the highway.

Kea parked the jeep alongside a large body of water ponded by the folds of the moraines. She and Julie walked across the outwash plain searching for the ice tunnel. They found one entrance to a tunnel directly across the river from them, but it would mean they'd have to hike over to the lateral margin and double back again to reach it. She stared into the shadowy mouth of the glacier with trepidation. The overhang above the river was low, barely a meter above the surface, the turbulent water frothing with silt and ice crystals. There was a small stretch of sands where the ice touched the bank, but the interior of the glacier was cloaked in shadow.

"If they went in there..." Julie ventured.

Kea knew that if they really had been that foolish, if they had crawled up the bank and into the ice tunnel... her mind slipped into panic mode, the rush of dreadful possibilities spiraling through her head. The ice underfoot here was unstable, possibly deadly, not to mention the threat of flood, or a simple misstep into the waters. The thought of trying to follow them, of losing someone else, after Bruce...

Why is this happening? Why now?

"…why aren't there any footprints?" Julie finished simply.

Kea's mental train of panic careened in sudden confusion, as she noticed that the stretch of sand leading into the cave was indeed pristine. The skin of sand was unblemished, sprinkled only with gravel and cobbles. There was no sign of anyone. She sputtered, at a loss for words. "Then where the-"

A hearty, high-pitched peel of laughter reverberated above the sandur.

"Bonnie," Julie commented.

The sound came not from the cave, but from behind them, away from the glacier, across the stretch of small rumpled hills, where a little hotel lay nestled beside the ring road and the moraines. Its simple roof and white walls contained only a handful of rooms, as well as an area with windowed walls that overlooked the glacier and contained, among other things, a bar.

She headed back towards the jeep. "I'm going to kill them."

***

They found Bonnie and her buddies knocking back pints of beer at the wood-paneled bar of Hotel Svína. Inwardly fuming, Kea waved hello in response to their cheers of greeting, wishing she had brought the tire jack to wield above her head like a berserker delivering bloody justice. Since there were a couple of other guests sitting at tables, she contented herself with a little nod and sat down at the bar alongside the volunteers. She noted Julie sidling over to the relative safety of Erik's side.

"What on earth do you think you're doing?" Kea demanded quietly, her voice cracking in anger.

Bonnie looked from her beer to Kea and then back again. "At this exact moment? I'm having flashbacks about coming home late from prom with a couple of tight ends. I think that's probably the last time I've ever heard anyone address me in that tone."

"We thought you'd gone into the ice cave," Julie explained. "We thought you were in danger."

"Have you seen that thing?" Bonnie wrinkled her nose in disgust. "It's nasty, just mud and yuck. We weren't going to go crawling in there."

"The guy who gave us a lift warned us that it was only safe in winter," Jon waved to the bartender. "Unlike Bonnie here, who didn't quite scroll all the way down to the bottom of the webpage when she pitched the idea." He waved around at the bar. "He's the one who recommended this place."

"How could you not have told us about a hotel?" Bonnie was beside herself with indignation, "I mean for God's sake, we're camped in a swampy field, when there's a perfectly good taproom right here!"

They're safe, Kea reminded herself. *Everyone's perfectly safe, calm down.* She nibbled from the bowl of peanuts, using the momentary distraction to settle her voice. "We're camped for nearly four months, the price would be astronomical," she said defensively. "Not to mention, there wouldn't be enough rooms for everyone."

"You could have at least given us the option," Bonnie persisted.

Kea felt as if she was trying to reason with a truant child. "How on earth did you think you were going to get back to camp?"

"Dunno." Bonnie shrugged. "Hitchhiked again probably or walked. It's only a couple of miles."

Before Kea could unleash a suitable response, Jon intervened, holding out a pint of beer and escorted her to one of the little tables located away from the bar.

She let herself be led away if only to mentally regroup and use the time to look for a blunt instrument with which to start hitting people. There was an ornamental paddle affixed to the wall that had caught her eye that looked hefty enough.

"Anyway, we had to fire Simon." Bonnie returned to talking to Erik, Kea's outburst already forgotten. "The guy broke into the company's lactation room and drank all the breast milk. What were we supposed to do, promote him?"

"So, what's it like?" Jon asked, bringing Kea's attention back to their table.

"Sorry?" Kea finally realized he was staring at her with, of all things, notable interest.

"The ice caves." It was obvious that he was trying to distract her, to calm her down, except once his startling blue eyes locked with hers, they had the exact opposite effect.

"It's… fine," she said, words eluding her. It didn't help that he was wearing one of those tight-fitting white knit shirts with the V-necks that exposed a swath of chest hair and a glimpse of the sharp edges of his pectorals. She found herself keenly aware of her own appearance: grimy ball cap, raincoat, and snow pants. Dressed to perform a rescue or deliver a throw down, not a tête-à-tête with a lick-the-mirror-handsome man sitting across from her. In a moment of true horror, it dawned on her that she had completely forgotten to put on deodorant.

"You okay?" Jon asked, still gazing at her.

"Yes." Kea found herself fixated on his nose – so firm and straight, it was impressive enough to prop up the Tower of Pisa. "Well, clearly no," she admitted after a moment. "But for now, I'm just glad you're all safe."

"You don't seem terribly glad." Jon took a sip of his drink, the foam leaving a trace of white mustache on his upper lip.

Kea fought down the urge to wipe it off with her finger, afraid she would look like a doting mother. "I think," she pondered instead, "someone needs to create a word to describe feeling tremendously relieved while still wanting to knock peoples' heads in."

"It's been a rough couple of days." Jon nudged her glass and raised his own in a toast. "To Bruce."

"To Bruce." Kea let it swirl around her mouth for a moment before swallowing. The beer was bitter and heady, but not unpleasant. She took two more pulls while Jon sat patiently, lost in his own thoughts.

"Sorry. We... I," she corrected herself, "was worried about all of you."

"Personally, I'm worried about all of us. It looks like we're living in a minefield." Jon pointed behind her, where the hotel owner had framed a collection of different maps each with different dimensions and frames, that formed a collage of Iceland. Highlighted on each were little red triangles representing volcanoes. "How do you pronounce this one?" He asked with all the innocence of a school kid holding an apple behind his back.

I know what you're doing, she thought, *and thank you*. "Eyjafjallajökull." She sat back in her chair slightly, relaxing into her professor persona.

"One more time?" His eyebrows contorted in a playful dance of confusion.

Kea laughed and repeated each syllable slowly. "AY-yah-fyad-layer-kuh-tel. 2010 was an amazing eruption," she reflected. "It truly would be a pity if the world forgot the event just because no one could pronounce it."

"I think we'll have to disagree on the amazing part." His teeth smiled a perfect smile, shining bright against his bronze skin. "I was stuck in London for nearly a week."

Kea nodded. When Eyjafjallajökull blew its top in 2010, not only did the eruption melt large volumes of the overlying ice - the resulting plume of ash and gas reached an altitude of more than thirty thousand feet. It caused havoc for the airline industry, stranding passengers and devastating profits.

"The main issue for planes is the ash, which is essentially just silica, or glass," she explained. "When it gets sucked into a jet engine, it can melt and fuse on the turbines, clogging the engines. London is definitely a safer option," she reflected. "Plus, amazing curries."

"Are we in any danger from Eya...Eya...?" Jon finally gave up. "From that volcano where we are now?"

"Not as such," Kea reassured him. He was still wearing that goofy foam mustache. "You passed that region on your drive out here, about two hours west." She pointed to another map where two small ice caps sat at the southernmost point of the island. "But we're here," she pointed to the largest ice cap. "Eruptions can occur throughout the island. It's what makes being situated on the Mid-Atlantic Ridge so exciting."

He stared at her with a raised eyebrow, a charming smile on his face.

"Iceland straddles a spreading center," Kea explained. "A ridge of volcanic activity that separates the Northern America plate and the Eurasian plates. It's the longest mountain range in the world, but it's all under the Atlantic Ocean, except here in Iceland." She traced the Mid-Atlantic Ridge, a jagged line that split the island into three regions. "Thingvallavatn Lake lies right on top of the Silfra fissure." She pointed to a lake just northeast of Reykjavik. "You can go snorkeling there, actually swim between the two plates."

"Have you ever done it?" He wasn't looking at the map anymore.

Kea found his intense stare unsettling. "No," she admitted. "I usually only have enough time and money to keep coming back to this same field site year after year." She stared at the array of maps, struck by their detail and variety. "I would like to make a trip around the entire island at some point, but I'll have to wait until the work is done."

Finishing his beer, Jon plonked the empty glass on the table and looked up expectantly. "When does the work end?"

"That," Kea chuckled, "is a great question."

"Well," Jon said softly, "let me know if you find yourself in need of company."

Kea flushed bright red. She drank from her glass slowly to buy herself time before attempting a response.

After the expedition, you can explore options, she told herself. *For now, volunteers are off limits.*

"I meant to ask," she began, desperate to change the subject. "Tony overheard you guys mention that someone…" She couldn't believe that she was going to even ask this. It must be the beer talking. "Someone parked their dinner outside of Max's tent the first night. Do you know who it was?"

Jon pulled back, puzzled at her choice of words before understanding finally dawned. His expression changed completely, as if she had thrown ice water in his face.

"I thought you knew," he said slowly.

She realized that she had misread his expression. It held only sadness. "Pretty sure it was Bruce. He hated Max. We think it was his final farewell."

"Bruce did it?" Disgusted and eschewing the visual that popped into Kea's head, she pressed further. "I assumed it was a rivalry between you guys and Corvis. Whatever did Bruce do it for?"

Jon shifted in his chair, as if not comfortable speaking ill of the dead. "Bruce blew a big project recently. Max couldn't fire him, because Bruce owned copyrights on some of the tech, but Max demoted him and knocked his salary in half. Not enough that he couldn't live on it, just enough to humiliate him." Jon nodded toward the sign for the restroom. "Back in a sec, I want to hear more about swimming in the rift."

At least I still haven't lost my power to drive men away, Kea thought. She noticed that Julie was practically sitting in Erik's lap.

One more week indeed, she thought, catching Julie's eye. *You and me both. Why can't men hit on me when I can actually do something about it?*

116

Jon's revelation lingered in her head. It was no less confusing or bizarre than everything else had been this trip, but still. *Bruce, what the hell have you been up to?*

Bonnie's voice grew louder, buoyed by the alcohol. "Look, we hadn't heard from her for weeks before we came here. Why on earth she wanted to go to Austria, I have no idea. I think she was just sick of Max hitting on her."

Kea's curiosity was piqued. "Tiko?" she chimed in.

"No," Bonnie turned to her. "Max was fixated on Andrea."

"Dunno about that," Erik laughed. "He's wrapped around Tiko like a wire brush now that Andrea's gone."

"What does that even mean?" Bonnie shook her head. "Tiko's just... convenient."

"Gone?" Kea struggled to remember the conversation she'd had with Bruce. She had assumed Bruce meant Andrea had just quit the company.

Bonnie waved a wad of cash at the bartender, motioning for another pint. "We got an email from her saying she'd resigned. No one has seen hide nor hair of her since. Bruce was gutted."

"I imagine anyone would be." Kea wasn't quite sure what Bonnie was suggesting.

"Well, yeah, but Bruce was particularly sweet on old Andrea." Bonnie bobbed her head up and down as if Kea knew exactly what she meant. "I think she was just upset how badly Max treated Bruce and just took some time off."

"Bruce and Andrea... were a thing?" Kea tried to digest this information. *Was that what ended his marriage? Or was it after?* She was beginning to think she had no idea who her friend really was.

"Couldn't say, dear, I'm in HR. We can't comment on those things." Bonnie tapped the side of her nose. "But he was devastated when she went missing, absolutely destroyed. His wife was going to get everything in the divorce, whatever was left anyway. No wonder he took a dive."

A part of Kea's heart buckled. She realized she had held out hope that there had been a mistake, that there had been foul play, that anything had happened, anything other than her friend committing suicide. She stared into the dregs of her beer, wondering at the sight of the little splashes that marred its surface. It was only then that she realized she was crying.

* * *

The bar shut at eleven. Kea loaded her band of miscreants into the back of the jeep and took them back to camp. Jon drifted off on the ride home, either due to jet lag, too many beers, or both. For that, Kea was thankful, as she had enough to think about right now without fending off any invitations to his tent. Or rather, she wasn't certain that if he asked, she would be able to say no.

She dropped them off at their tents before parking the jeep. The campsite was very still this late at night, although the perpetual twilight that inhabited the Arctic gave the world a dreamlike quality. The haunting cry of snipe, once alien and unnerving, she now found familiar, comforting.

Going native, her mother would have said.

She spied movement coming from Zoë's tent, the telltale glow of a computer screen. It gave Kea an idea. When she arrived at the tent flap, she realized she didn't quite know what to say. Finally, she whispered, "Knock, knock."

There was the sound of rustling, then zippers being fumbled. Zoë's face peered out, her eyes alert, but wary. "Hello?"

"Hiya," Kea said awkwardly. A second ago this had seemed like a better idea. "I was just, um, I was just wondering, could I have a look at yesterday's footage?"

Zoë looked at her oddly but nodded. "Cole's over at the visitor center using the Wi-Fi." She pulled open the flap to allow Kea to crawl into the tent and shoved her sleeping bag out of the way. "I already showed it to the inspector. He took a copy with him, but there was nothing to see."

Zoë's laptop was open, its screen filled with a paused frame of a television show or movie. "One sec." She shunted the window away with the mouse and flicked through some folders. "We lost Romulus pretty quick, but Remus got some great airtime. But nothing about Bruce, other than, you know, the body..."

Kea winced. "Can you pull it up now?"

"That's what I'm doing," Zoë replied curtly. "Here we go."

A close-up image of grimy boots appeared on-screen. The view shuddered and jerked as the drone shifted into position. Zoë fast-forwarded the video, and the drone suddenly spun upward into the air. On the glacier below, the rest of the drone team was gathered around Zoë. As the craft lifted higher, the edge of the glacier sprawled out beneath them, its irregular surface rumpled like a dirty blanket. The drone rose higher before crawling across the outwash plain, mapping the muddy edge of the glacier margin with its invisible lidar.

Zoë pointed on the screen to an area to the north, off camera. "I had Romulus heading up to that lake you asked about-"

"Lake Grænalón," Kea corrected.

"Yeah, that one." Zoë fumbled for the clipboard with the flight plan taped to it. "I think Romulus must've got caught in an updraft and bought it. I sent Remus on the other transect across the margin like you asked, but at a higher elevation... seemed safer, anyway." Zoë turned away from the screen. "What really happened up there with Gary?"

Kea rubbed her temples. "He was a diabetic and lied about it. Had a seizure."

"You looked severely pissed off." Zoë frowned. "You don't think he intentionally went into insulin shock, do you?"

"What?" Kea blinked rapidly. "No. I mean, yes, I'm upset... Upset that he didn't tell us he had the condition. That he put the team in danger. And then at Bruce. For the same reason and more. To do this to us... I just don't get people sometimes, you know?"

"No comment," Zoë said quietly, turning back to the screen. "Remus's about to enter the second pattern you asked for-"

"That there!" Kea yelped, jabbing a finger at the screen. "What's that?"

Zoë paused the smears of brown that were displayed on the screen. "Dirt?"

"Yes," Kea grinned. "Pay dirt! Come on, let's go tell others!"

Chapter 8

Day Four

THE NEXT morning, the main tent was swollen with the ranks of volunteers as they loaded up on breakfast. Kea stood at the rear, watching Lexie pack an Iceland-style field lunch: slices of cucumbers, tomatoes, and pepperoni on buttered bread. Bonnie and the two cousins were eating breakfast, giggling conspiratorially. Julie sat with her head bent over her laptop, no doubt preparing for the day's work. Across the heads of the volunteers, Kea saw Gary lingering at the open-door flap, staring out at the mountains, a mug of coffee in hand. Jon, eating breakfast, caught her eye and his face lit up with a big goofy grin.

Oh dear. She realized she, and the beer, may have led him on. *Going to have to have a chat at some point…*

Beside Kea, Amirah was tidying up some of the dishes, embracing her role as the unofficial team mother. The woman was wearing yet another fantastic silk scarf, as if, Kea thought, Amirah had a different scarf for each meal of the day. This one was steeped in dark maroon and glittering with flecks of gold. *Was this a breakfast scarf?*

Jon pushed aside a small carton. "Room temperature milk disturbs me more than a little."

"It's fine." Bonnie pointed at the label. "It's been irradiated."

Erik shook his head. "That's the opposite of fine. I'm not drinking nuked milk. And this yogurt..." He held up a small packet. "They drink it warm. Nasty."

"Everyone," Marcus bellowed, "your attention please!" He stood at the head of the long table, fully dressed for fieldwork, a clipboard in hand.

"First though," Kea interjected. "We'd like to say thank you to all of you for offering to stay and help, especially given the circumstances."

"Yes, absolutely." Marcus positively beamed with excitement.

Kea wished Marcus would dial down his enthusiasm a notch. It seemed wildly inappropriate. Even worse, she wished she didn't feel it too.

"Last night, we examined the drone footage, taken by our most excellent Zoë Forbes here." Marcus waved to Zoë, who fixed her gaze on her bowl of cereal, visibly uncomfortable with the attention.

"From the images, it looks like there was a minor flooding event over the winter, near the western-most river, the Blautakvísl," Kea explained. "It exposed a section of a cliff over a kilometer long which will provide us with a great exposure to map. However, this area is in danger of being washed away by the river, or by another flood."

Marcus highlighted the area on a map clipped to a whiteboard at the head of the table. "The flood has exposed hidden layers of sediment, providing us with a rare opportunity that could help us unravel the secrets of previous flood events."

"Basically," Tony added, "we're scrambling to action stations, and we need your help. The area is simply too big for us to map on our own with the time we have left."

"That's right," said Marcus. "We need to map this section as soon as possible."

"No glacier?" Nadia's disapproving pout implied Marcus should consider his response very carefully.

Kea loved that the teenager said what all the other volunteers were thinking.

"No glacier," Marcus replied, feigning disappointment. "But it should only take a day or two to map this section. I hope."

Looking around the table, Kea could see that Nadia wasn't the only one who seemed despondent. She sympathized. They'd come to see glaciers, not shovel mud. She was wise enough not to point out that in the first two days the volunteers had already been on two glaciers. Depending on the project, it was sometimes more than a week before most teams even laid a foot on the ice.

"We know it's a huge undertaking," Julie said, attempting to rejuvenate the team. "Each section will be photographed, sketched, and sampled. We'll do a proper sedimentary workup on the samples back at the university's lab."

"Today," Kea pressed on, hoping her enthusiasm was infectious, "we're going to train you all on how to become stratigraphers!"

The team appeared less than thrilled. Several turned back to contemplate their coffee and toast, blinking sleepily.

"If that weren't enough," Kea continued, grateful she'd saved the best for last, "our friend in the Met office called this morning. There's been increased seismic activity at Grímsvötn, which may signal an eruption!"

That got everyone's attention. Excited murmurs flitted around the tent with several repetitions of the question. *Are we safe?*

"Yes, yes, yes." Marcus was in his element now, Kea observed. An eruption, new project, and an animated crowd. It was better than Christmas.

"We're perfectly safe. We wouldn't take you out there if we thought otherwise. The seismic activity means that there is an influx of material into the magma chamber. It could melt the overlying ice in the Grímsvötn caldera, but remember, the caldera has to fill with enough water to lift the ice dam before water can flow out."

While activity under the ice cap was common, Kea knew the research teams always went to Iceland with their fingers crossed in the hopes that activity would coincide with their trip. Sometimes they got lucky and the dam lifted and there was a flood, although it was rare.

"It's carefully being monitored," Kea added. "We'll have plenty of notice should something happen."

"It does mean that we'll have to move quickly to map this section," Marcus pressed on. "Finish up your breakfasts, pack your lunches, and let's head out!"

Kea watched the team exit the tent. She wanted to take Jon aside, explain that she couldn't get involved, to just give her a week or so, but she found a hand on her arm. Julie steered her to the back of the tent away from the others. Unbidden, she poured Kea a cup of coffee and made a fuss of adding sugar and cream powder, talking softly under her breath the whole time.

"So, last night I downloaded the GPR data to my laptop." Julie nodded discreetly to where her computer sat next to the main table. "This morning, dead."

Kea frowned. "Dead as in you forgot to charge it, or *dead*, dead?"

"I plugged it in to charge overnight." Julie poured herself a cup of coffee, her hands shaking. "But this morning, I can't get the thing to boot up."

Kea cringed. Dissertation death by laptop failure happened more often in the field than anywhere else. "What about the memory card from the GPR? Did you have anything else on the drive?"

Julie shook her head. "I have all my projects saved to an external drive. Three actually, plus I synch up to the cloud whenever I can. I wiped the card, though. I thought I'd need the space in case we did any more fieldwork today."

Kea looked at the cup of coffee in Julie's hand. "If I drink this, I'll be bouncing across the sandur. I've already had two."

Julie shrugged. "You can dump it. I just wanted to keep busy in case someone was watching us."

"You really think someone would pull the plug on your GPR data?" Kea asked dubiously. "I don't think any of these guys have any interest in the sedimentology of a melting esker."

Julie looked at Reynard and narrowed her eyes. "I don't trust meteorite boy over there. No one gets that excited about meteorites…."

"True," Kea admitted. "Well, maybe Superman."

"You're not taking me seriously," Julie growled.

"Trust me," Kea said with a sigh. "Over the last two days, I've been taking everything far too seriously."

* * *

It took an hour for the team to load up the vehicles and begin the long ride on the Ring Road across the sandur. In her rear-view mirror, Kea surveyed her allotment of volunteers. They appeared to still be half-asleep, not having expected to be working today. As she drove them through the campground, she was relieved to see that there wasn't any sign of a press van. She wondered if the woman at EO HQ had been correct: what happened to Bruce would find its way into a few news blurbs and obituaries, but little else.

While the media loved tragedy, the EO woman said, they had little room in their headlines for suicides. At least, she admitted, when it came to regular people, seeming to imply that Bruce was no movie star.

Regular people. Kea found that the phrase stuck in her head as she drove. She still had a full team of regular people to look after, and she was paranoid about each and every one of them.

Today's site lay near the western side of the glacier. The jeep trundled across Route One, skirting along the front of the glacier, crossing first the Skeiðará and the Gígjukvísl rivers, then headed for the terrain tucked between the smaller, westernmost rivers, the Sula and the Blautakvísl. As they turned off onto a bumpy park track that shook and rattled the jeep as it bounced through the end moraines, the volunteers stayed quiet, sullen.

Kea was seriously concerned about the team's morale. She knew they were weary, but if she were honest with herself, she expected them to be... well, not wailing exactly, but in some way depressed. Yet they gave no sign. It was very peculiar.

Hopefully, the new work would be enough to distract them. The new field site was a long hike, but since it was safe and they had so much work to do, all hands were on deck. Even Gary was permitted on this trip.

For better or for worse, she thought.

They situated the vehicles at the edge of the hilly moraines. The volunteers filed out the jeep and gathered their equipment before starting their march across the endless broken hills and pitted terrain. The ice in this area had melted out long ago, making it difficult to find an even path across the chaotic ground.

Marcus led them down a gentle slope into the proglacial depression. To the north, low black peaks pierced the glacier's skin.

As they marched, Kea watched with interest who broke into groups. Tiko, Reynard, and Fernando clumped together, while Lexie, Derek, Max, and the cousins ambled behind at a more sedate pace, as if on a bar crawl. She saw Jon trailing behind and she intentionally slowed down. Eventually, he took the hint and paired up with Erik.

Kea found herself catching up with the edge of their group and started hiking alongside Lexie. Usually, the woman was glued to Derek, but now he was further up the track, speaking to Max in hushed whispers.

"How are you holding up?" Kea asked the reporter.

"Fine, I guess." Lexie shifted the weight of her pack and tightened its straps. "Busy couple of days, to say the least."

"I'm sorry I haven't had time to do a proper interview yet, what with everything..." Kea hoped she sounded sincere, even though she had been actively avoiding the woman. She needed time to get her own thoughts together, although she wasn't sure if she was having any success. Sleep had been fitful at best.

"No problem," Lexie said kindly. "We'll catch up once things settle down."

Kea nodded, scanning the terrain. "I haven't been out here in several years. This whole area has changed dramatically."

"Are you sure it's safe?" Lexie asked. "You guys keep mentioning the volcanic activity in one breath, then dismissing it with another."

"We wouldn't take you out here if we thought it was dangerous," Kea said, realizing too late she was parroting Marcus. "The Grímsvötn caldera is always fairly active," she expounded. "If there's any unusual activity, we'll be notified by the Met office and evacuated."

"If I recall from my article, it takes several days for the water to accumulate and breach the ice dam," Lexie said. "Is that the only danger?"

"There's always a chance that Lake Grænalón or other bodies of ice trapped within the glacier could suddenly be released due to an increase in volcanic activity or precipitation. However," Kea gestured to the expanse of streams and lakes in front of them, "we'll be perfectly safe where we're going today."

"Perfectly safe," Lexie repeated. "By going to a site where a flood excavated large volumes of sediment?"

"If you get a whiff of sulfur, let us know." Kea wrinkled her nose. "Hydrogen sulfide is often associated with a jökulhlaup, as well as acidity in the water. It's a result of gases released in the caldera."

"That's very reassuring," Lexie replied sarcastically.

"Doubtful though," Kea added. "But it pays to be careful, we are in a dynamic environment. Expect the unexpected."

As if on cue, a thunderous crack echoed from across the plain.

Lexie cocked her head, looking askance.

"Morsárjökull, dropping ice blocks," Kea said firmly, hoping she conveyed intellectual confidence. "We're perfectly safe, I swear."

***

"Okay guys, here's the exciting bit," Marcus held a large staff, its length marked by short intervals of red and white. The team stood around him in a loose semicircle, a river at their backs. "Now that you all have measuring rods, we're going to break this area into separate ten-meter sections. Everyone gets their own section to sketch and describe in your notebook. We'll be going around photographing the sections and helping you collect samples."

He stood before an embankment some four meters high that had been carved out by the flood. A wall of cobbles, sand, and ash, its face was characterized by numerous thin layers broken by large sections of boulders and gravel. The volunteers sat on small boulders, pondering the gray skies that loomed above their heads as he lectured about lithology, flood deposits, and fluvial processes.

"The techniques that we're employing today fall into a specialization of geology called stratigraphy," Kea continued. "This is the study of layers of rock or sediment, called strata. Stratigraphy examines the processes and timelines that deposited the material, whether by water, wind, or volcanic events."

Julie handed out a series of waterproofed cards printed with graphics to determine grain size and sorting, then pointed to the cut-bank where shifting flood waters had exposed a variety of thin- and thick-bedded rock layers. "We'll be examining the strata for layers that might be related to large flooding events and match them up to historic jökulhlaups that have been documented in this area."

"This section here, for example," Marcus pointed to a thick layer of strata. "See how this block has been ripped out from its section and embedded into the fine-grained section above? This is what we call a rip-up clast."

"Don't worry if you don't get it right away," Tony added. "Just don't let the rocks outsmart you. Remember, it's not rocket science."

"No, but it does take patience," Marcus reminded him with a glare. Turning back to the group he continued. "Nadia, you get the first section, Kea will photograph it while the rest of us go downstream mapping out one section at a time. Once you're done, please come show us, then we'll move you to another section."

"And in the grand tradition of geology humor, may the quartz be with you!" Julie called, receiving a chorus of groans.

The volunteers dispersed with not a little grumbling. The measuring poles clattered as they were dragged unenthusiastically against the cobbled ground. Marcus led the way downstream, counting off ten-meter intervals, while Tony showed the volunteers how to take a sample.

Meeting Nadia at the first station, Kea noticed her sour expression.

"Just place the rod there," Kea gestured, taking out her digital camera.

Nadia stared at the grimy wall of irregular black rock as Kea took photographs. "It just looks like mud to me."

"True," Kea smiled. "I do sometimes have difficulty explaining why I picked 'mud settling' as my field, particularly when everyone else is studying more exciting things like exploding volcanoes."

Nadia looked Kea up and down. "Well, I guess it wasn't for the fashion."

Kea pursed her lips and glanced at her own weather-beaten water-proof trousers and tattered jacket that had survived years of fieldwork. "Since you're young, I'm going to let that slide." She stepped closer to the wall and traced out the slivers of rock with her finger. "If you take the time, you can see that every thin layer is like a page in a book. Each one was laid down by different processes. It's up to us to figure out which one. The size of the grains, the position of the rocks, and the thickness of the layers all indicate conditions in the past."

"I still don't really see it," Nadia said sadly. "I mean, I can see that there are different layers and that some have different sized grains in them but..."

"It takes some getting used to," Kea reassured her. "Half the time, I can't figure out how some of these features were formed. But that's what I love about this place, the variety of processes and finding things I don't understand."

Nadia considered that for a moment. "Always something new?"

"Exactly," Kea answered with a smile.

"I get that... but..." Nadia grinned.

"But what?" Kea struggled to hide her exasperation with the young woman.

Nadia shrugged. "It still bores the crap out of me."

***

At the next section, Kea found Tiko perched on a small boulder, her feet tucked beneath her, sketchpad in her lap. A lunch bag was propped up against her knee. She munched absently as she drew the rock face, taking bites of something that looked all the world like a cigar with a length of string sticking out of it.

A hundred questions raced through Kea's mind as she approached the young woman. *What did you see? Why did you wait so long to say anything? What really happened?* She felt her heart rate increase, anxiety threatening to overwhelm her. *Calm, remain calm.* Kea blew out a long breath. *Try a different approach, one that doesn't lead to throttling a volunteer.*

"'Allo," Kea said in greeting. She sat down on a rock across from her. "What's that?"

Tiko looked up, startled, her mouth full of food. An expression of relief washed across her face when she registered Kea's approach.

"I'm sorry," Kea said, holding up her hands in surrender. "Only me. Are you okay?"

Tiko nodded, smiling around a piece of cigar, or at least a stub of something long and tan colored. Now that she was closer, Kea could see that it was dusted with flour or fine sugar. Tiko pulled a similar object out of her bag and offered it to her, a peculiarly long piece of white string dangling out of both ends.

"Churchkhela," Tiko said, holding it out again.

Kea sensed this was meant as an explanation. She accepted the gift with a raised eyebrow.

"Dried grape pressed together. With walnuts," Tiko explained around a mouthful. "Churchkhela."

Kea examined it again and realized the knobby bits along its length must be the walnuts. Taking a bite, she found the texture tough but one that softened the more she chewed. "Very tasty." She took another bite. "How are you finding our cooking so far?"

"You... try." Tiko smiled politely. Whatever had been troubling the young woman, talking about food seemed to calm her. "Cooking for so many people... is difficult."

"Never a truer word..." Kea dreaded the daily ritual. Except for fajita night, of course. That was sacred.

Obviously worried that she had offended, Tiko added, "You must try some Georgian cheese. I will make khachapuri, cheese bread."

"I'm not sure where you'd find Georgian cheese out here." Kea stared at the deserted plain that surrounded them.

"Not find," Tiko laughed. "Cheese in suitcase. I bring here with me."

It took Kea a moment to process that statement. "You brought cheese... in your suitcase?"

"Of course," Tiko sounded confused. "Only a couple of blocks."

"Well, let's not share that with customs." Kea tapped the side of her nose. "If anyone asks, we'll plead the language barrier." She dug into her pocket and pulled out something she'd been saving since the trip to Reykjavík. She held it out to Tiko. "Fair-trade."

"Sorry?" Tiko stared at the object, confusion on her face.

"Peanut butter cup," Kea explained. "At least I think it's fair-trade. Chock-full of preservatives, color dyes, and other awful things, but they are also rather wonderful."

"Thank you." Tiko carefully stowed it away in a pocket as if Kea had just presented her with a precious stone.

"Now then," Kea scooted closer to have a better look at Tiko's pad. "How's the sketching going?"

Tiko turned her notebook so that Kea could see her drawings. The outcrop was beautifully rendered with deft lines and fine detail. Sometimes the skills of the volunteers astounded her.

"That's amazing." Kea tucked her own notebook deeper into her jacket pocket, out of sight. "You've captured it perfectly."

"Yes..." Tiko agreed. It wasn't a boast, just stating a fact. "But what does it mean?"

"Aha!" Kea picked up a trowel and escorted Tiko over to the section. "Now you're speaking my language."

Kea tapped a layer of the cliff with the trowel. "See these cobbles?" Trapped within the fine sediment were small, elongated rocks that leaned against each other like toppled dominoes. "Each pebble has a long axis, an intermediate, and a short axis. By measuring, and averaging, the direction of the axis, not only can we infer the direction of flow when it was deposited, but also the conditions."

Tiko smiled politely, waiting for Kea to continue. It was the same look Kea used to give her grandmother when, in the later stages of dementia, the older woman vehemently insisted the family dog was a German spy.

"Okay, let me see..." Kea knelt on the ground and picked up some loose stones and spread them randomly over the sandy soil. "When the rocks are laid down by a stream, over time the water will orientate the long axis of the rock parallel to flow." She held a compass over the rocks and showed how to measure the long axis of the stones relative to magnetic north. "When there's a flood, however, there is usually a short burst of activity." She swept her hand across the cobbles, rolling them. "During all that turbulence, the clasts become poorly sorted. As the rocks are rolled along, the long axis of cobbles will orientate perpendicular to flow direction, a bit like logs of timber. By doing so, we can use our understanding of imbrication to discover the conditions that created them. See?"

Tiko ran her fingers across various patterns on the rock face as if skimming Braille. "I speak Georgian, Russian, French, and some English." She turned back to Kea, a mischievous grin on her face. "This is the first time I have read Earth."

Kea snorted, despite herself. "Don't let Julie hear you say things like that."

"Why?" Tiko looked at her curiously.

Kea pursed her lips. "She's not the biggest fan of cheese."

Tiko was silent for a moment then smiled. "More khachapuri for you!"

Kea couldn't help but grin at that. Then, in a softer voice, she asked, "How are you doing?"

"Tired, I think. Yes, tired." Tiko stared blankly at her notebook, as if not registering what was on the pages.

Kea hesitated for a moment, then decided honesty was the best approach. "I heard that you saw something that day."

Tiko's gaze remained fixed on her notebook as Kea spoke, her shoulders seeming to hunch protectively around it.

"And it seems to me that if you really had seen such a thing, you would have mentioned it to us much earlier…." Kea reached out and placed a hand on the notepad. "Tiko, did someone force you to say that?"

Kea knew she was reaching, pushing too far. She waited.

Tiko remained silent, her body language hesitant, like a cornered animal.

"Okay." Kea eased back to give her some space. "If you ever need to talk, just stop by my tent, anytime."

Tiko nodded, a faint smile on her lips. "Talking is not always so good, I think," she said slowly. "But thank you."

Kea patted her on the shoulder before taking photographs of the section and heading off to the next volunteer. Kea felt deeply troubled. The young woman who had enthused about Georgian cheese bread only moments before was gone.

As she walked, Kea wondered if Tiko was merely hesitant to get involved or was afraid of something. *Or someone?*

***

Kea wasn't surprised to see Fernando at the next section. The dapper Puerto Rican had been following Tiko around the camp the last couple of days like a smitten schoolboy. He stood at the cliff face, meticulously scraping loose sediment into a plastic bag. Filled sample bags were lined up at his feet, neatly labeled in handwriting that would have made a calligrapher weep with envy. Even as he dug into the cliff face, his dapper clothes seemed to somehow repel the fine dust that erupted in a cloud with each scoop.

Kea looked down at her own dirt-smeared waterproof jacket and marveled at how someone could remain so clean out here. It seemed almost unnatural. "How's it going?"

"So far so good." Fernando sealed the bag. He took out a permanent marker and labeled it as instructed with the date, section number, and distance measured from the bottom of the section. "It was entertaining to see you guys so excited this morning."

"Yes, well, this doesn't happen very so often." Kea waved a hand at the section. "We have to take advantage of these opportunities when they come along." She paused. "Although I do apologize if our enthusiasm was... out of place."

Fernando seemed to take her meaning. "In some ways, I barely knew him."

Kea couldn't help but shake her head. "It seems like no one did."

Fernando sealed another sample bag. "I work remotely, so I never met him until the other day."

"It's hard to imagine," Kea replied distantly.

Fernando looked at her oddly.

"I just meant that my department is so small." Kea nodded downstream where Marcus and Tony were conferring. "It's hard to imagine working with people and never meeting them." *Then again*, Kea thought as she stared at Marcus, *sometimes the pros could outweigh cons.*

"Telework's pretty standard in tech," Fernando said. "No commute, you get to just do your coding. Plus, you don't have to deal with all the office crap."

Perhaps Fernando has his own version of Marcus, Kea thought. "So, what's it like now?" she ventured. "With all of you actually together all in one place?"

"Joyous," Fernando answered drily. "Bruce is dead, and the rest of them don't seem to give a damn. It's wonderful." Catching her wounded expression, he added, "Sorry, forgot you two were friends."

"It's fine." She understood that sort of anger. In fact, she felt better that at least one other person from T3 had verbalized it. "I take it you worked with him?"

Fernando nodded. "Same division. Didn't have to go the way he did."

Kea noted that his tone seemed to shift from frustration to one of regret. "You don't sound too surprised though."

"Yeah, well…" Fernando appeared to struggle to find the right words. "He'd had a rough time lately."

Kea waited, but he didn't offer anything else.

What is with these people? Doesn't anyone other than Bonnie gossip about the workplace?

"Rough time?" she persisted. "At home or work?"

"Both really," Fernando appeared reluctant to go into detail. "Startups can be brutal. They take all you have, your savings, your nights, your weekends… It's all a gamble, hoping to either make it rich fast or get bought out by a bigger company."

"Either of those options in T3's future?" Kea asked.

"We were close to getting bought out a couple of months ago, but it all fell apart at the last minute. Bruce took it hard, but it hit Max harder. It was his deal. He got pretty angry."

Kea pictured Max's giant form and booming voice in a full-on rage. The Hulk phrase, '*You won't like me when I'm angry,*' echoed in her head. "That can't have gone over well."

Fernando shrugged. "Most things don't go over well with Max." He paused. "Why are you asking?"

That's my cue to move on and shut up, Kea thought. "I'm just trying to figure out how things got so bad so fast. You think you know someone…"

Fernando shook his head. "You never really know people. Ask my ex-wife."

Afraid as to what depths that conversation might delve into, Kea made her way to the next station where Erik and Jon were working next to each other. Despite the dark skies threatening rain at any moment, they had both stripped down to tank tops. Erik's arms were filled from shoulder to cuff with tribal ink. Jon's tattoos were just as plentiful but more random and unrelated. A dragon circled one bicep while the muzzle of a pistol hugged the edge of a pectoral.

Stratigraphy, Kea reminded herself. *I'm here for stratigraphy.*

She coughed to announce her approach.

Erik gave an up-nod with his chin in greeting. "Boss."

Jon kept his eyes down, and muttered hello. He must have noticed that she'd been avoiding him all morning.

I feel like I've kicked a puppy.

"How goes the battle?" Kea slung her bag down on the gravel and unzipped a pocket, digging for a new memory chip for her camera.

Erik waved a trowel. "Jon here thinks he's found some of your rip-up clasts."

"Really?" Kea straightened and hefted her camera. "That's exciting!"

"He hoped you'd be pleased." Erik lightly punched his cousin on the shoulder.

"Did he now?" Kea could have sworn Jon's cheeks reddened, although it was difficult to tell beneath the tan. "Let's see what he's found."

Silently, Jon pointed to a thick rectangular block of dark sediment that seemed to float in a matrix of sand and gravel. It was a meter across and twice as thick.

"I think you're right," Kea said slowly. "As you can see, this block of substrate was excavated from the underlying layer and incorporated into the matrix of sediment above, emplaced during the event. Probably by a jökulhlaup."

She looked up from her camera to see Jon looking proudly at his find. "Definitely well done." She pulled out her notebook and a sample bag, while the two men stood back and watched her work. "By the way." She hacked a clump of dirt out of the cliff and poured it into the little plastic bag. "I just wanted to say thank you again for staying. How are you guys holding up?"

"Shame, him going like that," Jon said, scuffing the ground with his boot.

"Yeah, a real shame," Erik agreed, but Kea glanced at him sharply, sensing humor in his voice.

Erik had the decency to look embarrassed. "Sorry, never could stand the guy."

Kea fought down the anger gnawing at her stomach lining. She kept her eyes on the sample bag as she labeled it. "You worked with him?"

"Yeah, he was our manager, but not like he did any actual work. Not that I saw. Still," Erik's tone softened slightly, "no one deserves to go like that."

"No," Kea replied, picturing Bruce's cold, bloated body. She shook her head as if to dispel the vision. She fixed her attention on the section. It was paper worth and needed to be properly documented. "Tell you what, why don't I finish up these sections and you guys can take a stab at the next ones?"

"Sure thing, Boss." Erik picked up his backpack in one swift movement and slapped a hand on Jon's shoulder. "Come on man, let the lady do her science."

Kea watched them walk down the river edge before she returned to the section, although her mind was elsewhere. *Did anyone like Bruce?*

"Why would you stay at a company where everyone hated you?" she asked the cliff. The only answer was a slow *tap, tap, tap* on the pages of her notebook as a drizzle began to fall.

***

A spattering rain harassed them throughout the rest of the morning, making lunch a dreary affair. The team huddled close to the cut-bank for the meager shelter it provided, scarfing down sandwiches and cold coffee. Those in need of the bathroom trudged back along the trail onto the elevated sandur to find a damp boulder to squat behind.

Section by section, the team pressed on slowly, mapping the length of the exposure. Under dripping hoods, they sketched on the waterproof pages of the notebooks, their fingers cold and wet. To their credit, none of the volunteers complained. Some even remarked on not being able to remember the last time that they had ever stood in the rain. As they worked into the afternoon, however, the mood of the volunteers began to sour. Even Fernando's perfect face became streaked with mud and grime.

Marcus and Tony scouted ahead, reporting that the exposure continued around the river bend, where it flowed into a lake. While they had made the traverse without incident, they recommended returning with some gear to ensure safe passage for the team. They all packed up a few hours after that, agreeing not to press their goodwill with the volunteers, particularly after recent events, and began the slow trek back to the vehicles.

Kea lingered behind to make one last sweep for the occasional discarded food wrapper. Or so she told herself.

Plodding slowly through the soft wet sands that nestled beside the riverbank, she climbed slowly up the gentle rise onto the sandur. The rain fell harder now, obscuring the distant forms of the volunteers. As they made their way in and out of the depressions, to Kea, they looked all the world like a slow-moving game of whack-a-mole.

She was becoming increasingly worried that Bruce's death hadn't been an accident. He had seemed so happy that day... But if someone had whacked Bruce, she didn't have any proof. Or motive. Or...

She raised her face to the sky and felt the drumming of the raindrops against her cheeks and sent her thoughts heavenward. *I'm sorry Bruce, I'm trying, honest. I just have no clue what I'm doing. Can you throw me a bone? Please?*

***

After returning to camp, the clouds unleashed a downpour unlike anything they had seen this season. People only left the safety of their tents for urgent sprints to the bathrooms or to dash to the main tent for meals. The main tent itself was stifling, filled with steam from the cooking and damp volunteers. Conversations were reduced to mutterings, with words few and far between.

"Where do we stand?" Kea asked the leads who had assembled at the rear of the tent.

Marcus had taped the sketches drawn by the team into one long panel. "On the plus side, they've mapped out half a kilometer already. It'll be another day at least, plus the bit around the river bend. That will be a bit trickier to get to." He pointed to the farthest transect, where the river bit into the edge of the cliff. "Tony and I have a plan to gain access. As far as the quality of the sketches, however," he used a finger

135

to show some of the cartoon-ish sections that had been drawn by the less gifted of the volunteers. "They're variable at best."

Kea had seen most of the sections in the field but laying them all out together helped wrap her head around both the scale and the features they contained. She would use a software package to mosaic together the photographs tonight, which would hopefully make up for any of the shortcomings of their artists. "That means what, another two days of fieldwork?"

Marcus grunted noncommittally. "At the present pace. The weather doesn't look good though."

Julie nodded. "The forecast says we're probably going to get another couple of days of misery at least."

"Manageable?" Tony asked.

"Hopefully," Julie shrugged. "Nothing drastic coming. Lots more rain off and on."

"And the team?" Kea had headed straight to the showers after returning from the field, long overdue for a scrub down. She had missed dinner, and the few volunteers who loitered in the main tent hadn't been very chatty. "How are they?"

"They seem okay," Tony ventured. "But they're not going to be having group sing-alongs anytime soon."

"Any word from the Met office on Grímsvötn?" Kea asked Julie, referring to the magma chamber.

"Same," Julie said. "Active, but just ticking over."

"We still need to get the MRS, the flow meter, and any other gear off the ice," Kea reminded them. "Getting Gary off was top priority, but I thought we'd be able to get back on the ice the next morning… Anyway, we might as well wait until the rain's over, just to be safe. Let's see if we can knock out the rest of the section in the next day or two, then re-evaluate going back up to retrieve the kit." Hearing her own voice, she wasn't certain if she was stating a fact or waiting for their approval. "It looks as though most of the Icelandic campers have packed up and left, which likely means we're in for more than a bit of rain. If it continues, the volunteers could decide to pack up as well. We'll need to do something to jumpstart them…"

Chapter 9

Day Five

Kea slid into the froth of bubbles and let the throbbing jets massage her sore spine. The room was filled with two large hot tubs, and the entire team crammed into every available inch. There was a chorus of sighs as the water, fueled by the local incinerator, soothed their weary muscles.

Today's field day had progressed in a similar manner to the previous one. Alternating between drizzling and spitting, the rain never reached the point where they had to cease work. She was impressed that most volunteers still had not complained as they mapped the section. While it was clear they'd rather be somewhere else, the novelty of the expedition, and the sheer volume of work, helped the time pass quickly. To reward them for their perseverance, the leads drove the team to the hot tubs, a twenty-minute ride west, near a local farm.

Kea had been first to clamber into the tub. Jon had stepped in beside her, providing a full Daniel Craig view of his tight-fitting swimsuit as he stepped into the water. She stared up at the ceiling as the rest of the volunteers piled in, trying not to notice the sensation of Jon's thigh against her own.

"I still can't feel my toes," Reynard held his foot above the water and waggled his digits.

Kea noted that a fine, dendritic tracery of tattoos reached from his arms, across his front and back, and all the way to his ankle. It was as if a tree had enveloped his whole body.

"None of them?" Tony asked.

"Just big one," Reynard said, shaking his head. "Feels numb."

"Trench foot," Marcus diagnosed.

"Trench foot?" The German struggled with the translation. "What is that?"

"Comes from the trench warfare during the First World War," Marcus explained. "Too much time in the cold and wet."

"Keep it warm and dry, and you should be fine," Julie advised.

"I have to admit," Bonnie said. "I thought it would smell."

"My foot?" Reynard asked.

"The garbage, you idiot," Bonnie said, splashing him.

"They burn all the trash over there." Julie pointed at a building hidden from view by the wall. "It's not very green, and certainly not geothermal, but it does give us loads and loads of lovely warm water."

"Best dry?" Reynard asked, still frowning at his foot.

"Best dry," Marcus assured him.

Kea considered the young man's response. *Was his English really that bad? Was he clueless or just acting?*

Reynard grunted and reluctantly left the hot tub, padding over to the bench to retrieve his towel. The group shifted clockwise to fill Reynard's vacant spot and Kea found herself pressed hip to hip against Zoë. Kea shifted slightly, but as a result only pressed closer to Jon.

You've got to be kidding. She closed her eyes and tried to focus on the jet of bubbles instead of the two warm bodies on either side.

"Are you lot going anywhere after the field season?" Kea heard Derek ask.

"Ever been to the penis museum?" Cole had obviously done his homework on the most important of Iceland's tourist options.

"I want to see the Museum of Sorcery and Witchcraft," Gary ventured. "They've got a pair of necropants."

Leave it to Gary to make it weird.

"Necropants?" Bonnie asked.

"Pants made of human skin," Gary expounded with macabre delight.

"That can't be true," Bonnie tutted. Then, "Where is this museum?"

Kea had only seen pictures of the necropants. The ghostly, translucent texture of them had made her skin crawl. "Marcus," she said before the conversation could devolve further. "Speaking of magic pants, have you told them the story of the witch of Hekla?"

"Ah, you mean Katla, I think," Marcus corrected. "The volcano Hekla is thought to be the gates of hell. Katla, on the other hand, was a far more interesting legend."

Kea had intentionally given the wrong name, knowing that Marcus would go into full-on lecture mode. She just wanted to relax and enjoy the warmth of the water, yet all she could think about was the soft sensation of Zoë's thigh on one side and the tickle of Jon's furry, muscled leg on the other.

Kea felt as if her sensory organs were going to overload.

Focus on the story, she reminded herself. *Focus on the story*.

"Once there was a monastery that had a housekeeper named Katla," Marcus began. "She was a fiery-tempered woman, mean-spirited and many called her a witch. It was said that she had a pair of magic pants that gave her the power to run across the land as fast as the thunder."

As Kea listened to the familiar tale, her hands and feet floated in the water, guided by the turbulent bubbles. She felt the brush of Zoë's hand against her leg.

Was that an accident? She couldn't tell. On her other side, she felt Jon's hand slide against her own. *Definitely not an accident.*

Kea desperately wanted to open her eyes, but she didn't know where it was safe to look. Instead, she kept them pressed tightly shut and forced herself to slowly exhale as Marcus droned on.

"A shepherd boy lived near the monastery and heard the stories of this Katla," Marcus continued. "One day when Katla was gone, the boy found that he had lost his flock. In a panic, he put on the magic pants and raced around the land. It was with great relief that he found his lost sheep and guided them home before Katla returned. He put the pants back where he had found them and returned to minding his flock. When she came home, Katla discovered what the boy had done and was furious. In a fit of anger, she drowned the boy-"

"Drowned?" Nadia asked.

"What?" Marcus paused for a moment. "Yes, drowned."

"That's not very witchy," Nadia protested. "Why not just, you know, zap him?"

"Anyway," Marcus said, clearing his throat loudly, "Katla had to hide the body, so she dumped it in a pile of grain-"

"-not magical," Nadia muttered.

"The boy," Marcus pressed on, "was hidden in the pile of grain so no one knew what had happened to him. Everyone thought he'd run away. Over time, however, the villagers began to eat the grain, and Katla became worried that they'd soon uncover his body."

Kea could hear Nadia ask about why no one smelled the poor boy first, something Kea had always wondered. She would have voiced support for Nadia, except her hand kept accidentally touching Zoë's knee. It was driving her insane.

"Afraid for her life, Katla put on her pants and fled up to the glacier, Mýrdalsjökull. She threw herself into a canyon and a short time later, a massive flood of water burst forth from the glacier, flooding the entire coast. The locals named the mischievous volcano after her and any time jökulhlaups burst out of Mýrdalsjökull, they blame the witch."

"She just ran away and committed suicide?" Cole sounded outraged.

Kea wasn't certain if the teenager really had a problem with the story or was merely siding with Nadia to curry favor. Kea had noted the way he had been gawking at Nadia's bathing suit all evening.

"I didn't say she died, just that she threw herself into a canyon," Marcus corrected. "She could still be up there, right now, waiting to unleash havoc."

"Are we done yet?" Nadia asked, bored.

Kea shook herself as she realized the question was directed at her. "Sorry, what?" As the attention of the whole team was now focused on her, she quickly pulled away from Zoë and Jon.

"The mapping?" Nadia asked again. "Are we going back onto the ice tomorrow?"

Kea had noted that out of all of them, Nadia was the least interested in, and the most vocal about, 'drawing mud.' It was obvious that she was eager to get back up on the glacier, or better still, just go home.

Thankfully, Nadia's question attracted the attention of the entire group, including the sandwich of sexy that Kea had found herself in. She felt both Jon and Zoë lean forward to hear Marcus' reply.

"Not yet," Marcus said. "There is one last section around the river bend where the cliff meets the lake. Tricky, but Tony and I managed to fix up the path using some planks."

"And after that," Nadia pressed, "back on the ice?"

"Probably," Marcus said noncommittally.

"Great." Nadia clearly didn't believe him.

Kea saw Andrei shake his head in dismay at his daughter's behavior. Beside Kea, both Jon and Zoë had independently decided by accident or choice to press in closer. Feeling her heart rate skyrocket, and desperate for a distraction, Kea re-joined the conversation.

"We really do want to thank you for all your hard work," Kea said, addressing everyone in the tubs. "We'd never have been able to map this section without you. It really is a tremendous find." Kea thoughts returned to the day of Bruce's incident. She turned to Zoë. "You know, it's been so crazy, I haven't even had a chance to watch the rest of the drone footage yet." She realized that she was babbling. "Anyway, who's for ice cream? It's on me!"

She leaped up before the others could leave the tub and made a dash for her towel. Glancing back, she caught both Zoë and Jon exchanging a bemused look, as if they couldn't quite work out what had just happened.

Join the club, Kea thought, as she fished in her bag for cash. Right now, she needed an ice cream sandwich followed by a cold shower. *Or a shower of ice cream sandwiches...*

***

Safe behind the glass windows of the spa, she watched as the driving winds bent the slashing rains into a forty-five-degree slant. The gray skies stretched from one end of the horizon to the other, with no respite in sight.

This is the real Iceland, she thought. *Yet another sight that Bruce never got to see.*

Looking through the frosted door of the freezer at the selection of treats, she found she couldn't decide what she wanted. In its reflection, she could see Jon and Zoë walking into the gift shop, still damp from the showers.

What do I want? Kea pondered. *A mom with baggage or a younger man who could have anyone he wants? Or both?*

Looking back out the window at the sodden landscape, she realized she'd lost her appetite.

Fernando joined her at the window. "You okay?"

"Yeah," she replied automatically. She didn't want to sound maudlin but couldn't help but add, "I just wish Bruce had seen this."

Fernando considered the dreary clouds and endless rains. "I guess. He's been talking nonstop about this trip. At least, I suppose he got to see some of it."

Kea turned, stepping too close, so fast that Fernando nearly spilled his drink. "You guys only joined at the last minute... did Bruce pick this trip?"

Fernando took a small step back and shrugged. "No idea, I'm just an IT guy. You'll have to ask the big boss." He nodded at Max, who was watching them, his expression unreadable.

"Yeah," Kea said doubtfully, "I'm sure I will."

***

Everyone seemed to move slower following their soak in the hot tubs. Once they returned to camp, the rest of the evening passed at a leisurely pace. In the main tent, cards were dealt, and coffee brewed. Across the campground, flaps were thrown open to air out the funk and damp that had been lurking within their walls.

Kea was surprised to see the sun breaking through in sporadic cracks of gold and orange as it hovered above the horizon. She took her work outside, setting up shop in a folding chair beside her tent. A duffel bag full of papers rested at her feet as she poured over the MRS data. After a half-hour of struggling to extract anything useful out of it, she gave up.

"Aliens," Kea declared to her tent. "Must be aliens."

"First sign of madness." Julie's voice floated over her shoulder.

"Look for yourself." Kea thrust the laptop at her in disgust. "Sense, it makes none."

Julie knelt beside Kea and scrolled through the data.

Realizing that she sounded like a mad person, Kea pressed her face into her palms. "It's almost as if the fields aren't returning to their original state... or perhaps they weren't normal to begin with."

"Could be fragments of something in the ice maybe? Or the ash throwing it off. A meteorite in the ice? I'm sure that's what Reynard would say." Julie turned the screen back to Kea. "You're the expert."

"Not at this," Kea said, frustrated. "I don't know what I was expecting." She thought again of the moulin and its position relative to the MRS. "Did you ever get your computer up and running again?" Kea asked, her attention still focused on her data. Or, rather, lack thereof.

"Yeah, someone had just unplugged it overnight. The battery was completely dead. That someone turned out to be Bonnie, who used the outlet to charge her DVD player." Julie shook her head in disgust. "It took a couple of hours of charging just to be able to turn my computer back on. Must be on its last legs. Anyway, I came over because I was wondering if you might want to talk."

"Talk?" Kea sensed a trap.

"About the other night," Julie said pointedly.

"Ah," Kea said.

142

"You wear your emotions like a bad suit. I can see every stain and wrinkle," Julie said in a sultry voice.

"Eh?" Kea glared at her graduate student. "My laptop isn't the only thing not making sense."

Julie laughed. "Amirah made that comment about you this morning."

"Thanks?" Kea replied. "I think."

"She mentioned that you still seemed a bit off," Julie continued. "And I have to agree."

"Am I?" Kea asked the tent for confirmation, then realized what she had just done. "Yes, I suppose I am." She clutched the laptop to her chest, hugging it for comfort as if it were a teddy bear. "I still don't believe Bruce committed suicide, but I have no proof. No smoking gun, no motive, not so much as a sausage."

"But you do have a witness," Julie reminded her.

"Yes," Kea agreed, remembering her conversation with Tiko. "And that's odd as well. Tiko seems more out of sorts than the rest."

"Well," Julie said, "you would be too if you had seen it happen."

"But why wait so long before telling anyone?" Kea asked. "Even if she thought he was just clowning around?"

"Amirah said something else," Julie said, checking to make sure there was no one around to overhear. "Apparently Tiko didn't want to tell the police anything. She was too afraid to speak to them. Amirah had to convince her."

"When I brought up Bruce with her," Kea considered, "she really didn't want to talk about it."

"Maybe," Julie said with a shrug. "From what I've heard, police in many countries don't always… behave how we'd expect them to. When you see something, it's sometimes safer not to get involved."

"I suppose. Since Tiko's with T3 and Amirah's with Corvis," Kea reasoned out loud. "It's just weird to see them…"

"Working together?" Julie finished. "Why don't you try asking Tiko?"

"Me?" Kea asked, puzzled. "I tried already. Sort of. I didn't get anywhere. Why does it have to be me, anyway? Why not you?"

"We're about the same age," Julie reminded her. "You've got the whole motherly thing going on."

"Piss off," Kea snapped.

"Seriously, you should talk to her," Julie replied in a kinder tone. "You shouldn't be so afraid to talk to people about something other than science."

Kea nodded. "I'll talk to Tiko again in the morning."

"I didn't mean just Tiko," Julie said with a knowing glance at Zoë's tent.

"For goodness sake, am I that obvious?" Not waiting for a reply, Kea opened her laptop. "Leave me alone with my aliens."

"Don't turn your back on them," Julie said as she walked away. "You know what they say about aliens with probes…"

"I can assure you," Kea called after her, "that if I do find an alien, I'll blow it out of the nearest airlock, cause I'm not in the mood." She reviewed the MRS data again for a few more minutes before shunting it off screen. The thought of Tiko watching Bruce fall to his death still haunted her. Once again, the position of the teams on the ice, the terrain, and the distances that separated them, filled her head, creating a mental map. Everything seemed off somehow.

If only…

She dove into her tent to find Zoë's USB drive. Nestled within one of the folders was the terrain file automatically generated during every flight, derived from the aerial photographs that were mosaicked over the top.

As she loaded the file into a geospatial software package, Kea shook her head in amazement. Even five years ago, this amount of data would have seemed like a geologist's pipe dream. Within seconds, the sandur, the lakes, and the front edge of the glacier margin materialized on her screen, beautifully rendered in three dimensions.

It was merely a partial transect of the vast region, but the image was detailed enough for her to drop pinpoints on the approximate locations of the three teams from the first field day – her own team near the wildlands, Marcus and Tony's team at the sample site, and Zoë team at the drone's launch site.

Tiko had been on Zoë's team, so what could she have seen?

Kea entered in a two-meter eye height to approximate a person standing on the ice. Running the line-of-sight query, she waited impatiently as the software rendered the results.

When the process completed, the screen filled with red, mostly due to the '*No Data*' portions of the region. However, bubbles of green appeared around each team, demarcating what the people on the ice would be able to see.

Since her own team was located near a depression in the ice, visibility was mostly limited by the walls of the canyons. Marcus' team had a much wider swath of green. Kea frowned. Both Marcus and Tiko's teams did intersect, although the region was pockmarked by areas of red where crevasses and moulins curved down into the glacier.

Could Tiko have seen someone jumping around up there?

Kea double-clicked on the icon for Tiko's team, and the worldview lurched from the bird's eye view to the perspective of the drone team on the ice. She panned across the screen, shifting the view this way and that. While it was possible from Zoë's location to view the area where Marcus' team had been, it was awfully far away.

Could she really know for sure it was Bruce? What had he been wearing? They all had the same red EO jackets under the hi-vis vests, hadn't they?

Realizing she was none the wiser, she stowed away her papers and secured the computer in her tent, tossing the USB after it. She needed someone to talk to and could only think of one person. The one person she'd swore she'd never talk to again.

Chapter 10

KEA PULLED nervously at her bangs as she listened to the laptop dial the number. She had driven a jeep over to the visitor center and parked as close as she was able to use their Wi-Fi. As it was, the signal was only strong enough to carry her voice but not her image, for which she was grateful.

Don't pick up. Don't pick up. Don't pick up.

Click.

Damn.

"Hiya!" she said, trying to sound cheerful. She sat scrunched up in the passenger seat, her computer tucked against the dashboard. She stared at an avatar of her ex-boyfriend's face: fair hair, blue eyes, light brown scruff, and big jug-handle ears. Adorable.

Damn. Damn. Damn.

"Everything okay?" Jason asked.

"Yeah," Kea said automatically. "It's just been a long couple of days."

"I heard about the guy topping himself." He sounded concerned.

"Really?" Kea didn't think Bruce's death had made international news.

"Old friend from UC Burlingame sent me an email," Jason explained. "Mentioned... the drama. You okay?"

Kea tried to formulate a response that encompassed the roller-coaster of emotions she had experienced over the last few days. In the end, she was so tired that all she could manage was, "Yeah."

"We haven't talked..." Jason paused, "in a while."

Since you walked out on me.

"I can't really talk to anyone here about it," she explained. "I think I just wanted to talk to someone who was... not here."

"What happened?" Any awkwardness about receiving a call from her appeared to be overridden by his interest in Bruce's death.

"I'm not sure," Kea considered. "As far as we can tell, a depressed volunteer decided that Iceland was a great place to commit suicide. Jumped into a moulin – a great big hole, waterfall thing in the ice."

"Well... at least no one else was hurt," Jason said. "Did you know the guy?"

"Once, a long time ago, but I'm beginning to think I don't know anything about him at all. Not now." Kea remembered Bruce's first day on the ice, his face lighting up with wonder. "He was nice. I mean, he was okay I guess." If she were brutally honest, had he not just died, she would have added '*he was a bit boring really,*' which seemed too terrible to say now. "He didn't seem *that* depressed."

"You can never tell what's going on inside someone else's head," Jason offered.

Indeed.

A hundred different arguments from their break-up leaped to mind. She decided to let the remark pass. "It's just, I just can't shake the feeling that it might not... Well, a woman here said she saw him die..."

"She saw it happen?" Jason's voice noticeably perked up.

"She said that she saw someone jumping around on the ice at least," Kea amended. "They found the body in one of the lakes."

"I'm sorry. Sounds awful." Judging by his tone, Jason seemed saddened that she didn't have any further gruesome details.

"It's just these people, these volunteers," Kea floundered, trying to pin down her emotions. "Some were his co-workers, and they don't seem the least bit bothered by it all."

Jason made a *tut-tut-tut* sound with his tongue against the roof of his mouth, the noise that had driven Kea crazy when they lived together. "What's the name of the company?"

"T3. Thauma... something... an IT company." Kea wished she could remember. "Another company, Corvis Engineering, is out here with us as well. I don't think any of them knew him."

"Well, depending on the coworker," Jason said not unkindly, "I wouldn't exactly be gutted if one of mine died. Particularly if it was my boss."

There was a long pause as Kea tried to think of what to say next.

"You think someone offed him, don't you?" Jason said at last.

Kea shook her head, then remembered he couldn't see her. "No, not really. I mean, it's possible, but it would be very stupid. Too easy to be seen, for one thing, not to mention his ex-wife had the note he left her. I certainly believe he was suffering from depression about his marriage being over. I just, I dunno, I wish they felt upset about it or at least felt *something*. I'm glad they stayed to carry on the work, I really am, but it's almost as if nothing's happened."

"How's everyone else handling it?" Jason's voice stuttered, as if the connection were interrupted.

"Well, Tony's been acting pretty weird, even for Tony," Kea reflected. "He was up on the ice, as was Marcus when the guy... jumped."

"They just let him jump?" Jason asked, incredulous.

"No," Kea said, exasperated. "The ablation drill got mucked. They were busy repairing it and the guy just wandered off. You know how boring it can be out here sometimes. They thought he just went off to relieve himself. They spent an hour trying to repair the drill when..." she broke off, remembering how much of a crisis Gary's incident seemed at the time. It felt so long ago now. "Things got confusing, very fast."

"Did you talk to the woman who saw the guy jump?" Jason pressed.

"I'm a geologist," Kea protested, "not Perry Mason."

"Miss Marble then," Jason offered.

"Marple," Kea corrected him.

"Not as punny," Jason said, no doubt wearing an evil grin.

They both laughed, a bit too hard for what the joke merited, then lapsed into a long silence.

Sitting in the jeep alone, thousands of miles apart, she felt a pang of regret.

"If you want my advice," Jason said eventually, "follow the money."

"You're an accountant," Kea replied. "That's all you ever say."

"True," he acknowledged. "I'm not a forensic one, although I do know a couple. If you'd like, I can ask them to do some research on the companies. But if memory serves, you never wanted my advice," he paused. "So, why are you really calling?"

Ouch. Kea sighed. When they were just talking about Bruce, she had been surprised how easily it was for her to slip back into conversation with Jason. Now, confronted by his question, her throat seemed to swell shut as she groped for words.

"I... I just wanted to," Kea found she didn't really know why she'd called. *That he'd sound happy to hear from her? That he wanted to get back together when she returned home?* "Just wanted a voice of sanity. I feel like I'm losing mind."

"Gotcha," Jason said in a tone that conveyed his disinterest all too well. "You mind if I get back to dinner now? It's only six here. I've got a date with Laura tonight."

Kea must have suffered a minor stroke because she found herself apologizing automatically. *Laura? The blond anthropology graduate student with the Heidi-pony tails?*

Completely numb, all she could find to say was, "Thanks for listening."

"No worries. Kea..." Jason hesitated.

"I know," she said wearily. "Be careful out there. I think it's too late for that."

Too late for Bruce anyway. Judging by Jason's tone, too late for them as well. As politely as she could, she said goodnight and signed off.

Desperate to turn her mind to something other than thoughts of Laura, Kea surfed the web looking for information on T3. '*Connecting the Internet of Things to the Real World of Things,*' was all she gleaned from the '*About*' page. The company appeared to specialize in anything and everything, from hand-held devices to enabling refrigerators and dishwashers to talk to each other, to helping heat a house more efficiently.

In fact, from what little she could discover, the company seemed to provide services for any industry, including the military. However, despite the wealth of information, she couldn't figure out what they produced. The website was calorie-free when it came to content. Searching for Corvis Engineering returned even less information.

It was as if the companies didn't want anyone to find them.

She sent the website addresses to Jason via email, along with all the names she had for the teams, including a mention of Andrea, last name unknown, hoping his forensic accountant friend might be able to dig up something more interesting.

Kea tucked the tablet away and started the jeep. It was midnight and the evening light possessed a dusky quality that she didn't want to spoil, so she kept her headlights off as she drove through the campground. Parking as quietly as possible, she returned to her tent and picked up her kit bag.

The campground bathrooms were mercifully empty of people. As she brushed her teeth, she began to wonder again what really had transpired up on the ice. Marcus and Tony were working on the drill, or so they said. Bruce was there, of course. Plus, Derek, Reynard, and Jon. Reynard was the only Corvis member up there with all those T3 guys, and she couldn't really picture someone as friendly as Reynard playing any part in Bruce's death.

Or was that wishful thinking?

Assuming not, that left Derek and Jon. Both were capable in size and mass to take on Bruce if they had too. She really hoped it wasn't Jon. She still wasn't sure how she felt about him, but those big puppy eyes kept drawing her in. As well as those shoulders...

Kea contemplated her reflection in the mirror. Both Zoë and Jon were beginning to take up too much space in her head these last few days. While Jon was a volunteer and therefore off limits, Zoë was just assisting the project, not technically a volunteer. The trouble was, Kea had no idea what was going on in Zoë's head.

What, she asked herself silently, *is it that you want?*

Jason. Still the same old answer. She still wanted Jason, and he clearly wanted nothing to do with her. Zoë and Jon offered the potential opportunity to break the cycle, as both were fair game after next week, but that wouldn't be fair to either of them.

She gave herself a disapproving frown before heading back to her tent. Walking through the grass, she noticed the light of Zoë's laptop in the dome of her tent, glowing like a tempting beacon.

Tomorrow, she thought. *I keep saying that, but when will that tomorrow ever come?*

She was so intent on her thoughts that she nearly collided head-on with Bonnie. The woman tried to step out of her way, but the contents of her large cardboard box spilled out onto the grass.

After a very undignified yelp, Kea apologized. "Sorry, I was miles away. Let me give you a hand."

"No worries." Bonnie bent to pick up the cardboard box. "I seem to always be dropping things around you!"

Kea stared at the gray, banana-sized objects in her hands. "Um, I don't mean to pry, but may I ask why you're carrying a box full of plastic sharks?"

"Oh, these?" Bonnie waved one in the air. The toy's jaws contained a ferocious set of rubbery teeth that jiggled threateningly. "Just got them in the mail today at the visitor center."

"You had the sharks shipped here?" Kea asked, dazed by Bonnie's priorities. "On a camping trip?"

"Of course, dear," Bonnie shook her head. "Couldn't fit them in my luggage. Can't have a horror-palooza without them! Where would the fun be?"

"Horror-palooza?" Kea asked, wondering where Bonnie was headed with this.

"Horror film fest. Showing movies in my tent all week. Tonight's Shark Night." Bonnie beamed. "You're welcome to join if you like. Max, Derek, and Erik are coming. Jon as well," she added with a tacky wink.

"Thanks, but I'll have to pass." Kea handed her the last of the fallen toys. "But I admire your energy, I mean, after, well you know."

"What do you mean? Oh," Bonnie hefted the box. "Look, I had these pre-ordered and scheduled to arrive before I left. It takes ages to get stuff shipped out here. I mean, I'm not like heartless or anything like that."

"Never mind," Kea apologized. "I didn't mean to imply anything. I know not everyone knew Bruce very well."

"Phwah!" Bonnie scoffed. "Know him, of course I knew him. Wish I hadn't. Couldn't stand the man. Pain in my ass, he was."

"Really?" Kea paused, a shark in hand.

"I'm in HR," Bonnie said as if it was the most obvious thing in the world. "I got all the Bruce-time because he kept filing complaints."

"Against who?"

"Everyone," Bonnie said. "Even me at one point. He was always complaining, grousing about everyone's projects, about the budget. Was all right for a while, but after his last project was a failure, he seemed intent on taking everyone down with him."

Although Bonnie echoed what the others had said, Kea fished for more details. "What kind of project? Government?"

"Hah!" Bonnie snorted. "There's no money in government these days. Their tech is years out of date. All the innovative stuff is in the commercial sector these days. I don't know what he was working on, not my area. I'm not usually pulled onto projects unless there's trouble.

People only come to me when they get hired, when they want to complain, or when they quit. But," she gave the box of sharks a jiggle, "I'm also in charge of recruiting and team building, and there's always time for a bit of fun! You sure you're not up for it?"

"Thanks," Kea tried to smile politely. "But I think I'm good."

"Fair enough." Bonnie strode back to her tent. "Will try to keep the screams from getting too loud!"

Kea shook her head, uncertain which was more confusing, Bruce's death or a shark-obsessed cougar. She heard a roar of male laughter as Bonnie entered her tent.

Kea slipped into her own tent and crawled into the warmth of her sleeping bag as the sounds of the movie began. It was beginning to look like sleep wasn't going to be an option tonight. Thoughts of Bruce filled her head:

Ruined projects.

Ruined marriage.

Angry co-workers.

Missing co-worker.

Motives, she thought, *there are a lot. Opportunity, there certainly was.*

Means... It's not like I'm looking for a revolver in a study, she considered, *the whole place could be a death trap.*

She thought back to the missing vest. *My only clue is missing and considering the vastness of the glacier, it's one I might never find.*

Propped up on her pillow, the friendly face of the stuffed little platypus grinned at her. She held it above her head.

"Tell me Pus, what was Bruce thinking? Was he really depressed, or was he killed?" The toy said nothing. "And why did he bring you? Was he really just too shy to give you to me, or are you a clue?" She tugged at its neck, digging her fingers into the stuffing, slowly at first, then tearing faster and faster, until there was nothing left but white fluff covering her face and pillow and inside-

Inside there was nothing. No message, no memory stick, no microdot, nothing.

"Sorry Bruce," she muttered sadly to the disemboweled platypus. "I have absolutely no idea what I'm supposed to be doing."

Chapter 11

Day Six

AFTER A rushed breakfast, the team descended on the last stretch of the exposure. The weather remained uncooperative, however, and rain fell every half hour like clockwork, puddling water around their feet and leaching away any remaining morale onto the sandur.

Kea made a point of moving between the different groups, trying to lighten the mood, and assisted with sampling wherever she could. The team was self-sustaining at this point, so it was just a numbers game until they finished. *'Never,'* each volunteer said, *'had two kilometers seemed like such a vast distance.'*

Around mid-morning, she encountered Tiko on a boulder, busily sketching. The young woman smiled quickly in acknowledgment, but kept her gaze firmly focused on the cliff face.

Kea listened to the sound of the pencil as Tiko scratched it against the rough, water-resistant paper of the field journal, letting the silence linger while she tried to decide what to say. She had been up all night trying to work out different theories, different scenarios – even one where Bruce and Bonnie had a torrid affair. However, wherever her mind went, her thoughts always returned to the same question. "Tiko, what exactly did you see that day?"

A hush fell as Tiko paused. Kea could hear the *ticker-tap* of grit blowing against the cliff. Behind them, the river gurgled and chuckled as the wind rucked its surface up into lapping waves.

"I've been trying different view shed models, using three-dimensional line of sight software to recreate the locations of the teams and what they could see," Kea continued. "Looking at the model, it is possible that you saw something, but the distance... is puzzling." Plucking a couple of peanut butter cups out of her pocket, she slowly unwrapped one. "I'm not saying it's impossible, mind, but I really just wanted to ask, what was it you think you saw? If anything at all?" She popped a candy into her mouth and watched Tiko closely for any reaction.

After a moment, Tiko continued sketching, as if by ignoring Kea, she could pretend that the conversation never took place.

"It occurred to me," Kea continued softly, "that it's also possible that someone made you say you saw something that day. That someone is threatening you somehow."

Tiko stopped sketching and turned to stare back at her, an unreadable emotion trapped within her soft brown eyes. If pressed, Kea would have to describe it as pleading.

"I'm not going to say anything," Kea said calmly, aware that Tiko's eyes now darted up and down the river as if searching to see if anyone could overhear their conversation. Sensing that Tiko was still unwilling to speak, Kea tried one more time. "Tiko, he was my friend. I just want to understand what happened."

Imperceptibly, Tiko shook her head, her loose curls trembling ever so slightly.

Fear, Kea thought. *She's terrified*. She placed a peanut butter cup carefully on Tiko's pad. "Well, sometimes a picture can say more than any words." She stood up slowly. "And yours are always lovely."

Kea left Tiko staring quietly at the dark cliff face as the rain spattered around them. Glancing back, she noticed that Tiko had turned her notebook to a fresh page and started to sketch again.

***

Max was sitting on his pack as if it were a throne.

Kea noted that his notebook lay in a plastic bag at his side, while the rest of the bags remained pristine and sample-free. "How goes the stratigraphy?"

"I never thought I'd miss running proposal teams," Max replied, a sandwich clutched in his hands. "But it's a much drier job."

Although the leads had noticed a decline in the quality of the sketches and documentation among the volunteers as the weather had deteriorated over time, Max had never appeared to put too much effort into any of the tasks in the first place. It wasn't that he was phoning it in exactly, but his demeanor seemed to simply suggest that he had people to do this sort of thing. It was as if he was waiting for his staff to show up and take over so he could get on to something more meaningful, like presiding over a board meeting or cutting a ribbon for a new supermarket.

"The weather should be clearing soon, if only for a little bit," Kea said, recalling the morning's weather forecast. Despite that, looking at the dark clouds overhead, she wasn't certain they had nailed it this time.

She pulled out her own notebook and began a quick sketch of the section. "Did you request this trip?"

"Nah," Max shrugged. "But felt I should lead by example, especially for a non-profit like you guys, so I came when asked."

"Aren't you in charge?" Kea asked, her attention distracted by the contents of Max's section. Despite his questionable company, it contained several interesting conduits where the floodwaters had forced material up through the overlying strata. She pulled out a bag and started taking samples.

"COO," Max said proudly, pulling out another sandwich. "Chief of Operations."

"Very swank." Kea pretended to sound impressed, or at least interested.

"Twenty-five years' experience," Max yawned. "I know how to get things done, whatever it takes."

"That sounds a bit gangster." Kea leaned the measuring pole against the cliff for scale and took some photographs to examine later. She noted the locations of the samples in her notebook. "So why Iceland?"

"Movies," Max replied firmly.

"Not the first time I've heard that..." Digging out a permanent marker, she labeled the sample with the date and location number. "Most people want to drive a car across the ice lagoon after that Bond movie, but we mostly get fantasy buffs these days."

"Not my thing," Max shrugged. "Not sure who selected this expedition for the company."

"Mmmmm...." Kea said around the marker. Science aside, she realized that she wasn't getting anywhere with this line of questioning. As she tucked away her notebook in her pocket, it suddenly occurred to her to check to see if Jason had dug up anything on Max or his company. "I think it's time to break for lunch, if you have anything left to eat..."

Using her radio, she called for the others to break for lunch. While they all sat down to eat their damp lunches at their sections, Kea trotted back across the plank board bridge Marcus had built. She moved along the cliff to a point where she could climb up a small rise and get cell reception. Only half a bar, she noted, but it the signal was strong enough to download an email from Jason:

'Haven't heard back from my friend yet on T3. Did some digging; looks like they're a front company for a small development firm based out of Seattle, founded by Alex Huxem, although he passed away a few years ago. T3 is mostly contracted out by the big tech corps for special projects. Not much else out there on the web, not publicly traded, no press. Hope it helps, careful out there. –J

P.S. There is an Andrea Lane listed as a former board member, although she had filed articles of incorporation for a new company about two months back. Looks like she was going to try her hand at a startup, some tech firm called based out of Europe, QuantSol Inc, but can't find anything on it…'

Kea put away her phone. *Huxem, eh? Maybe Max wasn't really in charge.* She looked back down into the valley. She knew a Huxem. Two, in fact.

***

"Hello, boys," Kea called as she rounded the river bend.

"Doc," Erik and Jon returned Kea's greeting in unison. The cousins were sitting on a couple of rocks at the base of the cliff, the river not a meter from their feet. Just to get near them meant she had to do a bit of boulder hopping along the river's edge. When she reached their site, the ledge was so narrow that she found herself almost pressed against them, suddenly reminded of just how big these two men really were.

"How goes the dig?" She sat down on a small boulder in what she hoped was a disarming pose. After a moment of unsuccessfully trying to shift into a comfortable position, she opted for her normal, if somewhat, slouched posture. She put down her clipboard to prop her bag up between her feet and rummaged for her camera.

"Not bad," Erik said, trying to shelter his food from the sporadic raindrops. "Not awesome, but not bad."

"The weather here is variable, I'll admit," Kea smiled. "Least so far. I've spent a lot of time in the Pacific Northwest, and it's like this all the time there." Kea handed Jon a ruler and snapped a few pictures of the section with the guys in the shot for scale. "Where are you guys from?"

Jon looked at her oddly.

Kea realized then that while she had been lecturing at them for days, she rarely made any attempt to be social with them in the field. Well, Erik at least.

"We're both out of Denver," Erik admitted, "but the company's HQ is in Seattle. Been there a couple of times, but it's not much like this place."

"How long have you lived in Denver?" Kea asked, doing her best to ignore Jon's lingering stare.

"About ten years." Erik squatted down by his bag and pulled out a length of jerky.

"How long have you been with the company?" Kea stowed her camera to protect it from the rain.

"T3?" Erik considered. "Just the last few years."

Rain continued to pepper the sand and cobbles around them. Intent on their food, the men didn't seem eager to expound.

Kea found it difficult to think of any questions other than the one she really wanted to ask, *'By any chance, did you have any reason to try to kill Bruce and make it look like a suicide while you were on holiday?'* There didn't seem to be a subtle way to work it into the conversation. Besides, it wasn't as if Erik had an opportunity that day, so it couldn't have been him. *Please don't let it be Jon...*

Almost afraid of the answer, she asked, "Why did you guys pick Iceland anyway?"

The two men exchanged glances before staring at her, their mouths frozen in mid-chew.

"I mean," Kea said quickly, tripping over her words, "we almost had to cancel this field team, then about three or four weeks ago, you guys pop up unexpectedly and save the day."

Erik smirked. "We don't choose these things. The company made the call. Granddad used to insist that we do something for charity every year. I think Max just wanted us to keep up the tradition in honor of Grandad, but it's probably...."

"Tax write-off," Jon finished.

"Usually, we do something more like helping out at a charity event. I didn't know EO existed." Erik glanced up at the gloomy sky again. "Mind you, I'd rather have done the dolphin monitoring project in Florida."

But Max had just said he didn't choose this expedition. Unless he was lying, of course. "Who picked this trip? I assumed that you…" Kea found herself backtracking in case she was too direct, "like you said, you could have picked a project that had much better weather."

Jon and Erik both shrugged.

"Dunno," Erik said. "Have to ask Bonnie that."

"She might have arranged it, but I don't think she chose Iceland," Jon corrected him.

It was the most she had heard him speak in days. Since the pub, or at least since she started actively avoiding him at any rate. She had been meaning to take Jon aside and explain her hands-off rule for volunteers on expeditions, but instead she kept delaying the awkward conversation.

"Yeah, that'd have to come from much higher up," Erik agreed.

"Higher up?" Kea asked, confused. She had assumed these two might have owned a portion of the company based on what Jason had said, or maybe their parents. Still, maybe they answered to someone else.

"Maybe Bruce?" Erik offered. "Would make sense, if he wanted to off himself here."

Kea ignored the last remark. "Bruce was higher up than you guys?"

"On the last project." Erik added, "Although Max took over, near the end."

Back to Max again. She wanted to ask about Andrea but didn't want to play her hand, so she offered a hunch instead. "Did Bruce ever mention to either of you two about starting his own company?"

"No," Erik said defensively. Shifting his weight, he flexed in a way that she found intimidating. "Why are you asking?"

"We just like to learn more about how to appeal to other companies," Kea fumbled. "To help us figure out how to recruit more teams next year…" She hadn't thought this through. She'd never needed an exit strategy before. She tried one more time, more tactfully. "Again, I just wanted to say how sorry I am. We just… we never… these teams are intended for the opposite of… what Bruce used it for."

"We get it," Erik said. "Nothing to do with you guys. What he was stupid. And selfish."

"Any idea why he did it?" Kea asked.

158

Erik shook his head. "He was an odd one, never understood what he was up to half the time."

"Did he say anything before it happened?" Kea asked Jon. "I mean, you were there."

He shook his head slowly again and folded his thick arms across his chest. The flirtatious man she had shared a drink with at the bar had vanished. "Nothing."

The spatter-pat-patter of rain slapped against the surface of the river, the only sound in the thick silence that followed. It was obvious that the conversation was at an end.

"Right." Kea levered herself off the rock. "Well, I better keep checking everyone's work."

"Don't you want to see ours?" Jon held up his field notebook.

"Yes," Kea said quickly. "Yes, of course." She flipped through the little book and made a cursory examination of his sketch. She handed it back with a forced smile. "Well done, you. See you on the way back."

She picked her way along the river's edge until she joined Julie, who was having a snack at the base of the cliff. It was only as Kea put down her pack that she felt the adrenaline drain out of her, shaking her limbs and lifting her stomach into her mouth.

"You okay?" Julie asked, her mouth full of granola. "You look all pink and balloon-y."

"Yeah," Kea said. "Learning to sleuth is harder than it looks." She brushed Julie's questioning look aside. "Never mind." She shook her head and squatted beside her. "I better keep my day job," she sighed. "Any chance you have an extra candy bar?"

Julie tossed her a miniature bar of chocolate. "You're up to some-thing."

"I'd like to be," Kea said as she struggled with the wrapper. She tugged on it with her teeth. "I don't really know what questions to ask. Tiko's upset about something, but in fairness, she always seems to be. It crossed my mind that someone like Max might have forced her to make up a story about seeing Bruce fall, just to keep the company out of the papers. Aside from that... Yes!" She gave a little cheer as she managed to rip open the wrapper. "As far as I can tell, they all worked with Bruce, but none of them seemed to like him. In fact, anyone on Marcus' team that day could have knocked him off. My bet is on Jon though, as he's probably the only one strong enough to knock over poor Bruce."

Julie, Kea noticed, was looking at her with wide eyes, her mouth frozen in mid-chew.

With a sense of dread, Kea turned around to see Jon standing behind her. He held out her clipboard silently. His expression was cold, his eyes unblinking.

Not knowing what else to do, Kea took the clipboard out of his hand. She heard her voice thanking him politely as if someone else was using her vocal cords. Then she turned and sat down, closing her eyes as she listened to him walk away.

"That," Julie ventured, "was more than slightly awkward."

"Well done me..." Kea choked down the last glob of chocolate and chased it with a drink of water. "Ya know, I think he really must have fancied me after all," she considered. "I really only screw up big time when people actually give a damn. Glad to know I haven't lost my touch."

"You really think he might have killed him?" Julie asked.

"I don't know." Kea took another long drink. "I lack both motive and method. As well as zero evidence. And you know what that means."

"Someone's getting away with murder?" Julie sounded almost hopeful.

Kea shook her head. "It means Bruce really did kill himself."

Chapter 12

LATER, SITTING at the edge of the river, Kea watched the last group of volunteers scramble for the shelter of an outcrop. She remained in the open, listening to the rain pepper her hood. She felt hollow inside. If anything suspicious had happened to Bruce that day, she hadn't discovered what it was. Propping her chin on her knee, she wondered what she was doing.

Something odd was definitely going on between the company teams, but she still had no idea what. Kea ran through the list of the people on Marcus' team on that fateful day: Tony, Bruce, Derek, Jon, and Reynard. None of the other teams on the ice had been within a kilometer of Bruce. Not that she seriously believed any of them was a killer, although she wouldn't put anything past Derek. Her conversation with Jon and Erik had been unsettling, but they might have just been put off by her clumsy attempts at sleuthing. Tony was a bit of a prick, to be sure, but he had never even met Bruce until this week, nor had Marcus.

What's harder to accept, she wondered, *that Bruce killed himself or that I think I could have somehow stopped him?*

God Complex, she remembered from Psych 101. *Or worse, am I so fixated on trying to solve a nonexistent crime to avoid thinking about the ruin that is my love life? Healer, heal thyself.*

She waited until the rain abated before approaching Derek, Lexie, and Tiko, who were busy sketching out the last of the sections. They were the last team, which meant everyone could wrap up soon. Realizing she didn't have much time left to ask questions, Kea made a beeline to Derek's station.

"Hiya." Derek grinned as Kea peered over his shoulder at his field notebook. "Like what you see?"

Kea frowned. "I didn't realize the strata had that many... curves."

Derek laughed and examined his work. "Not bad though, eh?"

"I wouldn't know," Kea admitted. "I've only ever seen Lexie with her clothes on."

"Shame," Derek tutted. "You're missing out." If he cared whether Lexie heard, he gave no sign. He flipped the page back to his section sketch. "Was this more what you were looking for?"

She pulled a face as she looked at his work. He was, it had to be said, a decent artist. More importantly, all the sections had been sampled, marked, and were bagged at the foot of the cliff. "Looks like you're done for the day."

"Yeah, figured." Derek made an odd sucking noise and spit a wad of chewing tobacco onto the cobbles. He looked across to the next section where Lexie was working. "Thought I'd find a way to kill some time."

"We'll be finishing soon." Kea checked her watch. "Hopefully before the sky opens up again."

"Is that it for the season? Or are you going back up on the ice?" Derek sounded genuinely concerned.

Kea pointed up at the sky. "Everything depends on the weather. We need to collect our gear, so we have to go back up. The rest of you are free today to leave of course, but we're thrilled so many of you decided to stay."

Derek grunted. "Most of us had plans to hang out in the city after the fieldwork and see a bit more of the country. But even that costs a fortune. Not to mention it's the height of the tourist season. Everything's booked solid for the next few days. You're doing us a favor by letting us stay on."

Looking at him squatting at the base of a filthy cliff being drenched by constant downpours, Kea found it hard to conceive the man was in any way grateful, but she let it pass. "Well, after everything that happened, we do appreciate it."

"Dumbass..."

Kea assumed Derek was referring to Bruce. "Did you two not get along?"

"Not get along?" Derek was visibly angry. Kea had only seen the lewd version of Derek, so the change was startling. "His stupidity destroyed two of my Lancet prototypes."

"Lancet?" Kea asked.

Derek eyed her curiously, then changed the topic. "Managers always want to save a few bucks to make themselves look good. Never understand the real cost."

"You're an engineer?" Kea asked, forgetting to cover the surprise in her voice. To be honest, he seemed so constantly lewd and randy, she discounted the possibility of his brain being able to capable of anything else.

Derek tapped his crooked nose with a finger. "More than just a pretty face, love. Engineer and project lead. Three years' worth of work down the tubes, thanks to Bruce. The fat fanny."

Means, motive, and opportunity. Kea checked off the boxes in her head. He was not the best person to be standing next to out in the virtual middle of nowhere. She looked up the length of the exposure and noted that Lexie and Tiko were starting to pack up their gear.

"Right, well," Kea took a couple of paces back and pulled out her camera. "Why don't you head back. I'll wrap up here."

Derek cocked his head. "If I wanted to kill the bastard, I'd have done it looking him in the eye, not kicking him in the back."

Judging from the harshness in Derek's tone, she got the impression that he was speaking from personal experience. She looked away quickly and began taking pictures of the section.

Kicking Bruce in the back? She thought. *How did he know he was kicked?*

After the moment that it took to regain the use of her vocal cords, she croaked out, "Noted." Time to leave. She tossed a quick, "See you back at the jeeps," over her shoulder as she walked further downstream. Out of the corner of her eye, she saw him heft his pack and begin the slow walk back.

There were another twenty or thirty meters of section left, but from their brief reconnoiter earlier that morning they had determined that the exposed sediment appeared to be unremarkable. The rain had discolored the section, making it easier to see the different strata, giving her a good excuse to take a few more pictures. Mostly, however, she was giving herself more time to put some distance between her and Derek and, although she was loath to admit it, to let herself calm down. Her hands weren't just trembling from the cold.

***

After another five minutes, the sky began dumping heavy sheets of rain, forcing Kea to slide her camera into a protective baggie and pull out her walkie-talkie. "Ready to head out? Over." Tony, Marcus, and Julie replied in the affirmative. "I'm bringing up the rear," she continued. "All volunteers have headed back to the jeep. Meet you there.

Over." She tucked the radio into her jacket and performed a final sweep for sample bags, trowels, or anything else left behind.

Trudging along the edge of the embankment, she felt the apprehension she'd experienced with her encounter with Derek subside as the wind and rain forced her to focus simply on walking. She watched as water filled the swarm of boot prints left in the mud by the volunteers. Soon they would be washed away by the swollen river, and with them the stratigraphic sections.

Sadness touched her heart for a moment as she realized that she'd never see this stretch of land again. It had been one hell of a find, particularly if they could correlate it to other historical accounts of flooding in the area. She only hoped they had collected enough data. It was only then that she realized how quickly she had slipped back into work mode, and how she had once again easily pushed any thoughts of Bruce aside.

"What the hell is wrong with me?" she asked the sky, feeling the gentle tap of raindrops splash her face.

"For a start, your breath could strip the paint off a car," chirped a voice from above.

Blinking furiously, Kea spied a purple hooded head poking up above the embankment. It was Nadia, peering down at her, scraggly strands of hair dangling down from the darkness of her hoodie.

"What are you doing up there?" Kea demanded.

"You're taking ages." Nadia threw a leg over the edge of the cliff and started sliding down the embankment. "They sent me back to check on you."

"No, don't- the section!" Kea protested too late. The teenager scrambled down the last few feet, arriving beside her in a cloud of rocks and sediment.

Kea shielded her eyes from the churning dirt, cursing silently. Cupping a palm between her nose and mouth, she sniffed her own breath.

It wasn't that bad, was it?

She frowned at Nadia. "There's a reason we made this path, young lady."

"Young lady?" Nadia sneered. "Are you a nun or something?"

Kea shook her head. It was too damp, and she was too tired to waste energy reprimanding Nadia. At least, she told herself as she surveyed the damage, they had documented the section already. She reached out a hand to steady her. "Don't make me sound like my mother. It's not a pleasant experience, for either of us."

"Can we head back now?" Nadia pleaded.

"You better walk three paces ahead of me," Kea cautioned, "otherwise, I might chuck you in the river."

"Moody," Nadia pouted. "You and everyone else."

"Better days," Kea said as they continued walking along the path, "I have had."

"Everyone started moaning on the way back about having to come back out tomorrow," Nadia said, appearing quite happy to rat out the others. "I thought we were done?"

"Who said we'd be back?" Kea asked.

"Marcus," Nadia replied.

"News to me," Kea replied, attempting to hide her irritation. The section was done, and she had informed him as much at lunchtime. "Some people never listen."

"People can be so annoying," Nadia agreed, oblivious to the sidelong look Kea shot her.

Arriving at the T-junction where the path straddled the edge of the lake, the clouds unleashed their cargo, drenching the air with thick drops of water, heavy and cold. Kea saw that the two-by-four planks Tony and Marcus had laid down the day before to assist the crossing were still there. It had slipped her mind that they would have to take them back. She sighed. Even with Nadia's help, the planks were too heavy to carry, given the weight of her pack, which meant they would have to return another day. Still, she considered, they could at least shift them so they weren't washed away.

"Give me a hand, will you?" Kea crossed over the planks. Warily eyeing the cold glacial lake below, she knelt in the mud. Gouging her fingertips into the space between the wood, she tugged, but suction held the wood firmly in place.

Wrinkling her nose in disgust, Nadia sunk her hands into the goo and pried out the other end. Together they pulled. Grudgingly, the planks popped free, accompanied by a series of grotesque sucking noises.

"I'm never going to get this crap out of my nails," Nadia moaned. "I'd murder for a long bath."

"You and me both." Kea reached out her hand and helped the teenager out of the mud. Together, they picked up the planks and walked across the last stretch of bridge. "Don't worry, on the way back to the airport, there's a thermal lagoon. You can soak until your heart's content-"

The earth fell out from under them.

Kea's hands scrabbled against the hard gravel as she tumbled down the embankment toward the water. There was a heart-stopping moment of nothing before she felt her palms push through a hard, flat surface. Then a cold black wall slapped against her face and swallowed her whole.

The shock of the icy water burned as it slid beneath her clothes, scalding as it flooded down her back. She screamed again, causing a fountain of bubbles to vomit out of her mouth. Kicking fiercely with the leaden weight of her boots, she shoved her head above the water, gasping for air. She clawed at the vertical cliff of loose sand, desperate to pull herself back up, but the soft, wet sediment bled through her hands. The slope was too steep, she realized. Her attempts only resulted in an avalanche of sand and gravel that spilled onto her face, blinding her.

A shriek nearby signaled that Nadia had not yet drowned. Kea felt a surge of adrenaline rush through her. She tried once again to find her own footing, but the water was too deep here, the current too strong. Heaving in a gulp of air, she found herself sinking beneath the surface. Thrashing frantically, her limbs felt heavier with every movement as her energy was leached away by the cold. Once, twice, she breached the surface. Without thinking, she sucked in a deep breath before slipping into the dark once more.

The breath gave her a moment to think. Or perhaps it was the realization that she didn't have the strength to reach the surface again. Her limbs flailed about her in a wild panic, but her mind no longer played a part. She felt detached, as if she were watching everything happening from a distance. The strangely calm sensation allowed her to consider the problem.

The slope was too deep here, she needed to move further along to where the embankment leveled out. She allowed herself to be pulled along with the current, kicking repeatedly, finding that her feet felt heavier with each stroke. She was still sinking deeper.

Her pack was filling with water, she realized slowly, pulling her down to the lake bottom. Fingers numb with cold, she fumbled for the pack's release clasp, a tight sodden tentacle of nylon that clung tightly around her chest. She yanked it free. The pack dropped away, and she felt suddenly propelled her upward. Breaching the surface once more, she took several quick, trembling breaths before striking off along the shore, kicking with her legs and grabbing at any rock to pull her along. Five yards. Ten. Twenty. Finally, her feet hit firm substrate, and she battered her hands against cobbles, trying to gain purchase on the bank.

A yelp caused her to look downstream. A bundle of purple clung to a boulder in the middle of the river. Nadia. Although she was unburdened by a pack, she appeared stranded, mewling like a wet kitten.

Get them back alive, Carlyle's voice echoed in her head. Without giving herself time to reconsider, Kea shoved off from shore, swimming desperately towards Nadia. Her body was already numb, but she used the current to assist her, steering as best she could with her leaden legs. She blew out jagged breaths between each stroke, her teeth chattering furiously. Unfortunately, she misjudged her momentum and slammed into Nadia, knocking her grip off the rock. The teenager thrashed wildly, latching onto Kea, her arms forming a death grip around Kea's throat.

"Okay," Kea managed to spit out as she pulled Nadia's arm away so she could breathe. "It's okay."

They floated with the current, and Kea used the opportunity to swing the girl behind her. Gently lifting Nadia's chin with the crook of her own arm, she used her other arm start to paddling back to shore. "Come on," she whispered, "we can do this together. Kick, just keep kicking."

Just keep kicking, Kea repeated over and over in her head. She didn't think she could make it. The glacial meltwater that fed the river meant the chilling cold might consume them at any moment. Her arms ached and her hands were so numb that she wasn't even certain she was holding Nadia anymore. Only Nadia's repetitive swearing informed Kea that she was still with her, still conscious.

Kick. Kick. Thud.

Kea bellowed as her boot thwacked against a rock. Cursing, she pushed upward and found purchase with her other foot. A bend in the river ahead had caused sediment to accumulate, giving her enough ground to start slagging toward the shore. She half-crawled, half-walked into the shallows. Nadia, appearing to regain her strength now that they were out of the water, helped her stand. They wobbled like contestants in an awkward three-legged race as they stumbled through the shallows before splaying out on the cobbles.

"I," Nadia gasped as she spat out a mouthful of glacial water, "hate," her words juddered from between her quivering jaw and chattering teeth, "nature."

Kea ignored her. The storm pelted the earth and water around them. Her arms were still shaking uncontrollably. She ripped off her jacket, its sodden weight slapping against the ground. Tugging at the pocket that held the radio, she tried to pull apart the Velcro to get to the zipper but found she was just pawing uselessly at the nylon fabric. Her fingers refused to feel, to bend, to yield. She wanted to scream in frustration, but she could barely manage to draw breath. At last, she was able to pull open the Velcro with her teeth. She yanked back the zipper, coating her lips in grit. Pulling out the radio, she watched in horror as it dripped water and mud onto the sand. Cursing, she flicked the power switch. Nothing.

"What's wrong?" Nadia asked, her voice barely a whisper.

Kea felt the radio slip out of her hand and thud into the mud. She closed her eyes and felt the raindrops patter on her eyelids. "Nothing," she said at last. "They're coming. Just hold on." She rested her head onto the rocks, surprised at how comfortable they felt. "Don't fall asleep, just hang on. I just need a few minutes to get my strength back…" She trailed off as her mind slipped into the shadows and she felt the arms of sleep embrace her..

Chapter 13

DARKNESS.

Warmth.

Naked.

Kea did a mental doubletake.

Yes, she realized, *very naked*.

She let out a long groan and inhaled slowly, aware that she was still shaking. Her nostrils filled with the scent of patchouli that stirred long-buried memories. It took her back to the days of noodles, pot-filled dorm rooms, and the crisp scent of autumn leaves.

"You know," Zoë whispered into Kea's ear, "if you wanted to get naked together, all you had to do was ask. Throwing yourself into a lake does smack of desperation."

"I didn't know it was an option." Kea felt cold, clammy, and distinctly uncomfortable. Her hair was wet and freezing. The corrugated floor of the jeep beneath the flimsy emergency blanket dug into her back. "Besides, there's nothing romantic about this."

Zoë repositioned herself so she could look Kea in the eye. "How long has it been?"

Kea looked down at her chest, saw that Zoë was only wearing her underwear. Kea looked up again quickly, and unable to meet the woman's gaze, settled for staring at the ceiling of the jeep instead. "You'll have to be a bit more specific.'

Zoë laughed. "I was actually referring to hypothermia treatment."

"First time on the receiving end. We had a volunteer get hypothermia once," Kea said, remembering a previous field season. "But that wasn't due to anything so exciting. Just from walking, exhaustion, sweating, and wearing the wrong clothes."

"Never had anyone leap into a glacial lake before?" Zoë teased, but her tone was warm, her smile kind.

Still quivering, Kea struggled to remember what had happened. "I didn't leap exactly..." She looked around the inside of the jeep. The engine was still running, the windows steaming up.

I'll never live down the rumors.

"Wait a sec..." Kea thought back to Zoë's initial response. She waved her fingers back and forth in the air between them. "This was an option?"

Zoë laughed. "I suppose it could have been... if you'd asked."

Kea didn't quite know how to respond to that. "Nadia!" She shouted suddenly "Where's..."

"It's okay." Zoë prevented her from leaping up. "She's in the other jeep, warming up with Amirah."

Kea looked around the dark interior of the jeep. Dark gray light from the rainy skies seeped through the foggy windows, settling in a haze across the benches and random bits of field equipment. "How did we get back here?"

Zoë kept the pressure on her arm as if afraid Kea would try to bolt again. "Gary found you. Don't you remember?"

"I..." Flashes filled her mind. Images of arms pulling her up, the sensation of being pressed against polyester jackets, the sounds of voices yelling into the rain, stumbling over the cobbles. "It's a bit of a blur."

Zoë grinned. "We took turns helping you back to the jeep. Cole picked up some of the gear you dropped. Not sure what happened to your pack though." She fell silent for a moment. "What did happen?"

"What? Oh, sorry," Kea shook her head. "I was thinking about my camera. It's at the bottom of the lake. Damn." She closed her eyes again, trying to recall the moments before the fall. "To be honest, I'm not sure. I was carrying the planks and must have tripped. Or the last boards gave way, I guess, but I could barely get the first set out, they were stuck fast. I couldn't see much in all the rain and mud." She paused, "I can't imagine how they gave way so easily. The rain could have washed away some of the soil I suppose, or... someone could have dug them out and put them back to make them look like they were fine."

Zoë frowned. "Why would anyone do that?"

"That's the question," Kea agreed. "Why would anyone want to..."

"Kill you?" Zoë asked, incredulous.

"If that was the intent. Maybe not even me. Can't be sure." Kea groaned. "Maybe Nadia? Although I was the only one left to cross the boards, until Nadia came back. I can't seriously imagine anyone..." She shook her head. "Never mind, it was just an accident. My mind's been seeing menace everywhere lately, after what happened to Bruce."

"Okay," Zoë said slowly. "Even if it wasn't an accident, who would ever want to kill you? That's pretty extreme."

"I'd like to think the list wouldn't be very long." Kea thought grimly. "Marcus despises me, but not enough to kill me. I think." She considered the vile looks Marcus had given her since she started working at the university. "At least, I'm ninety-percent positive he wouldn't kill me."

"Anyone else?" Zoë stroked Kea's bangs out of her eyes with long, delicate fingers. "Anyone else hold a grudge?"

"Not that I can think of." Kea trembled under her touch. "Although I'm not at my best right now."

Zoë fixed Kea with a firm stare. "There's something I need to tell you." She paused, her eyes flickering up to the ceiling of the jeep. "Cole... look, this isn't easy for me... Cole found something in Bruce's tent."

"What?" Kea pulled back abruptly. "Why?"

Zoë sighed. "Not a proud mother moment. He'd heard about Bruce, figured he was on antidepressants. Once they found... the body and were bringing it back, Cole snuck into his tent." She closed her eyes and let out another long breath. "Basically, he broke into a crime scene to steal Bruce's drugs."

"Well," Kea considered, "for one thing, it's not a crime scene. It was a suicide, and even if it wasn't, Bruce died out on the ice. Don't over-guilt this." She realized that had sounded more reassuring in her head. "Did he find anything?"

Zoë nodded. "Fluoxetine. I had to look it up online. It's a common antidepressant. And he found something else."

"You already have a captive audience," Kea commented. "You don't have to ratchet up the suspense."

"The drugs were in a little pack, you know the kind you wear around your waist?" Zoë continued. "Cole left the passport in it, thank God, but he took some money. Not all of it. He didn't want to make it look like Bruce had been robbed, but he took a couple hundred."

"Smart kid," Kea remarked.

"Like I said," Zoë frowned, "not a proud parent right now. Anyway, he also found something else, a ticket."

"A ticket? To what?" Despite her interest, Kea shuddered as another chill fluttered through her body.

171

"Well, not a ticket exactly. It was a receipt for a flight, tucked in with the cash." Zoë pulled the blanket tighter. "I knew Reynard went with the others on a flight that day, so I asked him about it today. He said Bruce had already gone up and had such a 'fantastic time' he booked a ticket for another flight, but there wasn't time to go up that day, and he'd have to go up the next day."

"The day he died." Kea began to see Zoë's point. "Why would a guy with a death wish buy a *second* ticket for the next day?"

Zoë nodded. "Reynard said that they offered to give him his money back, but Bruce insisted he'd be back to use it the next day and wanted to keep his place in line. I know it's not much," Zoë conceded, "but it is strange."

"We have a lot of strange happening around here," Kea agreed.

"And now," Zoë looked around the vehicle, seeming to refer to their close quarters, "if someone really did just have a go at you…"

"Why didn't you tell the police this?" Kea sputtered.

Zoë laughed. "Let's go back to the part where my son stole drugs from a dead guy." She shook her head. "Besides, I didn't start putting it together until now, and it still doesn't mean anything. As for Cole, I don't know what to do."

Kea saw the light in Zoë's eyes fade whenever she talked about her son. Not a parent herself, she found she couldn't think of anything to say to comfort her.

"I guess I'll sort out a punishment for Cole once we get home," Zoë said doubtfully. "I already have been drug testing him randomly, but that wasn't enough apparently. To be fair, I don't think he's ever gotten his hands on Fluoxetine before. I doubt he even knows what it is. He just wanted to up his street cred with his friends. They're not exactly Mensa candidates."

"We have to tell the authorities," Kea insisted. "I can say I found it in the tent." She winced, remembering that she had told the officers she would pack up Bruce's belongings and ship them back to his wife. After that awful mess of a night, she'd put off the task repeatedly. She may have inadvertently provided Cole with the opportunity he needed.

"It's not much to go on." Zoë stared into Kea's eyes inquisitively. "I mean, what are we saying? A suicidal guy comes out here to kill himself and is so blown away by the beauty of the place that he decides not to do it?"

172

"Stranger things..." Kea thought back to the first morning. "You know, that morning, Bruce was all energetic, up early, excited."

"People who are severely depressed," Zoë began slowly, "when they do get all excited, that's when you should start to worry. It means they're ready to carry out their plans."

Kea raised an eyebrow.

"Cole sees a therapist," Zoë explained. "So do I. He warned me what signs to look out for."

"Ah." Kea wasn't sure how else to respond to that. "If Bruce may have changed his mind about killing himself..."

"And then someone killed him anyway." Zoë nodded. "Why? And why try to kill you? Why now?"

"Someone thinks I know something, or saw something, I suppose," Kea pondered. "They may have thought Bruce did too."

"Is there anyone else who might have a reason to want to kill you?" Zoë asked, serious now.

"More people than I thought," Kea replied, thinking back to her conversations with Erik, Jon, Derek, and Max. "Who was the last person to cross the planks, the last person back at the jeeps? Was it Jon?"

Zoë shook her head. "Honestly, I can't remember. Between the rain and everything, I really wasn't paying any attention. I can ask around though."

"No," Kea said quickly. "Best not. It may actually have been an accident, but even if it wasn't, I'd rather not let whoever it was know I'm suspicious."

Zoë shook her head. "You sure you're okay?"

Kea looked around. "I'm naked in the back of a jeep in the middle of the sandur wrapped in an emergency blanket... but I am alive. I think that'll have to qualify for okay for now." She looked Zoë squarely in the eye. "And for that, I want to say, thank you."

"Thank Gary." Zoë reached for her clothes.

"Yes," Kea said. "I'm sure that will be... a unique conversation."

"So, about tomorrow..." Zoë started sliding out of the blanket and reached for her underwear that was strewn across the bench.

"Tomorrow?" Kea, uncomfortable watching Zoë dress, turned her back.

"I need to go back on the ice to look for Romulus," Zoë explained.

173

"Ah..." Kea had forgotten about the drone or at least given it up for dead.

"I took a stab looking for Remus on the sandur," Zoë continued, "but no luck. I think it may have wound up in a lake. I have a better idea where Romulus might be. I was just waiting 'til we got back up on the ice again."

"It might be a bit tricky," Kea began, thinking of the logistics of traversing Romulus' route on foot.

"That drone cost six grand," Zoë remarked flatly. "Remus was another eight."

Kea was glad that Zoë had turned away so that she couldn't see her flinch. "Well then, I guess tomorrow is Romulus' lucky day."

Chapter 14

KEA WAS sequestered in the front seat of the jeep on the return trip to camp, spared from a barrage of questions from the volunteers. Nadia was dropped off at the main showers, while Marcus dropped Kea off in front of the research hut. It wasn't until she'd waved them away and locked the bathroom door that she felt safe. She stepped into the hot spray of water and watched the mud and grit pile up in miniature dunes against the sides of her feet. The adrenaline, and her strength, had been completely sapped away.

Along with any hope of logical reasoning.

Emerging damp and sore a glorious half-hour later, she discovered that Julie had left a bag of clean clothes and sneakers outside the door. Once dressed, she found herself staring at her reflection in the mirror, wondering again what on earth she was going to do next.

"All I really want," she told herself, "is to sleep. And a five-course meal." The woman looking back at her seemed unimpressed. It was as if her visage knew that the only meal in her future was most likely a damp peanut butter and jelly sandwich.

Outside, the evening clouds had been shoved aside by the brisk winds that gusted off the icecap. As she walked back to the tents, a thick towel slung over her shoulders, she hugged herself even as she felt the warm caress of the sunlight on her face. The cold nightmare of the river seemed an impossible memory, one that belonged to someone else.

Arriving at her tent, she knelt by the zipper and nearly poked out her eye with a puffin's beak. She blinked. The brass puffin regarded her stoically. The hiking stick was lodged into the ground, its length partially obscured by the doorway of her tent, presumably left there by Marcus. She held it up to the sky and inspected the staff. It seemed much lighter than she expected. She slotted it back into the hole in the ground and patted the little bird's head, before going back to the main encampment.

Entering the main tent, Kea was greeted by a thunderous cheer. Glancing around the circle of beaming faces and pink cheeks, she deduced that Marcus must have broken out one of the bottles of whiskey, a prize traditionally reserved for the last night of the field season.

Amirah handed her a shot of the Black Death. Kea raised it in a toast and gulped the burning fluid down in one go. Smiling and waving politely, she moved past the crowded dinner table, making a beeline for the bowl of chocolate pudding.

Life, she thought, *was too short to wait for dessert.*

She plopped down at the end of the table, waved away the kind words and questions and savored the chocolate sweetness of the pudding. As she slurped, she watched as the others finished their supper and transitioned into the obligatory drinking games. People were stuffing their faces with food, laughing, washing dishes, and getting skunk-drunk. It seemed so utterly normal.

After the incident in the river, she knew what she wanted.

I can't do this anymore, she thought. *Either I see monsters in the shadows that aren't there, or worse I'm putting people in danger by asking so many questions. I just want to finish the work, go back home, and start re-building my life.*

Kea watched Zoë supervising Cole as he washed the dishes, his mother's expression weary but determined. Jon stood beside them, helping to dry the dishes with a grimy washcloth.

Even if I have no idea what that future should look like.

"Everything all right?" Marcus sat down across from her, a mug in his hand.

Kea looked at him. He seemed concerned. Odd. She was now only sixty percent sure he might have tried to kill her by shifting the planks. Of course, the concern could just be an act to throw her off. She cranked her suspicion rating back up to seventy-five percent.

"Fine and dandy," she replied automatically. "Just lost my footing." She couldn't be certain that wasn't what had happened. "Must be getting old."

"You gave us quite a scare." Marcus regarded her curiously. "Well done saving Nadia. Quite remarkable."

Kea nodded but hated how patronizing he made the compliment sound. Looking at him now, he seemed so harmless, so small. She could tell that he expected her to thank him for giving her Dr. Carlyle's staff, that she should be grateful for his gesture, for his generosity.

Too little, too late, she thought.

"Marcus," she said calmly. "I know you're trying to publish without me, and I've gotta say, that's pretty messed up."

His mouth gaped open, his jaw bouncing uselessly as he searched for words.

"I'll happily co-author with you on it, which I highly recommend," she continued, "because I have additional data from this season that will make for a more complete record."

Marcus' expression was a beautiful picture of confusion and apprehension.

"You clearly enjoy leading these teams, and I have no desire to take that away from you," she went on.

Nor have I enjoyed any of this experience.

"I'll speak to Dr. Carlyle about appointing you as the lead on all future expeditions once we get back," she finished.

"Why are you..." stammered Marcus.

"I've decided it's all about pudding." She pushed aside the empty pudding bowl. "My life needs more time for pudding and less of this." She waved her hands in the air between them. "Whatever this is."

Marcus slowly put down his drink, laid his hands out on the table and studied his fingers carefully for a moment. "Kea, after I left the service, I have been working very hard, despite what you might think. Between my family and work, I get very little sleep. I have four children, two of whom will be going to college soon..."

No one told you to have kids, Kea thought automatically. She winced, repulsed at her own gut reaction.

"You're younger than me, have more energy, more determination and yes," Marcus paused, "are more talented than anyone else in the department. I have no doubt that you're going to get promoted to Professor, but don't think that I'm not going to at least try to compete."

The fight or flight impulses that Kea normally had ready to brace against Marcus' attacks deserted her. Even her exhaustion couldn't keep a bemused expression off her face.

"Okay, while it may not seem proper to leave you out of the publication," Marcus admitted grudgingly, "in fairness, I did re-process the data myself, and I did work with the engineering department on a new model. Besides, you have so many other publications already, I'm sure it wouldn't make much of a difference."

Kea, although still slightly numb, realized that this was as close to an apology as she was likely to get. "Thanks. I think?" She shook her head, wondering if when she woke up the next morning, this would all turn out to be a dream. "All I really want is to go to bed." She turned but paused, watching through the tent flap as Derek chased Reynard around the lawn, spraying him with a fire extinguisher that he must have nicked from the supply tent. "Ermm... Can you, ya' know, adult?"

Marcus laughed. "Drunken volunteer safety duty. I got this."

Kea nodded and started toward the exit.

"Hey." Max caught her arm. Judging by his motions, and his breath, he was already drunk. "You're not going to stay for the party?"

"Not tonight, thanks." Very calmly, Kea plucked his paw off her arm and continued on her way.

Time, she thought, *is too precious for this.*

She caught sight of Julie and Amirah looking at her with concern, but thankfully they left her alone. Spying the profile of a certain man, she sighed softly and forced herself to walk toward him.

Gary sat alone outside his tent, eating his dinner off a plastic plate held between his knees. He seemed to be staring out at the main campground, where campers lazily moved back and forth between the bathrooms and the visitor center as the day wound down.

He took all his meals alone, Kea realized suddenly. She had been so busy this week that she had not noticed. Normally, she made time to make sure the outsiders felt welcome, or at least made an effort to include them. However, nothing about this week, she reminded herself, had been remotely normal. "Evening."

"Evening." Gary returned her greeting but offered little else. Instead, he turned back to contemplate the shifting sky.

"I heard you found us out there." Kea waved out to the glacier. "I just wanted to say thank you."

"Of course," Gary said an odd tone in his voice. "Terribly easy to lose your footing out there."

Kea wondered then if he was the one who moved the boards.

Unlikely, she concluded.

Their relationship, if there was one, may not have gotten off to the best start this week, but she doubted Gary would bother setting a trap, let alone bother to rescue them. She shook her head to clear it. "Well, thank you again. I'm just glad you were out there."

Gary nodded once more and tipped a finger to his chin in acknowledgment. As the laughter reached them from the main tent, she noticed that he seemed more than content to be left alone with the sun on his face and the glaciers at his back.

She took a moment then to look around her, to remember where she was and how fortunate she was to still be here, still living and breathing. She felt a wave of anger flow through her body at the thought that someone might have tried to take it from her. Anger at whatever, or whoever, had taken it from Bruce when he had only just discovered it.

"Sorry Bruce," Kea whispered to the wind.

Regrets, she thought as she turned away to head for her tent, *I have a few.*

"He's a queer one," Gary croaked.

Kea followed his gaze to the edge of the campground. Tony was skirting the edge of the trees, carrying a large pack of some kind. She honestly had no clue where he was going at this time of night.

"Yes," Kea said thoughtfully. "He really is." She toyed with the idea of following him, of finding out what he was up to, but found she was too exhausted. Besides, it most likely involved Ísadóra, and the less she knew about that, the better.

Tomorrow, she thought *Tomorrow will be a better day.*

Chapter 15

Day Seven

KEA WOKE in her sleeping bag feeling like an overcooked burrito. Despite the glow of sunlight that illuminated her tent, a glance at her phone showed that it was only four in the morning. Unable to fall back asleep, her mind kept replaying the events of the past few days. Was she was going crazy? Maybe there really wasn't anything going on. Or should she run around screaming for everyone to run for the hills, to keep them all safe.

They're going to be fine, she told herself over and over. *They'll have the day off, then tomorrow they'll be on the first shuttle back to the city and then fly home.*

For the funeral.

Kea looked across at the jumble of clothes, food wrappers, and notebooks that comprised her tent floor. Platy sat half-buried in a pile of laundry. Its fur and stuffing torn asunder, it regarded her silently with its one good eye.

Unable to stand its accusatory gaze any longer, she wormed out of her sleeping bag and routed through her gear until she found a sewing kit.

"This may hurt a bit," she warned, as she threaded the needle, "but I can't have you lying around like this." She tucked the stuffing back in and sewed it back together as best she could. "There you go." She propped him up on her pillow. Truth be told, she was terrible at sewing. The result was less platypus, more purple teddy bear-zombie hybrid. However, he had two eyes and a smiling face again.

For the first time in days, Kea felt like she had accomplished something.

She glanced at the clock again. Still early.

Staring at the ceiling of her tent, she felt her mind slipping away, her thoughts spiraling once more into a mess of fear and confusion.

"Nope," she announced. "Bored now. I'm not lying around freaking out. I'm not doing this." She pulled on some clothes and grabbed the toy. "Come on, Pus, let's get some work done."

***

Crawling out of her tent, she walked through the campground, picking her way between the maze of tents in the haze of the mist. Yellow depressions in the grass marked the sites abandoned by the Icelanders, a worrying sign of the bad weather still to come. While the sky was bright, clouds hovered around the periphery of the ice cap, coloring the horizon a charcoal gray. Skirting the campsite as quietly as she could, she made her way to the main tent. As she had hoped, it was empty. A quick scan of the whiteboard informed her that Julie had arranged a trip to the hot tubs later that morning. *Bless her.* Some of the others had signed up for various hikes up to Skógafoss and Morsárjökull, which meant they would be gone for quite some time. The rest would be sleeping off a hangover before packing up to head back to the city and begin their 'real' vacations.

She took advantage of the time to make toast, slathering it thick with marmalade and dollops of margarine, and brewed a large cup of tea. Thus armed, she dug out the maps, booted up her computer, and did what she had come thousands of miles to do: she got to work.

She received her first surprise when she discovered that Julie had not only already uploaded the GPR data of the esker, but also the measurements of the exposure collected by the volunteers.

Someone else, Kea suspected, *wasn't getting any sleep either.*

She examined the three-dimensional model of the esker that burrowed into the ice. While the GPR transects still needed to be cleaned, she got a general sense of its dimensions. There was a minor deformation due to ice melt, but the structure as a whole remained intact. Previously, Kea had only ever studied eskers after the ice had retreated, leaving nothing behind but a jumble of rock and mud. She noticed that the proximal crevasse fills were also captured at depth by the GPR data. They rendered as numerous, almost box-like features nestled around the esker, their cavities jam-packed with sediment.

Julie had struck dissertation gold, Kea thought. The model on the screen might provide insight of how different phases of the flood added to the feature, adding layers as the water and sediment rammed its way up through the ice before bursting out through the margin and finally receded as the supply of water dwindled. For now, though, Kea was interested in other locations on the sandur where similar landforms may have existed to get an idea of where the next flood may emerge.

She scanned the map and identified a couple of landforms on the outwash plain comparable to Julie's assemblage of structures. To the west lay the ghost of an esker-like ridge. It was farther south, abutting the mountain wall. *Maybe an esker, hard to tell, perhaps the sign of another previous flood outlet.* The crevasse fills they mapped last week seemed far too delicate a feature to have survived anywhere else.

She frowned and pulled up the photographs of the section Erik and Jon had mapped. There in the exposure wall she saw a cross-section of the crevasse fills preserved in the sediment, which meant the outlets were moving progressively eastward in response to the glacier's retreat, as they suspected. *But how far?*

"What are you looking for?" Julie stood beside her, frowning at her GPR data on the screen.

Kea swore. "You scared the crap out of me." She turned back to the data. "I'm trying to figure out where it will go next."

"The glacier?"

Kea shook her head. "The next flood." She considered the map again. "The glacier margin has retreated, what, nearly a kilometer in some places, since the 1996 eruption, right?"

"And lowered vertically." Julie grabbed another map from the file drawer and laid it on the table. "Here's the surface and subsurface maps from the radar flights the Met office did back in 1997."

Large in scale and coarse in resolution, the profiles gave an estimate of the ice surface and the valley floor it rested on. Kea compared estimates of some of their recent survey points on the ice. "Already more than two hundred meters lower, just in these few locations. Which completely changes the pressure regimes."

Julie pointed to the map. "And we know from the carpet-bombed sandur that when the glacier was advancing the floods occurred all across the front margin." Her finger slid along the margin, finally stopping near the middle of the glacier's snout. "The main outlet of the 1996 flood was here in the central area, but the next one could really be anywhere east or west of it."

"I know that," Kea said quietly. "I was hoping to narrow it down to a couple more likely options."

Julie brushed the 1997 radar map with the back of her hand. "Three generalized profiles do not a provide a detailed subsurface. I can't model anything off this."

Kea traced the edge of the margin with her finger again, attempting to mentally piece together everything she had seen in the field. "Those upwellings to the east, it could emerge there."

"What on earth happened to him?" Julie had spotted the repaired platypus.

Kea grunted. "I'm trying to piece my life back together."

"I think we're going to need to find you a better seamstress," Julie commented. "Otherwise, I hate to think what your sex life will wind up looking like."

"This is the most likely spot." Kea tapped the ice valley near the east where the upwellings were most abundant, and the ice was the thinnest.

"It could just as easily emerge in any of these spots here," Julie randomly tapped three spots along the margin. "The deposits left within and below the ice during the last flood are still there and could deflect drainage a hundred different ways. Plus, the ice has lowered, among a dozen other factors. We don't have enough data of what's going on under the ice to even begin to model it."

"I know," Kea agreed. "I just have a hunch."

Julie arched an eyebrow. "Willing to make a bet?"

Kea didn't get a chance to answer, as Marcus threw open the tent flap and headed for the coffee pot.

"Just got a call from the Met office," he said, lighting the gas burner. "More activity under Vatnajökull over the last few days apparently, although they said they've had trouble with a couple of the monitoring stations. Looks like just a few minor swarms at this point, a sign of more activity under the ice cap. We could see some flooding in a few days."

"Or in six weeks, after we're long gone." Kea stared into her tea and watched the steam shimmer and blur.

"That's fantastic." Julie was visibly bubbling with enthusiasm as she headed out of the tent. "I'll go tell Tony."

It was Julie's first time at the site with volcanic activity, Kea remembered. *Oh, to be young again.*

"I thought you'd be more excited," Marcus said, as if implying that Kea's mood was somehow now important to him.

Perhaps my nearly dying had that effect on him, Kea pondered. Assuming, of course, he hadn't been the one who tried to kill her.

Stop it. Stop.

She forced a smile. "Sounds like a minor eruptive event at least. I guess I just feel like I've had enough excitement for one field season." This wasn't the first time that they'd had similar warnings only for there to not be a major flood weeks or months after they left. "Let me know if they think there might be enough meltwater to float the ice dam."

"Even though the others are headed back, we can still pack a couple more days of research in. You should still have no trouble making it back in time..." Marcus blew out a long breath, leaving off the phrase *'for the funeral.'* "I have some proposals for next season that I've got to knock out this morning before giving the team a sendoff. I'll hole myself up at the cafe at the visitor center. You?"

"I still feel a bit... odd." Kea played the tired card. She really didn't want to have a conversation right now. Too many things were still going around in her head, like *'Did you try to kill me yesterday?'* "Catching up on a paper or two sounds brilliant, but I've still got to get my gear off the ice. Might snag Tony and Julie to help and one of the volunteers. Speaking of, did I miss anything else last night?"

Marcus shook his head. "It got pretty tame after midnight or so. Caught Gary washing his socks in the washing basin though. Not sure how long that's been going on."

Kea pulled a face at her now empty teacup. "Oh lord."

"Indeed." Marcus smiled again. "He knocked back quite a lot of the whiskey. Not sure where it was all coming from, to be honest. He told quite some interesting stories. Did you know he used to work in Hollywood? He used to work with a lot of celebrities and was in a couple movies."

"Sorry?" Kea wasn't sure how to digest that piece of information. "I would never have guessed."

"Goes to show," Marcus said, "never know what people have hiding in their pasts."

How true that is, Kea thought.

***

Kea exited the tent head-down and nearly plowed straight into Zoë and Cole. They were both wearing their EO jackets, but Zoë's hair was drawn up into a tight ponytail, a sharp contrast to the unkempt brown locks of her son. Behind them, looking equally disheveled, Nadia and her father stood side by side, rocking on the balls of their feet, eager to get inside the warmth of the tent.

"Morning." Kea gave Zoë a genuine smile. She tried to give Cole her best equivalent, even though she couldn't help thinking, *Yes, you and everyone else know that I was naked with your mother last night. Now stop staring.*

"Morning." Zoë mumbled, not fully awake yet. "How are you?"

"Not bad," Kea replied, not wanting to dwell on the aches that had seeped into every muscle during the night. "Surprisingly. Mostly I just want to avoid everyone for a bit and try to focus on getting back on track with work. How are the others?"

"Haven't seen anyone else up yet," Zoë said. "I think everyone is taking advantage of having a chance to sleep in." She waved her son into the tent, stroking his hair as he passed. "Time for a shower. You're starting to stink."

"He can have my slot," Kea offered. "I think I hogged enough of the camp's water last night trying to thaw out."

"By the way," Zoë handed Kea a field notebook, "Tiko wanted me to give you this."

"She was really sweet," Nadia commented. If she'd been traumatized by her adventures the previous night, she gave no outward sign. "I'm going to miss her."

"Miss her?" Kea asked.

"Sorry, thought you knew." Nadia waved in the general direction of the highway. "She and Reynard left about an hour ago."

"What? Why?" Kea's confidence floundered. *Why does no one bother to tell me anything?*

"She spoke to her father last night," Andrei explained. "After hearing about the recent... events, he insisted that she head home. They caught a ride with some campers back to the city."

"They can't just leave..." Kea groaned. Still, the inspector had said everyone was free to go. "I wish she'd have said something. Wait, Reynard too? I didn't realize they were a couple."

Nadia and Zoë exchanged a conspiratorial glance.

"Kea." Zoë said with a wry smile, "You know Reynard's gay, right?"

Kea rubbed the bridge of her nose. "I really never thought about it." *I really am completely oblivious sometimes.* She let out a long

185

breath, trying to take in the new information. "Reynard left because he was afraid too?"

"Nah," Nadia shook her head. "I think he was pissed Derek was ignoring him after they, you know."

Kea threw her hands up. "Wait. Wait, just wait a sec. You're saying Derek and Reynard-"

"Yep." Nadia nodded, already bored with the conversation.

"Derek," Kea repeated slowly. "The guy who hits on every woman he sees?"

"Yeah, well, Derek hits on everyone he sees," Zoë remarked pointedly. "Anything with a pulse really."

"When did all this start?" Kea demanded, unreasonably offended that someone else would have the nerve to explore their sexuality during her field season.

"On the ice that day," Nadia said. "While Marcus and they were drilling, they were off doing some of their own-"

"Nadia!" Andrei cuffed his daughter lightly on the shoulder.

"Oi!" Nadia yelped. "They did! Least Reynard said they did. The last couple of days though, Derek has been all about Lexie, now that she's paying him attention."

"I'm beginning to think," Kea sighed, "that I've no idea what's going on here at all." She started walking away.

"Where are you going?" Zoë called after her.

"Research," Kea said, tapping her nose. "Right after I make about a dozen phone calls to EO about my little dive and let them know about Tiko and Reynard."

"Okay." Zoë hesitated. "But what about Romulus?"

"Don't worry," Kea reassured her. "We'll get your drone this afternoon."

Zoë nodded her thanks and slipped into the tent. Andrei followed close behind, leaving Kea to survey the campground that was only just beginning to stir. It seemed unnerving, somehow, to see it so empty. Tiko and Reynard had just bailed without warning, like canaries in a mine.

Not to mention, Kea thought, *if Reynard and Derek had nipped off into a crevasse that day for some canoodling... that just left Marcus, Tony, and Jon near the site of Bruce's death.*

If she were completely honest, she didn't know if she could rule out any of those three as suspects. She fumbled with her phone to call up the Eco Observer main phone number and resigned herself to a morning of paperwork.

***

Kea stared unenthusiastically at her laptop's display. The latest draft of her submission filled the screen, covered with highlights, comments, and callouts. She'd spent a half-hour revising the paper and hadn't even gotten through the first two pages. The requested alterations to the diagrams alone would take at least three solid days. She pulled up a game on her phone and knocked out a couple of rounds, trying to clear her head. At least EO had been fine with Reynard and Tiko leaving; they were adults, they'd paid upfront through the company and had left of their own accord. Besides, everyone would be gone by tomorrow anyway.

Watching the icons on her screen explode, she realized that her brain was still too numb to be productive. She slumped back against her sleeping bag and stared around the tent, and found her gaze drawn to Tiko's sketchpad.

Flipping through the drawings, she found herself in awe once again at the young woman's ability to delicately capture the intricate layers of the rock face. Each one was signed in the bottom corner as if Tiko expected to appear in a gallery someday.

Kea thumbed through the volume until she reached yesterday's sketch of the exposure. While the attention to detail was still excellent, the drawing appeared rushed. Examining the signature, Kea realized that instead of Tiko's name and the date was scribbled a number that looked like an IP address followed by '/lancet,' in tiny print.

Lancet. The same name Derek had mentioned, Kea remembered. Too tired to bother going to the visitor center, she activated the hotspot on her phone, extra fees be damned. She entered the ip address into a browser but found herself looking at a web page with nothing on it except the T3 logo and a login screen.

Kea searched through the rest of the journal but found nothing that resembled a username or password. Turning back to the screen, she scrolled down and saw a familiar seal at the bottom of the page. It was a tiny circle with the drawing of an ant and a blade of grass with a field of stars in the background. The same one as Max's tattoos.

Clicking on the icon got her nowhere. Typing *Admin* or *Guest* into the login produced similar results. At a loss, Kea searched on '*lancet.*' It returned hundreds of results, including several obscure medical journals. She spent the next ten minutes clicking through the pages but found herself none the wiser. She tried combining 't3' and 'lancet', but that resulted in nothing more revealing. She returned to the drawing Tiko had left her, then searched on the terms 'ant', 'grass', 'night', and 'lancet'.

Dicrocoelium dendriticum returned immediately. A parasite known as the Lancet Liver Fluke.

Kea spent the next five minutes totally grossed out learning what Mother Nature did to her poor creations. She was both repelled and fascinated.

The fluke lived in the livers of infected sheep and then laid eggs that wound up inside the sheep's feces. Through a complex cycle, snails ingested the feces and the eggs, before extruding them as slimeballs. These tasty morsels were then eaten by ants, who would have their brains hijacked by the parasite. Every night, the parasite used its mind control to force the ant to climb up a blade of grass and clamp onto the end, waiting for it to be consumed by the sheep, thus completing the circle of life.

A very twisted circle of life, Kea reflected.

While she knew very little about what T3 did, she doubted it had anything to do with animal behavior modification. Most of the people that she had met on the team seemed to be a developer or programmer.

Perhaps it was a code name for a virus they were developing. Or an anti-virus?

She headed outside. She needed to get some fresh air and clear her mind. It was raining, of course, but only a light drizzle which suited her. There was nothing so soothing as having a quiet walk in the mists and fog. Slipping on a couple of outer layers, she grabbed her toothbrush and headed to the bathroom.

It was only then that she noticed the cluster of people gathering around the research hut. She jogged toward the crowd, a sense of dread growing in her stomach. Muttering spilled around her as she pushed through the campers pressing against the entrance to the hut. "What's going on? What's happening?" she asked anyone who would listen. None of the faces were familiar to her.

"Accident, in the shower," said one.

"Some kid slipped," said another.

"Did you see all the blood?" said a young boy with a British accent, smiling delightedly.

"What? Who?" Kea shoved her way to the center of the crowd. The concrete path was dark with a puddle of vivid crimson. The color was jarring, out of place, rich and violent. She couldn't, however, see any sign of anyone injured.

"They're gone," a familiar voice filled her ear. "Headed for 'Klaustur." Amirah was by her side, holding her arm.

"Who?" Kea turned on her, grabbing her shoulders. "What happened?"

"Cole," Amirah said gently. "He's fine, he's okay. Marcus and Zoë took him to the medical center at Kirkjubæjarklaustur. Julie went too. Everyone's okay." Her deep brown eyes implored Kea to remain calm.

"That," Kea yelled, pointing at the pool of blood, "is not okay!" She realized that the crowd was staring at her. The muttering continued, but no longer about the blood, about her.

Amirah folded Kea into a hug and pressed her head against her neck. She cupped her fingers around Kea's ear and whispered, "Cole slipped in the shower and broke his arm. It's a bad break. He cut his head too, so there was bleeding, but they stopped it, and he's in good hands. They'll both be okay." She pulled back and looked Kea firmly in the eye. "And so will you. Yes?"

Kea found strength in that look, saw echoes of her own mother in those eyes. "Yes," she managed at last. She realized she was shaking. She looked around at the crowd of people watching her. "I'll be okay." She nodded at them and made herself walk into the hut. She gave a smile that she hoped conveyed the message, *'I'm not a loon. Please go about your business,'* but she was fairly certain that she wasn't pulling it off. Once inside, she tried to put their looks behind her. She needed to get cleaned up. In so many ways.

The research station was usually crowded with biologists, thick with the heady smells of cooking and laundry, but now it seemed eerily empty. She slipped into the unisex bathroom and made hasty work cleaning her face. Rubbing her temples, she could feel the pressure of a headache building within her skull.

I should have done something, she thought.

189

Should have what? she knew Jason would have countered. *What would you have done? Held Cole's hand in the shower? You can't be responsible for everyone, for everything.*

But I do, Kea answered silently. *I don't know why, but I do. And I always seem to fail.*

Her mind held no reply, the only sound the *thump, thump, thump* of her own heart.

Kea turned to leave the bathroom but instead found herself turning the corner to examine the shower stall. She wasn't sure why, but she lingered at the threshold.

Don't know how to stop... Jason's voice echoed in her head.

"Shush you," she muttered aloud. She pulled open the door and knelt by the puddle of blood that still clung to the edges of the drain.

Kea had seen enough blood before in her life and found it nauseating at best. Now, however, she found herself drawn to the shiny, red globules that trembled as she knelt against the edge of the floor basin. It seemed unworldly somehow. So much darker, so much richer than she remembered. She leaned closer, entranced but careful not to touch it.

How did Cole manage to break a limb in the shower?

The base of the shower was metal, cold, and sharp, true enough, but what on earth was he up to in here? Remembering she was dealing with a teenage boy, she flinched. Putting her hands against the wall, she levered upward, examining the stall as she did so. There were steel handles bolted to the walls, but even then, it would take quite a fall to...

Her foot rocketed out from under her, causing her to swear as she slid onto her backside. "Christ on a stick," she swore in relief. If she hadn't had her hand braced, she would have been the second casualty in the medical center.

Carefully, she used the handle to pull herself upright. Then, bracing both hands against the wall, she pressed her boot to the shower floor. It slid across the surface with frightening ease.

Puzzled, she knelt again, this time resting her knees outside the stall. She ran a finger along the metal floor, careful to avoid the blood. Examining her skin, she saw an odd iridescent shimmer. She rubbed her thumb against her finger. It slid, like graphite gliding across a sheet of paper. She gave it a sniff. It didn't smell like soap or grease. It was almost metallic.

Familiar, she thought. *Maybe...*

She headed off with long, confident strides out of the hut and across the campground. She hurried over the wet grass, weaving through the team's tents until she reached the cache of supplies that they kept behind the main tent. There, under the awning, sitting within the chaos of wrenches, screwdrivers, and cables were two spray cans of petroleum-based lubricant. She popped the lid off and took a whiff.

It was the same scent.

Kea felt a strange sensation flow through her, a mixture of relief and anger. Yes, Cole had been injured, but for the first time, she had proof. Proof that she wasn't crazy, that someone was actively trying to...

Very slowly, she put down the can into the mess of the other supplies, conscious of how visible she was to the rest of the campground. She stared at the equipment, trying to come up with another reason that she would be here. Her hands lingered on the jar of chocolate spread, then drifted around the assortment of tools. Selecting a metal clipboard, she walked around to the front of the main tent. Flipping open the cover, she dug out a pen and rummaged through the forms inside, doing her best to look busy, purposeful.

I am occupied, she broadcast, her head bent over the forms.

It was certainly true that Cole's accident meant that she had a great deal of paperwork to fill out for Eco-Observers. With any luck Marcus was on the phone with them now. Not to mention filing a report with the authorities, if she was right about the lubricant. First, though, she needed to check one thing. She made a show of shuffling through paperwork for a bit longer, then gave an audible sigh and nipped back into the main tent. She skimmed the whiteboards and saw that her name was still on the shower rota for, she glanced at her watch, about thirty minutes ago.

The thought chilled her. If someone had deliberately done that to the shower, they weren't after Cole. Someone was after her. A chemical test to confirm the presence of the oil would take some time, Kea reasoned, before she was struck by the sheer ludicrousness of the concept. *Death by shower? What was the point? Who would be stupid enough to even try something like that?*

It was then Kea saw Tony, walking away from a tent partially hidden behind the line of bushes. He hadn't seen her, or at least she didn't think so. It looked like he was headed for the visitor center, but his motions were furtive.

He's definitely up to something, she thought, remembering his actions the night before. She hurried after him, clutching the clipboard to her chest, relieved to be doing something at last, but still no closer to understanding what was going on.

Chapter 16

KEA TRAILED Tony to the visitor center but lost sight of him in a churning busload of tourists. She used the opportunity to call Eco-Observers via the center's phone. It turned out that Marcus had indeed already alerted them and she was assured that the medical center in Kirkjubæjarklaustur was expecting Cole. The voice of the staff member who helped her fill out the accident form was very soothing. Paperwork rarely had that effect on Kea, so she knew that she must have been rattled to the core.

She used the visitor center's fax machine to send the completed form to headquarters. Waiting for the confirmation receipt to print out, she sat in a chair at the front desk, watching the tourists mill in and out. The mundane atmosphere made all the drama of this morning somehow seem surreal.

Did anything happen at all? The thought stuck in her head for some reason. She pulled up the number of the police on her phone but paused before dialing.

Paranoid, she thought. *I'm just being paranoid. This sort of thing doesn't happen. I just have a feeling and some oil.*

"A smoking gun," she muttered to herself, "it is not. Maybe it's time to give up." Reflexively, she glanced at her watch.

Oh crap.

Realizing the time, Kea sprinted out of the visitor center. The research hut was a quarter mile west, and when she reached it, she was panting for air. Staggering to the entrance of the unisex bathroom, she saw the *'Closed'* sign and swore. She stumbled through the door, nearly bowling over the cleaning woman.

"Hello?" The young woman, alarmed at Kea's entrance, took a step behind her cart.

Kea peered over the woman's shoulder. Too late. The shower stall had been scrubbed clean, no sign of blood or oil. The tiles almost sparkled. Any evidence had been washed down the drain.

Now I really will seem crazy.

"Can I help you?" The cleaner asked. Her words were hesitant, as if addressing a child that might burst into tears at any moment.

"Sorry." Kea took a long breath, forcing herself to calm down. "I just thought..." She looked at the slight blond woman, her tiny frame dwarfed by the cleaning cart, her expression one of confusion. "I thought I left my bag," she finished.

***

The cooling taste of the vanilla ice cream gave Kea something to focus on that was deliciously real. After slugging back to the visitor center, she had hit the café for a snack and a chance to think. *If I'm going insane*, she reasoned, *calories are the least of my problems.*

Sitting behind the counter while Ísadóra was on a smoke break, Kea stared absently at the phone again, her mind in a fog. The noise of the tourists and children wandering through the visitor center was familiar, reassuring. Her gaze lingered on the campground map taped to the desk. The research hut with the shower was on the far western edge, she noticed, just off the map. The entrance to the shower meant that anyone could have gone in and out unobserved.

Kea considered the implications. While it was possible that Bonnie, the person before her on the rota, had slicked the shower, it seemed unlikely, unless she was dealing with the dumbest criminal in history. Leaving one's name on the whiteboard screamed a bit too much of '*I did it,*' than a convincing double bluff. She scanned the map again, first studying the EO campground, then letting her gaze spiral out toward the edges. She paused at a campsite located close to the tree line where she had seen Tony loitering earlier, marked with the letters '*TJ*'.

Maybe Tony's not schtupping Ísadóra after all, Kea thought. *He wouldn't really be stupid enough to rent out a separate campsite under his own name, would he? Unless Ísadóra knew. Were they both using the tent for said schtupping? What on earth is he playing at?*

"Why is everything always about sex?!" Kea asked the room.

The tourists paused in their conversations to stare at her.

Kea hurried out as fast as she could, no longer caring what anyone thought.

***

"You rat bastard," Kea breathed. She stood in the middle of Tony's second tent, staring at its contents. She hadn't broken in exactly. She had knocked. Lightly. On the fabric. Then, seeing that only half-inch had separated the zipper from the securing end, she had hesitated from opening it, worried about invading his privacy. Until she saw what was inside.

She heard Tony step into the tent behind her.

"What are you..." Tony's voice drained away.

Kea grabbed the front of his shirt with one hand and jabbed her finger in his face with the other. "You filthy little turd."

"I don't know what you're talking about." Tony's eyes narrowed.

She was floored. He didn't even have the decency to look apologetic. She waved around at the tent floor. It was covered with sample bags and maps. "You're stealing our data!"

Tony shrugged. "I just took some samples to analyze later. I'll still have to do all the work."

"You're using our funding to acquire samples," Kea yelled. She remembered the GPS transects she had seen him doing that first afternoon along the margin of Skaftafellsjökull. "And doing surveys... you were going to publish without us."

Tony shook his head. "Don't be-"

"Christ," Kea cut him off. "You really are Marcus' protégé. To think, this whole time I thought you were acting weird cause you were shagging Ísadóra."

"Ah..." Tony averted his gaze.

"Oh, for Christ's sake..." Kea groaned, praying Ísadóra's father didn't find out. Not to mention Tony's girlfriend back home. "This day just keeps getting better and better."

"It's not that big a deal," Tony protested feebly.

"You stupid prat!" Kea seethed. "You know, I actually thought you were the killer! And all this time, you've just been," she picked up a sample bag and tore it apart, scattering the contents throughout the tent in an explosion of black dust, "screwing around!"

Silence followed, punctuated only by the rattle of tiny pebbles on the canvas floor of the tent. Tony stared at her, and for the first time, his expression became one of honest bemusement.

"Ummm..." Tony met her eyes for the first time. "What killer?"

***

"Are you going to tell me what's going on?" Tony asked. "I feel like I'm missing something here."

"Welcome to my world." Kea desperately wanted to hit him. As they jogged across the campground, Tony followed in her wake, firing

195

question after question. She ignored most of his babbling, answering only the bare minimum. An idea was forming in her head. She sprinted the last few meters, the grass slippery under her feet from the nonstop drizzle of the rain. She slid onto her knees, tore at the zipper, and shoved herself through the flap. She grabbed her laptop. The battery was dead. "Hell."

"What is it?" Tony asked from outside of the tent. Kea ignored him. In the dim light, she rummaged through her sleeping bag, clothes, and assorted mess of candy wrappers. Finally, she spied Zoë's memory stick peeking out from beneath a pile of socks. Grabbing it, she scooted backward out of the tent and turned to Tony. "Your laptop, now."

***

In contrast, Tony's tent was immaculate.

As if Kea needed another reason to hit him.

She knelt in front of his laptop but paused before handing the data stick to him. It was still possible that Tony had tried to kill her, and that this data stick was exactly what he was after. She almost hoped it was true because she was looking for a reason to rip his throat out. Even as the laptop hummed to life, she knew she would be disappointed. Tony was manipulative, greedy, and self-serving, but she doubted he had the balls to kill anyone. She handed him the thumb drive. "Here."

Tony slid the drive into his computer and, sensing her mood, wisely said nothing. She pointed to the folder labeled *Remus*. He launched the .mp4 file and maximized the viewer window. They sat back on their haunches, watching as the screen filled with a sooty white expanse of ice crystals. After a few moments, the drone lifted into the air and Kea could see Zoë and the rest of her team members standing around the launch site. The camera tilted as the drone banked, before zipping across the front of the glacier to begin mapping its pre-programmed transects.

"I've seen this bit already," Kea said impatiently. "Go forward."

The screen flickered with stuttering images of the outwash plain and the glacier margin. Lakes, icebergs, stream channels, and deformed ice-melt topography flitted on the screen. The grid flight pattern meant this scene was repeated several times as the drone mapped the area. Recognizing the portion of the video where she had discovered the section that had been newly excavated by the flood, she said, "Slow it down, just a bit. I haven't seen past this bit."

Tony nudged the controls and they waited as the drone painstakingly continued its flight path. "What am I supposed to be looking for?"

Kea folded her arms across her knees and rested her chin in her hands. "I honestly have no idea."

Tony looked sideways at her. "I'm still a bit weirded out you thought I killed Bruce."

"I'm still not sure you didn't," she muttered quietly.

"I've got two eyewitnesses," he continued. "And my dad is a great lawyer."

"Two?" Kea asked.

"Marcus was with me the whole time with that friggin' drill," Tony said, his facial expressions communicating how much he had enjoyed that experience. "And Jon."

"Jon?" She closed her eyes.

"Yeah," Tony said. "He was trying to help us fix it the whole time. Nice guy."

Kea shook her head. "I really am an ass."

"Eh?" Tony asked.

"Nothing." Kea shook her head. "I just have an apology to make."

"Yeah," Tony grunted. "Still waiting for mine."

The video showed nothing other than muddy streams and slumping melt out terrain. The same scene played out over and over as the drone completed its grid across the field site. While the geomorphology was gorgeous, and certainly the best imagery they had ever had of the region, it was not, she considered, worth killing for.

She had Tony play until the viewer window faded to black and the file reached its end. The Replay icon pulsed questioningly on the center of the screen.

"Do you want to see it again?" he asked, obviously hoping that she wouldn't. His body language suggested that he would be much happier if she got out of his tent and left him alone. "Should I try Romulus?"

Kea shrugged. "Didn't that one crash right away? I'm not even sure Zoë added the file to the drive."

Tony clicked through the folder. "It's here, but it's only two megs. There's probably not more than a couple minutes of footage." He pressed *Play,* and another grit-filled expanse filled the screen as the camera zoomed upward from the launch pad. Then it rotated, flying northward up the glacier. It didn't get very far before it wobbled like a drunk seagull and plummeted down onto the ice and the video cut out.

"That was..." Tony trailed off.

"Anticlimactic," Kea finished for him.

"What did Zoë say happened to it?" he asked.

"Lost signal, or a sudden updraft from off the glacier knocked it out of whack." She had promised to retrieve the drone from the ice today, but that depended on being able to locate it. She reached out and played the scene again slowly, frame by frame, hoping to get a better idea of where it had crashed.

She advanced through the frames once more, pausing as Zoë's face appeared on the screen during launch. There was nothing abnormal around her or the rest of the team and no one appeared to be missing a safety vest. She used the few moments of video to examine the slope of the ice as the drone headed northward, noting the patterns of drainage as they flowed across the ice in twisting rivulets.

She played the video again, then paused just before it began to wobble. The camera was pointed up-glacier. If she squinted, she could make out the blurred red dots of her 'Apple' team in the wildlands, but nothing else. Depending on how high the drone was flying, and how strong the wind was, she would have to search a half a kilometer area to find it.

Tony shook his head. "Not gonna lie. I was kinda hoping for a video of Gary shoving Bruce down a moulin."

She shot him a stern glare.

"What?" Tony protested. "The guy gives me the creeps."

"If every creepy guy was a murderer, our entire Physics Department would be behind bars," Kea said despite herself. "Gary wasn't anywhere near them. He was busy nearly dying with me. Besides, I know Gary was wearing a vest."

"Vest?" Tony asked.

"Whoever knocked Bruce into that moulin, I think either Bruce took their vest with them or at least damaged it to the point they had to get rid of it as evidence." She ignored his bewildered expression and turned back to the screen, searching for something, anything. If she couldn't find anything on this drive, then she had no idea what her attacker was after. She counted the red blobs. "Six in the valley," she muttered, "and on the rise... seven. That's not right. Or maybe it is, I can't see everyone, the topography is crazy here."

"What is it?" Tony peered closer at the screen.

"There weren't..." She couldn't discern faces on the images, only the blobs of the yellow high-visibility vests and red jackets they all wore. She counted again. The numbers didn't add up.

Two blobs too many.

"Give me that," She pointed at Tony's backpack, which was tucked neatly against the wall. Waving aside his protests, she dug out the clipboard all the team leads carried. She flipped through the maps, trying to find the field plan. "Where did you put the ablation stakes?"

Tony lifted the back page and pulled out a photocopy of a topographic map. Coordinates were marked with little plus marks in red pencil. "Here, there, and here."

Kea estimated the position of her apple team.

Too far away. Couldn't be them.

She felt deflated, frustrated again. "That's it? Your certain you didn't go any further west?"

"Err..." Tony frowned at the map. "We did, but the rig blew out on the last hole, remember. We never put down a stake."

Kea froze. "Where was that?"

Tony waved a finger uncertainly over an area half a kilometer away from the last position. "Somewhere over there. We didn't take a marker, it seemed pointless. Anyway, we lost signal."

She examined the relative position on the map. "That means that your team was only a few minutes' walk away from the northern end of my team's field area!"

"Yeah, but we never went down there," Tony protested.

"*You* didn't," she pointed at the blobs, "but maybe someone did. How long were you guys fiddling around trying to get the rig to work?"

He shrugged. "I'm not sure. Close to an hour."

Kea needed him to be certain. "All of the volunteers were right next to you the whole time?"

"Like I said before," Tony reminded her, "some went exploring and taking pictures. Some went to go to the bathroom. I was more focused on getting the rig working again. You know how Marcus gets. I only remember where Jon was because he was helping with the cable."

Kea could see that Tony was flustered. He didn't like talking about how he and Marcus should have been paying more attention to the volunteers, to Bruce. He obviously didn't want to have that conversation again. Instead, he pointed to the collection of blobs on the screen. "That could be anyone."

"Yeah," Kea agreed. *It might even*, she thought, *have been someone from my team, potentially doubling the list of suspects.* She only had Nadia's word on the whole Derek-Reynard canoodling bit as well. "We don't know who they are, but at least now we know where they were going."

"We?" Tony asked. "Gone a bit royal all of a sudden."

"You're coming with me." Kea glared at him, her nostrils flaring as if daring him to question her. "I want you where I can see you." She scooted out of the tent on her knees, painfully aware that he was staring at her backside. She felt her anger rising, which did nothing to help prepare her for what she had to do next.

***

"Could I have a word?" Kea watched as the tent's flap unzipped in irregular, jerky motions. Jon stuck out his head, blinking in the light. His hair was tousled up into spikes, and tattoos snaked down across his bare torso, disappearing out of sight into the depths of his sleeping bag.

Kea did her best to keep her eyes firmly on his and not contemplate the unseen part of the tattoos. She hadn't expected him to still be asleep. "Sorry about this…" Having never been in this position before, she wasn't quite sure of the appropriate phrasing. "I just wanted to apologize for, you know, the whole 'accusing you of murder' thing."

Jon blinked a bit more then peered around sleepily. "Um. Yeah. Okay." He inhaled a deep breath, flexing as he did so.

Kea found her gaze straying southward again. "That aside," she continued, "I need to ask a favor…"

***

Kea stood on the cliff, looking out across the depression to the dark edge of Skeiðarárjökull, which rested across the horizon like a storm cloud. As the wind blew against her face, its breath was flecked with minute specks of grit that peppered her eyes, causing her to blink and weep. In her mind, she could picture the depression filled with the raging floodwaters of the 1996 event. She could imagine the shifting forms of tumbling ice blocks as they crashed into each other like billiard balls. She could even hear the bellowing cracks that would have rocked the valley as the flood ripped through the ice margin.

She knew the facts, having typed them repeatedly into every paper. She could recite from memory that the torrential flood had covered seven hundred and fifty square kilometers, with a flow that had a peak discharge of fifty thousand cubic meters per second, transporting nearly two hundred million tons of sediment.

She could picture all those events, here in this wonderful valley.

What she could not imagine, however, was what Bruce had been thinking when he died. Or worse, what could have driven someone to kill him. That level of despair, or that amount of hatred, was simply beyond her conception.

"Are we really doing this?" Tony stood beside her at the edge of the embankment.

"I promised Zoë I'd get her drone back." Kea glanced at her watch. It was two in the afternoon. Plenty of time. "Plus, my equipment's out there as well."

She scanned the outwash plain with a pair of binoculars. The sandur and the glacier were both devoid of any signs of life. The sun was still bright, but clouds scudded across the ice, hugging low to the surface. Judging by the weather, this may be their last chance on the glacier for at least another year.

"Don't worry," she said, forcing herself to sound optimistic. "We'll be back in time for tea."

"I meant, are you sure about him?" Tony nodded at Jon, who was beside the jeep, lacing up his hiking boots.

"We can't carry the MRS and the other gear off the ice by ourselves. He's the only other person left in camp that we can place at the time Bruce died," Kea reasoned. "You vouched for him, remember?"

"But he's with T3," Tony grumbled.

"That's exactly why I asked him to come." She hefted the puffin staff and took a few sample strides. It was difficult to set up a good pace, but in a pinch, she could at least thwack someone with it. She folded it back up and clipped it to her belt. "I want answers."

"Do you trust him?" Tony continued in a low voice.

"Nope," she replied breezily. "I don't trust you either, but I'd rather have you where I can see you." She moved to the trailer, unlocked the toolkit, and extracted the compressor. She pulled out some flares and tucked them into her pack as well. "I left our route with Ísadóra and Marcus, well, on his voice mail. They should be back in a few hours." *If Cole really is okay*, she reminded herself.

"You sure you didn't see anyone out there?" Tony hefted his pack and strapped the waistband tight, keeping a watchful eye on Jon as he did so.

"Not unless they parachuted in." She waved her hands around the empty dirt parking area beside the Háöldukvísl dam. "Come on, let's get this over with." She started down the hill, kicking up little clouds of dust with her boots. "Otherwise, I'm going to have to find a creative way to come up with six thousand dollars to replace Zoë's drone."

"The MRS is worth at least fifty grand," Tony's voice drifted down to her.

The enthusiasm in his tone made Kea wish she had throttled him. "Yes, Tony, thanks for that." She watched as he bounded ahead of her, his leaps gouging out huge explosions of the soft sands.

"Why on earth did you ever pick him?" Jon asked. He was taking small, measured steps down from the parking area behind her.

"In theory, for his knowledge of igneous petrology." Kea watched as Tony made a final giant leap off the slope, struck his foot against a small boulder, and landed in a heap. Upside down, he flailed about like an upended turtle as he tried to right himself. "And comic relief, apparently."

Jon snorted. "This is gonna' be a long day."

"Indeed," she agreed. "And I didn't."

"Didn't what?" he asked.

"Pick Tony. He's Marcus' prodigy," she replied, moving farther downslope. "Julie's my grad student."

"So, you do have good taste." Jon sounded flirtatious for the first time since she had accused him of murder.

"From time to time," she said with a tight grin. Below them, Tony was slowly pulling himself up off the ground, unharmed. "Looks like he's vertical again."

The rest of the hike across the rocky floodplain was spent in silence as they focused on navigating the terrain down the terraces and around the vast kettle holes. The lake crossing was uneventful, the silence of the glacier punctuated only by grunts of exertion as they took turns with the oars. Beaching the craft, they secured it to a boulder before continuing their hike up the esker and out onto the snout of Skeiðarárjökull.

During their march across the plain, Kea had kept both men in front of her. Now that they were on the glacier, she led at an angle, keeping them both in view whenever possible. She didn't think either of them would try anything, not now that everyone knew they were out on the ice. She did not, however, want to put temptation in anyone's way by going near any convenient crevasses. She made sure to walk on the other side of Tony, so if Jon did try anything, he would have to go through Tony first.

Kea kept her gaze on the ice around her, searching for anything that might be out of the norm. As she walked, each step crunched loudly under her boots, the harsh sounds muffled by the winds that burned her cheeks. She followed the route they had taken on their first day on the ice until they arrived at the point where the team had split into groups.

"Which way?" Tony asked.

She pulled out her topographic map. Heading further west would eventually bring them to the wildlands, home of the twisting canyons and apples. Team Kea. Heading north would allow them to follow the team that installed the ablation stakes. Team Marcus. Or, as Kea had christened it, Team Bruce. Somewhere in the middle lay poor Romulus.

Hoping that following in Bruce's path might provide insight into his final moments, she pointed north and waved for Tony to take point. "Lay on, MacDuff."

Another hour passed before they reached the third stake and stopped for a snack. She squatted on the heels of her boots, sitting as close to Jon as she dared. The sky spat unenthusiastically on them while they ate. Tony, leery of them both, sat at a distance, noisily chomping an apple.

"Thanks for coming with us." Kea cradled her flask between her knees.

"I'd feel safer if Erik were here," Jon said around a mouthful of a protein bar.

"Sorry." Kea hoped her apology sounded sincere. "I wasn't comfortable risking one volunteer, let alone two." *Plus*, she thought, *I can vouch for you at the time of Bruce's death; I have no idea what Erik was up to.* "But thanks again. With no Marcus, we wouldn't have any hope of getting the kit back."

"Look," Jon pulled off his hat and ran his fingers through his tangled mass of hair. "About your friend. I've been there…" He looked up at her, his ruffled locks and wide eyes making him look like a lost child caught in the rain. "But don't use it to push everyone else away. It won't help."

Kea nodded. She wanted to tell him about the ticket receipt, about what happened to her at the river, about Cole and the oil, but she found she still didn't really trust him. Not yet.

Once they finished their snack and packed up, they headed out toward the last location on Tony's map, the site where the ablation drill had failed.

Kea quickly grew weary of the sight of Tony's behind as he trudged across the glacier ahead of her, but there was little else to see. The surface of the ice was far from flat but was folded together into an undulating expanse of rumpled black and white hills that obscured everything else. Jon caught her staring at his rear too often, so she focused on her feet, taking care not to slip on the wet ice.

After a good twenty minutes of walking, she noticed Tony pausing repeatedly. She increased her pace to match his. "Are we lost?"

"I'm looking for a three-inch hole drilled into the ice with no marker, no lat-long, and no GPS signal." Tony smacked the GPS device in his hand. "It was somewhere in this area, I swear." He waved up at the western edge of the valley walls that loomed above them. "We were between those two ridges, I remember that. We're very close."

Jon nodded but offered nothing in the way of guidance.

Kea poked her head out from under her hood so she could see the screen of the GPS unit. The readings flickered in spastic twitches, the digits unreadable.

Just like mine did when I measured the stream channels that day.

"I think you're right." She pointed a kilometer down the glacier toward where her team had been chasing apples. "Let's head down that way. Spread out, let me know if you see anything unusual."

They started walking down the glacier, keeping twenty meters apart. The rain increased, changing from a light spatter to a full-on downpour, rapidly decreasing visibility and making each step treacherous.

Kea tried to imagine the scene as Bruce had seen it on that day when it had been sunny and warm: with the bright blue sky above and the crystalline expanse of the glacier glittering underfoot.

Where would I go if I were Bruce? What was he thinking? Did he want to be as far away from the group as possible? Did he want to take a picture, to find a cliff to jump off, or just a quiet place to pee?

In the end, she realized she would never know. She settled for simply walking, letting gravity guide her down the most obvious, and safest path, down the ice.

Perhaps, she reflected, *Bruce had done the same.*

***

As they moved across the ice, the sound of water became louder, finally building into a roar. It took Kea a moment to realize that the rain was still only a drizzle. The noise was coming from up ahead, drawing her closer. Somehow, Kea wasn't surprised when she found herself standing near the northern ledge of the vast moulin she had found the day Bruce died. Water poured off the ice ledge to cascade down into the maw of a gaping dark hole, its center obscured by mist. She carefully skirted the edge of the abyss and peered into the darkness, listening to the sound of the falling water. If she had seen a bloody mark the last time she was here, it was gone now.

Wait, was that a scuff mark by her feet, she wondered, *and another there?*

She shook her head. She was no tracker. This landscape was so dynamic, its surface could change on a daily basis. If there had been any activity, she doubted if there was any way she could detect it.

She spied the black, insect-like stick still wedged in the ice. Using the walking staff to brace herself, she was able to reach down into the moulin and pull the object toward her. Examining it in her hand, it was not organic, nor igneous in origin. Definitely manufactured.

"You think it happened here?" Tony joined her by the moulin.

"It certainly could have," Kea tucked the object into a sample back in her pocket, out of sight. She shifted a couple of paces away from him, just to be safe. She tried to recall the location of the moulin on the aerial photographs in relation to the lake. "There are several moulins in this area and numerous crevasses, but maybe…"

She imagined Bruce standing here, looking over the outwash plain, the shimmering hint of the ocean beyond. To the west, cliffs loomed above the edge of the glacier while to the south lay the hidden valleys and canyons of the wildlands, obscured beneath a cloak of fog and rain. Along the snout of the glacier, the lakes shimmered like pools of dark obsidian, reflecting the darkness of the clouds above. *What had he been doing out here?*

"I've no idea..." she answered herself aloud. She stared down at the wildlands, regretting that they hadn't come via that way. It would have saved a great deal of time. For all their wandering across the ice, they hadn't, as far as she could tell, discovered anything. Certainly, no sign of Romulus.

"I can't see anything." Tony walked carefully away from the edge of the moulin. "There's almost no point in this weather."

Kea was certain that he would follow that shortly with '*Let's go home,*' a refrain he'd been chanting for the last twenty minutes. She knelt, examining the canyons of the wildlands below. The sinuous twists and turns of the streams that down-cut into the ice created an almost impenetrable maze, but her eye was caught by a flash of color. Her flow meter.

Bruce would have been able to see me.

"Maybe Bruce wasn't headed back to the drill, but was headed toward us," Kea breathed. "Toward me." She turned and looked westward, where the glacier sloped away from view, its surface stuttered by elongated crevasses. She headed along the edge of the wildlands, with Tony and Jon following close behind.

As they moved westward, the swooping arcs of ice grew steeper, the crevasses wider, extending up to two meters in width and at least thirty long. The chaotic topography forced them to walk up and down their irregular lengths until they could cross. The rain fell in gray curtains so thick, that if a crevasse hadn't opened up before her and made her pause, she would never have seen what she didn't know she was looking for.

"I thought Romulus was red..." Tony's voice trailed off beside her.

Wedged into the lip of the crevasse, where the glacier ice pinched together, lay an oblong object less than two meters in length, its matt gray form was twisted like a giant piece of fusilli pasta. Its skin glistened in the rain, almost reptilian. The object's narrow length and unusual form made it invisible against the dirt riddled surface of the glacier. A gash had been torn along its length, exposing innards of silver and black. The winds pulled at its fragile form, threatening to tear it away from the grip of the crevasse.

It almost looks alive, Kea thought as she clipped the walking staff into her frame pack to free her hands and pull out her GPS. Watching as its display flickered uncontrollably, she retrieved a paper map from inside her jacket and read off their approximate coordinates to Tony. As she watched, he used his phone to enter them into a text message addressed to Julie and Marcus and hit *Send*. The hourglass icon spun on the screen as it attempted - and failed - to connect to the network.

"Guessing that's not a coincidence," Tony observed, staring at the object. "What is it?"

She stepped closer, leaning down carefully. While the rain had started to ease, falling in intermittent gusts, the thing's exoskeleton trembled with every breeze and raindrop, making it difficult to discern any markings, although she spied a tracery of fine circuitry running along its skin.

"Well, it's not alien." She examined the area where the surface ruptured, noting the way the skin seemed to bleed a viscous blue fluid. "At least, I don't think so." Leaning out carefully, she could almost reach it. "Jon, what do you think?"

Studying his face, she noted that he didn't appear as confused as they did. If anything, he looked worried.

Not a coincidence indeed.

Jon stood silently beside them, as if deciding what he should say. She shifted another meter away from him, her shields up. She was surprised when he put a hand to his forehead and groaned.

"It's not supposed to be here," Jon answered finally. "This... this shouldn't have happened."

"Is that yours?" Tony pointed at the thing.

"No," Jon shook his head. "We don't make those. We don't make anything."

"That's not an answer," Kea snapped. "What is it?"

"Suborbital drone," Jon answered. "Basically, an experimental communications relay. Sort of, except it's not."

"Could you be less specific?" Tony asked in exasperation.

"It's more of a cuckoo..." Jon trailed off, unwilling to divulge anything more.

A cuckoo? Kea struggled to remember her biology classes. The cuckoo laid eggs in other birds' nests. When the egg hatches, it tosses out the other eggs and chicks from the nest. Her mind leaped back to the tattoo on Max's arm, the image of the ant on the blade of grass. A parasite controlling its brain. "A lancet," she breathed. "It infects and controls the brain. But the brain of what? Other drones?"

Jon looked at her in surprise. "Yeah," he nodded. "It infiltrates different communication systems of the Face-Google fleets up there." He waved up at the sky. "We developed the software for the chip, but Corvis built the components. It allows the drone to pass as one of them, taking in and reading the data – or changing the data, depending on what the customer wants. It can even interfere with the commsats entirely, taking out a whole network, if you decide you want to take down the competition. Plus, if you're trying to track it, it can jam or scramble any signals in the region."

"Which is why our tools are all screwed up." Tony tucked away his useless phone.

"The drone's batteries should be nearly dead by now," Jon said sadly. "Looks like the solar collectors were damaged during the crash."

Kea leaned back, steeling herself to run.

Was Jon telling them all of this because he was going to dispose of them?

Jon's eyes were wide open, his hands trembling. He didn't appear threatening. If anything, he seemed afraid. Still, at least he was talking for a change.

"If you didn't build it," she asked carefully, "what does T3 have to do with it? Why is it here?"

Jon shook his head. "I told you, I don't know why it's here. We just designed the software. Corvis did the hardware, they never let us anywhere near the thing."

"And Bruce? This was his project?" Kea asked.

"Our team built the nav systems and the infiltration-ware. This isn't the first one to bite it." Jon frowned. Leaning carefully over the crevasse, he stretched out an arm to the device, but it was still out of reach. "Bruce told us it went down in the North Atlantic, lost at sea..."

"Is that thing why you're all here?" Tony asked angrily. "Why didn't you just go get it yourselves? Why do you need to drag us into this?"

Jon stepped carefully as if herding a terrified cat, watching the strange form tremble in the stiff wind. "I swear, I didn't know it was here. They said it was lost, irretrievable. Believe me, you don't want to be near this thing."

"Why? What's inside?" Her stomach clenched at the thought of accidentally exposing her team, or herself, to radiation or whatever else the thing might be carrying.

"It's not dangerous, in itself," Jon replied cryptically. "It's who might be after it."

"For God's sake!" Kea, afraid that she would start thumping someone, rammed her fists into her jacket's pockets. "Can you just tell us-"

"Look out!" Tony cried.

The device leaped out of the crevasse and darted straight at Kea's face. She yelped, swatting it away in terror. Frantic, she ripped it out of her hair. The torpedo-shaped projectile bounded away, skittering across the ice. It traveled about thirty meters before finally nose-diving into another crevasse. The rear portion of the drone poked up above the ice, its tremulous wings fluttering in the winds, as if ready to take flight again at any moment.

Calmer now that the drone was a safe distance away, Kea discovered that her hand was still tangled in her hair, her fingers stuck to a heavy, sticky mass. Using her free hand, she put the small stick into her pocket and gently teased the goo-encrusted object out of her tangled hair.

"I think I can reach it," Tony called as he and Jon trotted after the drone.

"Wait," she called after them, but her voice was lost in the wind. In her hand, she held a strange black globule, its glutinous surface matted with strands of her hair. She must have torn it out of the drone when it hit her. It was only a few centimeters long, but glistened with oil, or moisture. Repulsed, she resisted the urge to toss the thing onto the ice and mash it with her boot.

Corvis built this drone, she reasoned, *Bruce came here for this, and someone wants it back very badly. Any part of it could be valuable.*

Wrinkling her face in disgust, she tucked the thing into her jacket pocket in a bag with the black stick then joined the others at the side of another narrow crevasse.

"That," Tony pointed across a series of dark fractures in the ice, "is going to be a pain."

She was surprised at how tiny and frail the drone appeared. *No wonder neither the drones nor the search team had spotted it.* "How did you even expect to find it out here?"

"We didn't," Jon reminded her. "But maybe Bruce knew it was here." He seemed to consider the idea for a moment before dismissing it. "Honestly, I don't think he did. He can't have had any clue. He would have said... but with Corvis showing up here, I think we all suspected something was going on."

"But why not just get it yourselves?" Kea seethed. "Why did you have to involve us?"

"I told you, *we* didn't," Jon pleaded. "If we wanted it, we would have just landed it at our test site in Arizona. My guess is someone wanted to make it look like a crash, retrieve it, and sell to the highest bidder. They probably didn't count on how difficult it would be to find it here, let alone get across the margin to look for it." He kicked at the ice like an angry child, knocking chunks into the crevasse. "Corvis was working on a portable remote guidance system that could have helped them find it, but we only saw the schematics. We didn't have one."

Kea eyed the dark shadows that lurked within the crevasse. "I don't want to die trying to reach that thing. Besides, Zoë will kill me if I don't find Romulus but... hang on a sec..." Maybe it was the cold, maybe it was the effort of processing so much new information, but her thoughts were sliding slowly like treacle through her head making it difficult to piece everything together. "What did this remote look like?"

"Small, black, about so long," Jon said, measuring a few inches between his fingers. "Look, we can't stay here. Trust me, we must leave. They'll come for it."

"Who's they?" She felt the outline of the stick in her pocket. She must have launched the device when she clenched it. She gently squeezed it, then paused, worried the drone might leap into the air.

Wait a minute.

"Did you say this thing may have been screwing up readings in the entire area for more than a month?" she asked.

Jon nodded.

She felt her stomach convulse in panic. "We have to get out of here. Now."

"Look," Tony leaned into her, and pointed along the crevasse toward the drone. "All we have to do is cross up there where it merges, then come down the other-"

Her head exploded with light as Tony's head crashed into hers. She felt a tremendous weight slam into her chest that knocked her straight into the gaping crevasse. She reached out to Jon, her hands grabbing his jacket for support, realizing too late that they were both falling into the darkness below.

Chapter 17

WRONG WAY around! Wrong way around!

That way up! That way up!

Kea's body sent a torrent of messages to her brain, overloading it.

Breathe! Breathe! Just breathe!

Calm. Stay calm.

In.

Out.

Warm water trickled along her temples, slithering across her skin and puddling in her ears. Her heartbeat thudded inside her head, making it impossible to think, to focus.

Upside down! Wrong way around! Upside down! Get right side up!

The impulse to panic was overwhelming. Her frame pack had saved her, digging into the opposing sides of the crevasse, its straps pinning her shoulder against an icy wall. Her glasses had been knocked off her face in the fall, leaving her dislocated from the world around her. Although nearly blind, she could hear the echo of the water falling into the emptiness below, eager to consume her.

Stop.

Focus.

What else?

Not alone…

Something else had halted her fall. She could make out splotches of red polyester and a haze of pink. As her eyes began to adjust to the light, her cold fingers pressed against the wet slickness of a jacket. She traced the sleeve until she reached the collar. Gently, she pulled at it, slowly turning the face toward her.

The pink blur resolved itself into Tony's head, his neck bent at an unnatural angle, his eyes wide. Empty. Lifeless.

Retching, she pushed herself away, swaying back underneath the trickle of warm water that dripped on her head. She let out a long breath. Tony's pack, wedged into the ice beneath them, had helped cushion her fall, but she may have killed him in the process.

Not now. Not now, don't do this now. Crying. Stop crying. Stop-stopstop.

The chattering of her teeth alerted her to the fact that her body was shivering uncontrollably.

How long have I been here?

She didn't remember blacking out. She tilted her head up, shielding her eyes against the gray glare of the sky, and found herself looking up at Jon.

He was dangling above her, rivulets of his warm blood dripping onto her face. She jerked back, frantically wiping her face in horror. She clapped a hand over her mouth to stop herself from screaming.

Was their attacker still up there, listening? Was there more than one?

Holding her breath, the fear of what waited for her above and the certain death below threatened to drive her insane. She focused the pain that burned in her shoulder, the strap of her pack still biting into her flesh.

Listen. Listen. Listen.

The rain. She could hear the patter of the falling rain as it trickled down the sides of the crevasse.

Nothing else.

She was alone.

Squinting up at Jon, Kea could discern a lurid red gash arcing across his forehead. The gray sky beyond him was just a vague smear. Near-sighted, she couldn't clearly see anything unless it was less than a few feet away.

Like Jon's face.

Shuddering, she closed her eyes and tried to steady her breathing. She had no idea how much time had passed, but it was clear that if she stayed here much longer, she would die. If she went up and her attacker was still there, she would also likely die.

Decisions, decisions.

She listened and waited.

Rain continued to fall in a steady drizzle. Wind gusted through the crevasse every few minutes, as if the glacier below was exhaling. It was impossible to hear much of anything else.

Hopefully, if the attacker was still close by, they can't hear anything either.

Very slowly, she pulled her knees into her chest and stretched them out again, placing her boots on either side of the crevasse that narrowed below her. Gingerly, she shifted her back against the ice, easing the pressure off her throbbing shoulder. Using her good arm, she released the strap and slid out of her frame pack. Pulling the small daypack free, she looped its strap around her neck, careful to avoid her injured shoulder. She unzipped the main flap of the frame pack and extracted items she thought might come in handy, including the emergency blanket and compass. The walking stick appeared undamaged, so she clipped it to her belt.

She focused on the task at hand, trying not to think about her trembling fingers or the infinity that seemed to stretch below. Or Tony's body growing cold beneath her.

Stop! Just stop. There's nothing you can do. Just get out. Just get the hell out of here. Get help.

She edged a couple feet upward so she could reach Jon. Feeling for a pulse, she was delighted to find his skin still warm to the touch. Pulling up his eyelids elicited no response, but he was very definitely alive. She took out a large bandage from the pack. Using her teeth to tear it open, she pressed it against the wound on his forehead, hoping it was worse than it looked. She hated to leave him, but if she didn't go for help, they could both die down here.

Using her feet and knees, Kea edged her way along the crevasse, out from under Jon and away from Tony. She didn't - *couldn't* - look back. She extended one knee forward, shifted her good shoulder a few inches, then moved the other knee. Knee, shoulder, knee. Repeat. As she crawled along, every motion felt like her shoulder was being stabbed with an ice pick, but she forced herself to keep going.

After what felt like an eternity, her knees raw and her legs quaking with fatigue, she hoped that she had gone far enough. Sparing a glance back at the blob that was Jon and Tony, she estimated that she had only moved about ten meters. Enough, she hoped, that if she showed her head again above the ice, no one would think to look in her direction.

Shifting so that her back was against the ice, she pushed her feet against the opposing wall, knees bent. Very slowly, feeling like she was the Grinch trying to shimmy up a chimney, she began to climb. She judged that she only had to ascend about three meters, but as the gap grew wider, she found herself pausing to rest more frequently. Because of her exertions, her teeth had stopped chattering at least. Although she wasn't confident that was a good sign.

Finally reaching the surface, she inched her head above the ice. The sky was darker now, and the rain poured down heavily, angled by the strong winds. Off to her left, she saw a bright blotch of red.

A jacket.

She ducked down again, waiting. After a minute, hearing no sign of approach, she dared to look again. In the distance, someone, the red blob, had their back to her.

Pulling herself up until she could rest an elbow on the ice, she took some weight off her stiff legs. The figure was about fifty meters away. Judging by the size, it looked like a man, crouching over the alien object that appeared to still be stuck in a crevasse. Squinting, she could only discern that the man's back was to her.

Stay or go? Either hide and wait for him to leave and pray he wouldn't come back to finish the job. Or run.

Now or never.

Kea didn't stop to think, didn't give herself the chance to question, she rolled out onto the ice and made a dash for the wildlands. She kept her gaze on the gray landscape ahead of her, beneath her, anywhere but behind. Her boots flashed under her as she ran, the jolt of each step causing her shoulder to pull and scream with pain. She moved as silently as she could, praying that the wind and rain were covering the sounds of her steps. Ahead, the dark smear of the wildlands opened before her, inviting her in. She knew them better than anyone. She could lose him there. At least she hoped she could.

She chanced one last look backward as she ran down into the valley of the wildlands. The man was yelling in frustration, stamping on the machine, kicking its broken body down into the crevasse.

She kept running, sliding down into the first valley, slipping down into the depths. She let gravity speed her way downhill as she fled, using her remaining good hand to slow herself on the curving, twisting channels of ice. As she fled, her mind returned to the sound of his voice. One she knew well.

Fernando.

***

Kea didn't run through the wildlands so much as fall down it. She swerved through the canyons propelled by gravity, her feet finding purchase through luck rather than skill. As the channels widened out around her, she tried to judge how far down-glacier she had come.

Without her glasses, she felt as if she was finding her way through a fog. The walking stick was a blessing, helping her keep her balance and push her way along the channels. She kept moving, always alert for the sound of footsteps behind her.

Sliding to a stop at an intersection of three channels, she found a slope gentle enough that she could scrabble up using only her knees and her good arm. Poking her head up above the ice, she could see nothing but the gray of ice and clouds. Fernando, if he was following, was still hidden below in the labyrinth of the wildlands. She heaved herself up and jogged across the open ice, heading eastward. The oblong shape of the lake gradually came into view on her right as she stumbled downslope towards the esker and the Double Embayment.

Drawing closer, she could discern the yellow blob of the raft on the water's edge. She quickened her pace, each step gaining more traction as the ice beneath her feet turned to cobbles, then gravel, then sand. She skidded to a stop on her skinned knees beside the raft, swearing as she groped for the oars. It was only then that she noticed *both* rafts anchored on the shore.

Of course, he used the other raft. It's not as if he swam here.

It was then that she understood why Fernando hadn't just grabbed the drone before, why he waited for them to come first. He needed the compressor. They had been so focused on looking westward, they had never bothered to look behind them.

She glanced over her shoulder. Still no sign. During her sprint across the open ice, she had been exposed, but she had hugged the lower slopes as best she could, hoping that the topography and rain kept her cloaked from sight. Not that it mattered. They both would be headed here. Yet she had bought herself a head start and didn't want to waste it.

She attempted to untie the rope that was anchored around a small boulder, but her fingers were numb and lifeless. The coarse nylon knot was bound tightly by the weight of the raft. She quickly resorted to using her teeth to pull it free, desperate.

This has to work. It has to.

During her flight through the wildlands, the stabbing pain in her shoulder made her realize that reaching the raft first wasn't enough. There was no way she could row across the lake with only one arm. She would be paddling around in circles. Round and round. If Fernando had a gun, she would be a sitting duck. While she had no idea where he might have managed to procure such a weapon, Iceland didn't exactly sell them at the local hardware store, she didn't want to take the chance.

Giving the knot a savage tug with her teeth, it finally gave way. She sagged against the raft, nearly crying with gratitude. She yanked the rope free and dragged the inflated raft the last meter to the water's edge. *Almost done.*

She pulled off her bright red jacket, wincing as she maneuvered her injured arm through the sleeve. Left wearing only her windbreaker, she kept the camel pack and a few other small items before tossing the daypack into the raft. She positioned the pack upright against the rear of the raft and wrapped her jacket around it. Hastily, she tugged a life jacket around her creation and with a firm shove of her foot, set the raft adrift into the lake, watching as a gentle current carried the boat slowly away.

She squinted at the lump of her pack. It was, she hoped, enough to suggest the shape of an injured Kea huddled in the raft.

Not very convincing, she thought worriedly. *And I'm the blind one.*

She waited for one heartbeat. Two. Three. The raft wasn't moving into the lake far enough to create the illusion yet, but she couldn't hang around to wait.

It could fool someone, she admitted. *If that someone was Mr. Magoo.*

She considered the remaining raft. She could either let him get away or just push the thing into the lake and strand him here with her, which would mean her death.

Tony. Bruce. Cole. Jon. Nadia.

She exhaled a long breath and made up her mind.

The edge of the raft was only a foot or so away from the water's edge. Leaving the anchor rope attached, she nudged the raft closer to the lake until the base was roughly five centimeters into the water. Then, lifting the edge of the raft, she wedged the hilt of her pocketknife into the sand beneath it. Gently, she lowered the rubber base down on top of it, careful to ensure the blade didn't yet puncture the raft's skin.

Glancing around to make sure the coast was clear, or at least as far as she could tell, she sprinted away from the water's edge, heading eastward across the irregular face of the glacier. She rounded a tongue of the ice margin, praying that it would shield her from view. Her breathing was labored now, the adrenaline fading. Kea was desperate for a rest, but she settled for swearing frequently under her breath, using it as a mantra to urge herself on. She plodded on as fast she could, hoping to put as much distance between her and the lake as possible. She knew where she had to go, but she was worried Fernando would be heading there too.

Roughly five minutes later, as she was stumbling across the ice, she heard a scream of rage echo across the glacier. She smiled grimly, imaging the blade of her knife puncturing the raft. She couldn't be sure of Fernando's fate, however, so she kept moving.

***

Kea moved eastward as fast as the dared, aiming for a region where she knew the lobe of the glacier bridged the depression, touching the outwash plain and letting her cross to freedom. She had only been here once with a team doing a reconnoiter a couple of years ago. Even then, the landscape had been sickly, riddled with shallow lakes that pooled on a fragile skin of ice.

During that expedition, she hadn't fully realized just how thin the ice was here, nor how close she and her team had been to falling through into the frigid waters. Now, as she followed the curve of a trough in the glacier surface, she was comforted to see the familiar random pattern of jagged ice sheets stabbing upward into the sky. At their base, several little pools of water were scattered across the white landscape, their dark surfaces tickled from below by cascades of bubbles. She'd made it.

She knew that these fountain-like pools were formed by the upwellings of water coming from under the ice. The topography of the terrain beneath the glacier ice meant that this was the low point in the massive valley. The resulting overburden pressure of the glacier was enough to super cool the water and force it upward into fountains of free-flowing liquid ice.

Another paper I haven't gotten around to writing, she realized in dismay. It seemed so trivial now.

Conjuring up a mental map of the chaotic landscape, she picked her way carefully down into the lowest part of the valley. She put her weight on each step gingerly, testing the ice with the walking stick, and listening for sounds of cracking. Her progress was infuriatingly slow.

She found herself continually looking over her shoulder for any signs of pursuit.

Fernando would be cold, wet, tired, and furious. At least she was counting on that. With any luck, the stunt with the raft had made him angry and irrational. This was her only chance.

In her present condition, she would never win a race across the sandur to the jeep. In her sprint across the open ice, she had only spied the red blob of his jacket once or twice. While the occasional sight of him caused the taste of vomit to edge up her throat, the lack of gunfire was reassuring. If by some remote chance he had gotten his hands on a firearm, perhaps her little trick with the raft had caused him to drop it. However, if he had been paying attention during their field lectures, he knew where she was heading. There was only one way off the glacier.

Stepping as close as she dared to a patch of thin ice, she placed the camel pack on the ground. She drank a long pull of water, then stuffed as much of the bag's contents as possible into her jacket before tipping it over onto the ice. She scattered some wrappers and tissues around to make it look as if she'd dropped it in a rush, mentally apologizing to the glacier for littering.

She retraced her steps away from the bag, hoping she had bought enough time to hide. Each slow step she took across the ice was agony, her heart *thump, thump, thumping* in her head. Finally, when she was sure that the ice would bear her full weight, she used the last of her energy to sprint up the northern side of a little depression.

Keeping low to the ground and moving as quietly as she could between the jagged peaks of ice, she cursed her poor vision. The triangles of ice served as adequate cover as she worked her way to the far side of the depression. She was nearly halfway along the edge of the valley when she saw the red glare of Fernando's jacket as he entered the valley behind her. She tucked herself behind an ice block and held her breath, hoping he hadn't spotted her.

She counted to fifty before sneaking a look. Although blurry, she could discern Fernando approaching her bag. His pace was slow, measured, his boots testing the ice. She hissed obscenities through clenched teeth. She had taken too long. She had hoped to be on the other side of the valley by now, just a blob retreating into the distance for him to recklessly pursue.

He came to a stop a few meters away from her bag. She couldn't be sure, but she got the impression that he was surveying the valley around him, as if sniffing the air. She ducked back behind the ice, her eyes closed. Mentally, she willed him on.

Just keep walking. Just a little more. Just grab the bag.

"Nice try," Fernando's voice boomed through the air. The fact that he was yelling meant that he still didn't know where she was. Or at least she hoped not. Unfortunately, she was close enough to him that she couldn't move without him hearing. She waited. It was his move. She was out of options, and if she was right about her theory about the drone causing havoc with the seismic sensors, she might be out of time as well.

The silence stretched out interminably. She imagined Fernando turning slowly, hunting for her.

"I never wanted to hurt anyone," Fernando shouted. Judging by his tone, he sounded as exhausted as she was. "I just needed to get across the lake to the drone. I could have been gone a week ago, if you had just left the rafts inflated."

Kea bit back a response, resisting the urge to scream. Stillness reigned on the ice, broken only by the crackle of the rain on the surface, as constant as television static. Finally, she heard the *crunch, crunch, crunch* of footsteps as Fernando walked around the little valley. The acoustics of the area were unnerving. She couldn't tell if he was walking further away or closer. Perhaps he was just circling, looking for her.

"Bruce didn't know I was reading his emails." Fernando's tone became conversational as he walked. "None of them did. No one pays attention to the IT guys unless they're too stupid not to know who to map their printer. I knew Max fudged the budgets to keep us on schedule. I knew it was the reason the code in the prototype wasn't ready, why it crashed. Knew he blamed it on Bruce. I knew all about the company that Bruce and Andrea were setting up, trying to get rich off the next launch. When those two next-generation drones crashed, I knew where Bruce was trying to send them. I was even able to alter the landing coordinates.

"I didn't mean to hurt him. He freaked out when he found me out here with the remote control... I just knocked him around a little to scare him. He fought back. Even tore up off my vest. He ran away from me but wound up leaping straight down into that pit. Was awful."

Kea thought she detected genuine sorrow in Fernando's voice, but the fact he was telling her anything only terrified her more. He would never let her leave, not now. The crunching of his icy steps continued. She pictured the valley in her head, trying to remember the location of the weak spots, hoping the terrain hadn't already changed since she had taken the aerial photographs last week.

"I knew he didn't think he was coming back," Fernando laughed, a nervous cackle, thin and creepy as his voice edged up an octave. "He saved drafts of his suicide notes on his desktop at work." He tutted scornfully. "Things not to do on company time... could give a guy like me ideas. I have to admit I was so sure that someone had heard the screams, but then Gary spazzed out. It was all just a mess."

There was a pause and more crunching. If she had to bet, he was standing about four meters to her left.

She pressed her face against the ice, trying to flatten every centimeter of her body, praying that she was shielded from view. The harsh, crystalline granules bit into her cheek, numbed her flesh. She heard the slow breath of the glacier, the susurration of the rainwater trickling down into the ice, the shifting of the grains beneath her head... and something else. A sharp ~*crack*~ that rattled through the ice.

Willing to make a bet? Julie's voice echoed in her head.

"I'm sorry." Fernando sounded weary, as if he didn't want to be here any more than she did.

Kea winced, offended by his feeble attempt at an apology, but there was no time to process that, no time for anger, no time forgiveness. There was no time for anything.

The sound came again, closer now as the pressure wave shifted its way through the glacier. A short distance up the ice, the internal drainage was shifting as metric tons of water lifted the ice, forcing its way into every cavity and crack, about to inundate the very valley they were standing in.

God dammit, Kea mentally screamed at the skies above. *I've waited my whole career for this, and now it happens? What the hell did I ever do to you?*

She felt the subtle shift of the ice beneath her feet.

Screw it. Now or never.

Her knees shaking, she pulled herself up from the ice block and stepped into view.

"You killed them!" Kea spat, trying to act as angry as she possibly could, finding that it came all too easily. "You nearly killed me!"

Fernando was standing right in front of her, far closer than she expected. She carried on ranting, to keep his attention. Even with her bad vision, she could see the outline of the ice ax he brandished in one hand. "You knocked us into a crevasse for God's sake. I nearly drowned in that river, nearly froze." It was with some satisfaction that she noted that he seemed drenched, courtesy of her raft trick. "And what about Cole? He could have broken his neck!"

She wasn't certain, but she thought she could see Fernando frowning in disapproval, as if irritated.

"Needed to get you out of the way and off the ice." He smiled, but his words lacked the certainty of before. "I just want to get out of here, like you."

She poised to run but paused. *One chance. One last chance to find out.* "That thing... what is it doing here?"

Fernando just shook his head, casually slinging the ax to rest on his shoulder. "Didn't exactly go to plan. Didn't count on the winds... nor the rivers." He took a step closer.

A familiar tang of sulfur burnt Kea's nostrils.

Oh, for God's sake, she realized, *this was really happening. Christ.* Adrenaline, already pumping through her veins, raged through her body. Every instinct shouting, *Go! Go! Go!*

"You wanted to sell it, didn't you," she pressed impatiently. "You're doing this all for some goddamn corporate espionage, aren't you?" Her eyes darted up and down the valley. *Out of time*, she thought. *We're running out of time.* "Who are you working for? Who wants it?"

Fernando didn't answer. He took another step closer, the crackle of his boot on the ice a sinister whisper.

Kea hesitated. If she turned and ran up the slope behind her, she knew for certain that he would overtake her. She only had one other option.

She forced herself to exhale slowly.

She wondered if this was how the witch Katla had felt in that moment before unleashing the fury of the mountain on the villagers.

Dear gods, Kea thought. *That woman had some balls.*

An echo of thunder cracked through the valley.

Now!

She bolted toward the camel pack that lay in the middle of the valley. She ran as fast as she could, her limbs flailing, her shoulder screaming. She was dimly aware of Fernando following behind her, the heavy tread of his boots on the ice gaining on her with every step. As she neared the pack, she angled her path to step just around it, where she remembered being able to walk safely, then sprinted for the valley wall opposite.

From behind her, she heard Fernando crunching through the crust of the ice followed by a splash. He shouted in anger, but the sound of his footsteps barely slowed. Glancing back, she could make out that he was closing the gap. He seemed to have lost the axe at least.

That wasn't the trap now. Just the distraction. She was waiting for something else.

The dark green cliffs bordering the easternmost edge of the glacier promised safety as they loomed out of the clouds in front of her. She sprinted toward them, her breath exploding out of her lungs in gasping coughs. She didn't have to make it all the way to the edge of the glacier. She just had to make it out of this valley, out of this channel.

A toxic belch of sulfur engulfed her, causing tears to stream from her eyes and scald her lungs. She kept running, hearing Fernando close the gap between them, the sound of his boots thudding on the ice right on her heels. Panic urged her forward. She ran up the valley's icy wall and lunged for the lip. Dangling from her one good arm, she kicked against the ice with her feet, desperate to gain purchase. She shoved her other arm over the edge, screaming as pain shot through her shoulder.

In a span of less than two gasping breaths, Fernando was on her, pulling at her legs, trying to yank her down into the valley. She kicked and screamed and wept in frustration as she felt herself sliding back down.

The world around them roared in fury.

In the valley below, a wall of ice and water, a jökulhlaup, tore through the little valley, ripping apart the glacier ice and scouring the walls of the outlet channel. The waters roiled against them, battering Kea's legs with blocks of ice and gravel. Her feet jerked free suddenly as Fernando was forced to release his grip. She rolled up and over the edge of the valley, scrambling away on all fours, driven by primal terror as she tried to escape the noise, the destructive power of Skeiðarárjökull, and the horror of what she had just done.

Chapter 18

KEA LAY on her back, looking up at the leaden clouds that hovered in the sky. She'd wrapped herself in a silver emergency blanket from her medical kit and, after a protracted fight with her sodden laces, tucked her boots underneath her to keep them warm. She chewed a candy bar slowly, as it was the only bit of food she had left. The sweet and salty taste of the caramel, peanuts, and chocolate were simultaneously profound and mundane.

Over the ridge, she could hear the floodwaters receding as the jökulhlaup drained into the depression, flowing out through the newly active river channels and, eventually, out to sea.

I should probably be taking notes. She still felt lightheaded as the adrenaline high began to fade away.

It hadn't been a particularly large flooding event, not by Skeiðarárjökull's scale, but that was the closest she had ever been to a jökulhlaup. The recession of the glacier upslope meant that the outlet had shifted away from the usual Skeiðará outlets. If the drainage channels had shifted any further, she would have been trapped on the glacier. As it was, she could cross through the abandoned Skeiðará channel and head back to the jeep, although it would take some time.

She groaned at the thought.

More walking.

***

Her soggy feet squished with each step as she walked across the outwash plain. She pictured a mug of warm tea waiting for her in the main tent, calling to her. That was all she wanted. That and a long shower. In a hotel. At the resort by the airport.

It was only as she mounted a small rise that she realized that she had lost the walking stick. It was probably washed out to sea, along with Fernando.

Dr. Carlyle's going to kill me.

The thought made her giggle again.

Exhausted, she thought. *I'm exhausted, and possibly suffering from hypothermia. Again.*

As she walked, the wind, cold and sharp, blew in great gusts, nearly toppling her into a kettle hole. Having lost the feeling in her toes and feet, she felt drunk, watching in wonder as her legs seemed to move of their own accord, as if they belonged to someone else.

Come along, come along, she sang to herself repeatedly. *Keep moving. Must keep moving.*

The journey across the proglacial depression was much shorter this far east, where the sandur and the glacier pinched together. The floodwaters had indeed drained into the Gígjukvísl river, allowing her to walk across the narrow point where the ice still abutted the outwash plain. As she climbed up the slope to the elevated outwash plain, the winds grew stronger, the gusts more frequent. The rain continued to drizzle down, sapping the last of her energy reserves.

Jon.

The thought of him dangling unconscious in the crevasse kept her moving. She had to get to a radio, get help, and get him out of there.

When the red blob of the jeep finally came into view, she nearly gave a shout, but she was too tired to manage anything more than a quiet *"Wheee!"* as she stumbled down the hill. After fishing the key out of the rear wheel well, she unlocked the door and crawled into the driver's seat. She started the engine and put the heat on full blast.

The radio had been ripped out of the console.

Thank you, Fernando.

Rummaging in the glove compartment, she pulled out her spare glasses. They were five years old, with scratched lenses and an out-of-date prescription, but would do the job of getting her home, albeit with a migraine. She pulled off her waterlogged boots and socks, and rested her bare feet on the vents, taking a moment to savor the warmth.

Knowing Jon's life was in her hands, she reluctantly placed her feet on the pedals, released the brake, and slipped the jeep into first gear, starting the long journey back home. As she steered the vehicle down the embankment, she let the feel of the tires in the worn tracks guide her. With this much rain, it was slow going. Clenching her hands on the wheel, she peered ahead as the jeep rolled downhill, the worn shock absorbers allowing her to feel every rut and hole.

As awareness returned to her limbs, her mind started to spin again. There was little that she could do for Jon until she reached the main road and flagged someone down. She shook her head, still unable to process that Tony was really gone and irrationally angry that he had left her with such a mess.

Dammit, Tony. Now I'll have to tell Ísadóra everything, and Jennifer too, you stupid…

Her head slammed into the window, knocked sideways by the force of the impact. The Jeep rolled onto its side, before settling onto its roof. Kea fell upward against the ceiling, the engine still revving, the heat still blasting. The horn bleated a single unending tone as the world twisted and screeched around her.

Stunned, she found herself lying on her side, her glasses miraculously still on her face, staring out of the shattered windshield. She had landed on her injured shoulder, causing her to cry in agony. Over the sound of her own screams, she heard the roar of an oncoming vehicle. Panicked, she clawed her way out of the cab and pulled herself out into the mud. She rolled into the ditch beside the road and tucked her head into her knees just as a tremendous hammering pounded the earth around her. Sprawled in the muck, she watched in shock as a shiny blue SUV rammed into her jeep for a third time.

Her ears rang from the impact and she was dimly aware of a stinging sensation coming from her hands and feet. Kea was horrified to see a dozen small glass fragments from the windshield glistening in her skin.

There was a screech as the other vehicle came to a stop. The driver emerged to inspect the wreckage of the jeep. Even from behind, Kea knew that silhouette: Lexie.

What the hell?

Kea must have made a gasping sound that caused Lexie to turn toward her. The woman stomped down the muddy embankment, brandishing a tire jack.

Before Kea could say anything, Lexie lunged at her.

Instinctively, Kea dodged to the right. The blow slammed into the ground beside her, more due to Lexie misjudging the depth of the ditch than Kea's evasive maneuver.

The jack thudded into the mud with a wet squelching sound.

Kea kicked out in a panic, trying to crawl away, but only managed to entangle her legs with Lexie's as the woman worked to lever the jack out of the mud. Lexie came crashing down on top of Kea in a sprawling, cursing heap.

Kea rammed an elbow into Lexie's throat and rolled over her attacker, scuttling away on all fours. In her haste, she wound up sliding further down into the ditch, landing with her back wedged against the jeep's ruined fender.

At the sound of groaning, she turned to see Lexie curled up in a ball, both hands clutching her neck and sobbing.

It was her, Kea realized. Lexie had been the one who set the trap at the lake, who had slicked the shower with grease. She had been working with Fernando on this. She had been his ride out here today. She had been here waiting for him to get back this whole time. She must have seen Kea coming and rammed her jeep.

Still dazed, Kea stared at the battered grill of Lexie's vehicle. She wondered if Lexie had even been on the bus when the team arrived that first day, or if she had just been waiting in the parking lot and joined the crowd.

How far back did this go? Were there others?

"Give it to me," Lexie's voice was a feral growl as she uncurled and rounded on Kea.

"What?" Kea shouted in frustration. "What is it you want?"

"Give it to me." Lexie was poised to pounce, her teeth bared like that of a rabid dog. "Now."

"I don't have anything!" Kea raised her bloodied hands, splaying them out to show that they were empty. "I don't know what you're talking about."

Lexie levered herself up off the ground and wrenched the tire jack free. She held it up with both hands above her head, ready to slam it into Kea's skull.

"Wait!" Kea pleaded. Every inch of her body ached with pain. She knew she couldn't survive another attack.

Talk it out. Keep her talking.

"We found the thing, the drone," Kea admitted. "Then Fernando attacked us. Tony's dead. Fernando killed him."

Lexie paused, waiting.

Kea couldn't discern her expression. She tried again. "Why is it worth killing for?"

"The chip," Lexie spat at her. "Where is the chip? He wouldn't have left without the chip."

Kea felt herself slump further into the mud. It was all so pointless. So many people dead for money, for industrial espionage. She felt the vast weight of exhaustion settling on her.

So tired. I'm so tired. Just leave me alone, I just want to lie down and sleep and never wake up.

Instead, weary beyond caring and just to screw with Lexie, Kea asked, "How much is it worth to you?"

"Give it to me!" Lexie demanded, spittle flying from her mouth.

Kea could tell the woman was on the edge of losing whatever sanity she had left.

I'm going to die here, she realized. *She's about to kill me, and all I want to do is roll over and fall asleep.*

Kea started babbling, trying to talk herself out of her shock, trying to reason her way back into reality. "Fernando was willing to steal the tech and sell it to a rival company and split the money with you, right? If he was willing to kill for it, to do all that, I'm thinking my price is going to go up the longer you talk." A thought slipped into her head. "Are you even a real reporter? Did you set this whole thing up? He told you it would be an easy retrieval, didn't he? Just didn't count on not being able to get up on the glacier."

"Easy?" Lexie spat. "Are you insane?"

Yeah, Kea thought stupidly. *I'm the crazy one.*

"Fernando was part of the T3," Kea continued, stalling for time, "What's your connection to him?"

More silence. A very familiar awkward silence. Kea had caught more than one faculty member with a student in her time. She knew that look. "You're with him, aren't you? You were together before all this…"

"The chip," Lexie said, raising the jack again. "Now."

"Fernando kicked the whole thing down into a crevasse," Kea said, the words tumbling over each other "It's gone. It's all gone."

"He would have taken the chip out first." Lexie looked searchingly at her. "Where is he? What happened?"

"Fernando came after me, but," Kea paused, uncertain how Lexie would take the truth, if it would push her over the edge. "He got caught in a jok… an outburst flood. He's not coming back. Not ever. Whatever he had, it went with him."

Screaming in fury, Lexie slammed the jack down. Kea curled up into a ball, putting her hands up to protect her face. It was all she could do. It was all she had left.

The jack clanged into the jeep and bounced off into the mud.

Kea peered through her hands to see her attacker walking back to her jeep. Dumbfounded, she watched Lexie start the vehicle. A moment later and Lexie was gone, nothing more than a pair of taillights receding into the gray fog that blanketed the sandur.

Chapter 19

KEA SQUATTED underneath the jeep's rear fender, watching the rain fall. She sat cross-legged in the mud, her bare feet tucked underneath her for warmth. After Lexie drove off, Kea crawled around the gravel and muck in a daze searching for her boots, until the numbness began to fade and her feet prickled with the cold. It was a two-kilometer walk to the main road, and without footwear, she knew she would be hypothermic, not to mention slice her feet to ribbons.

I should get up, she thought. *Jon's out there. He needs help. Now.*

"I will," she told the rain that tapped a gentle rhythm against the metal above her head. "I just need to rest, just for a moment." She leaned her head against the jeep, her eyelids heavy. "Just for a little while…"

Snap.

She blinked, dazed. A riotous twitch of color tickled her nose.

"That scarf," Kea couldn't help but say, "is amazing."

"My dear, we simply have to take you shopping." Amirah helped Kea out of the mud. "There's so much more to the world of fashion than Gore-Tex and flannel."

Kea felt herself being first carried, then tumbled, into the back of a jeep.

Another snap of fingers.

Kea groaned, slowly regaining focus.

Amirah stared back.

Kea blinked, shuddering with cold. She was finally aware of the blanket around her, of Julie beside her, and Marcus at the wheel. She felt the gentle roll as they slowly rumbled along the dirt road. "Sorry," she said stupidly. "I think I nodded off there for a bit." She accepted a thermos filled with lukewarm coffee. "Um… Not that it's not great to see you, but what are you doing out here?"

"When we got back to camp, she," Marcus nodded at Amirah, "insisted we come out to find you right away."

"I noticed Fernando and Lexie hadn't come back, so I was worried something might be up." Amirah placed a hand on Kea's knee. "I'm glad you're okay."

Okay. Everything's okay, isn't it? Kea's thoughts were as heavy and leaden as her hands.

"Map!" she blurted suddenly. "Give me a map. And a pencil!"

After some rummaging, Julie pulled a natty map out of the glove box. Kea eyeballed the coordinates and scribbled them down along the margin of the map. "Call for search and rescue. Jon's still up there, in a crevasse, just here, a few meters down. Should be visible from above."

"And Tony?" Julie asked.

Kea shook her head. She waited until Marcus called for help before informing them of the events that had transpired over the last several hours leading up to Tony's death. Noting the peculiar look on Amirah's face, Kea thought it best to leave out specifics about the chip and controller. Instead, she focused on Fernando, the flood, Lexie's attack, and her subsequent disappearance. She found some consolation in the news that Cole was recovering at the hospital with his mother.

Julie rounded on Amirah. "What the hell is wrong with you people?"

Amirah ignored Julie, her intense gaze focused instead on Kea. "You found it up there, didn't you?"

"Found what?" Julie implored.

Kea nodded.

"Well then," Amirah sighed. "There we are."

"Are what?" This time it was Marcus who bellowed at the woman.

"I'm afraid that I'm bound by a nondisclosure agreement," Amirah said simply.

Despite the profanity that followed as Marcus and Julie vented their frustration, Kea kept quiet, thinking. Finally, she lied. Slightly. "Fernando told me everything."

"Did he now?" Amirah shrugged. "Well, since the police are on their way… still, I can neither confirm nor deny."

Kea raised an eyebrow.

"I'm *this* close to braining you right now," Julie, always more proactive than Kea, had unclipped the mini fire extinguisher from beneath her seat and brandished it above Amirah's head. "After two bodies, what's one more?"

"Three," Kea corrected sadly. "Three bodies."

Amirah sighed. "When the first prototype crashed, T3, Max tried to pin the blame on our team, citing a hardware defect."

"Slimy," Julie commented.

"Indeed," Amirah agreed. "We did our own investigation and discovered that there was a bug in the navigation software, or so we thought at the time. It was also revealed that T3 had been behind on their deliverables but had fudged the numbers to hide it. Once we found out, Max blamed Bruce, slashed his salary, and threatened to cut him out of any bonuses unless the next launch was successful."

Catching Kea's questioning look, Amirah added. "Bruce and I did exchange some… information, occasionally. In Max, we had a common enemy."

Kea nodded, but Julie still looked lost.

"The two companies were working on a new kind of drone," Kea explained, suddenly more tired than she could remember. "Bruce and Andrea, a co-worker, had planned to sell it, and another one, I think. They'd already set up another company and were planning on a getting a new start with the money, except Fernando caught on…" Sitting out there in the mud, she had a long time to think, to put together the puzzle. "I guess since he was the IT security guru, he could see every communication they sent."

"So, they crashed it on the ice," Julie reasoned slowly, "to sell it on the black market? Or copy it?"

"But Fernando altered the coordinates of the crash," Kea said, remembering his words before the flood. "Knowing that Bruce was feeding Max a story that it was gone all together but knowing it had landed somewhere else."

"When we got wind of T3 'volunteering' here," Amirah added, "we realized the crash data had been altered, much like everything else. Max told us that one drone had crashed in the North Sea, the other in Europe, both irretrievably."

"Do you think Max knew what Fernando was up to?" Julie tried again.

"I thought so," Kea said, "until Lexie showed up. Maybe Fernando was trying to go into business for himself, now that T3 is essentially wrecked. Or maybe they're both working for him. Or someone else?" She eyed Amirah, wondering what the quiet, scarf-obsessed woman knew. "I guess we may never really know."

"Tony…" Julie trailed off, seemingly having trouble processing what had happened.

Kea tugged the blanket tighter around her shoulders, luxuriating in its warmth. Either the terrible coffee or her brief nap in the rain had given her a tiny burst of energy. Her thoughts were a little clearer. "Does anyone else at camp know anything about what happened to me?"

"Not really," Julie considered. "Only that you guys hadn't come back yet. Why?"

"Nothing," Kea said slowly, "I was just using my little gray cells…"

***

Kea sat in the main tent, considering Max across a mug of hot cocoa. She had asked Marcus and Julie to keep the others outside to give her some time alone with him. In the end, she knew whatever it was, Max would get away with it. Most likely, she would never speak to him again. Would never know.

Not unless she looked him in the eyes.

Max sat opposite, his arms folded across his chest, his breathing low and measured. Air whistled out of his nostrils, but he remained otherwise silent. With her good hand, she idly drew a figure on a blank sheet of paper. The pencil scratched on the paper, the loudest sound in the tent. Outside, the rain had stopped. Somewhere over the sandur, the rescue helicopters were whirling, hopefully rescuing Jon near the coordinates she provided.

Kea turned the paper around so Max could see it. She had drawn an image of an ant sitting atop a blade of grass, the same as his tattoo, with the words *Dicrocoelium dendriticum* written beneath.

Max's eyes narrowed, but he gave no other sign of recognition.

"Let's say for a moment," Kea said slowly. "Just for the sake of argument, that I had the chip."

"Sorry?" Wide-eyed and smiling, Max gave nothing away.

Either Max was genuinely clueless, she observed, or an excellent liar.

"Let's say I had the chip," Kea repeated, recalling Lexie's words. "For a moment, let's pretend that I have it in my pocket. How much, hypothetically, would that be worth to you?"

Max tilted his head, looking askance.

"None of this falls under my area of expertise," Kea admitted. "But I'm fairly certain that flying a drone into Icelandic airspace probably violates all sorts of rules, not to mention that it's a drone that jams communications. Or that it's one that can capture and alter any communication that passes through it."

Still, Max said nothing. He seemed impatient. His eyes darted to the tent's entrance, as if suspecting someone to walk in at any moment.

"But I think it's more than that." Kea traced the outline of the ant with the pencil. "I think your team designed the system to act like a parasite that can infect and control other communication drones, just like the lancet. It infiltrates the other fleets up there in the sky, the Face-Googles. It pretends to be them, feeds you all the information you need. And whenever you like, you can control them. Or take them out altogether. Maybe even alter the data being transmitted back…"

She studied Max, looking for any sign of admission or denial. Ice-blue eyes stared back. His lashes were jet black, but his eyebrows were already flecked with gray.

"But does it actually work, I wonder?" Kea attempted to scrutinize a man who specialized in being inscrutable. "Or did you botch this last launch of drones like you did the prototype? Did you know Bruce and Andrea were trying to get their hands on it?" He said nothing, and Kea found herself firing off more questions, more theories. "Were you planning to sell it yourself? Is Fernando working with someone else altogether? Who is pulling the strings, I wonder? Did you really succeed?"

No response.

It was like talking to a refrigerator. One that didn't even have the decency to hum.

"Of course," she continued, "I imagine your company could claim that the drone crashed here as an act of industrial espionage. That Fernando was working for another party, so that none of it was your fault. Insured, I suppose. Still," she added, using her best scolding professorial voice. "the reputation of crashing multiple drones could ruin your company. Plus, you haven't been able to get your hands on the hardware to make a considerable profit. It makes me wonder again, how much is this chip worth to you?"

"Hypothetically?" Max answered at last.

"Hypothetically," Kea nodded.

"One chip alone, for a device that you speak of, for the materials and programming," Max said, choosing his words carefully. "For a technology like that and for the information that could be on it, would be worth around ten million."

Kea blinked. Twice.

"Hypothetically, of course," Max replied quietly. "If it even works."

"Hypothetically," Kea echoed. She lifted her hands and extended her arms. "Because, as you can see, I have nothing in my pockets."

Max smiled beatifically, showing off his perfectly bleached-white teeth.

It gave her the chills.

"That's a shame." Max rose from the bench to leave.

"It is possible," Kea continued, causing him to pause, "that Fernando and Lexie were acting alone, but maybe there was another buyer. Someone unknown. However, it's also possible that they were acting under your orders. It's also possible that you threatened Tiko to make a false statement to the police against her will about Bruce committing suicide."

Max wisely said nothing.

It was as if, Kea thought, *that he knows I have Julie's cell phone taped under the table recording every word.*

Chapter 20

AFTER BEING questioned by the police, Kea filled Julie and Marcus in on her conversation with Max, or rather the lack thereof. As she talked, Marcus poured out measures of whiskey for each of them into plastic mugs.

"Any sign of Lexie?" Kea asked before downing the shot.

Marcus shook his head. "The inspector said they haven't had any word. I can't imagine she'll make it off the island."

"What about Jon?" Kea asked, fearing the worst.

"Nothing yet." Julie had just returned from the hive of police activity that infested the visitor center. "They're still out looking. No sign of Fernando either."

"I doubt he made it out of the jökulhlaup," Kea rubbed her neck with her good hand. "But I've come to the conclusion that I have no idea what to think anymore because somehow it always seems to be worse. Did they recover the drone thing?" She held out her glass for another pour. "Or Romulus for that matter?"

Julie shrugged. "They're not really telling me much. They've asked everyone to stay put. They want to talk to Tiko and Reynard as well. I gave them their phone numbers. I doubt they've gone far."

"You don't think they were involved too, do you?" Marcus idly rolled his empty cup on the table.

"I doubt it," Kea said.

"I did have a word with Bonnie," Marcus offered. "She didn't reveal much, but she did say that nearly everyone worked on different projects, so they might not have anything to do with this. The only ones who worked on the drone project were Andrea, Derek, Tiko, Max, and…"

"Bruce." Kea finished.

"So, Bruce finds the drone," Julie began, "and then Fernando finds him."

"Fernando can't let him tell the others he's seen it," Kea added.

"But why not just go and get it?" Julie asked. "Why did they need us to get out there?"

"For all we know, they may have tried to get to it earlier," Marcus conjectured. "Without the rafts, they wouldn't be able to get across the lake. I imagine Fernando was just hoping to wander off at the appropriate time while we were on the glacier and retrieve the chip. Bruce must have interrupted him."

"And because of that, and mapping the strat section, we didn't even go back on the ice for days," Kea reasoned. "The weather didn't help, of course."

"So, what?" Julie asked. "He just wanted to grab the tech and sell to the highest bidder?"

"Maybe that's where Lexie came in," Kea expounded on a theory she had been working on. "Not only the getaway car, but she could sell the stuff, with no connection to Fernando at all."

"Picked a hell of a place to crash," Julie remarked.

"I'm sure they would have preferred somewhere more convenient," Marcus almost sounded offended. "Although sometimes when you try too hard to make something look like an accident, the results aren't what you anticipate."

"I don't think Lexie told Fernando about her stunt dropping me in the river," Kea said. "Or the grease in the shower."

"She was probably just trying to get you out of the way," Julie ventured, "to ensure we stayed off the ice for a couple of days so they could pop across and get it."

"Bit messy." Kea considered the haphazard way fieldwork often went, improvising around weather, resources, staffing, floods, and eruptions. "Although that's usually the way things are around here. But I don't think she had it in her to be a killer." She remembered the thud of the tire jack slamming into the mud beside her head. "Thankfully."

"They were probably planning to just wait it out," Marcus said. "Maybe go to Reykjavik and grab a raft there to bring back, but with the news of the eruption they had to move up their agenda?"

"Maybe," Kea answered softly. "For a while, I thought Andrea and Bruce were in it together, wanted to start their own company, or maybe thought Max was up to something and just wanted out. We may never know."

"And Max," Julie pressed. "You really think he was the one giving the orders?"

"I think..." Kea broke off, remembering the look in Max's eyes. "I think he knows what's happened. Does that mean he was the one who came up with the plan? I'm not sure. As for who the buyer is, I'm still in the dark. Some competitor somewhere? The police may find out."

"Even if they do, they may never tell us." Marcus poured out a few more measures of whiskey and raised his cup in a toast. "To Tony."

Kea downed the alcohol, wincing as it burnt the walls of her throat. She hadn't mentioned Tony's other activities with Ísadóra and had decided that she never would. The truth wouldn't make anyone any happier.

"Okay." Kea held out her mug for another. "What happens next?"

Marcus poured her a generous portion. "Well, Julie here will take you to the medical center and get that shoulder checked out. Then it has been recommended by Eco-Observers that this session should be shut down immediately."

"Yes," Kea said. "Well, the volunteers are already heading out, and we should go home. That would be the reasonable thing to do."

Silence hung in the air for a long moment.

"Well, I mean," Julie scrunched up her forehead. "We came here to study floods and well, we just got exactly what we hoped for."

Marcus poured himself another drink. "I did tell them that it would take a couple of days to take down all the equipment. We can probably get some great measurements, but," he paused, looking at Kea, "not all of us should go back out there."

"What me, with my little broken wing?" she asked with a smile. She had made some decisions of her own on the drive back, ones she intended to follow through on. "Watch me fly."

***

"Knock, knock," Zoë called.

Kea spun around on her knees to face the pair of skinny jeans that blocked the entrance of her tent. She peeked out of the flap and saw Zoë standing there, awkwardly clutching a large cardboard box.

"ICE-SAR brought back your MRS equipment," Zoë said, crouching down. "Marcus had it loaded in the trailer. He also asked me to deliver this." She put the box down on the grass and peered inside the tent. "Did you finish packing?"

"Nearly." Kea shifted slightly to hide a massive pile of unwashed clothes. Since her encounter with Max last night, things like laundry seemed so unimportant. She nodded at her injured shoulder. "Just taking things slow. How's Cole?"

238

"Spoke to him an hour ago on the phone." Zoë shook her head. "Couldn't be happier to not be camping. Aside from the broken leg of course."

"Glad he's okay," Kea replied, her mind still on Tony. Another funeral to attend.

Zoë shook her head. "Marcus was just telling me stories of you going all hard-core interrogator on Max. I can't quite picture that somehow."

"No?" Kea shoved the pile of laundry into a garbage bag as best she could with one hand. "Well, I guess I'm not entirely sure who I am anymore."

"Deep." Zoë sat on her heels as Kea crawled out of the tent on her knees. "Any chance I get to meet the new Kea?"

Kea stared at the lumpy plastic bag of clothes, wondering if she should transport it home or just burn it. "I'm not sure you'll like her. I'm not sure I do."

Zoë paused. "This new Kea... Does she like chocolate cake?"

Kea scratched her nose, considering. "I'm fairly certain all iterations of me like chocolate cake."

"Then we'll get along fine." Zoë stretched out a hand and helped Kea stand.

Above them, the undulating peaks of Öræfajökull blazed in the sunlight, the sky clear of clouds. While the rain had left the night before, the grass around them glistened with dew. Most of the volunteers had packed up, leaving yellowed squares of grass as the only fleeting memory of their existence. Amirah, Gary, Andrei, and his daughter were waiting for the afternoon bus, having been given permission by the police to leave. Max was in custody for further questioning, as was Derek. Jon, located by the rescue team, had been taken back to Reykjavik at top speed to get his injuries treated.

The end of another field season, maybe the last.

"I meant to ask..." Kea found that after all she had been through, she was still afraid to pose the question. "If you could stay just a little longer..."

"What for?" Zoë asked with a smile.

"Any chance you'd like to go on a little plane ride in about..." Kea checked her watch, "five minutes?"

Zoë laughed. "As long as we're back in a couple of hours, I need to get back to Cole." She turned and walked to her tent. "Oh, Kea..."

Kea paused, worried Zoë had changed her mind. "Yeah?"

"Aren't you going to open your present?" Zoë asked before disappearing into her own tent.

"What?" Confused, she turned to examine the crumpled cardboard box. Kneeling, she unfolded the top flap stenciled with the ICE-SAR logo printed on it. Within she found a life jacket, her daypack, and her jacket neatly folded up in the bottom. She unzipped the pocket and pulled out the baggie that held the remote control and the peculiar globule.

She stared at the tiny thing in the palm of her hand.

I'm holding ten million dollars.

The greasy sheen of its alien skin stuck wetly to the edge of the bag. It seemed like such a grotesque thing to build with all that money. Not worth Bruce. Or Tony.

She would have to give it back, of course. Probably. Of course, she would.

Right now, however, she had to see a girl about a plane.

***

Kea let out a whoop as the little Cessna lifted off the bumpy gravel runway and shuddered into the air. Nestled within her fleece, her shoulder ached with every jolt, but as the mountains rose before her, the pain fell away, forgotten. The tramadol the doctor had given her helped, of course.

During the night, Kea had lain in her tent, trying to map out her future. Between thoughts of Fernando and Lexie, what had happened to Bruce, Tony, and Jon, she had decided that it was time to just move on. To find a research site somewhere more accessible. Somewhere tropical even, near a beach.

Now, as she soared through the sky, Kea felt elated. With Zoë's help, they propped the camera against the window to document the modifications of the river channel caused by yesterday's jökulhlaup. As Skeiðarárjökull spread out below her, she remembered why she loved this place so much. No one could ruin this for her. She would never let them.

Who am I kidding? I'd be bored stiff on a beach within a weekend.

As the plane banked for another run, she looked down at Skeiða-rárjökull, the magnificent glacier that seemed now like an old friend.

I'll be back, she concluded. *After, perhaps, just a quick trip to the beach with Zoë.*

Epilogue

"CAN I help you?" Ísadóra asked. She was desperate for a cigarette, but this guy in the rumpled yellow rain slick wouldn't leave the
gift shop. He didn't seem to be buying anything, just walking around
poking at things and generally weirding out the other tourists in the
visitor center.

"I said, can I help you?" she repeated.

He turned. It was one of those Eco volunteers, she remembered.
The old one with the wild hair and the nose shaped like a bent spoon.
Although Ísadóra had been introduced to all of them on their first day,
she couldn't recall his name.

He walked toward the counter, waving his gloved hands as if cast-
ing a spell. "It's late, isn't it?"

"Late?" Ísadóra glanced at her watch. It wasn't even noon yet. The
shuttle bus to Reykjavik was still idling outside the visitor center. Unfortunately, he didn't seem to be in any hurry to get on it.

"Terribly late." He snuffed the air in disapproval, giving Ísadóra
an unpleasant flash of untrimmed nose hairs. "This is no way to run a
business."

"Kúkalabbi," Ísadóra swore under her breath.

The man slapped the counter sharply, causing her to jump.

"Language, young lady," he scolded in a quiet whisper. "I expect
better service in your country."

Ísadóra stared at the old man. His eyes which a moment before had
been distant and unfocused now burnt blue and bright. Even his accent
had changed, becoming hard-edged and foreign.

"I would like that." He pointed to a toy puffin in a box on the counter. "And the postage to mail it."

Ísadóra nodded and quickly rang up the sale, eager for him to be
away. She handed him the customs form and a pen. She watched as he
hurriedly filled out the information, his handwriting consisting of
nearly illegible looping swirls of cursive. She noted the final address,
totaled up his costs, and waited impatiently while he counted out exact
change.

"When does the mail get collected?" The man's irritation was evident, his fingertips tap-tap-tapping on the countertop. "I thought they'd be here before now."

"The mail goes on the bus." Ísadóra nodded at the Reykjavik shuttle. "He's collected already, but you can give it to him."

"I'll take that." He snatched the package out of her hands before she had a chance to seal it. He stalked out of the visitor center, leaving Ísadóra to exhale a sigh of relief. Despite wanting to be as far away from the man as possible, she watched through the window as he stopped outside near a bin and dumped out the furry toy.

As if sensing that he was being watched, he shifted his body so that his actions were shielded from view. The old man, Gary, Ísadóra remembered, pulled a plastic baggie out of his jacket and presumably stuffed it into the postage box. He then strode over to the shuttle and handed the driver the sealed parcel before hopping on board himself.

A few minutes later, Ísadóra stepped outside for a smoke, watching as the vehicle pulled away from the visitor center and vanished up the little road to Route One.

Germans, she reflected, *were so strange. Who wears gloves in gorgeous weather like this?*

***

Across the campground, Kea's tent flap lay wide open, its flimsy skin fluttering in the cool breeze. Her bag of clothes had been ripped apart, her undergarments threatening to take flight with each stiff breeze. Her sleeping bag lay splayed out on the ground, her pillowcase turned out and her daypack upended. Atop the mess lay her field jacket, its pockets turned out, their contents emptied.

High above, the tiny plane was nothing more than a speck, keeping watch on the beast of Skeiðarárjökull that slumbered below.

R.J. Corgan

Acknowledgements

To Matt for believing in me, to Kate for listening, to my parents for their support, to Maeghan Kimball for developmental editing, Aimee Child for copy editing, to Rory for the title, to my brother for Georgian food, and to Scott, for everything.

Thanks to Dr. Andy Russell, Dr. Andy Large as well as partners in crime Dr. Andy Gregory, Dr. Matthew Burke and Tim Harris. Special thanks to Dr. Fiona Tweed – your hard work, enthusiasm, and dedication is an inspiration for generations of students. Thank you for letting me explore your world.

Finally, this book would not be possible without the hard work of hundreds of volunteers over the years or the kindness and generosity of the families who have dwelt at Skaftafell for nearly a thousand years.

If you enjoyed this book, please leave a review on the the website of your choice.

Lastly, if you'd like to volunteer to assist scientists on expeditions there are numerous non-profit organizations that you can join!

Cast

Burlingame University Glaciology Department
Dr. Kea Wright
Dr. Marcus Posner
Dr. Carlyle (former project lead)
Julie
Tony

Thaumaturgical Telecommunication Technologies (T3)
Max
Bruce
Jon
Erik
Derek
Fernando
Tiko
Bonnie

Corvis Engineering
Andrei
Nadia
Amirah
Reynard
Gary

Contractor
Zoë
Cole

Reporter
Lexie

Park Staff
Ísadóra

Glossary

Beheaded – the term for the lower part of a glacier that, during retreat, may become separated, due to topography or burial by sediment.

Black Death – slang for Icelandic potato mash vodka.

Dirt Cones – mounds of dirt-covered ice, created by uneven melting due to the presence of sediment or ash that may serve to insulate the ice, resulting in uneven topography.

Englacial – term used to refer to processes or features located within the glacier.

Esker – a sinuous, ridge-shaped feature formed by the deposition of sediment by water moving through, or below, the ice.

Geomorphology – the study of the earth surface, including landforms, geology, and surficial processes.

Gloop – slang used to describe sediments that have become supersaturated with water.

Ground Penetrating Radar (GPR) – device that determines a glacier's internal structure by sending radar waves into the ice and recording the return time of the reflections.

Inverted topography – the deposition of sediment on the ice, and subsequent melting, which may result in the topographic reversal of high and low features in the landscape.

Jökulhlaup – Icelandic term for glacier outburst flood; may be generated by the sudden release of water impounded within, below, upon or adjacent to a glacier and may be volcanic, lacustrine (lake), or pluvial (precipitation) in origin.

Kettle hole – depression, usually circular, formed by the melting out of ice blocks that have become stranded or completely buried by sediment during a jökulhlaup.

Kirkjubæjarklaustur (or 'klaustur) – a small town in southern Iceland; closest medical facilities and a hamburger joint.

Kúkalabbi – Icelandic term for scumbag; 'poop on two legs.'

Meltout – the melting out of sediment above or within the glacier.

Moraine – referring to the region across the front of a glacier, composed of ice, sediment, rocks, and boulders deposited by the ice; alternatively, a lateral moraine is found on the sides of the glacier as the ice scrapes material off the valley walls.

Moulin – hole in the ice where surface drainage flows down into a glacier.

Magnetic Resonance Sounding (MRS) – surveying technique used to measure the level of water in an aquifer by applying an electric field to water molecules, then measuring how long it takes for the water molecule to return to its original state.

Munter – slang term to describe a person impaired by alcohol or other drugs; ugly.

Sandur – Icelandic term for outwash plain in front of a glacier.

Snout – slang term referring to the front edge of the glacier.

Subglacial – term used to refer to processes or features located beneath the glacier.

Supraglacial – term used to refer to processes or features located above the glacier.

Surge – rapid advance of a glacier.

Tephra – volcanic ash.

Thaumaturgical – magical.

Tuya – Icelandic term for the flat-topped (table-top) volcanic mountains formed beneath the ice.

Wildlands – the name Kea has given to the heavily ash-covered western region of the glacier covered by an extensive drainage network of streams and canyons.

Recommended Readings

For more information on Skeiðarárjökull:

Skaftafell in Iceland: A Thousand Years of Change by Jack D. Ives, published by Ormstunga (2007).

For more information on glaciers and glacier landforms:

Glacial Landsystems, edited by David J.A. Evans, published by Arnold (2005).

For more information on the 1996 jökulhlaup and the resulting landforms:

Icelandic jökulhlaup impacts: Implications for ice-sheet hydrology, sediment transfer and geomorphology by Andrew J. Russell, Matthew J. Roberts, Helen Fay, Philip M. Marren, Nigel J. Cassidy, Fiona S. Tweed, and Tim Harris in Geomorphology (2006).

For more information on GPR and the esker at Skeiðarárjökull:

Structural controls on englacial esker sedimentation: Skeiðarárjökull, Iceland by Matthew J. Burke, John Woodward, Andrew J. Russell, and Jay Fleisher in Annals of Glaciology (2009).

For more information on supercooling:

Glaciohydraulic supercooling in Iceland by Matthew J. Roberts, Fiona S. Tweed, Andrew J. Russell, Óskar Knudsen, Daniel E. Lawson, Grahame J. Larson, Edward B. Evenson, Helgi Björnsson in Geology (2002).

Additional Location Maps

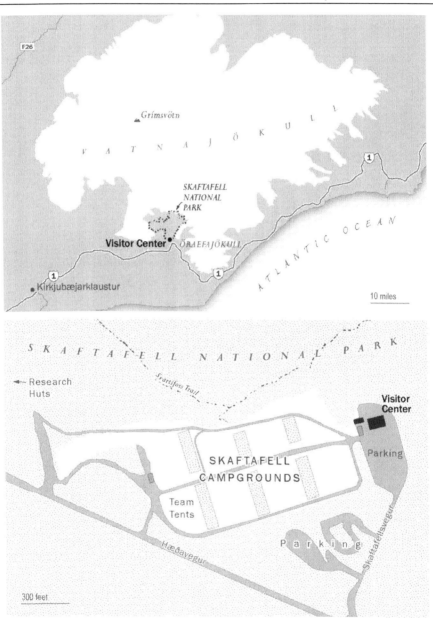

Made in the USA
Las Vegas, NV
08 September 2023

77261963R00155